D1519842

LEGEND RISING

GALACTIC GUARDIANS BOOK ONE

JONATHAN YANEZ

BOOKS IN THE GALACTIC GUARDIANS
UNIVERSE

STAY INFORMED

Get A Free Book by visiting Jonathan Yanez' website. You can email me at jonathan.alan.yanez@gmail.com or find me on Amazon, and Instagram (@author_jonathan_yanez). I also created a special Facebook group called "Jonathan Yanez' Reading Wolves" specifically for readers, where I show new cover art, do giveaways, and run contests. Please check it out and join whenever you get the chance!

For updates about new releases, as well as exclusive promotions, visit my website and sign up for the VIP mailing list. Head there now to receive a free stories.

www.jonathan-yanez.com

ONE

"I HURT MYSELF TODAY, to see if I still feel," Johnny Cash's rendition of Nine Inch Nails' song played through the radio in that same slow, sad cadence. It was a song I'd learned to understand deeper than I ever wanted.

I had mixed feelings about staying and listening to the whole track in my parked rig or getting down at the Flying J rest stop and grabbing a quick, probably non-nutritious meal.

It was one of her favorite songs and I didn't want to think about her right now. I turned off the engine and climbed down the front steps to the dirt ground.

It was late in New Mexico right outside White Sands Naval base. To be honest, the place kind of gave me the creeps. There was something just not right about that area of the world. I'd heard all the conspiracies, of course: government testing, aliens, even interdimensional portals.

There was no doubt they were doing something they didn't want people knowing about, but I also doubted they had little nude green men running around.

I crossed the parking lot where other trucks were

bedding down for the night, some plain and straight from the manufacturer, others chromed out with a full set of chicken lights like my own. I fully intended this to be my last stop. There was a frozen burrito in the Flying J with my name on it and maybe a Mountain Dew.

As soon as I opened the door to the rest stop, I knew there was something wrong. The Flying J was on the smaller side as far as these things went. I'd been to every rest stop from San Diego, California to Augusta, Maine. I'd seen rest stops with barely enough room to fit a toilet and cashier up to ones that you would have thought were a full-on shopping mall.

This one was smaller with restrooms in the back, a handful of aisles, and the cashier next to the front door.

Right now, that cashier was a young man with a face full of pimples, shaking as he stuffed bills into a coffee pot. You heard that right, a coffee pot. It still looked warm by the way the cashier palmed it from hand to hand like he was playing hot potato.

Another man held a handgun to his chest, screaming at him so quickly, the words seemed to come out together.

"Hurry, hurry, the money in the pot, all of it." The man holding the gun looked at me with wild eyes. He pointed the gun in my direction. "Oh snap, oh snap, you, you get over here. Hands up, hands up!"

I'd always wondered what the odds were that I'd be party to a robbery one day. I knew it had to happen sooner or later. Out on the road more than I was home. Who am I kidding; the road *is* my home.

Entering thousands of gas stations and rest stops over the years, it looked like the odds had finally swung my way.

"You deaf, man?" The guy with the gun was erratically moving from pointing his gun to me and then the kid packing the coffee pot with bills. "I said, you deaf, man? You want to die today? You want to die today?"

I lifted my hands as adrenaline jolted through my system like a bad gearshift.

"Over here, over here," the man with the gun said, motioning with the weapon for me to stand in front of the cashier so he could see us both. "Let's go, come on, let's go."

I was no John Rambo. I had no experience in the military, either. I'd never even been in a fight, unless you counted getting beat up while I was blacked out drunk.

I didn't.

I walked over to stand in front of the cashier, hands still in the air. I got a better look at the man holding the gun to my head. He had to be in his thirties or forties, with dragging pants, chains around his neck, and a sports jersey two sizes too big.

"Here—here, that's all of it," the cashier said in a shaky voice. He handed the coffee pot full of cash to the man with the gun. If I didn't have a gun pointed at my head, I would have thought seeing a coffee pot full of cash was funny. Apparently, our braniac robber didn't anticipate needing something to put the money in when he arrived.

A puddle of spilt coffee by the coffee machine told me all I needed to know. If I weren't so scared, I'd be kind of mad how much coffee had been wasted.

"All right, all right, all right." The man with the gun bobbed his head as if he heard some kind of beat in his mind. He was about to go when he thought better of the idea and motioned to me. "You, your wallet, ring, empty your pockets. Let's go, let's go."

I started sweating when he mentioned my ring. Thus far, I had planned to stay out of this whole ordeal. I didn't want anyone to get hurt. Money would come and go, but lives wouldn't. I knew that better than most.

"Slow, slow, hurry, hurry," the man said, wiggling his gun from my head to the pot.

"How am I supposed to go slow and hurry?" I growled as I slowly and quickly reached for my wallet and dropped it in the coffee pot.

"And the ring, the ring," the man said looking at my wedding finger. "I swear to God I'll kill you. Drop the ring in the coffee pot."

I had to stop from shaking. There was no way I was giving up my ring.

"Come on, you're going to die for a ring, man?" the guy with the gun asked, stepping closer and pressing the barrel into my forehead. "You some kind of slow inbred? What, your wife give this to you? Your slow inbred wife gave this to you and it means something?"

Tears stung my eyes at her memory.

"What, are you crying?" the man asked. "Are you crying? Are you going to die because of this ring?"

Sadness turned to anger like a flip of the switch. I was ready to go. I'd made peace with that a long time ago. Without her, I was just a shadow in this life anyway.

"You willing to die for this ring?" The man pressed the barrel of his gun harder into my head. "You're going to die for this ring?"

"No," I told him under the halogen lights and the bright-colored chips in the aisles to our right. "You are."

Fueled by years of repressed anger, I moved into action.

Too slow.

Eating frozen Tacos Culos Locos beef burritos and flaming hot Cheetos didn't exactly make me the spitting image of the perfect athlete. By the time I lifted my hand for the gun, the guy had already squeezed the trigger.

CLICK!

I heard the sound even as I grabbed at the weapon with both hands, bulling the man backward. I guess those extra cheese puff pounds were good for one thing. I had to outweigh the robber by fifty, maybe sixty pounds.

I pushed him back, not really sure what my plan was. Apparently, I didn't need a plan. I forced him back right into the puddle of coffee he'd emptied for his money container.

The robber's athletic trainers slipped on the dark liquid and he went back hard. I heard his skull crack against the edge of the coffee stand so violently, I'd be amazed if it didn't do some serious damage to his skull.

I fell on top of him. The coffee container full of money dropped to the ground and shattered. Tiny glass pieces shot out in all directions.

"Oh, oh," the kid behind the counter was yelling.

I wasn't really sure what he was going on about, but I was sure there was no way I was going to let the robber under me up.

Through shards of the broken coffee pot digging into my hands, I secured the handgun and threw it behind us. I was ready to...what? Try to wrestle the guy into submission or choke him out? I didn't know what to do next, but I didn't have to know.

The would-be robber under me was out cold. A puddle of dark red blood poured from the back of his head, mixing with the brown hue of the spilt coffee.

"Yes, yes, nine, one, one?" The casher, to his credit, had his cell phone in his left hand and with his right was already going to secure the discarded firearm. "We need help. Someone just tried to rob us."

I heard the sounds of the conversation through a daze. My head hummed. I felt sick from the adrenaline. With shaky hands, I reached for my wallet through the broken glass of the coffee pot.

I stood up, not sure if the guy below me was dead or just unconscious.

"Yes, yes, he's down," the cashier was saying through a panicked voice. He held the gun on the unmoving robber now. "A trucker, I think, someone knocked him out. What's your name, sir? Sir, what's your name?"

The yelling pulled me out of whatever mental fog I was in. Later, I'd realize I was in shock. I looked down at my hands covered in glass and blood.

"Sir, are you okay?" the cashier asked me. "Help's on the way. Sir, can you hear me?"

I'm not really sure to this day why I ran. I was confused, numb, still so hyped up on adrenaline. I just knew I didn't want to be there. I didn't want to find out if I'd killed the guy or not. Because I had wanted to kill him for a moment.

I ran.

I hit the door at full sprint, heading for my truck, the shouts of the cashier chasing behind me.

It was late now. The New Mexico sun was gone, showing off a vast array of stars and a half moon.

I was breathing hard by the time I reached my Peterbilt 379. The adrenaline was still there but beginning to wear off, reminding me I had glass in my hands. I ignored the pain for a moment longer, climbing up into my rig. The engine roared to life and I was gone out of the parking lot like a bat out of hell.

Do you really want to die? You knew he was going to

pull that trigger. Did you want to give up? Are you done? What would she think of you? What would she say if she knew?

More thoughts crashed through my mind. I felt like I was going to throw up as my stomach rolled. I found my way onto the highway and pressed the accelerator, gaining momentum to reach the max speed limit allowed.

It was later than I thought, only a few vehicles near White Sands occupying the lanes. Blood smeared across my steering wheel. I shifted again and hit the gas.

The road was my home, my rig, my sanctuary, and for a brief moment before I was taken, I began to calm down.

It's going to be okay. It's going to be okay. You didn't do anything wrong. You helped that kid back there. That guy you tackled isn't dead. He's just knocked out. It's going to be okay, I told myself.

I couldn't have been further from the truth. One moment I was rolling through White Sands on a dark highway. The next thing I knew, a bright white light filled my rig from the windshield inward and I was taken.

TWO

THERE WAS no holding it back now. Already I felt sick from the conflict at the Flying J; after the white light hit me, I couldn't hold it in. I vomited all over my chest, lap, and steering wheel.

I'm not sure if you've ever experienced Chef Boyardee ravioli coming up, but let me tell you, it stings.

There I was coughing and hacking, trying to see the road in front of me as I lost my lunch. Except there was no road in front of me at all. I blinked back the tears that came with intense vomiting, hitting the brake and trying to make sense of what I was seeing out of my windshield.

There was no sense to be had, not here. The road in front of me, other vehicles in my rearview mirror, the night-time stars overhead—all gone.

I stomped my foot on the brake again. If I was having some kind of mental episode, I wanted to make sure I didn't harm anyone else. There was no need. My rig wasn't moving. The engine was dead.

I sat there for a moment longer, breathing hard and trying to figure out what was going on. My mind ran through the possibilities, from alien abduction to government test and, who knew, maybe I was dead. Maybe the robber at the Flying J had killed me right there. Maybe everything that happened after was just my entrance into the afterlife.

It would be a pretty bad afterlife if I was throwing up Chef Boyardee ravioli all over myself.

"Max Tyco," a voice that sounded more robotic than human boomed from somewhere outside my rig. "Max Tyco, please step out of your vehicle. You are in no danger. You are among allies."

I froze, really wishing I would have taken a pee before fleeing that Flying J. I swallowed hard, trying to see what was outside my truck. I had no idea where I was.

Dark walls, maybe? It looked like I was in a massive room with dull illumination coming from the ceiling. It was difficult to see anything more.

"Max Tyco," the more robotic than human voice called again. "Please, we understand this is a jarring transition for you, but your time as a guardian has already begun. Please step out of your vehicle."

My mouth was dry, which was weird, since it had been full of vomit a minute ago. I still couldn't see anyone out of my windows. I didn't want to abandon the supposed safety my home on wheels brought, but I couldn't exactly stay there for the rest of my life, either.

"Where—where am I?" I asked, opening my door a crack to ask the question. "Am I dead?"

I closed the door as soon as I uttered the words to the dark room beyond.

"No, Max Tyco, you are very much alive," the voice answered. "Currently, you are on Oni. I told you, you are among allies. If you would step outside of your vehicle, perhaps it would be better if we discussed things face to face. Would that put you further at ease?"

I thought about this in my truck, realizing how silly it was to think that I could be any safer inside my rig than outside. I mean, whoever this thing was or whatever it was happening to me had what? Lifted my entire truck off the ground and disabled it? If it wanted me dead, I would be.

I swallowed hard, opening the door to my rig and stepping down. If I thought I'd be able to see any better once I was down, I was wrong. All I could make out was an empty room the size of a warehouse with black walls at the ends and that same dim light coming from a vaulted ceiling above.

"All right," I said with a shaky voice, cleaning the vomit off my chin and hands. There wasn't too much I could do about it on my shirt and jeans. "I'm out. Who are you? What did you do to my truck?"

"Your vehicle was disabled when we teleported you aboard Oni," the voice answered. "That is also the reason for the return of your digested food through your mouth hole. Teleportation at first can be a jarring experience. Please refrain from screaming like a small child when you see me. It's important to have an open mind. I am your ally. You'll do well to remember that."

I prepared myself to see the most horrifying specimen of nightmare fuel possible. I figured if I expected to see some giant mutant hybrid spider, then whatever I was really going to witness couldn't be that bad.

A portion of the wall in front of me opened or receded into itself, revealing a bright white square of light. Something or someone small moved through the doorway and headed in my direction.

I clenched my fists, not to fight but to further brace

myself as my mind tried to find reason in the events transpiring around me. Government conspiracy was still on the table, as well as alien abduction and mental break. It was possible I had finally gone off the deep end. Maybe I was crazy, but crazy people didn't know they were crazy, right? They thought they were the sane ones.

"It's important that you forget all you thought you knew before and start with a blank slate," the voice said as the being approached. "It'll be easier for your mind to accept these new things you see if you can let go of the truths you thought you understood."

"That's really confusing for a guy who just vomited on himself," I said, squinting as I tried to get a better look at the thing coming my way. "What are you?"

"My name is Tem Fan," the creature said as I finally got a good look at it. The robotic hint to his voice was gone, making me realize he had been speaking through the room's speakers or some kind of electronic device up until now. "I must say I am very excited to meet you. I am the historian assigned by the High Council to follow you and Rima Noble on your journey."

Everything Tem was saying took a back seat to what my eyes were trying to convince my brain was real. Tem had to be five feet tall, with slender shoulders and a robe twice his size.

He was a reptilian mouse, if I had to put a name to him, with big black eyes and ears that came out the sides of his head, more like small wings. There was no nose I could see and a little mouth. He used said small mouth now in what I guessed was a smile. Shorty stubby white teeth showed through.

I wasn't really the pass-out type, but neither had I ever come into contact with an alien species. My knees felt weak as I realized I was face to face with an extraterrestrial. Aliens were real!

A metal collar hung tight around Tem's throat, translating his words. I saw his lips move and heard high-pitched squeaks come out that were then translated by the device into English.

"Oh right, the translator will be of no need as soon as you drink the all-water," Tem said, bringing a thin hand to his throat. "It translates my tongue to your language. I have drunk the all-water so I can understand what you are saying in my own language. But I'm getting ahead of myself, aren't I?"

"I, uh—so aliens, huh?" I asked, still unclear on what exactly was going on here. "Does the government know about you, or are you going to do any weird butt stuff to me?"

"Weird butt stuff?" Tem cocked his head to the side. "Why would we do anything weird to your butt?"

"You know, all those stories about alien abductions and —probing," I said, trying to control my breathing. "Is there any chance I'm hallucinating any of this?"

"I am not interested in doing any poking of your booty hole," Tem said, lifting both hands in what I guessed was the universal sign of 'no, thank you'. "I'm not that kind of Ublec. You are not hallucinating, and neither are we working with your government. The alien species your government has discovered are ones we haven't even come in contact with. The universe is a massive place. We are here for you on order of the High Council, Max Tyco. You have been selected to be a guardian."

"Back up. Did you say our government does know about aliens?" I asked incredulously. "I knew it."

"Yes, but you're missing the much larger picture here,

Max Tyco," Tem answered with a look like I was disappointing him. "Come on, I know it's a lot, but follow along with me here. You've been selected to be a guardian. Do you know what that means?"

"I have no idea, but I'm pretty sure you have the wrong guy," I said, feeling a sense of relief that this might all be some kind of crazy intergalactic mistake. "The only thing I've ever been selected for is jury duty, and even then, they dismissed me. I think I know what's going on here. I think you picked up the wrong guy."

I heaved a grateful sigh of relief as I headed back to my rig.

"If you could just drop me off where you picked me up, that would be great," I said. "I won't tell anyone any of this. To be honest, no one would believe me anyway. Well, nice meeting you, Tem. Good luck with the High Council and the guardians and all of that."

I sat back in the puddle of vomit in my seat and buckled my seat belt. Hands at ten and two. I hoped beyond hope he would just send me back.

"Max Tyco, born May 22nd, 1985 to Brandon and Megan Tyco?" Tem asked from outside the vehicle. "Born in Visalia, California?"

My heart sank. I closed my eyes, trying to make sense of it all. There was no denying it wasn't a mistake. Whatever hope I had of going back to a normal life was gone. They wanted me for what? I wasn't sure, but it was me.

"Married to Christina Tyco on May 10th," Tem continued rattling off truths about my life. "Christina Tyco deceased on—"

"That's enough, that's enough," I said, knowing what came next. "So you have the right Max Tyco, but I still think you've made a mistake. I'm just a guy."

There was a lot of huffing and puffing from the other side of my door. Tem almost gave me a heart attack as his alien head popped up on the other side of my window.

"The High Council never makes mistakes," Tem said, fogging up my window. "I'm sorry for what happened to you, but you are capable of more than you know. That's why you're here. That's why you were chosen. Now can you help me down off the exterior of your door? My muscles are made for note-taking and turning pages, not climbing."

Reluctantly, I opened the door and helped Tem off my rig as I left the driver seat once more. The little historian weighed almost nothing. When we were down, he revealed a square glass datapad from the insides of his cloak. The datapad sprang to life with symbols I didn't recognize scrolling across its screen.

Apparently, the symbols meant something to Tem because he began muttering under his breath as he took notes.

"Human smells foul, struggling to accept new reality as expected, insists on being probed," Tem said under his breath as he continued to work. "Will need extensive physical training as he has really let himself go."

"Hey," I said. "I'm right here."

"Right, of course," Tem answered, reaching into his robe again and handing me a glowing blue vial. "The all-water. You'll need to drink it before she comes. She's not as— understanding as you and me. She'll expect you to know what she's saying. She hates using translators."

"What is it?" I asked, examining the vial. I wasn't exactly used to gulping down glowing liquid given to me by aliens on a day-to-day basis. "All-water?"

"Yes, down it goes," Tem said, beginning to sound rushed for the first time. "Instructor Rima Noble allowed me to ease you into your new reality first, but she's on her way now. The all-water will allow you to hear your own language being spoken when others talk to you. Please, Max Tyco, hurry. Instructor Noble is not known for her patience."

"Right, right, okay," I answered, popping the cork on the vial and taking a whiff.

"Oh, that's not a good idea." Tem cringed as I smelt something ten times worse than vomit waft from the vial. "Sorry, Max Tyco, I should have warned you."

The same square of white light somewhere further down the warehouse room caught my attention. Someone far larger than Tem stepped through the door and approached.

"Hurry, hurry, please," Tem said, motioning with his hands. "Please drink or she will not be pleased."

THREE

I WASN'T REALLY sure who this Instructor Noble was, but I gathered she wasn't to be messed with. I weighed my options. I could refuse to take the elixir and see why this woman was so feared, or I could obey and get it over with.

Already in the last few hours, I'd been held at gunpoint, vomited all over myself, and abducted. I doubted things could get much worse. Plus, if the stuff in my hand was poison, Tem could have killed me ten times over since I'd arrived.

I threw my head back, taking the concoction with a grimace. It tasted like rancid cherry cough syrup, just not as thick. It gave me goosebumps as it went down my throat.

I started coughing. My head felt fuzzy as a migraine came on.

"You'll be fine in moments," Tem reassured me as I crumpled to my knees under the pain. My skull felt like it was splitting in half. I pressed my palms to the sides of my head groaning. "This is part of the process. It will pass, Max Tyco. Give it a moment."

I was vaguely aware the woman had arrived and was

speaking with Tem as I suffered in silent agony. Saliva ran down the corners of my mouth as I winced, trying to keep myself from falling into unconsciousness.

"By the ancient ones," a woman sighed. "I thought he'd be in better shape. I'm getting too old for this."

"Oh, he's not too bad," Tem said encouragingly. "He can learn. The High Council is never wrong."

"They are never wrong, but neither am I a miracle worker," the woman answered. "Look at him, moaning like a child. Is that—vomit on him? Did the human vomit all over itself?"

"His transition was rough," Tem answered. "He'll get used to teleporting."

The pain in my head was finally beginning to subside. I looked up with one eye cracked to get a good look at this Instructor Noble. She was tall, maybe even as tall as I was. Tattoos lined her arms and on her skull between thick braids. Her sleeveless shirt showed off toned arms and hard muscle. Right now, her jaw was set as she stared down on me with disgust.

I wiped my mouth, getting to my feet.

"You're bleeding," she said, looking at my palms where the broken coffee pot cut me. There were still small pieces of glass in my hands. "Why are you looking at me like an idiot? Tem, did he drink the all-water or didn't he?"

"Oh he did, he did," Tem said, coming over and patting me on the arm like a proud parent. "He's been doing great, considering everything we're putting him through."

"Listen," I began under the hard stare of the woman. "I know you have the right Max Tyco and this High Council doesn't make mistakes, but what exactly have I been chosen for?"

Although I spoke English in my head and the words

came out like I heard them, both Tem and Instructor Noble were able to understand what I was saying.

"You've been chosen to become a Rowki Guardian," Instructor Noble said, waving her hand to the ceiling. Tem took out his datapad and began hitting keys.

The warehouse type ceiling above us transitioned from dull light to a picture of the universe. Small lights floated in the room now as the hologram took on life, not just on the ceiling, but all around us in the room itself.

I saw planets, black holes...the wonders of the universe I had only ever witnessed in pictures or videos.

"Since the inception of the universe, the Rowki have staved off the pull of darkness and kept balance," Instructor Noble continued as star systems and galaxies flew past us. "Our fight takes place in the very first galaxy to ever be created, the Ragmar Galaxy, the center of the universe."

Planets and stars whizzed by until we were in front of one galaxy in particular. Bright vibrant greens, oranges, and reds, just to name a few of the incredible colors, made me forget everything in the presence of their wonder.

"It is the fight here in this galaxy at the heart of the universe that matters the most," Instructor Noble went on to explain. "Here, we hold back the darkness. Here, Rowki give their lives. Here, the repercussions of battles won and lost ripple outward to the rest of the universe."

I stood open-mouthed as Tam took us around the Ragmar galaxy, clearly enjoying the look of utter amazement on my face.

"Cool, right?" Tem asked. "So cool. I remember the first time I saw it."

I just nodded along, my breath stolen in the pure beauty of the Ragmar galaxy.

"Rowki are chosen from across the universe to come

here and train," Instructor Noble finished. "We are chosen not because of our will to fight, our experience, or our physical prowess. I mean, that much is clear; just look at you. We are chosen for the depth of our potential. You, Max Tyco, as hard as it may seem, have the potential to be something truly great if you only apply yourself."

"Potential?" I repeated the word like I had never heard it before. "I don't know. I don't know what potential I can reach."

"And you may never know if you don't apply yourself," Instructor Noble answered. "Not all who are chosen make it past training. You have to be willing to apply yourself. Many have washed out, unwilling to do what it takes to reach their full potential."

"What does that mean?" I asked. "They die?"

"If they fail to complete training, we send them back to their home planets," Tem answered. "Everyone the High Council selects is capable, but few truly reach within and dig deeper."

"So I get a choice in this?" I asked, stunned. "I mean, you don't have to kill me if I say no, or wipe my mind?"

"We don't want you here if you don't want to be here," Instructor Noble said with a raised eyebrow. "Being a Rowki Guardian is a privilege."

"Well, if there's not going to be any hard feelings, then thank you, but no thank you," I said, throwing up my hands with relief. "I mean, it sounds very interesting and all, but I'm just a trucker. I'm just a guy who's maybe eaten one too many soft serves in my day. I'm good. I'll go back."

I turned toward my rig, imagining they would teleport me back just like they'd teleported me here in the first place. If everything went as promised, this would all be a very confusing memory.

Padding bare feet caught my attention as Tem ran to my side before I climbed up into my rig.

"Max Tyco, Max Tyco, please wait a moment," Tem said, pulling gently at my arm. "I know this is all so much to comprehend, but you have it in you. I can see it, Max Tyco. Instructor Noble can see it, too. You have to stay."

"See what?" I asked, slowing my movement but not stopping. "Potential?"

"Yes," Tem answered, nodding his head so fast, it became difficult to track. "Please, give it a chance, Max Tyco. If you decide after you've given it a chance that it's not for you, you can go back."

I'd reached my truck, pulling myself upward and opening the door to my cab. I had no intention of stopping until Tem opened his mouth again.

"Do you have any regrets, Max Tyco?" Tem asked quietly. "Do you carry any losses with you?"

"You know I do," I said, gritting my teeth. "You have all my information."

"If there is even a one percent chance that you may regret this later, give yourself grace in this moment to try," Tem said in a voice that told me he meant every word. "If it doesn't work out after you give it a chance, you can go back with nothing lost. If you go back now, you will live with the uncertainty of what could have been for the rest of your life. Do not add to your regret. We both know you carry enough to crush any man."

I felt anger again, mostly because I knew Tem was right. I was a lot of things, but I wasn't a quitter. As much as I hated admitting I was wrong, somewhere in the back of my head, I knew I'd regret leaving now.

I mean, how many people got the chance to see another galaxy? I'm betting that list was pretty short. I let out a long sigh, wondering what she would have told me to do. She was always encouraging my introverted nature to go out and put myself in situations that may seem uncomfortable at first, but would help me grow.

If she were here, there was no doubt she would have wanted me to stay and give this a chance.

"Okay," I said, climbing back down from my truck.

"Okay?" Tem asked, surprised and excited at once.

"Okay," I repeated.

"Oh, Max Tyco, this is so exciting!" Tem shouted, practically jumping up and down. "Instructor Noble, Max Tyco has agreed to begin his training."

"Oh joy," Instructor Noble said in a monotone way that made me think she didn't mean those words at all. "Well, if you're ready, then we should begin."

"What, you mean, like, now?" I asked. I still smelt like death from the vomit, and while the blood had stopped dripping off my hands, there were still tiny glass particles in my palms that needed to be dug out.

"I'm sorry, did you need a nap, perhaps a massage or a fruit beverage?" Instructor Noble asked.

"Well, actually, if I could get a change of clothes and a bandage..." My voice trailed off as Tem stepped on my foot. I looked at Instructor Noble's deadpan stare. "Oh, you're being sarcastic, aren't you? I don't know you that well yet, so I wasn't sure."

"Five minutes," Instructor Noble said with a smile that reminded me of those nature channels when a predator is about to pounce on its prey. "Five minutes and then your training begins."

FOUR

I WASN'T sure when the last time I had seen real physical exercise. I think I had a gym membership a few years back but never really went. It just made me feel better knowing that I had access. I would always lie to myself about going sometime soon, but "soon" somehow evolved into Netflix binging and nacho cheese Doritos.

I spent the five minutes Instructor Noble gave me changing into clothes Tem provided. He also brought back something that looked like tweezers and a solution that stung when he cleaned out my wounds.

"Son of a nut cracker," I growled as Tem dug the glass out of my hand, poured the salty-smelling solution on, and wrapped my hands. "What is that?"

"It's urine from a species called the Insectoids," Tem said as he wrapped my hand in clean white bandages. "It is widely used to clean infection."

"Wonderful," I answered. "Why did I even ask?"

"One minute," Instructor Noble said, just staring at me as I began to undress in front of her.

"You want to look the other way or give me a bit of

privacy?" I asked, taking off my shirt and replacing it with a sleeveless shirt that wrapped in the front like a gi. "You know? Leave something for the imagination?"

"Please," Instructor Noble rolled her eyes. "I am hundreds of years older than you. Your species is not one I find attractive."

It was easy to forget Instructor Noble wasn't human. She looked human enough, minus the head tattoos and the thick braids. Now that she mentioned her age, I could see it. White in her hair, wrinkles around her eyes and mouth. Her eyes were the dead giveaway. I was surprised how I'd missed them before, probably because looking into them was like looking into the sun if the sun was made of cold steel. There was wisdom there, wisdom and fury.

I went along my merry way, stripping off my clothes and changing into the ones provided. Tem handed me what was basically white shorts to go along with my sleeveless gi and a long strip of white cloth to keep the gi closed. Running shoes that conformed to my feet like magic rounded out my new outfit.

I was reminded of the shoes I'd had when I was younger with a pump on the tongue that would tighten the shoe. These were like that, but I didn't have to do anything except slip them on and they hugged my foot like an old friend.

"Oh, snap," I said, bouncing up and down on my toes. "What are these shoes? They feel amazing."

Tem looked as though he were going to respond when Instructor Noble cut him off.

"Tem, initiate course zero, point zero-one," Instructor Noble said, disregarding my question. "Training has begun."

Tem nodded with that quick motion of his again and

smiled as he took out his datapad and pressed a few commands.

At once, the room brightened. The dull lights overhead were turned on max, making me blink a few times until my pupils were used to the light. The entire room was made of the same dull black material.

I did a double-take when walls of varying height began to rise from the floor of the room along with what looked like a pull-up bar. They grew from the floor as if someone had filmed a plant sprout from a seed and then played it at a thousand times speed.

These structures rising from the ground appeared around the perimeter of the room. Instructor Noble looked on with a satisfied grin. Tem gave me an encouraging nod. "You can do this, Max Tyco. I know you are capable, if you are willing."

"To find true peace, the war must be won from within," Instructor Noble told me, motioning for me to follow. "I'll be conducting conditioning over your mind, body, and spirit. Tem will give you instruction over the history of our order. Axeleron will instruct you in weapons training and combat."

"Bless you," I said, trying to lighten the mood.

Instructor Noble either didn't think that was funny or didn't get the joke.

"Who's Axelemonimum?" I asked.

"Axeleron," Instructor Noble corrected.

"Right, that's what I said," I answered. "Who is he, or she?"

"Axeleron is the captain of the Ursonian guard," Instructor Noble said as if that was supposed to give me answers to all my questions. "He is our link between the

Rowki and the Ursonian Corps that supports the Galactic Government."

"Nope, nothing, still not getting it," I told her. "Who, the what, now?"

"Save your questions for your time with Tem, human," Instructor Noble answered. "Your days will be structured for you as follows. Your wake up time will be five am sharp. At five thirty, after a morning meal, we will train and condition for two hours. You will then have weapons training with Axeleron for another two hours, then instruction with Tem for four hours, with a break for another meal with him. We'll follow that with two more hours with me and then after your nighttime meal, you will have a few hours of free time before bed and the process repeats."

"Wait, is that four hours of exercise?" I asked incredulously.

"Six, if you include weapons training with Axeleron," Instructor Noble answered. "And trust me, his training will in ways be more unforgiving than my own."

"I've seen commercials on TV where you can get a solid burn going with just fifteen minutes of a workout," I answered, trying to reason with the woman, who was clearly off her rocker. "I mean, maybe we can do some heavy stretching and jumping jacks to start."

The entire time we'd been talking, we were walking to the far side of the warehouse where a red line six feet in length appeared on the ground.

"This is the start and finish line for each circuit," Instructor Noble said, rolling her head from side to side. "Usually, I would start with stretching, but you talk too much and I don't think I can take much more of that at the moment, so we'll begin our first circuit. Then, when you're sucking in breath trying not to die, once we're done, we will stretch."

I had about a dozen more questions to ask at the moment, but the death stare I received from my mentor was enough for me to rethink my current plan.

"Behind the red line," Instructor Noble began. "Go when I say. It doesn't matter how slowly you move as long as you don't stop. You are capable of going all the way. Become the victor of the war within."

If I was expecting some kind of pep talk, that was it.

"Go," Noble said, taking off at a jog beside me as she already began to travel the perimeter of the course. She moved like a freaking gazelle, long legs so graceful and easy, it was as if she were gliding over the air itself.

"Go, Max Tyco, go!" Tem cheered me on from the side-lines of the course.

I took my first step and fell on my face. My upper body wanted to move faster than my lower body was prepared to travel. I picked myself up, hoping Instructor Noble hadn't seen that and hurried to catch her.

There was no catching her. She was a goddess of phys-ical exercise sent down to torment me. Along the perimeter of the track were stations set up for pull-ups, wall climbs, even two square indentions in the ground I would learn to love to hate. They were for stopping to do pushups and sit-ups.

Instructor Noble always made sure to stay ahead of me, but not too far ahead that she couldn't look to make sure I was doing all my reps.

Sweat poured into my eyes and down the back of my neck.

There were walls to get over: two feet, four feet, and six feet high. I threw myself over one after the other. I learned each square indention in the ground was ten push-ups and each circular indention was ten sit-ups.

My body was screaming. Muscles I didn't know I had were staging a rebellion. I think I pulled something in my butt halfway through. My lungs burned like someone put gasoline on them and then set them on fire.

"Find your 'why'," Instructor Noble told me when she saw my arms shaking at the second round of push-ups. "I can't do that for you. That's something you'll have to discover. Find out what pushes you forward. Find that, hold on, and for the love of the ancient ones, learn how to control your breathing. You sound like a stuck Moronian when you run."

I wanted to yell at her, curse her out and then some, but there was no oxygen to spare. I was having a hard enough time breathing, much less trying to have a conversation with the woman.

When we reached the pull-up station, I really gassed out. I couldn't even manage to do one, much less ten. I watched as the inhuman being in front of me managed to do not just ten but twenty pull-ups at once.

She dropped down to the ground, barely breaking a sweat for the first time. When it was my chance at the bar, I jumped up to grab it. The steel rod felt cool in my hot, sweaty palms. I took a deep breath and pulled.

Nothing happened.

I took another deep breath. *Come on, Max, come on, you can do this*, I shouted in my head.

Nothing.

In my mind, I imagined I was doing all the correct motions. I was pulling, just nothing was happening.

I kicked out my legs, trying to get some momentum. I dropped off the bar, panting.

"You'll need to lose some weight and build upper body strength if you're going to be able to pull your own girth," Instructor Noble said with disdain clear in her voice. "We'll double up on the sit-ups and pushups to make up for the pull-ups. If you can't get all the pushups on your feet, then doing them on your knees will be acceptable for now. Continue, human."

I wasn't really sure how I made it around the entire perimeter of the warehouse and back to our red start line. I crossed the line and collapsed, seeing stars. I couldn't suck in air fast enough.

"Good job, good job, Max Tyco," Tem said, appearing over me as I lay on the ground staring up toward the ceiling. "I knew you could do it. Here's some energy. Here, you need to recharge."

I accepted the bottle from Tem, not really sure what I was agreeing to consume, but knowing my mouth felt like a desert at the moment. The liquid actually wasn't that bad. It tasted like a cross between water and a fruit I couldn't quite place.

"Here we go, here we go, all right," Tem said, helping me to a sitting position. He put his hand on my back and the other on my arm. He came away grimacing at the sweat on his hands and rubbing them on his cloak. "Oh, oh my, that's gross. Why do you leak so much?"

Sure, I wasn't able to get my pull-ups in and I felt like that run shaved off a few years from my life, but I had done it. If I could do this, then technically, each day should get easier. Maybe I would get stronger as time passed. Yes, with enough rest, I could do this. I needed some down time to recover and then tomorrow I could try it again.

"Two minutes," Instructor Noble said as she bent from

her waist letting her arms hang low and touch the ground in front of her. "You'd do best to mimic my stretching."

"Two minutes for what?" I asked, struggling to my feet. I got a whiff of what I smelt like and nearly passed out. If I was going to be working out like this, then I needed way more deodorant. "Do we eat in two minutes? I could really go for a Snack Pack right about now."

"Two minutes and we run the circuit again," Instructor Noble answered.

FIVE

NUMB, that was what I felt like when we were done. I felt numb, exhausted, and bruised. Like my whole body had just been put in a dryer on high.

When Instructor Noble called a stop, there were no high fives or well dones. She told Tem to make sure I was up at five am the next morning and then just left.

Tem did his best to make up for her harsh manner, even seeming a bit embarrassed on her behalf. He brought me something that tasted like meat and a bowl full of some type of green vegetables.

His little datapad seemed to be able to reconstruct the room into whatever we needed. With a few command clicks, the perimeter of the warehouse disappeared and a shower room lifted from the floor.

I was in the square black room with hot water pouring from the middle of the ceiling. It was great, to be honest, at least twice the size of the driver showers I was used to using at the rest stops across the country.

"I can construct anything out of the training room," Tem called out to me from the other side of the shower room. "Would you like a bed, a hammock, a couch, even? I did some research on what humans prefer to sleep in. It would be a bed, correct?"

I stood under the spot where the hot water poured from a square opening in the flat black shower ceiling that had grown into existence moments before.

"It would be a bed," I answered, so tired I felt delusional. "But I have a bed in my rig. I can sleep in there. It's what I'm used to."

"Of course," Tem answered. "You pilot this 'rig' across your planet carrying, what, supplies and foods?"

"I drive it across my country," I answered just standing there and enjoying the water washing away layers of sweat. "I drive for a company called Amamart. I carry everything from food to drinks, clothing, and supplies."

"Fascinating," Tem said with an energy I didn't know at the moment. "I'm going to pass a cleaning ingredient and applicator to you through the shower. Also, may I recommend lowering the heat of the water? Studies show cold water will do more for your immune system, recover aching muscles, and other such benefits."

I watched in awe as a circular bar of cream soap along with what looked like a little rough bag grew from the ground and came up in the corner of the shower.

"No, I think I'll stick with the hot water, for now," I said, putting the soap in the bag and starting to scrub myself. The stuff was awesome. It smelled like a cross between mint and heaven.

"As you wish," Tem answered. "Well, I'll leave you to it, Max Tyco. After you shower, you should really get some rest. You have a full day tomorrow. I know Instructor Noble can be a bit harsh, but give her some time. She really does care, if you can believe that. She's been—she's been through a lot, but that's her own story to tell."

"I get it," I answered, scrubbing the rough bag over my head and face, creating a myriad of soapy suds. "Hey, Tem? Why am I training alone? I mean, wouldn't there be other Rowki chosen? I can't be the only one in a universe of options."

"You are not, but—but again, that's another long story best left for another day," Tem answered hurriedly. "I must go now. Rest well, Max Tyco."

If I hadn't been so dog-tired, I would have pressed the issue. It was something that had been bothering me since my second circuit with Instructor Noble. If the Rowki were a universal order, then there should be hundreds of new recruits training with me, maybe even thousands.

I rinsed off, not knowing exactly how to turn off the shower. Lucky for me, some kind of motion sensor did that as soon as I stepped out of the square room. Tem had left a towel and I dried off before changing into my own boxer briefs and a shirt that read *Back to the Future!*

When my head hit the pillow, I was out, maybe even before my head hit the pillow. For once in a very long time, I wasn't plagued with nightmares of my past.

Sleep came and went much too soon. I swore I'd just closed my eyes when there was knocking on the door of my cabin.

I sat up blinking, trying to remember where I was. Events of the past day hit me like a tidal wave. I wasn't sure what to think at the moment, but the knock came again.

"Yes, yes, I'm awake," I said, rubbing at tired eyes. "Tem, is that you?"

"It is I, Max Tyco," Tem said from the other side in that same excited voice as usual. "We have thirty standard Earth minutes to get you ready before Instructor Noble will arrive to train. I thought today you might enjoy getting out of the circuit room and seeing our dining area."

The idea of leaving the room did sound good. It was one item on a long list of things I wanted to ask about today.

"That's a great idea," I said, climbing into the driver side seat and opening the door. Tem handed me my clothes that were the same sleeveless shirt of the day before, shorts and shoes. "Hey, Tem, what do I do if I have to relieve myself? I used the shower drain the night before, but that's not going to work this time around."

"I'm sorry, I'm afraid I do not understand, Max Tyco," Tem said, tilting his head to the side. He squinted his large black eyes, trying to discern my intentions. "Do you require a physician?"

"No, well, yes, after what my body went through. Every muscle feels like it served as a punching bag for Rocky, but right now, I just need a restroom, you know, a bathroom, somewhere to do my natural body functions," I asked, trying to get my meaning through. "You know, what goes in must come out."

"Oh, yes, of course," Tem said, bobbing his head. "I think I know what you're talking about. I think it's time for your own tablet, by the way. It will let you control things in this room and create various items like showers and such you may need. The tutorial is only a few hours, but perhaps tonight, I'll leave it with you to—"

"That's great, that's really great, Tem," I answered, getting down from my truck one aching movement at a time. "But right now, I really gotta go. I'm prairie dogging it right here. Can you make me a bathroom?"

"Certainly," Tem said, doing his magic over the tablet he held. A moment later, another black room sprouted to life beside the shower. "It has everything you might need pulled straight from your planet's internet findings."

"Thank you," I said, going over to the black door that slid open as I approached. The toilet looked normal enough, along with the black sink. "Hey, Tem, I need some toilet paper."

"Toilet paper?" Tem looked at me, confused. "Your pop culture shows evidence of three seashells being used to clean said rectum. Is this not the case? What is this mysterious toilet paper you speak of, Max Tyco? I must know more."

"Never mind, I got it," I said, stopping at the front of my truck for my utility knife and then trotting over to the rear of my trailer. Each step was a new definition of pain as a jolt of aching muscles started at my heels and worked its way up to the top of my head. I opened my trailer and headed inside. I forgot how packed the trailer was with crates of everything from energy drinks to alcohol and, to my great pleasure, toilet paper.

I cut through the heavy plastic wrapping on the crate of Charmin double ultra-quilted for your pleasure.

"Yeah, here's the good stuff," I said under my breath, speed-walking back to my new toilet area. "Come to daddy."

"Do all humans sweet talk their rectal paper?" Tem asked, confused at what was about to happen. "Is this a subculture I have yet to discover?"

After I was done in the restroom and washed up, Tem looked down at his tablet. If we were going to get a quick breakfast before training, then we had to hurry. For the first time since I'd arrived, I was invited out of the circuit room to explore the rest of the grounds.

We stepped out of the room into a wide hall that wasn't

black. It was a soft gray, with light set into the ceiling showing off clean walls and a cleaner floor.

"The Ursonians are the dominant species here, so try not to stare," Tem instructed. "They're the backbone of law and order around our galaxy. The muscle of the Galactic Government, if you would."

"I though the Rowki were the muscle," I asked, trying to keep up.

"Think of the Rowki Guardians as an order of very elite peacekeepers," Tem explained. "The Ursonians are more of the soldiers who aid the Rowki and act as support."

"Got it," I answered, entering a doorway to our left. As soon as I walked in, I saw bears. I mean, I knew they weren't bears. They were aliens called Ursonians, but still, for all intents and purposes, they looked like humanoid bears to me. They were massive giants.

They had to be seven to eight feet tall standing upright, weighing I had no idea; hundreds, maybe even a thousand pounds. There were a dozen or so of them standing and sitting on large benches, eating their meals.

They all looked over to me when I entered.

"You'reeeeeee starrrrrrring," Tem said in a low sing-song voice.

"Right, right," I answered, swallowing hard and following Tem to a far wall where a series of cubes were set with glass barriers in front of them. Above each glass window were command screens of buttons and options I didn't recognize

I could feel the eyes of the massive bear people boring into the back of my skull. I pushed away the idea of a steroid-induced Winnie the Pooh breaking me in two for a snack and started pressing buttons on the device.

"What would you like to eat, Max Tyco?" Tem asked,

eager to be of assistance. "These are food printers capable of making whatever your heart desires. They aren't in your common tongue, but I'm sure I can find you something close to what you're looking for."

"Great," I answered, stopping the random pressing of buttons. "I'd like some pancakes with a side of sausage, and throw in a few donuts too. I'm starving."

"Oh right, so that's not exactly on your meal plan," Tem said, reaching over and pressing a few buttons on the control panel. "Instructor Noble has you on a strict regimen of foods you are and aren't able to eat. But here, how about a tasty cup of brown water your kind enjoys and a double serving of what is it called? I did research on you and your planet trying to figure out what you'd be eating and our closest alternatives. Is it pronounced, eggs?"

"Coffee and eggs?" I asked with a sad expression as Tem scrolled through items that resembled calories and sugary goodness. "How about just one donut, Tem, just one."

"Sorry, Instructor Noble would choke us both with our intestines if she knew we were going off your designated meal plan, but as an added bonus, I'll see if I can sneak some breakfast meat in for you," Tem said as if he truly believed this was some favor he was doing me. "Just don't say anything, but I think we have something close to sausage you'll enjoy."

I saw the shadow over my shoulder before I witnessed the massive bear creature in the glass reflection. I could feel its presence too, if that was a thing. My hair stood on end.

"Hey, new meat, I was using that food printer station," a deep rumbling voice said. "Move aside."

SIX

I TOOK a deep breath then turned around to see a giant Smokey the Bear looking down at me with glowering brown eyes that matched his fur. Like the others of his kind, he wore a tight-fitting gray uniform. Short fur did little to hide boulder-like muscles and a neck so thick, it was the size of my torso.

I had to crane my neck upward just to look at him.

"Hey, no problem here, Care Bear," I said with a shrug, moving to the other food printer on my left. "I can move over."

"No, no, you will not," Tem said, sucking in a wave of air. "This is a Rowki Guardian. He has been chosen by the High Council. You will show us some respect or else."

"A Rowki Guardian, oh no," the Ursonian asked in mock shock. "Not a Rowki, oh my, I'm so sorry to you and your entire race. What are you anyway, some kind of mushy pig species?"

"Nope, nope, I'm a human but no problem here. I'm just going to eat my designated meal plan quietly," I said, motioning to Tem to zip it. "I don't want trouble."

I held my breath, hoping against all hope that that would be the end of it. Wishful thinking. Even as I moved over to the next food printer on my left, another massive Ursonian sidled up to his buddy. He showed off a smug smile with plenty of teeth.

"He was going to use that one," the first Ursonian said.

"You know what, I'm not even really that hungry," I said, putting my hands up in the air and backing away. I'd been through enough over the last twenty-four hours. The last thing I wanted to do was get used as a punching bag for a creature that outweighed me by hundreds of pounds.

Tem made a sharp sound that sounded like he was sucking in a large amount of air at once.

"Why, I've never...this is going in a report. A full report," Tem said, looking up at the Ursonian's insignia over the left side of his chest. "Sergeant Bull, is it? Well, you can rest assured that you will be getting a harsh talking-to by your captain."

"You Rowki are all the same, you and your historians sent from the High Council," Bull said with a sneer, looking between me and Tem. "You come in and use the Ursonian Corps like a disposable meat grinder, sending us to the front lines to do your bleeding and dying while you swoop in to take all the credit."

The mess hall was completely quiet now as every eye in the room took in the altercation.

"That is just untrue," Tem said, shaking his head. He came up to the stomach of the Ursonian, but that didn't stop the historian. "Yes, the Ursonian Corps has been the backbone of the Galactic Government, but they have always worked hand in hand with the Rowki when the light was in jeopardy. Have you forgotten the battle of Delm when the Rowki Guardian Alita sacrificed her life to save the

Ursonian unit assigned with her? What about the conflict on the fire planet Haydar, when Jora Two-blades forbade the Ursonians to go with him because the danger was too high? Or when Alexander Tambascia went to help the surrounded Ursonians on Kulgi when the Hage overran their position? He is a hero to this day and still suffers for his sacrifice."

I wasn't really sure what Tem was talking about, but it seemed to have an impact on Bull. He swallowed hard and looked around as if he were embarrassed for a moment.

"Yeah, well, I've lost plenty of brothers and sisters in the corps following orders from the GG and the High Council," Bull said, trying to save face. "Now get out of my way. I'm hungry."

Looking back, I'm not sure Bull even meant to shove Tem that hard, but his sheer size compared to the much smaller species sent Tem reeling into the food printer hard as Bull moved forward.

I acted without thinking.

"Hey, that's enough," I said, moving in front of Bull and shoving the much, much, much larger individual in the chest. Needless to say, my shove did nothing.

"What are you going to do about it—what did you say you were? Human?" Bull asked, leaning down so he was face to face with me. "Come on. Go ahead, I'll let you take a swing. You look like you want to hit me. So go ahead, hit me. You're a Rowki, aren't you? What, humans don't carry any sense of pride or courage? I bet your clan is very proud of you back home. Bet your father and mother and whatever you call a mate just are so—"

I did hit him. I was tired of his mouth and I was already as sore as I could imagine being anyway. My right hand balled into a fist and smashed him across the snout so hard, my palm came back tingling.

To my credit, Bull actually stood up straight, shaking his head as tears filled his dark brown eyes. A thin line of blood fell down his left nostril.

"Oh, oh, I'm going to enjoy this," Bull said, lunging for me. I saw massive paws the size of my head reach for my shoulder and a mouth so cavernous, I was pretty sure I could fit a whole arm in there reach for me.

This is it, the thought flashed through my mind. *This is how you go. Killed by aliens, eaten by a steroid-pumped gummy bear named Bull.*

But the impact never came. Instead of being rammed by a thousand pounds of muscle and teeth, Bull was lifted off his feet. I couldn't believe my eyes. Bull, the massive figure of strength and rage was lifted from the ground like a child.

A slightly smaller but obviously much stronger Ursonian lifted Bull off his feet and shoved him back. The floor actually trembled a little as Bull slammed into the hard mess floor. This new element to the situation stood a head taller than the other Ursonians, with a Mohawk shaved into his hair. He wore the same grey-colored uniform as the others, but with a different insignia over his chest. The dense fur over the parts of his body I could see was a chocolate brown.

I thought there might be a fight, but apparently, this new Ursonian carried some kind of weight. Immediately, every Ursonian in the mess hall stood to attention, slamming a right paw over their chest.

Even Bull, who, after recovering, looked ready to pulverize whoever had just thrown him to the side, dropped his lower jaw. Immediately, he stood upright and pounded his chest with his right paw.

"Captain," Tem said, righting himself and shaking off the adrenaline surge. "Thank you, sir, it's a good thing you came when you did. Our newest Rowki here was about to lay into members from your unit. I'm sorry to say it, but they may have gotten hurt."

The captain didn't say a word but regarded me with a raised eyebrow as if to say, "Really? This thing?"

I held the captain's gaze. There was so much in those shrewd eyes. I saw intrigue, doubt, and maybe a little aggression. It was starting to get a little awkward, me shaking out my fist that throbbed with pain after laying into Bull, and the captain just staring at me as if he were looking not at me, but inside me.

"Oh, how rude of me," Tem said, talking with his hands as if he were some kind of symphony conductor. "Max Tyco, may I introduce you to Captain Axeleron Akel of the Ursonian Corps. Captain, this is Max Tyco. He has been selected as the newest member of the Rowki Guardians."

"Hello," I said, not sure if a wave or a handshake or a bow was appropriate. I don't know why I decided on the bow; maybe I'd watched too much sci-fi in my day and it just seemed fitting. As soon as I bent from my waist, I regretted it, as Bull and his counterpart snickered.

I stood up looking at the captain, who didn't bow in return but did dip his chin.

"I'm sorry, Max Tyco, you don't know. The captain has taken a vow of silence," Tem explained.

"Of course he did," I said, catching my surprise and trying to mask it. The last thing I wanted to do was piss off the strongest Kodiak in the room. "Well, that's certainly—certainly a noble calling."

The captain pointed behind me to the food printers,

then threw a thumb over his shoulder followed by a finger across his neck.

I wasn't sure if he was telling me to steal second base or giving me some kind of military hand gesture. Either way, it was all Ursonian to me.

"Right, right, thank you, Captain," Tem said, turning back to me. "He says we should get you something to eat. We have training with Instructor Noble next. If you're late, she's going to slit your throat."

SEVEN

SOMEWHERE AROUND THE first or second sprint, I was regretting that extra helping of eggs. Between the third and fourth laps around the torture track, I lost it.

"Is your species prone to expelling their meals?" Instructor Rima Noble asked. "If so, how did you manage to gain so much weight?"

"I'm fine, thanks for asking," I said, spitting the last pieces of regurgitated egg from my mouth. "And no, humans aren't prone to throwing up. I've just been teleported to an alien planet and now made to exercise until my guts are staging a revolt."

"Interesting," Rima said, wiping the sweat from her forehead. "Now get up and stop regurgitating all over my training floor."

The woman sure had a backward way of motivating, but it seemed to work. The more she pissed me off, the more I wanted to prove she was wrong about me. Pull-ups were still a no go. If I could feel my chest, I would have been proud of myself. I think I did more pushups than the day before. Truth be told, I wasn't really sure. All I focused on was not passing out and whatever task was immediately in front of me.

Rima called a halt as I lay on my back in a puddle of my own sweat, trying to do more sit-ups.

"That's enough," Rima said, hopping up from her own set of sit-ups like she still had all the energy in the world. "We want you left with something for Axeleron to use, not a stinking puddle of heavy breathing and sweat."

I was going to bite back with something, but I was too tired.

Tem scurried up with his ever-present datapad and whispered something to Rima. The two held a hushed conversation of which I could only make out every few words.

"He's...not ready..." Rima said.

"Morale boost... good for him..." Tem answered.

"Pathetic...poor excuse for a—"

"Hey, I can hear you," I said, forcing myself to my feet despite a wave of pain from every sore muscle in my body. "Just thought you should know. I'm literally feet from you."

"Tem thinks you should be told all the truths with nothing held back," Rima said, crossing her arms over her chest. "I think you're a little weak-minded to handle it all."

"First of all, we need to work on your people skills and fat-shaming," I said to Rima, too tired to even care if she made me do another circuit for talking to her like that. "Second of all, I'm still standing. I think if I can take talking bears and nearly getting jumped at breakfast, I can take whatever it is you have cooking up next. Hit me."

Poor choice of words on my part.

Rima moved too fast for me to tell her it was a human expression. She lunged forward and slammed her fist into my left shoulder so hard, I lost all feeling in the limb.

"Ugh, what the f—"

"Rima!" Tem shouted, cutting me off. "That was an Earth phrase for us to tell him more information."

"Oh, I see," Rima said, not looking sorry at all. "Well, now I know for next time."

"Holy potatoes," I groaned, gingerly moving my arm as feeling returned. "I think—I think you might have popped it out of—socket."

"Highly unlikely," Rima said, rolling her eyes. She placed her hands on my arm and pulled.

More pain rippled outward from my shoulder, threatening to take me to my knees again.

"No, you're fine," Rima said, turning her back to me. She waved for me to follow. "Come on, you think you can handle more? We'll see."

"Is she always like this?" I asked Tem as soon as I could stand straight.

"Violent, aggressive, short-tempered?" Tem asked.

I nodded as we both followed in the wake of the Rowki Instructor.

"Pretty much," Tem said with a shrug. "She's been through a lot. We all have."

Of course I had more questions, but I decided to let them go for now. Something told me that, for a very long time, I would always have questions that needed to be answered.

Both Tem and I followed Rima out into the wide, brightly-lit corridors. I had no idea where we were going, but Tem seemed to be content that Rima was leading us in the correct direction.

We passed a few Ursonians, who seemed to respect Rima. At least they slammed a paw to their chest and nodded in her direction. When they saw me, their mouths opened and they tried not to stare. I guess I was as much an alien to them as they were to me. Apparently, humans didn't get out in the universe very often.

We stopped at the end of the corridor where a series of cylinder-shaped indentations were made in the wall. I noticed Ursonians getting in and out of the cylinder-like pods as if they were elevators. Clear glass casing closed the moving cylinders, allowing everyone to see who came and went.

Rima stepped into an open cylinder pod and motioned us inside. Unlike elevators on Earth, there was no music. Rima touched a pad next to the opening. A glass door slid into place and the floor moved beneath our feet, sending us upward.

Now I thought it might be appropriate to ask one of the many questions battling to the surface.

"Where are all the other Rowki Guardians or those like me, in training?" I asked both the historian and the instructor. "I mean, if they are the law and order around this galaxy, shouldn't there be hundreds of them? Thousands?"

Tem and Rima exchanged a look I couldn't read. Was it worry? Definitely hesitancy.

"Maybe we should table this discussion for another time," Tem answered. "There is a lot going on that we still need to make you aware of."

"No, hit him," Rima said, using my own term. "Hit him with the truth. Did I use that correctly?"

"You did," I said, pretending I didn't flinch when she said the words.

"The Rowki are not as numerous as they once were," Tem said slowly as we continued to move upward in the cylinder. We passed level after level, making me wonder exactly how big this building we were in actually was.

"Wars, conflicts, splintering of the order itself has led to a decrease in our numbers."

"Not to mention the rigorous training it takes to become a Rowki," Rima added. "It seems fewer and fewer are willing to take up the burden and the amount of suffering required to become a true Rowki Guardian. The path is narrow; the way is steep."

As this new information sank in, our cylinder came to a stop at our designated floor. What I saw as the glass doors opened took my breath away.

The entire floor, at least this room, had glass walls on either side of a wide chamber. Those glass walls showed me that we weren't in a building at all. Neither were we on a planet. We were on a massive ship.

I felt my jaw drop, but I didn't care if they saw it or not. All I cared about was seeing what was on the other side of the glass wall.

As a child, I could remember dreaming about going to space. I would look at the sky and imagine what it must be like to travel amongst the stars, and now here I was.

Like a man in a trance, I walked over to the glass wall and allowed my eyes to drink in the beauty of this new normal. There were so many stars and planets of varying colors beyond the glass wall, I was caught under the spell of their wonder.

An excitement gripped me then, as well as dread. I would have thought the two were mutually exclusive, but I would have been wrong. Stars so bright they were hard to look at gave way to green, red, and purple planets.

The clear glass wall around the room allowed me to see it all in a near-panoramic view.

"We're not on a planet at all," Rima said after giving me

a moment to try and make sense of it all. "We are aboard the starship *Oni*."

"Oni means hope," Tem offered, arriving on my other side. "We are on a mission to give hope. That's what the Rowki truly stand for, if you want to boil it down."

"There are so many out there that need hope. So many without the light, living in a darkness of their own making, or of another," Rima said on my right. She stared out the window, not looking at me at all when she spoke. "When the world of men stands defenseless against the dark, send me. When the ancient ones come to reclaim their throne, send me. When all hope is lost and no one can see the way, send me. And when the light trembles to regain its feet, who will go? Send me."

I understood it was some kind of mantra or code Rima was repeating, but it did sound familiar.

"That is the code of the Rowki," Tem informed me. "You will be taught to repeat it as well."

"We're already on our way to the planet that needs help," I said, realizing my window for training was limited. "How long do we have?"

"The *Oni* jumps in and out of faster-than-light travel," Rima answered. "It's not good for any of our species to be placed in FTL travel for more than a few days at a time. At this pace, we'll reach our destination in two weeks' time."

"Two weeks," I repeated as if I had never heard those words before. "Two weeks? Is that enough time? Will that be enough time for me to train?"

"Well, that's up to you, isn't it?" Rima asked.

"Where are we going?" I asked the next logical question. "Two weeks to prepare for what?"

"Well, look at the time," Tem said, fishing out his ever-present datapad from the folds of his cloak. "The captain will be waiting for us in the weapons room. Come now, Max Tyco, we must get going."

"Training for what?" I repeated, not allowing the conversation to be manipulated this time. I stared hard at Rima until she turned her head to look over at me. "Where are we going?"

"We're going where we're needed the most," Rima answered, moving away from the window. "You'll be told when it's time."

That was it. Rima went to one cylinder and left the level. Tem directed me to another. No matter how much I pressed him, he just shrugged and said that Rima would tell me in her time.

I was reminded about all those movies and TV shows I'd watched where some government agent would use the word "classified" to answer a question they didn't want to answer.

I was a bit annoyed to say the least. If I only had two weeks to get ready, it seemed like I should know what I was getting ready for.

Instead of answers, yet more punishment awaited me. Tem directed our cylinder to move to a floor somewhere in the middle of the ship, if I was guessing correctly. We stepped off onto a busy corridor heading for a massive side room that roars and great huffs and groans came from.

I thought those meatheads at the gym who purposely let their weights fall and yelled out when they lifted to show off were concerning. Not that I had been to the gym in a few years, if I'm being honest here.

But the roars and groans coming from inside this room came with clashes of steel on steel. I even heard weapons being fired, not with the traditional boom or crack of any gun I was used to, but with a *pew pew* noise.

Tem and I walked into the room on our right where two heavy steel doors that reminded me of a bank vault stood open. Inside was the training area with a swarm of Ursonians working on everything from hand-to-hand combat, to bladed and ranged weapons.

There was so much to see, I didn't know where to look first. What was even more overpowering was the stench of sweat. The whole place smelt like a gym bag. For me to recall that scent was saying something.

Ursonian males and females threw each other around on thin mats to our right. The females of the species were nearly identical to the males. The only thing I did notice was they were slightly smaller of stature, with more curves and more of their bodies covered than their male counterparts.

It seemed clothes were optional in the hand-to-hand area. Many of the males had stripped off their gray uniforms, favoring a kind of boxer brief situation covering up their goods.

Likewise, the females did the same for their lower body, with a kind of sturdy sports bra for the top.

They traded blows as they sparred and threw each other to the ground. It was immediately obvious there were no punches held here. The females and males gave as good as they got, roaring and grunting as they trained.

As Tem and I walked past, we were regarded with a series of curious, not quite hostile expressions.

"Remember, don't hold eye contact. It's rude to stare," Tem said, smiling and nodding as we continued on. "They haven't seen a human before, so you can imagine what you must look like in their eyes."

"Right, right," I said, doing my best to look at them and smile then look away.

On our left, a range opened up where Ursonians fired off bladed weapons. Oh, you heard me right. This war-loving race found a way to incorporate blasters with their blades.

Axes, mauls, sledgehammers, and spears seemed to be their favorites, or a combination of them. Out of the very top of the weapons, a blaster opened to provide the user a ranged weapon.

Bright red bolts flashed from a firing line to targets down range with that same *pew pew* sound I'd heard earlier.

"The best of both worlds," Tem said as he saw me eyeing the range. "Ursonians prefer a simple weapon that will provide them with the opportunity to engage with an enemy at range as well as up close. The standard is what we call a Mauler T-19 with an ax head on one end and a spike on the other. Out of the top, a blaster barrel is equipped to target enemies at range."

"Seems efficient," I said, catching sight of Bull at the end of the firing line. I wasn't really sure if it was him or not, not to sound speciesist, but I was still getting used to telling the Ursonians apart.

The thing that tipped me off was that this bear was gingerly touching his nose. When he saw me, he lifted an upper lip and pointed his Mauler T-19 in my direction.

EIGHT

THE BLOOD in my veins went cold. He wouldn't, would he? Bull turned his snarl into a smile when he saw the blood drain from my face. It seemed even the bear wasn't that crazy. He pointed the barrel of his weapon down and acted as if he were just inspecting the weapon when Tem looked over.

Bull did draw a line across his neck with the first digit on his right paw, however.

"What are the odds that 'you're dead' means the same thing to humans as it does to bears?" I thought out loud.

"While I don't have an answer for that, I'm happy to say we are here," Tem answered, opening his arm up to the back corner of the training area where Captain Axeleron Akel stood with his Mauler T-19 in front of a pair of thickly-muscled bear soldiers. "It seems the captain is just finishing his latest instruction."

As the two warriors squared off against the captain, a circle formed with other soldiers eager to see what would happen.

"Two to one odds that neither of them even lands a

single hit on the captain," a female Ursonian said to her counterparts. "Come on, three to one."

"No way," a gruff voice answered from the Ursonian next to her. "You've taken enough of my money, Ero."

Ero looked over to me. "Well, as I live and breathe, that human pig species is here. Hey, Rowki-in-training, care to get in on the action?"

A few of the Ursonians around Ero looked over at me with intrigue, but quickly turned back as to not miss the fight.

"Sure," I said, willing to grab the lifeline of friendship Ero offered, even if it was to take my money. "I'm not really sure what you use as currency, though."

"Credits, my mushy friend," Ero said. "Cold hard credits."

"Don't have any credits, but I have a case of Red Bull in the back of my rig," I answered. "I'll bet you that."

"What's Rip Bell?" Ero asked, scrunching her eyebrows. "Is this some kind of human pig trick?"

"I'm not a pig," I said, shaking my head. "No, it's a drink."

Ero nodded and looked like she was about to say something else, then the harsh clash of metal on metal sounded.

Tem's eyes were already glued to the fight as sparks flew from the warriors' weapons.

"Axeleron is the weapons master," Tem explained without moving his eyes from the fight. "Each week, he has an open invitation for one or a pair of opponents to take the title from him. So far, no one who has challenged him has been able to defeat him."

A few seconds into the fight, I could see why. As Axeleron's opponents came in and out, the captain moved with deceptive speed. More than just quick, the captain flowed from one action to the next. A parry on his left transitioned to a kick to the sternum to the opponent on his right, and then another parry and strike of his own back to the first opponent.

For a creature as large as the captain to move with such grace was a mystery all its own. I had to blink a few times to try and discern how a being hundreds, if not a thousand pounds could move with the poise of a ballet dancer.

The captain brought the rear staff portion of his weapon under the jaw of his first opponent, snapping the soldier's head back with a sickening crack. The unlucky Ursonian staggered, then fell to the floor with a crash.

The remaining soldier moved in, trying to take the captain off guard. Axeleron saw the movement out of the corner of his eye, side-stepping out of the way. He turned that side step into a full circle, using the end of his weapon again to lash out and catch the base of the skull of the soldier stumbling forward.

There was another sharp thud and the soldier went down. Half the crowd groaned, the other half cheered as credits were exchanged.

"He's never lost," Tem said with obvious admiration. "Every week, he holds these open invitations for challenge, and he's never lost, not once!"

"Yep, yep, he's a legend," Ero said, eyeing me up and down. "So this Rum Bum, where is it? You have it on you? Time to pay up, human pig species thing."

"No, I don't have it on me," I explained. "They're drinks. Like, a case of drinks in my trailer."

"Mmm hmm, well, I got to go, but I'm holding you to your debt. I can swing by later tonight when my shift at the med bay ends. You better be good for it. I've never had Rum Bum before," Ero said.

"Not Rum Bum, Red Bull," I corrected her as those gathered dispersed. "I'm good for it."

Ero nodded, going over with a few others to help the concussed victims off the mat.

Tem took the opportunity to give me some last-minute instruction before I met with the captain.

"I'll help with translation where I can," Tem said. "Although the signs the captain does use are generally easy to decipher. He's brutal but kind. He'll make a great teacher for you. Be respectful and pay attention. You'll do fine."

I couldn't help but think Tem was like a proud parent sending his young off for their first day of school.

As the others left, the captain caught my eye and gave me a short nod. I returned the gesture. He wore the normal dark gray uniform, but this one was missing its sleeves. Boulder-like shoulders and arms the size of my waist were clear to see, as were the many scars that lined his limbs. Patches of fur were missing, telling stories all their own of the battles the captain must have endured in his time.

He wore his rank over the left side of his chest. I couldn't read it, but I imagined the symbol of his unit and perhaps the word "captain" in his language. The symbol was three slash marks coming down in a diagonal pattern.

The captain opened his right arm to take in the wall beside him and behind him. We were in the corner of the training grounds where the walls were stacked with hundreds of bladed weapons in neat racks.

I saw plenty of Mauler T-19's as well as knives, blasters, and even shields.

I examined them and looked back to the captain, eyes wide and nodding. "Yes, lots of weapons. I see them. Also, I should just let you know I bruise easily, so if you were wondering if you shouldn't knock me unconscious, that might be a good idea."

The captain, unlike the stern Rima Noble, actually smirked at my joke. He pointed to my chest and then behind him at all the weapons again.

"Oh, you want me to pick one?" I asked.

He nodded.

"Okay, then, let's see," I said, getting closer to the weapons. I had beyond no idea what I was doing. I'd been to the range a few times growing up, but I didn't own a firearm. I carried a knife in my rig for protection, but that ended up mostly for opening boxes and packages.

I glanced over at small blasters that looked like hand-guns, axes the size of my head, and the rifles, and settled on the largest blaster I could find. It was a heavy number, something that looked like a shotgun crossed with an ax.

"How about this one?" I asked, hefting the weapon off the wall. I could barely hold it. "This one looks like a winner. Tem, what's this one called? The Destroyer of Worlds, Eviscerator 2000, Annihilate Ultra?"

"That's the Peaches 2.0," Tem said, "but I don't think you're going to be using that."

"Huh? Peaches?" I said, repeating the word. "Why can't I use..."

I let the words die in transition from my brain to my mouth as I looked over at the captain.

He examined me with a raised eyebrow as if he just found me with my hands in the cookie jar. Or, in this case, all over Peaches 2.0.

"Or not?" I asked. "You said pick something."

The captain nodded, reaching for what looked like a steel baton from a small rack on the side of the wall. The baton was nearly lost to view as his massive right paw covered the weapon from end to end. He gave me the baton and motioned for me to give up Peaches.

"Really?" I asked, obeying. It felt like some kind of punishment, going from the weapon that looked straight out of a futuristic *Terminator* movie to a baton no larger than my forearm. "What am I going to do with this? Lead a marching band? I'm not Daredevil."

The captain placed Peaches back on the wall and reached for his own baton weapon. He activated a button on the shaft I didn't see. Immediately, the baton's ends sprouted from the weapon, forming not a baton, but a bo staff at least six feet long. Captain Akel twirled the weapon in his hands so fast, it ceased to be a staff and transitioned into a blur.

He slowed his movement a moment later and made sure to show me the correct grip. Once I pressed the groove in the middle of my own baton, it transitioned to a staff.

Learning from the captain was a lot easier than I'd first anticipated. Where Rima was harsh and condescending, the captain was patient with me. When he wanted me to do something like adjust my stance, he would first look to himself, modeling what he wanted me to do. If that didn't work, he'd adjust my hands and movements.

It felt strange to be so close to a being I was pretty sure could crack my skull with one hand and not be afraid of him.

At multiple points in our training, the captain would look to Tem to translate, using his hands to form words the little historian understood.

"He says your lack of an exo-skeleton will make armor mandatory when you're out on the field," Tem translated the captain's gestures. "You'll have to rely on speed, cunning, and force of will to win the fights in front of you. Strength isn't exactly your species' specialty."

"Thanks, I think," I said, having to agree with the strength part. If the Ursonians were any indication as to what waited for me out there in the universe, I knew the captain was right.

)

NINE

THE REST of the lesson was learning how to use the weapon to strike vulnerable parts like the head, eyes, nose, throat, joints, and groin. It seemed humans and Ursonians were quite similar when it came to where we hid the family jewels.

I learned to direct oncoming attacks instead of meeting them head on and trying to stop them. I didn't need to absorb the energy from the captain's staff when it descended on me if I could move to the side, or even impact the trajectory of the blow by a few degrees for it to land harmlessly next to me.

As we trained, we gained our own group of looky-loos who no doubt wanted a first glance at the human Rowki in training. I tuned out their mutters and talk. Having them there didn't seem to bother the captain and I wouldn't let it get to me either.

By the time we were done, I'd received a few bruises to my hands where the captain's staff came down on me and I didn't adjust correctly. He gave me another souvenir as well, a slight concussion when he threw me to the ground to demonstrate takedowns with the staff.

Otherwise, I didn't think I did so bad.

At the end of our training, the captain looked over to Tem and nodded.

"That's enough for today, more tomorrow," Tem said from his seat on the ground, making notes in his datapad. "We don't want to be late for our lesson and lunch before Rima Noble's hand-to-hand combat instruction to end the day. Let's take a quick break for food, though. You've burned through a lot of calories already today."

"No, of course not," I said, rolling my eyes and wiping the sweat from my forehead. "We couldn't have that, could we?"

Tem looked at me, blinking a few times as if he couldn't grasp the concept of sarcasm, but didn't know if I was trying to be serious or not.

I pressed the slender button in the middle of the baton and tried to hand it back to the captain.

The captain shook his head, closing my hand over the weapon and pressing it back toward me.

"You want me to keep it?" I asked. "Are you sure?"

The captain nodded.

"Thank you, Captain Axeleron Akel," I said. "Can I just call you 'Cap' for short? That's a, and if we're going to be..."

I just let that thought die as the captain shook his head with a frown.

"No? Okay, we'll work on that," I answered.

I thanked the captain again and then made my way with Tem back to the mess hall. I could smell myself, and it wasn't a good scent, either. I wasn't exactly a fan of taking multiple showers a day, but maybe I should start rethinking my stance on the matter.

The mess hall was as busy as ever. I was too tired to worry about the Ursonians staring at me. Instead, I sat down with my meal-plan-approved plate of what looked a lot like chicken and salad. It tasted a lot like chicken and salad as well, as if the recipe had been given to someone who had never had it and they put it together as best they could.

Tem seemed super happy about it as he stared at me taking my first bite.

I tried to ignore him, but he was sitting right across the table from me.

"What?" I asked, chomping on the lettuce.

"Well, what do you think about the food?" Tem asked, nodding. "Is it good? It's good, right?"

"I mean, it tastes healthy, if that's what you mean," I answered. "I could go for a cheeseburger and chili cheese fries right about now."

"No, no, this is better for you," Tem reassured me. "I studied what your species needs to eat to be healthy and strong, then inputted the ingredients into our food printers to give you some semblance of human food."

"Hey, what are you eating?" I asked, looking over at Tem's plate. It didn't really look that great—some mass of meat and oozing liquid—but it smelt like pizza. "Give me a bite of that."

"No, no, no," Tem said, protecting his food. "You wouldn't like this anyway, Max Tyco. It's not human food. It's a dish shared only with my people, the Ublec."

"It smells good, though," I said, leaning over with my eating utensil, which was basically a spork. "Come on, just a taste."

"Max Tyco, don't you dare," Tem squeaked, trying to

fend me off while hovering over his tray at the same time. "It's not in your designated meal plan. It's not in your designated meal plan. Resist the urge. Resist the urge!"

We both felt someone staring at us at the same time. Tem and I glanced over to see Rima Noble standing at our table looking at us with a flat stare, shaking her head.

I had my spork stuck in Tem's Ublec dish with one of his arms in my hands. On his part, he was trying to shove me away.

Fixed under Rima's death stare, I cleared my throat and sat back in my seat. Tem coughed in his hand. "Right, so we should get going to the Well of Enlightenment and begin our next lesson."

"Well of Enlightenment?" I asked. "What is that? It sounds relaxing. Tell me there are no more pushups or staff training at the Well of Enlightenment."

Rima seemed satisfied and went to a food printer to gather her own meal. Probably piss and broken dreams for how cheery she was.

"You'll be happy to know your body will be given a rest," Tem answered, hurriedly eating his food now with a distrusting eye in my direction. "Your mind, however, will be opened in a way you have yet to experience."

"What is it, like drugs?" I asked, munching on my chicken-like meal. "You're going to make me eat some mushrooms and go talk to the jolly green giant in the sky?"

"Mushrooms are an ingredient in the cocktail," Tem replied. "Come now."

I followed him as we walked to a conveyor belt that took our dishes through a series of stations where robotic arms cleaned and washed them before depositing them back somewhere behind the food printers.

I followed Tem to the cylinder-shaped lift and, this

time, we went down instead of up. We stepped off at a lower level that wasn't as brightly lit as the rest. It was more of a blue light than white. A sense of dread crept over me as we exited. There was no one else on this level. Memories of all the sci-fi horror movies I'd come to love over the years washed over me.

"Uh, hey, Tem?" I asked, holding my closed extending staff tightly in my right hand. Not that I could effectively use it in a fight after a day of training, but it was all I had. "Why is there no one else on this level?"

"This level on the *Oni* has been designated for Rowki use," Tem explained. "Both Rima and I have our personal quarters here, as well as the Well of Enlightenment."

That didn't make me feel any better as we traveled down a series of corridors then made a right and a left, ending at a pair of closed metal doors. Tem placed his hand on a pad set in the wall. A hiss escaped as the metal doors separated from the middle and slid into the walls.

To say the scene was ominous would have been putting it lightly. I couldn't help but think this reminded me of when Luke Skywalker was training with Yoda and about to go into that tree place to face the Darth Vader that lived in his mind.

"Maybe this isn't such a great idea," I said hesitantly. "I mean, this is day one of training, right? At least our first full day. Maybe we visit this on day ten or a hundred. Better yet, maybe we just skip this part altogether."

"There is nothing in the well that you do not bring yourself," Tem said, walking into the dark room. "You must learn to confront your demons. To find lasting peace, one must first be willing to wage the battle within."

"Wow, that's deep," I said, taking my first step into the room.

Motion sensor lights lit the chamber as Tem and I stepped inside. Dark green illumination filled the room, which was smaller than I first thought. On the left side of the space, what looked like a scientist's lab was set up, including tools and ingredients I didn't recognize. In the center of the room and to the rear was a reclining chair, and on the right side was a computer with a wall of screens.

"Our past does not define who we are today, but we would be remiss in saying that it does not play a part, Max Tyco," Tem said, going over to the left side of the room where he began mixing ingredients. "We are all shaped by our experiences, but it is finding meaning and learning from those experiences that drives us forward to be the best versions of ourselves that we should focus on."

The walls of my mouth were dry. Beating down my body with rude teachers and care bears was one thing. Going into the deepest parts of my mind was another. There were events and memories there I made a conscious effort to ignore.

Tem sat at a chair, working with ingredients. He wasn't kidding about the mushrooms either. A small pot sat under a blue light with the fungus growing out of it. A red-capped mushroom with yellow dots was removed and crushed up in a circular glass bowl.

My hands started to sweat.

"Tem, what exactly is this going to do to me? This well of enlightenment? What is it?" I asked nervously. I didn't even care if he heard the hesitancy in my voice. Tem was the closest thing I had to a friend on the ship. "It's going to make me hallucinate?"

"The well will place you in a deep sleep and bring to the forefront of your mind whatever you must overcome to be at peace with yourself," Tem explained, crushing the mushroom in the glass bowl with a glass tool. He added powders and liquid to the mix with expert hands. "The ingredients being used are the mushrooms from Valka, sleeping powder from the moons of Aderan..."

Tem went on, explaining where the ingredients were from and what they did, but he lost me at Valka. I was too busy thinking about her. I'd suppressed so many memories for the sake of my own well-being just to survive. Thinking about her now? I wasn't really sure what that would do to me.

"Rowki have been taking this for thousands of years," Tem was saying as I tuned back in. "It's safe."

Tem stood up from his seat with the bowl in his hands, directing me over to the kind of reclining chair in the back of the room.

"While you are dreaming, what you see will be recorded for future study if you so wish," Tem instructed, motioning to the wall of monitors. "Come, sit and breathe."

"Tem," I said, swallowing hard as I sat in the chair and took the bowl in my hands. The stuff looked lumpy and smelled like spices and mold. "Tem, there are things in my past I don't want to remember. I'm not sure I can do this."

Tem took a long breath as if he were measuring his words before he spoke.

"Max Tyco," Tem began. "I know all about you and your past. I did my research before you were taken aboard the *Oni*, as any good historian of the Rowki would. I know what you've been through. I know the demons you face."

I clenched my jaw, shaking my head.

"I can't make you enter the Well of Enlightenment," Tem explained with a soft voice. "But I know if you refuse, you will be sent back to Earth. I know how much pain you carry. I know that pain will never go away, but maybe,

maybe you can use that pain for something good. I never met her, but I read all about her. What would she want you to do? Perhaps if you cannot do this for yourself, you can do it for her. For them."

Tears stung and itched my eyes as I stared into the bowl. They splashed down my cheeks. I began to think about events so long ago, events I'd repressed through booze and distraction because anything was better than dealing with them over and over again.

"It's ready when you are," Tem explained. "Breathe deeply in through your nose for a count of six and slowly out through your mouth. The act will sync your body and mind. You'll only need to do it two or three times before you will feel the effects."

"You can do it for her," I said through blurry vision. "You can do it for them."

I counted to six, breathing in slowly through my nose. I couldn't keep my hands from shaking. If Tem saw it, he didn't say anything. I knew what my demons were. I understood what waited for me.

I counted to six, exhaling the spiced mold smell, and did it again. I felt sleepy. Vaguely I remembered Tem taking the bowl from me as I reclined in the chair and then the most vivid dream I'd ever experienced came for me.

TEN

I DIDN'T HAVE the greatest memory. That was a double-edged sword. Right now, I saw it all as clear as me being there. I wasn't really me in this dream. I saw myself and her as memories of my past flooded my waking mind as I'd feared they would.

I met Christina freshman year of high school, and we were inseparable as outcasts that only had each other. We ate lunch together, walked to school together, and even nerded out about playing video games together, and the latest board games, card games, or films. If it was science fiction or fantasy, you bet the two of us were into it.

She saved me during those years. She was all I had. A mother who lost interest in the idea of having kids left when I was young. A father crushed by the stresses of this world started working sixty-hour weeks, trying to support us. When his body was present, his mind was lost in the bottom of a bottle. All I had was her.

"Seriously, I'm going to talk to him. This isn't okay," Christina said from beside me in the high school's cafeteria table. "He's not supposed to hit you. Parents aren't supposed to hit their kids like that."

"I'm fine," I said, touching the place over my left eye where my father had laid into me the night before. "It's not really him when he's drinking. You've seen him sober. He's just, he's under a lot of stress and—"

"If you make another excuse for him, I'm going to punch you myself," Christina said. "I live in a group home. I've never had a mom and dad, but I know they're not supposed to punch you. I'm going to do something about it."

"Please, not yet," I said, moving my square pizza slice around on my tray. "I'll talk to him, or just leave next time he's getting drunk. It won't happen again."

"That's what you said last time," Christina sighed, rolling her eyes. "Promise me. If you need to get away, you go out the window or something. Call me and we'll meet up."

I swallowed hard and nodded.

"Ah, isn't that cute," Chad Snyder's voice said from the next table over where he sat with his friends. "The two nerds are going to get it on and have baby nerds together. Wait a minute, Tyco, does she beat you? What happened to your eye?"

I didn't say anything. I knew feeding bullies was the worst thing you could do. Christina didn't hold the same outlook.

"The same thing that's going to happen to your eye if you don't mind your own business," Christina shot back. "Does making fun of people make you feel better about yourself somehow? Who hurts you or degrades you so much you feel like you need to take it out on others?"

Chad opened his mouth and then closed it again. Instead of an answer, he cracked some kind of joke about me and Christina having some kind of super loser spawn and went back to his friends at his table.

"Don't worry about them," Christina said, rubbing my arm. "We'll be okay. You'll always have me. We have each other. We'll be okay. Like Doctor Who and his assistant. Just to be clear, I'm the Doctor in this analogy."

That made me smile.

"Like Superman and Wonder Woman?" I asked.

"Just like that," Christina agreed.

I watched this memory take place in front of me. I saw the freckles on her cheeks, her bright eyes so alive with joy and light despite her having every reason to hate everyone. Growing up in the foster system should have broken her, but it only made her stronger.

I stood there in the corner of the cafeteria near the back of the room where we always shared our meals. We were so young. The image in front of me twisted and evaporated like smoke dying in a light breeze.

The next scenes were only snapshots, like a picture instead of reliving an event. I saw us falling in love, her going to community college and graduating with her AA degree, and me working at the local grocery store.

We were married and happy. Money-wise, we didn't have much, with her teaching and me stocking shelves, but we were happy, so happy. We had each other and that was all we needed.

I shook my head. The lump in my throat grew as I understood the timeline of events and what would take place.

Our love had grown over the years and we wanted to start a family of our own. Years of trying to have a baby and falling short sought to drive a wedge in our marriage, but we were too strong to let it. Our relationship bent but never broke.

The scene of the night it all happened conjured around me like a bad magic trick.

I saw myself and Christina in a heated argument in our one-room apartment.

"Tem!" I screamed out. "Tem, enough! I know what happens next, enough! Get me out. Get me out of here!"

Nothing.

The truth was, even though I knew what happened next, the details were so buried in my psyche, I didn't remember exactly what I said that night. I saw it all now.

"Listen, I just need some time to process it all," Christina said with a long exhale. "You don't know what it's like. It's me that lost the baby after so many years of trying, and all those tests and being poked and prodded. All the sickness. *I* lost it."

"We'll figure it out," I answered. "Of course I'm sad, but we'll figure this out. It's not your fault."

"Tell that to my body," Christina sighed as tears welled in her eyes. "Why doesn't my body want to have a baby, Max?"

"We can always adopt," I answered. "We've talked about it before. We don't have to put ourselves through all of this again."

"I just need time," Christina said, shaking her head. "I know you're trying to help, but I just need time to think through all of this."

We stood there in our little apartment family room that barely had enough room for a couch, table, and TV. I didn't know what to say. I wanted to comfort her more, but I also knew Christina worked through things differently than I did.

I watched my wife and me going through all of this again. Panic seized my gut as if this was happening in real time instead of a memory long past my control.

"Don't let her go," I said to my past self. "Don't let her go. Why did you let her go?"

My past self didn't know what else to do. I remembered feeling that way. I remembered the helplessness. Anything I wanted to say to her didn't seem like enough. After getting the news we'd lost that baby after years of tests and trying, everything else seemed trivial. It wasn't like I could ask her if she wanted to just sit down and watch some Netflix.

"I think I just need to take a walk or drive," Christina said. "I just need time to work through all of this, Max. I'm not like you. I can't just focus on the next thing to do. I need to sit with this."

"Okay," my past self answered. "If that's what you need."

"You shouldn't have let her go!" I yelled at my past self, rushing forward to block Christina from going. I knew this was all out of my control somewhere, but now, in the moment in this lucid dream state, I thought maybe I could stop her and change things.

Christina reached for her keys and headed to the door.

"Stop her!" I screamed to my past self who just stood there like an idiot. I ran for the door, blocking Christina's path. "No, stop, just stay. Stay and think about it. Don't go. Don't go. Chris, please don't go."

Christina passed right through me as if I weren't there at all. She opened and closed the door forever.

I was a man lost in his sorry. I was a madman in my own dream.

"Come back!" I yelled, reaching for the now-closed door. "Come back!"

When I tried to open the door, my ethereal hand just passed through it. I was left to live out the hell of the next twenty minutes and what was doomed to follow.

My past self let out a deep sigh and headed for his phone and then sports on the television.

"Do something, call her back," I said in a whimper, all the fight out of me now as I waited helplessly. I'd never felt so defeated. Whether it was Tem or my own psyche having mercy on me I wasn't sure, but time sped up now as we headed toward the end.

The scene in front of me vanished. I saw a glimpse of me getting the phone call. The manic drive two blocks down where the crash happened. Then I was there at the scene with our little Mazda 3 smashed so violently, it didn't even resemble a vehicle anymore.

There was glass everywhere, the lifted SUV that struck her in the intersection. Her body was covered with a tarp on the side of the street. Police and paramedics, firemen and the ice cream.

Why did I fixate on the ice cream? She had gone to get ice cream for us after our fight. She knew my favorite, cookies and cream, and mint and chip; a double scoop lay melting on the black gravel of the road, seeping into cracks and crevices unexplored.

My past self howled and cried not like a man but like an animal. I forgot I sounded like that. I forgot what a man can sound like when his heart is ripped out of his chest along with any sense of joy to come.

ELEVEN

I WOKE in front of Tem, screaming like a banshee. Sweat covered me from my brow to my palms. I was panting my throat raw, telling me I had been screaming for some time.

"Max Tyco, Max Tyco," Tem said, rushing to my side from his place in front of the screens. "I'm sorry. I'm sorry, Max, but this is what you brought with you. This is what you hold repressed. This is what you must come to peace with if you are to truly become a Rowki Guardian."

I sat panting, not knowing what to think or do. I was pissed that I had let Tem talk me into this, confused as to what I was supposed to do with my past if not bury it, and finally, exhausted.

Tem went to his shelf of supplies and came back with a cup of water for me.

"Drink and breathe, Max Tyco," Tem said. "Drink and breathe."

I accepted the water and took down a long draught before placing it on the seat beside me. I focused on six seconds of air in through my nose and six seconds out through my mouth.

Tem and I just sat in silence.

"You can see now the way of the Rowki is not just mastering one's body, but one's mind and spirit," Tem said slowly. "We can teach you how to be at peace with who you are and with your past."

"I shouldn't have let her go," I said, thinking back on the memory now that was still so clear. "I let her go when she was angry. I shouldn't have let her go, Tem. Why did I let her?"

"Max Tyco, please, please release me, you're hurting me," Tem said.

I looked down to where my hands held Tem by each shoulder so tight, my hands shook. I didn't realize I had even taken hold of the smaller historian.

I let go, staggering off the table. Rubbing my eyes, I tried to get my head right.

"You must find peace in the past if you are to be able to live in the present," Tem said meekly from his place by the chair. "You must accept and overcome."

"So what, you want me to relive that nightmare over and over again? Because I have, Tem," I spat. "I have, and it leads me to the bottom of a bottle every time, just like my father. It's better to not think about it."

"The past is something to be gazed at but not looked directly on, like the sun," Tem answered. "Recognize it for what it is, accept it, and then move on. It only destroys you because you refuse to even think about it. Instead, you've been as you said, dealing with it through substance abuse. True strength is dealing with it on your own two feet."

I stood there just shaking my head.

"This is enough for today," Tem said with a worried sigh. "Max Tyco, I wish I could have afforded you more time, but it is the hour for your final training sessions of the day with Instructor Noble."

"What?" I asked, trying to remember the day's structure. "How long was I under? It couldn't have been more than ten, twenty minutes."

"Nearly four hours," Tem said, motioning me to follow. "Come, Max Tyco, the day is almost over and then you can rest."

I thought I knew what professional athletes must feel, the hours of training every day. I felt depleted and sore as my muscles and joints ached all the way back to the upper floor and the training room where my truck still sat.

Rima was there waiting for us. She leaned against my rig, tapping a foot when we entered.

"You look horrible, Tyco," she said, glancing over to Tem. "Did he find it?"

"He found it, first time," Tem answered. "Just like we thought."

"Found what?" I asked, a little peeved they were treating me like a child.

"The things holding you back," Rima answered. "You need to accept them and let them go."

"Right, so all of you are suddenly psychiatrists?" I asked, now pissed off instead of just a little annoyed. "You two have the only thing you loved in the universe ripped away? Did you have a chance to stop it, and you did nothing?"

Tem looked to the ground.

Rima held my stare with a wild rage in her eyes.

"We all have our stories, Max Tyco. Do you think you are the only one that's lost something?" Rima asked through gritted teeth. "We've all lost. Some of us, everything. You think you're special? You're not worth crip. Oh, I'm going to enjoy this session. Get ready for hand-to-hand combat training."

Tem used the datapad in his hands to turn the right side of the training room into a futuristic sparring section. A dummy sprouted from the ground that felt like soft rubber when I hit it.

"Your stance is sloppy," Rima said as we went over to the striking object and stood in front of it. "Knees slightly bent, left in front of the right. Hands up and open. Let me see you punch."

I let out a right that I thought was pretty decent.

"Turn your hips into the punch; put your full weight behind it," Rima explained. Torque your fist on the point of impact. Don't try to hit the object; drive through it and hit the other side."

Information was coming at me so quickly, but I tried to grasp and implement it all. Unlike Akel, Rima was not patient or kind about her instruction.

"You look like a child learning to walk for the first time," Rima huffed. "If this is the best the universe has to offer, then we're in trouble. Breathe out through your mouth when you throw your punch. Breathe in when you reload your strike. Again."

And so it went for the first hour and the second, Rima giving me two points of instruction and one criticism with absolutely no praise.

I didn't need her praise; that was not what I craved most at the moment.

"Hit it like you mean it," Rima said as I made contact with the dummy in front of me over and over again. "Use it. All that pain and anger you feel. All that remorse and regret. Don't allow it to consume you. Instead, you use it, here and now, for something good to come out of the event. Feed from it, Tyco. Again, again, again. Let me hear you."

"Raw, raw, *raw!*" I grunted as I landed blow after blow. The skin on my knuckles tore and blood smeared the dummy as I struck over and over again, lost to the pain and numbness in the moment. I'm not sure how many times I hit the target at the end—a dozen times, more? All I knew was my chest was heaving and my hands were a bloody mess by the time Rima shoved me from my place in front of the bag.

The woman was much stronger than she looked. She pushed me so hard, I lost my balance and landed on my butt.

"I said enough," Rima bellowed. "That's enough for today, Tyco. Rest; tomorrow will be harder."

That was it, no good job or well done. Rima left me there sweating and bleeding on the floor.

Tem was immediately by my side. He looked at my bloody hands and shook his head. "I'll get medical here right away. When you're able, we should also get you showered and to the mess hall for sustenance."

"I just want to be left alone," I answered, still catching my breath.

It must have been the way I said it that gave the historian pause. "Max Tyco, I—"

"Tem," I shouted louder than I intended. "Please, I'll be fine. I just need a moment to think."

"Of course," Tem said, adjusting his datapad. "I'll leave the shower area up for you and have a meal left just inside your doors. Your own datapad is waiting for you in the rig as well. It gets better, Max Tyco. The first few days usually break new recruits, but it does get better."

I had a few smart remarks that came to mind, but I was

beaten down both in mind and body, and to be honest, there was only one thing I really wanted at the moment.

I waited until Tem left and headed to my rig. On the manifest, I remembered seeing a pallet of booze I wanted to get my hands on. I just wanted to escape. I wanted the pain of the memories to stop. I needed them to stop. I didn't want to remember. I didn't want to have to deal with all of this here on an alien ship. I just needed to let go.

I unlocked the rear of my rig and jumped in, ignoring the pulsing pain coming from my fists. The pallet I needed was to the rear and on the left. Cellophane wrapping gave way to my knife as I cut through and opened the box and freed one of the bottles.

It could have been anything, but it so happened to be whisky. I broke the safety seal, twisting the cap as fast as I could, and tilted my head back, lips pressed hard to the bottle. Fiery, burning ecstasy scorched my throat, promising me reprieve in minutes.

I coughed, lowering the bottle and heading down to the rear of the rig. I hated turning into my father in this way, but the only other option was to sit with my pain. The shower and eating food were a blur as I found my way to the bottom of the bottle, numbing my pain for a moment. But that was the thing with alcohol, it was like trying to put a band aid on a broken hose. You were just going to need to keep replacing that band aid.

In my stupor, I managed to find my way to my bed in the rig and passed into quiet oblivion. My dreams were of her. The way she smelled, her laugh, the feel of her in my arms. Whatever that Well of Enlightenment did, it opened my repressed memories so I could see her so clearly, remember so vividly. I hated and loved it at the same time.

TWELVE

I PROBABLY WOULD HAVE MISSED the alarm on my new datapad if Tem hadn't come for me. Between the amount of whisky I took in and the way my body felt, I think I might have slept all day.

And so the cycle of training twelve hours a day and drinking myself into a stupor at night began. Hangovers weren't much of an issue for me, but as I saw the bottles of whisky in the boxes depleting, I knew sooner or later I was going to have a serious problem on my hands.

Tem knew. He had to smell it on me in the morning, but he didn't say anything. Day by day, I was getting stronger. Akel praised my improvement with the staff. Rima heckled me less. My lessons with Tem transitioned from the Well of Enlightenment to history lessons of the Rowki.

Ten days in and I started to notice the soreness beginning to diminish. I was down a few pounds of fat, and while I was far from Chris Hemsworth, I noticed my pants fitting looser and my level of cardio increasing.

Say what you will about the meal plan they had me on and the torture they called training, it was working.

At the moment, I sat with Tem in another room at the lower level of the ship. This one was so large, it was almost comical that Tem and I would be the only ones using it. A circular sphere rose from the middle of the room and acted as a projector as Tem explained to me the rich heritage of the Rowki and why they were so important.

"Throughout time, factions have broken off from the Rowki Order. The most notable and dangerous of these factions are the Sait," Tem explained. The orb projector in the middle of the room showed off a group of menacing black-cloaked figures wielding weapons of their own that ranged from blasters to swords.

"Why'd the Sait break off?" I asked from my La-Z-Boy-like chair. I convinced Tem this was the standard classroom style seat. I don't think he totally bought it but was willing to concede the point. "Let me guess, they had enough of the authorized meal plan?"

"No, no, but good one," Tem said, going from a smile back to being serious in a heartbeat. "The Sait don't believe in balance. They don't care about the good and the bad; they only want to service themselves."

"You should choose different words; that just sounds wrong," I cautioned.

"They only look out for their own interests," Tem said, looking over at me for approval. "Better?"

"Better," I agreed.

"The Sait kill and take what they want using the power they learned from the Rowki. They are ruled by their emotions, and as such, are our most dangerous enemy in the galaxy," Term explained. "Which leads me to sardonium metal."

"What kind of metal?" I asked, sipping from my water. After the initial meeting where I had to have my heart bashed in again at the Well of Enlightenment, my time with Tem was almost enjoyable. Like Akel, he was patient and let me learn at my pace. My time with Tem was quickly becoming my favorite part of the day.

"Sardonium metal is extremely rare," Tem said, maneuvering his fingers over his datapad screen. A hunk of rock was projected via the hologram in front of us. "It is said it comes from the heart of dying stars. Rowki are able to use and manipulate the metal over time."

It looked like a small meteor to me. I got that I was supposed to be amazed by the hunk of rock, but I was more interested in what Tem said Rowki could do with it.

"Wait, Rowki can manipulate it, how?" I asked.

Tem transitioned the hologram to show footage of Rima that appeared on a screen in front of me. She was breathing hard, blood coming from a spot over her left eye. A curved sword I had yet to see her carry rested in her hand. The steel shone with a white ray almost like a flame.

"It's better if I just show you," Tem explained. "This is Rima with her back against the wall during a mission at infinity's edge. She was penned in with a dozen Sarmirs about to consume her."

I sat up straight and leaned in as I watched figures from nightmares close in on Rima. They looked like scarecrows stuffed with metal shards instead of straw. A hard ticking sound came from them as they advanced around Rima.

Rima Noble didn't look scared in the least. If anything, she was even more terrifying than the Sarmir that hedged her in.

Unlike Akel, Rima moved with violence and stiff strokes of her weapon that nearly severed her opponents in half, sometimes decapitating them altogether. The magic happened when Rima threw her sword at an enemy. It stuck deep in its chest, spilling silver blood down its shirt.

As if it were pulled by a magnet, the weapon returned to her hand, where she used it to hack another enemy down. She tossed the weapon again, this time making a zigzag pattern as if an invisible force moved the weapon. The sword struck the heads of two, three, four enemies before returning to her.

"Oh snap, are you telling me we can control things with our minds? We have telekinesis?" I asked, standing up from my seat. "You should have started with all of this."

"Not all things; only the sardonium alloy," Tem corrected. "Instructor Noble discovered a small sliver of the sardonium and was able to melt it down into her weapon. She controls the sardonium; the weapon is only a vehicle moved by it."

"So like Magneto," I said with awe. "You're telling me I can control a certain type of metal with my mind. That's like Magneto; close enough."

"I know nothing of this Magneto you speak of, but yes, with training, in time, you will be able to control the sardonium," Tem said. "That is, if you can find some. It is a very rare metal and valued more than most."

"I am just made of questions right now," I said as the video of Rima kicking butt ended in front of us. "First, note to self, I really need to make sure I don't get on Rima's bad side."

"Too late," Tem said honestly. "I think the—sheet has sailed on that one."

"Ship, ship has sailed," I corrected the historian. "I think you mean ship."

"Do I?" Tem asked with a smirk.

"Next," I answered, moving along the conversation.

"How do you have footage of this? Someone was with Rima not helping but just videotaping it all?"

"It is important that when Rowki go into the field, as much is documented as possible," Tem explained. "The video you saw was taken by a hover camera. There will be a hover camera with us on our missions as well."

"And about this mission the High Council has us on," I said, trying to get more information out of Tem. "When do I get to know where we're going and why?"

"We'll know soon enough," Tem answered.

"Well, we're supposed to be wherever it is we're going in four days, so sooner rather than later would be nice," I pressed. "Besides, I think—"

The doors to our classroom opened and Rima stepped into the room. She looked pissed, but that was just the face I had come to know her by.

"Rima, hey, Rima," I said, feigning friendship. "We can control metal? When do we get to start learning that? When does arts and crafts begin?"

Rima gave me a blank stare and blinked a few times. She ignored me and just looked over to Tem. "I've received a message from the High Council. There's a system in need and we're the closest ones to it. We're being rerouted there. It shouldn't take us long, and then we'll continue on."

"Of course," Tem said, closing his datapad. "Should I call Captain Akel?"

"I already have," Rima answered. "Both he and his second are on their way here for a briefing. I have rerouted the *Oni* to the planet in need. We will arrive in hours."

My blood ran cold. Suddenly, I felt both Tem and Rima staring at me. I was only ten days into my training. Sure I could land a good punch and there were fewer rolls to my gut now. But it was ten days, not ten weeks.

"Tyco," Rima said with a cold, hard voice. "I need to know that you're ready. I haven't made an issue of your drinking because you continue to perform, but out in the field, I will not abide you being addle-minded when it could put others at risk. Do you understand?"

I was partly shocked she knew, partly offended and angry to be called out like this, but mostly upset with myself because I knew she was right.

"You deal with your past now," Rima went on. "You deal with your issues, and we're here to help you do that, but the training wheels are off. When we go down there, it's life and death. It's time for you to show us why you were selected as a Rowki. Prove it to yourself."

I wish I could have come up with something epic or funny to say in that moment to alleviate some of the tension. I had nothing. I just nodded.

"I know I've been hard on you, Tyco," Rima continued, holding my gaze. "And I'm going to keep on being hard on you. The strongest blades are forged in the hottest flames. You've had a lot of pain in your past. It's time to use that for something great."

Tem wiped a tear from his eyes. "They grow up so fast."

I wasn't sure if he was being funny or not, but I didn't have time to figure it out. The doors behind me opened again. In walked Akel along with the female Ursonian I had made a bet with my first full day of training. Ero was it? She had never come for her case of Red Bulls after the bet.

"Captain, Lieutenant," Rima said.

Captain Akel nodded to us.

"Rowki, Tem," Ero answered.

"Thank you for coming so quickly," Rima said, motioning for Tem's datapad. He gave her the tool right away. "We received news from the High Council that a planet in this system called Somu is in need."

We all watched together as the holo screen in front of us transitioned to a planet more water than land.

"There is a warlord who has overthrown the ruling government and made slaves of the local populace," Rima continued. "Our mission is simple: free the slaves, restore the monarch to power. We hit them hard and by surprise. We should be in and out within a day, two at most."

The screen followed Rima's words, showing a group of amphibian-type creatures who looked humanoid enough, with webs between their fingers, gills for ears, and feet that looked like flippers.

"The Somu empire has been allies of the Galactic Government for years. We won't let them down when they need us most," Rima continued. "Questions?"

"What's the size of the force we'll be engaging?" Ero asked.

"We're going to infiltrate their capital city with a small team and free their soldiers," Rima explained. "The forces we'll be engaging will be a few hundred at most, and taken by surprise."

Akel made a few paw motions that included grabbing his crotch and giving Rima the finger. I assumed both those things translated differently in this situation.

"Good idea," Rima told the captain as the two of them and Tem spoke about specific plan points.

"Hey, how come you never came to pick up your Red Bull?" I whispered to Ero. "I lost that bet."

"I did come," Ero said with a raised eyebrow. "When I arrived, you were naked and drunk in a deep slumber."

"Oh—oh," I said, coughing and looking away. "Well, I see, then. My—my bad. I still owe you those."

"Yes, you do," Ero confirmed. "I just have no desire to see your strangely unabashed nudity. I had to wash my eyes out with military-grade antiseptic usually reserved for cleaning bacteria from wounds. The image of your smooth naked buttock is forever branded into my brain."

"Okay, okay, I get it," I said. "I'm sorry. I'll get them for you. I won't be naked again."

As I said those last words, Rima, Tem and Akel finished their conversation and looked over to me with raised eyebrows.

"Oh, come on, you had to have just heard that last part?" I asked incredulously.

"Two hours," Rima said, heading for the door. "Tyco, with me."

I trotted next to the woman, grateful to be free from that awkward situation. I didn't want to have to explain my nudity to everyone.

I followed Rima out of the room. We took a left, heading deeper into the Rowki level of the *Oni*. I'd never been this deep before. My experiences here had been relegated to the Well of Enlightenment and Tem's conference room that we'd just left.

The lights were still, dim. It was quiet aside from the even footfalls of our boots.

"The Rowki have their own armory aboard each ship," Rima explained. "We'll need you outfitted and ready to go. I'll show you what you'll be wearing."

Doubt crept in my mind. The insanity of driving my rig just ten days before and now prepping to go into combat was not lost on me.

"Are you sure I'm ready?" I asked. "I'm not positive I've had the proper training."

"I can assure you, you have not been trained nearly well

enough," Rima explained as we entered a room on our right. "However, this is the time we have been given and experience is the best teacher of all."

My breath caught in my chest as we entered the Rowki armory.

THIRTEEN

SUITS OF SCI-FI armor stood shoulder to shoulder against the back wall. On the right, weapons sat against the wall, on the left, supplies.

The sheer number of armored suits reminded me again that the Rowki must be hurting for recruits. There were dozens of suits ready and only Rima and me to wear them. The armor reminded me of medieval protection, from the vambraces and shin guards, right down to the helmets.

The helmets were pointed forward from the nose to the chin, with breathing filters on each side. The visor ran sideways just over the nose and to the forehead, again reminding me of pictures of helmets I had seen knights wear in movies. The armor was a dull gray while the visor was red.

"Yours is first on the right," Rima explained. "I had it altered to suit you. However, you are more rotund than I expected you to be."

"Thanks," I said, not even looking over. My eyes were still taking in the suit of armor in front of me.

"The black synth suit underneath is already strong

enough to turn most blades or small caliber blasters," Rima explained as she moved to the other side of the room and her own suit of armor. "The dura steel plating on the outside will protect your vital parts. Dura steel can withstand direct hits from even large caliber rounds."

Are you really going to do this? I asked myself. *You're really going to suit up and go down to an alien planet to what? Kill some fish species and free other fish people? The whole time doing it with an army of steroided-out Winnie the Poohs?*

"It's normal to have second thoughts the first mission out," Rima said over to my left. "We all have had them."

I looked over and immediately closed my eyes. Rima stood as naked as the day she was born, bending over to pull the black skintight synth suit over her body.

"Uh, Rima, a heads-up next time would be appreciated," I said, feeling the heat rush to my face. Who knew alien physiology could be so close to humans'?

"Don't be such a child," Rima scolded. "We're about to go into conflict with one another. We have to be comfortable with seeing each other's no-no parts from time to time."

I realized here she didn't actually say no-no parts; it was just the way her words were being translated in my ears. Still, I couldn't help but crack a grin as I removed my own clothes and pulled on the synth suit.

I heard Rima huff a little as I undressed and began to slide on the cold fabric.

"What?" I asked defensively. "It's cold in here."

"You're putting it on backwards," Rima retorted with a raised eyebrow as she finished zipping hers on and began to place her armor over her chest.

"Oh, right," I answered, turning the black synth suit around and climbing in. The fabric was frigid and, to be honest, not very thick. I had yet to understand how something as thin as this could be responsible for saving me from a blade. "Rima, are you sure this is going to work? I mean, the synth suit doesn't feel very durable."

Rima went over to the side of the room and removed a dagger, approaching me with a grin I didn't like.

"Hold on, hold on," I said, understanding what she was about to do. "I don't need to see it! I—"

Rima brought the blade down on the left side of my chest. Where the dagger made impact, I felt a small amount of pressure but no stabbing pain or agony.

"Synth suits displace incoming force and spread it out across your body," Rima said, stabbing me a few more times for good measure. There was a satisfied look in her eyes as if she were fulfilling some kind of fantasy. "See?"

"Are you crazy?" I asked, taking a step back from Michael Myers. "What if this was a defective suit, or I moved to block and you stabbed me in the hand?"

"I was willing to take the chance," Rima said, sheathing her blade. She motioned to the rest of the armor. "Come on, I'll show you how to gear up."

I put my heavy-duty boots on while Rima secured the rest of my armor. Each piece practically clicked into place as if it were held magnetically by the synth suit. By the time we were done, there were only small sections between the pieces of armor that the synth suit would have to protect if an attack managed to get through.

The dura steel was much lighter than I anticipated. I did a few squats in it and general stretches to test its limits. There were none. However, I wanted to move the synth suit and dura steel plating allowed.

"Wow, this is some really intuitive stuff," I said, rolling

my neck around my shoulders. "I bet I look like a superhero."

"Helmet and extending staff can clip onto your magnetic belt," Rima answered, going over to the wall of weapons. I saw her add a small blaster and large sword to the knife she already carried.

I recognized the sword. It was the same one Rima had used in the holo video Tem showed me. The blade was long and slightly curved, with a white gleam in the metal.

"Is that the—the salmanion metal?" I asked in awe.

"Sardonium," Rima explained. "Yes, I see your lessons with Tem are paying off. Glad something is sticking."

"What's that symbol?" I asked, motioning to the mark in the blade that practically shone. "Is that a letter?"

"That is the sardonium," Rima said, whipping the blade sideways and letting me get a better look. "When Rowki find sardonium, it is melted down and imbued into their weapons via an ancient rune of the Rowki. This rune, my rune, stands for vengeance."

"That makes a lot of sense," I said, admiring the shining symbol. "If I had to pick a rune for you, it would be vengeance or death or... is there one for generally pissed off?"

That actually made Rima smirk, although she didn't answer. I took her pause as an invitation to ask more questions.

"Tem said, as a Rowki, we can control the sardonium with our—with our minds?" I asked. "How does that work?"

"It's a bond that you can create and master with the metal," Rima explained. "It's not used often, since the act requires an extreme amount of concentration from the user, but it can come in handy in dire situations. If you continue your training, in time, I am sure you will discover your own sardonium and learn to harness its power."

I looked at her expectantly, waiting for her to show me some cool tricks she could do with the weapon.

She stared at me, blinking a few times.

"If you see me nude while changing that is one thing." Rima scowled. "I will not stand here while you ogle me still."

"What?" I asked incredulously. "No, no, get your mind out of the gutter. I want you to do some Rowki tricks with the sardonium. Come on, like you did in that clip Tem showed me. I don't want to see you naked again."

I heard a deep inhale from the door as that last part left my lips.

Tem stood there with his mouth open in shock. He looked from me to Rima and back again.

"No, not again. It's not what you think," I said, waving my hands at the historian. "I just wasn't expecting to see Rima naked today."

I don't think that helped. Tem used a hand to cover his mouth.

"I mean, she was putting on her synth suit and I didn't know she was going to just go complete nudist on me," I said, trying to navigate the slippery slope.

"Should I come back?" Tem finally asked. "What happens in the Rowki armory stays in the Rowki armory, as far as I'm concerned."

"No, you're fine," Rima answered. "Apparently, Tyco has issues when it comes to covering his shame. What is it?"

"I just wanted to let you know the Ursonians are gearing up now," Tem answered. "Captain Akel will have his squad ready to meet us in the hangar bay in minutes."

"Good, we're nearly done here," Rima said, looking over

to me. She reached behind her on the wall of weapons and handed me an extending staff. That was it.

"Hey, I mean, I know I've only trained with the staff thus far, but how about some kind of blaster this time?" I asked. "If we're going down to do battle, I think I need more than a stick, here."

"You've only trained with the extending staff," Rima said without hesitancy. "Giving you anything else would prove dangerous to yourself and others."

I took the extending staff from her, albeit begrudgingly. Sure, I was okay with the weapon in a one-on-one fight when the other person had the same weapon, but we were going into a warzone, here.

I was about to argue when Rima headed for the door. "Come, our time is short."

Tem and I hurried after the woman. I noticed my small friend staring at me with admiration as we walked.

"What is it?" I asked. "Do I have some of my designated meal plan on my face? Whatever it is that you reconstructed to act as hummus gives me some serious gas. Wait, what happens if I have to toot in this synth suit?"

"The smell will be trapped in place until you remove the covering," Tem said without pause. "However, that is not why I am looking at you. I'm admiring your armor. There's nothing quite like the nobility of a Rowki in full kit."

"Thanks," I said, noticing the historian had yet to put on any of his own armor. "Aren't you going to be wearing anything to protect yourself?"

"Oh yes, my armor waits for me at the hangar bay of the *Oni*," Tem explained. "While the two of you and the squad of Ursonians prepare to head out, I will don my own protection."

If I could take solace in anything at the moment, it was the quality of soldiers I'd be going into battle with. Rima was no slouch. The simple image of thousands of Ursonians in full gear gave me an extra pep to my step. They made professional strong men look like children. We'd be okay.

"A squad," I repeated the word. "What is that like, a thousand? Two thousand soldiers?"

"Ursonian squads are made up of ten soldiers," Tem answered straight-faced.

I broke out laughing and slapped Tem on the shoulder. "Good one, that's a good one."

Tem began to chuckle as well. "Thanks, thank you. I try. I was voted class comedian when graduating from my historian academy. Why are we laughing?"

"Wait, you're serious?" I asked, stopping in my tracks. My laughter ground to a halt like worn brakes forced to perform on a runaway semi. "Ten. Ten Ursonians are going with us into occupied territory? That's it?"

"That's all we will require," Rima said as we followed her into a lift and headed for the hangar bay. "We're going into the city at night to free our enslaved allies. Once freed and with our help, they will retake the capital quickly and restore order."

Apparently, Rima felt nothing but confident about this plan. Going into war with ten bears, a trucker, a historian, and one Rowki didn't seem like a great idea to me. It made my stomach roll and I kind of had to empty my bowels with all the nervousness.

Why did I always have to poop when I got really nervous? What was the deal with that, anyway?

The lift took us to the last level of the ship. The hangar bay was a massive open room with ceilings that had to be five, maybe six stories tall.

The place was brightly lit without walls on either side, but with a red force field that shielded us from space. At least I guessed it was a force field. It was see-through red, nothing but dark space on the other side.

Inside the bay was a swirling movement of Ursonian soldiers. I thought the soldiers were big before. In their armor, they were freaking walking tanks. The Mauler T-19's, standard issue for each soldier, were being checked and rechecked before departure.

The ship the unit was gathered next to was thick, with stubby wings and a rear ramp. The dropship's rear ramp door stood open waiting for us to load inside. Captain Akel greeted us with a heavy thump on his armored chest.

Goosebumps rolled down my arms and I had that feeling of having to poop again as red light began to flash on our dropship and a siren sang a war cry.

FOURTEEN

IT SEEMED while talking was out due to Captain Akel's code of silence, making noise was not. The bear man rolled his shoulders back, looking at the ceiling of the hangar bay, and pounded on his armored chest three times in quick succession.

The squad of Ursonian soldiers around him followed his act and also let out a roar with each slam of their gauntlets on chest armor. The noise was so ferocious, it made my sternum tremble.

"Are you okay, Max Tyco?" Tem asked as he maneuvered himself into a heavy set of armor. "You look as though you've seen a spirit."

"I think I just pooped myself," I said, looking around the hangar bay at the Ursonians, who worked, completing their preflight checks and last-minute duties. "Actually, I'm going to run to the restroom real quick. If I'm not back in time, feel free to go without me. I can just jump on the next suicide mission."

"In," Rima said, appearing at my right side.

I fell in line behind the Ursonians. Lucky me, Bull was

one of the soldiers Captain Akel had chosen to accompany us on this mission. The massive alien specimen of muscle and teeth gave me a sideways grin, enjoying my discomfort.

"Don't worry, fresh meat," Bull said with a wink. "They say you don't feel the blaster bolt that ends you."

"Comforting, very comforting," I told him. "Great to know we buried the mauler and are starting off on a new foot."

I followed Bull and the rest of the Ursonians inside the rear of the ship. The dropship was bulky and wide enough to give us room to sit across from one another. The armor the Ursonians wore was very similar to my own. It seemed instead of synth under their gray metal plates, they wore only their fur, trusting their hide to turn any smaller danger. Their helmets were like mine and Rima's—a bowl helmet, wide visor with two pieces that came forward to meet at the front from nose to chin.

I was directed to a seat between Rima and Tem. The former already looked like she was in the zone, eyes focused and ready. The latter I had to blink a few times to believe. Tem was a walking marshmallow.

His armor, unlike the rest of ours, did not look as though it were made of any kind of actual armor. It was more like he filled a suit with air and then slapped a clear glass helmet on his head.

"Uh, Tem?" I asked, trying not to offend him.

"I know, I know," Tem said, shaking his head. "It seems foolish to go into a warzone without a weapon, but I am a noncombatant, only meant to document the happenings of the Rowki. I do not intend to fight."

The marshmallow alien even squeaked when he walked. He barely fit into the seat on my left.

Captain Akel sat across from us with Ero on his right

and then Bull and the others. He looked over at Rima and sent her a series of hand motions.

"Ready," Rima answered as the rear ramp door closed behind us.

My gut twisted again as the dropship lifted from the floor.

"Don't worry, they don't know we're here," Tem said, patting my hand, which had a death grip on the seat handle next to me. "Dropships are very reliable in space. I mean, there was that one time, but no one could have seen that coming; the faulty wiring, those that died in the vacuum of space... I mean—"

"Not helping," I told my friend.

"Right, right," Tem said. "Look out the window and relax."

The inside of the dropship was wide, with seats lining either wall. Behind those seats were oval shaped windows letting us see outside. I took Tem's suggestion and looked forward, past the walkway and over Ero's shoulder.

The dropship maneuvered through the hangar bay, clearing the red force field without a hitch. The blackness of space waiting on the other side of the force field enveloped us immediately, and we were headed down to the planet of Somu.

Across from me, Captain Akel gave Ero and Bull instructions via hand gestures. An uncomfortable thought hit me as the hum of the dropship and the thrusters tuned out any other sound.

"How does Akel communicate if he's not with us?" I shouted to Rima on my right. "I mean, what if we're separated and he has to reach us via radio or something?"

"Inside his helmet, there's a heads-up display," Rima said, pointing over to the vambrace on Akel's left forearm.

"There's a keyboard in there he can use to communicate if the situation calls for it. Although that shouldn't be necessary, as he'll always have someone with him to relay his order over the comms. Are you ready for this?"

"If I said yes, would you believe me?" I asked her.

"Not at all," Rima answered. "Let your anxiety make you even more focused. Do exactly what I tell you and you'll be fine. No one expects you to be a hero your first time out. Don't do anything dumb."

"Right," I said, thinking that may have been the first time Rima didn't put me down in a conversation.

"Oh, and try not to die," Rima added. "I've already invested a lot of time in you. I wouldn't want to have to scrape you into a body bag and start all over with the next recruit."

There it was. Rima was still running with a perfect record when it came to her tough love training routine.

"Ladies and gentlemen, Ursonians, Rowki, and the new meat I'm told is human, welcome aboard the Dynamite," a rather young voice said over the intercom. I could see a few smiles and grins from the Ursonians across from me as if they recognized the voice. "This is your humble pilot, Claw, speaking. We're expecting entry into Somu airspace in t-minus fifteen minutes. From there, we'll be flying low and slow down below their radar and coming in nice and easy a few miles behind the capitol. Please keep from puking and enjoy the ride."

"Huh, that pilot trope is pretty much true inter-species too," I said to myself.

The fifteen minutes until we entered the planet's atmosphere went way too quickly. I checked my helmet magnetically held to the left side of my belt and my extending staff on the right a few times. The seat I sat in was huge, thanks to it being made for an Ursonian four to five times my size. The shoulder and lap harnesses were self-securing or else I'd have been in real trouble. As it was, I felt like a kid in the oversized seat.

Rima handed me what looked like a rubber mouthpiece from a compartment she opened at her feet. I took the item with a question on my face.

"You'll want to put this in your mouth so you don't bite your tongue off when we descend," Rima warned me. "Flying can be tricky if you're new at it."

I looked at her in shock and then at the mouthpiece. I was no germaphobe, but neither was I eager to shove a piece of mystery plastic in my mouth. Who knew how many times it had been used before, or by whom or what.

"Join the Rowki, they said, see the galaxy and shove questionable pieces of rubber in your mouth, they said," I sighed.

"Hey, new meat!" Bull yelled from across the aisle. "Welcome to the suck."

Other Ursonians laughed good-naturedly. I knew no one besides maybe Bull actually wanted to see me suffer.

I shoved the rubber piece in my mouth as Claw's voice boomed over the speakers again.

"All aboard, hold on tight; we're about to head in," Claw said in an excited rush of words. "There's a storm below, so this should be extra fun."

I groaned and bit down on the rubber piece in my mouth harder. It tasted like old plastic and bad breath.

The dropship had thus far been rather smooth with the occasional wiggle or jostle. That was all about to end as the ship shuddered on descent. The dropship trembled as if it were caught in a death spasm. I closed my eyes, but that made things worse.

I grabbed on to my harness, trying to slow my breathing.

Four seconds in through your nose and four seconds out through your mouth, I thought to myself. *Hold it together. If this is how you go, then no amount of worry or stress is going to save you.*

Ironically, that thought was rather comforting. I had to stop spending so much time with Rima. That sounded like something she would say.

The windows had shown a view of space before, but as the dropship shook and rolled, clouds obscured my view. Rain began to patter and paint the window as lightning lit up the sky. What I thought might be thunder sounded. The sound of the thrusters was too loud now to know for sure.

Growls and grunts from a few of the Ursonians across from me added to the madness. I knew this species was crazy. I had seen firsthand how much they loved combat. They were a warrior race, there was no doubt, but they were working themselves into a frenzy, slamming their fists into their chests and roaring into the storm.

I found myself grateful for Rima and her questionably dirty mouthguard. I bit down on that sucker like there was no tomorrow as I was jostled in my seat again and again. Just when I thought the ship was going to break apart, our descent evened out, and although the ship still shook, the rolling and harsh jostling seemed to lessen.

"There we go; I thought we were about to join our ancestors there for a moment," Claw said over the speakers. "I have us approaching land now in two minutes; get ready to disembark."

I heaved a sigh of relief. The view I could see across from me out the window was nothing but gray sky, rain, and maybe an ocean? It was too hard to tell.

"We shouldn't get separated, but if we do, you head

back to the ship," Tem explained by shouting this to me from my left. "Do you understand?"

"Easy enough?" I answered.

Rain pelted the exterior of the dropship as we continued to slow our forward momentum. A moment later, we came to a complete stop. A harsh jolt told us we had landed.

"Here we go," Rima said, stretching her neck to either side of her shoulders. "Ready?"

The dropship's rear ramp door began to descend as we unbuckled our harnesses.

I decided to lie. "Yep, let's do it!"

FIFTEEN

CONTRARY TO WHAT I first believed, Rima, not the Ursonians, was the first off the ship. In my mind, it just made sense for the walking battleships to go first like linemen in a football game, followed by the much smaller running backs and quarterback. No such luck.

Rima was out the ramp door before it even touched to the ground. I was with her a moment later. I noticed Tem didn't have the same enthusiasm to follow us into the unknown. He decided to stay back and wait for the Ursonians to pile out behind us. Couldn't say I blamed him. He was a noncombatant, after all.

Rima trotted out, then Captain Akel's unit formed a perimeter around our dropship. Steam came from Rima's breath as she scanned the area.

We were on an alien cliff overlooking a crashing ocean four stories below us on one side. On the other side was a lush green plain stretching out as far as the eye could see.

I noticed while the Ursonians wore their helmets now, Rima still did not. I was half thinking about asking her about this when Captain Akel trotted up to us. He gave her a head shake and three fingers up.

"It's all clear here," Rima nodded. "You can tell your pilot to sit tight. Let's go."

Captain Akel nodded.

Cold wetness spattered over my head and face, running down my neck. Lucky the synth suit fit so tight, it kept the rain from traveling down my back and chest.

"Should we, I don't know, put on our helmets?" I asked

"Perhaps when the fighting starts, you can," Rima answered. "Now there is no need. Our plan is working. They don't know we're here."

Rima followed these last words by unwrapping a black hood folded into the shoulder of her synth suit.

It kept the rain out of her eyes as she looked over to me and motioned me to follow.

I obeyed, reaching behind my own shoulder, hoping to find the same hidden hood. It wasn't there.

"See, you're already learning to be better prepared next time," Rima said as we took point through the open landscape. "Stay low and move quickly. I have access to the long-range scanners on our dropship. There are no life forms close by; they will be soon enough."

"Right," I answered, glancing behind me at the moving line of Ursonians. "Shouldn't we, I don't know, let the monsters in full armor go in front of us? Why were we first out of the dropship?"

"Leaders lead by example," Rima said as she moved over the terrain that was less grass and more moss. "Rowki are first on the battlefield and last off."

The more and more I found out about the Rowki, the more and more I realized why they were in such short supply.

For the first time, I was thankful for all those many circuits Rima made me run in our training room. We weren't at a full out sprint, but a steady jog in the cold rain as we moved forward. I found it was easy to keep up with Rima. I knew ten days ago, I'd already be gasping for breath, carrying extra pounds on me.

In the silence of the rain, I was able to get my first good look at the planet of Somu. It was lush and green, slight rolling hills, and that same bright green moss that covered nearly everything. Here and there, plants and flowers poked up. Crimson coral mounds sporadically rose from the ground.

The landscape was beautiful. I could only imagine what it looked like in the light of the sun. Was I really doing this? Was I really on an extraterrestrial planet surrounded by foreign allies and going on a mission to liberate those in need? I tried not to dwell on it too much in that moment. I'd have time after this was all done to process what was going on. At least, I hoped I would.

I followed Rima in silence for another fifteen minutes before she called a halt, finding shelter behind a rock outcropping of what I assumed was coral. It looked close enough to the hard Swiss cheese-like substance to me.

Captain Akel and Ero joined us while the others around us found their own cover with similar coral outcroppings. I caught sight of Tem in the back with a black orb floating over him, recording everything. He gave me a thumbs-up.

I returned the gesture to the marshmallow-looking space cadet. His suit reminded me of the old-school first-generation deep sea diving suits, with the billowing body and heavy helmet.

"Twelve o'clock, you can see the wall. No doubt there

will be sentries monitoring the area," Rima said. "Darkness is coming soon. We'll use that to help us."

Rima looked down at her left forearm where a small screen rested. She pressed a button and a holographic map of the fortress appeared.

"I'll go in and open the doors for the rest of you," Rima explained. "Have your Ursonians secure the gates and be ready to move. To free the slaves."

Captain Akel nodded as Ero relayed the news to the rest of the unit.

I peeked over our cover and squinted through the rain. Rima was right, night was approaching quickly. The previous gray illumination was now fading to black. I could just make out a structure about a city block ahead of us. It was too far to be certain of what I was seeing, let alone who or how many guards might be there.

"No, I'll take him. He needs to learn," Rima was saying to Axel. "This is how the Rowki train the next generation of warriors."

It took me no time to realize they were talking about me.

Captain Akel did a sign like he was hanging himself.

My eyes went wide.

"Death is a risk for any one of us," Rima answered. "I appreciate your concern, my old friend, but this is a Rowki matter, not Ursonian. He'll live or die by the sword."

"Or live," I chimed in. "Maybe we should listen to Akel. I mean, if I get a vote—"

"You don't get a vote, Tyco," Rima answered. "Head low, move quickly, stay behind me."

I swallowed hard as Rima shrugged deeper into her hood and prepared to make her run.

"Hey, if you don't make it—I mean, we all think you will, but if you don't," Ero whispered in a way that I couldn't tell if she was joking or not. "No offense, but can I have the stuff in your hauling vehicle?"

I looked over at her in shock. Past her shoulder, I could see the other Ursonian soldiers hunkered down exchanging credits as bets were no doubt placed on the odds of me surviving the mission.

"I am offended," I told her in mock shock. I couldn't see her eyes past her helmet, but I focused on the red visor. "No, no, you can't have any of my stuff if I don't make it back. I want to be buried with it."

"Or I can just take it if you die," Ero said under her breath. "It's not like you'd know anyway. I still want to try some of that Red Rum."

"I thought we were making a real friendship connection here," I sighed, secretly grateful for the conversation distracting me from what I was about to do. "If I die and you take my stuff, I swear to whatever bear in the sky you worship, I'll come back and haunt you."

"Tyco, move," Rima said, vaulting over our coral outcropping and dashing over the open landscape.

I had just enough time to motion with my pointer and middle finger at my eyes and then back at Ero to let her know I'd be watching from the grave if things turned that way. I followed Rima a moment later.

My teacher made the jump over the shoulder-high coral barrier appear so seamless. I tried the same, my left boot catching on the ledge. I went down hard, the air knocked out of me.

I heard a collective gasp from the Ursonians behind me.

"I'm okay, I'm okay," I hissed, hiding my discomfort and taking off after Rima.

"I want twenty to one odds," I heard Bull say. "No, make that thirty to one odds."

I was too far away now to hear whatever was said next as I followed Rima's shadow in the distance. The woman was fast; no, the woman was superhuman or super whatever her species was. She moved like a wraith in the impending night.

I caught up to her, thankful again for my training. We moved quietly from cover to cover, always closer to the walls in front of us. With each step, the structure took on more and more shape.

The walls had to be three stories tall, made out of that same red coral material as the cover we found ourselves running between. This must have been a side entrance of some kind into the structure.

An oval gate with holes in it just large enough to stick your fingers though stood closed in front of us. It was wide enough for two Ursonians to get through and probably eight to ten feet tall.

On either corner of the wall, I could see a torch with at least two shadows moving in front of the light.

Rima headed for the rear corner. There was a final coral outcropping we hid behind before a twenty-yard dash to the wall would force us out into the open.

"Use it," Rima told me as I gasped for air next to her.

"What?" I asked.

"The events of your life, who you are. Use the pain. You are stronger than you think," Rima told me, staring at me from under her dark hood. "How many people have had to suffer the events you have? How many people know what it's like to grow up without a mother, an abusive father, and have their only hope snuffed out? That makes you stronger than you know. You lived through it all and you pressed on. Draw from that strength now, Max Tyco."

Rima was speaking so fast, I couldn't get a word in edgewise. Also, she was making way too much sense. Usually, talks like this fell under Tem's tutelage.

"Move to the wall as fast as you can," Rima told me. "Get to the gate and I'll be over and let you in in a matter of minutes. If anything happens to me, you head back to the others and tell them what happened."

"Okay, okay," I said, reaching for my helmet. "Should I put my helmet on now?"

"If it's your time to go, then it's your time to go," Rima answered. "No helmet or shield will protect you if your death day has arrived."

"Thanks. Very, very comforting in my hour of need," I answered, unclipping my helmet from my magnetic belt, then wondering if this was some kind of test.

"Move," Rima said, beginning her run for the wall.

SIXTEEN

I DECIDED against the helmet for the time being. I had never trained with one, and as far as I knew, we were not in any fear of being fired on at this moment.

Once more, I followed Rima through the night. The darkness was upon us now. Only a light spattering of rain accompanied our final run. I headed for the gate as instructed. Rima veered off to the right.

I ran as fast as my legs could carry me, trying to be as quiet as I could with each footfall. Have you ever tried to run full out on wet terrain in alien armor and do it quietly?

I'm sure I didn't actually sound like this, but in my own ears, each footfall was a heavy thud. My heart beat out of my chest as my adrenaline spiked. I sucked in oxygen as quickly and quietly as I could, still aiming for the gates. They were closer now, only ten yards away.

The idea that someone was drawing a bead on my exposed skull itched at the back of my mind. My tombstone was likely to say, "Here lies Max Tyco, human pig species. Should have worn that helmet."

To my right, I witnessed Rima reach her section of the

wall, and then the impossible. Rima carried her sword over her right shoulder, the hilt sticking up like a pirate parrot.

Without breaking stride, the sword moved by itself. The blade, humming a dull white, lifted from her sheath, maneuvering itself under her right foot as she leapt in the air. The blade turned sideways, caught her foot, and then propelled her upward.

It happened so fast, I had to be sure I wasn't hallucinating. The white blade was a flash and then it was gone.

I skidded to a halt, finally reaching my destination. I threw myself against the left side of the gate, panting hard. If I was supposed to put on my helmet or not, I decided to err on the side of caution.

I placed the bucket on my head as my vision immediately turned to red in the visor. Readouts scrolled across the top and bottom of the visor as well as on the right and left sides.

I wasn't going to try and figure out what it all meant, but one thing I was grateful for was the enhanced night vision. Still not as bright as day, I was able to at least see better. Why Rima or Tem didn't give me a heads-up was beyond me. It had to be part of the training.

I waited, expecting to hear...what, I wasn't sure. Maybe a muffled scuffle overhead, a cry cut short, or a thud as bodies hit the floor?

One second I was there trying to figure out if I should be hearing anything, and the next a body crashed to the ground beside me.

"Son of a—" I said, jumping back and slapping a hand to the helmeted area over my mouth. I nearly threw up looking down at the figure in front of me. It was tall and thin, with those same blue webbed hands and long webbed feet. Gills were where the ears should be.

The thing wore leather, or what looked like a dark fabric armor. A lone rifle lay broken under its body.

Then I did pee myself a little as the creature groaned. It shifted, reaching a hand to grab for my boot.

I'm not going to say I made a high-pitched scream when that happened, but Rima would tell me later she heard a small child cry outside the gate before she let me in.

I moved back, kicking the hand off my boot as the gate behind me clicked open and Rima walked out. She saw me, rolled her eyes, then brought her blade down deep into the side of the skull of the dying Somu at our feet.

Right before the blade went in, he gurgled one word. "Rowki."

I'd never seen anyone killed before. As a truck driver, I saw accidents all the time, even stopped to help a few, but they were already dead or just shook up. I'd never seen a life taken with my own two eyes.

It was a sobering feeling. Not like the movies would have you believe as the heroes walked through killing all the bad guys in sight. Rima had taken everything from this alien. Any chance of redemption for him was gone.

"Hurry," Rima said, ripping her blade free from the Somu's skull with a sick wet sound. She reached two fingers to her right ear where she must have put in some communication device. "Captain Akel, the gate is open. Secure our exit and free the prisoners. We're headed for the warlord."

I heard a series of clicks in my helmet that meant something to Rima. Whatever pre -conceived code she and the captain had seemed effective because Rima was content and ready to move on.

"We are?" I asked.

"We are," Rima answered. "Same plan."

"Same plan," I repeated.

The interior of the city was pretty ravaged. We made our way through streets littered with the bodies of men, women, and even children. It seemed the attack on the city couldn't have happened more than a day before. The bodies were swelling and a stench began filtering through my helmet despite the rain.

I could hear cries and screams now as we ran through the coral streets. There was manic laughter interspersed with those screams of horror. How those two competing sounds could live in the same space was a foreign idea to me.

"No, no, please!" a female voice said. "Please no, not my baby. No, please."

An alley between two buildings opened on our right. I could see two huddled figures on the ground and three larger beings around them.

Rima hesitated as the female voice pleaded again.

I couldn't believe Instructor Rima Noble didn't just go in there and start breaking skulls.

"Well, are we going to help them?" I asked.

"It's not our mission," Rima answered. "Dozens of these scenarios are going on throughout the city. The faster we free the local militia and kill the warlord, the sooner all of this ends."

"Are you kidding me?" I asked incredulously. "They're right here. You can kill them in like, three seconds."

"If you feel this strongly about it, then this is your test, Tyco," Rima explained. "I'll activate my beacon in your heads-up display. In the lower left side, you'll see a map directing you to my location. Be swift, show no mercy, for you shall receive none in return."

I was tempted to start breaking out with a nervous

chuckle. She really wasn't going to leave me here, was she? Rima turned and continued her run up the street.

Son of a gun, she was going to just leave me here. I was going to have to have a long talk with her if I survived the night. Her *and* this High Council of the Rowki. No wonder there were so few left in the galaxy. Who made it out of this kind of workplace training environment?

"No!" the woman screamed.

The sobs of a small child and the blood-curdling scream of the little girl drew me back to what was happening in the alley.

"They'll both make for a good price on the open market," a gruff voice taunted. "Demetr said we can keep whatever we find. But let's have some fun with them first, shall we?"

For me, now, it wasn't a question of if I was going to do anything, but how. I wasn't going to just stand by and let this happen, but how I planned to stop it was a different question.

I had ten days of training. Ten days. I could take one of them maybe, if we were both using extending staffs, but I could bet these guys were armed with some kind of blaster at least, as well as bladed weapons.

An idea so wild crossed my mind, I didn't want to try it, but it was all I had. Time was short.

"Leave them alone!" I shouted, walking into the ally. "By order of the Rowki High Council, you are to leave them be."

I discovered now the collar of my armor carried a translator in it as well. It changed my words for the beings in front of me. Why it did this for them and not Rima, Tem, or the Ursonians, I wasn't sure. Perhaps it detected who had consumed the all-water and who hadn't?

The all-water would let me understand their language, but unless they also drank it, my words would sound like gibberish to them.

All three men swung around now, pointing a variety of weapons at my face and chest. I was happy I decided to put my helmet on after all.

I got a better look at them now. All tall, with gnarly arms and that same black armor that left their thighs and upper arms exposed. They didn't bother with gloves, boots, or helmets either.

Their weapons were two of those longer blaster rifles and one smaller one. A pair of huddled figures wept on the side of the alley. I guessed they were a mother and her child. Seeing them there confirmed I was doing the right thing, even if I didn't live to see the next day.

"Rowki, Rowki are here?" one of the others asked the leader. "I didn't sign up to fight Rowki."

"Naw, the Rowki are dead," the third answered.

"What's this thing, then?" the gruff leader asked. "I don't know what you are, stranger, but you just made the worst mistake of your life."

I thought there would have been more talking. Not so much. They opened fire. I had enough time to reach for my extending staff and throw myself into the door on my right. I fell crashing to the ground amidst a volley of blue blaster fire peppering the entrance to whatever kind of house or store I had fallen in.

I scrambled to my hands and knees, hoping against hope this armor was as strong as Rima told me it was when we were gearing up. I was going to need it to hold, along with a few miracles if I was going to make it out of this alive.

The deluge of weapons fire continued. I crawled to the area next to the door hoping a stray round wouldn't find me.

As holey as the coral buildings were, they stood up to blaster fire pretty well, only chipping when a round hit them.

After what could have been the twentieth or thirtieth rounds, I heard a cackle of laughter and boots approach.

"I want that stick he was reaching for." The gruff voice laughed. "What was that anyway, a flashlight?"

I gathered my courage, gauging how close they must be by the sound of their voices. When I saw the first boot cross the threshold of the door, I sprang into action. Adrenaline made my moves clumsy at best but my first strike sure hit home.

Akel would be proud. I extended my staff at the same time as I rose to my feet and jabbed forward. The end of my staff caught one of the Somus in the throat. I heard something break as it staggered back, grasping at its ruined windpipe.

I followed my attack by moving forward and getting in close. In my mind, I had a better chance of winning if I closed the distance as opposed to further away where they could use their blasters on me.

My forward momentum took me right into the arms of the second attacker. I shoved him backward out into the alley, using my staff to strike him across the head as hard as I could and then back again with that same end. His shallow nose shattered in a shower of blood.

I heard the hard crack of a blaster going off behind us as the third Somu opened fire on both of us.

SEVENTEEN

ROUNDS HIT the back of my arms, head, and butt. Each round didn't tickle, but neither did it penetrate my armor. It felt like an Ursonian had a big foam bat and was beating me like I stole its pot of honey.

I would bruise for sure, but if that meant saving me from smoking craters in my body, so be it. My Somu friend I was caught in conflict with didn't fare so well. He took a round to the skull that caved in half his head as we fell to the floor.

Covered in the blood of the dead Somu, I struggled to find a way out of the conflict. A final round from the last attacker standing struck me in the side of the helmet so hard, I saw stars. Dazed, I lay on the alley floor trying to fight off the fingers of unconsciousness.

"No, oh great Father, no!" I heard a woman scream from somewhere past my foggy vision.

"What? Did you think this one was going to save you?" the gruff-voiced Somu still on his feet asked. "I don't know if he's a Rowki or not, but I just scored double. Armor and slaves."

I felt the helmet ripped off my head as the Somu took my near unconscious state for death.

"This will sell for a wicked price on the night market," the Somu cackled. "And now more credits for me since I won't have to split the profits three ways."

The young girl in her mother's arms began to sob uncontrollably. Her tears turned to screams as rage filled the little one.

"You're going to pay for this!" she screamed. "You're the bad one. You killed him. He was trying to save us and you killed him!"

"You don't shut your mouth and I'll kill you, you little filth," the Somu said, turning from me. "Maybe I shouldn't wait. Maybe I'll just teach you a lesson right here, right now."

The darkness in his voice promised pain for the little one if I didn't do something.

Get up, Max, I heard my wife's voice in my head. *Get up, Max.*

I didn't have time to assess if that voice was my own or I just wanted to hear hers so badly, I tricked myself into thinking it. I missed her so much. I hated and loved the Well of Enlightenment for giving me back such clear memories of her.

"I can't take an eye or a gill—that'll decrease your value as a slave—but what about the webbing between your toes?" the Somu announced, advancing on the mother and daughter. "You won't be needing that."

I rose to unsteady feet, unsure where my extending staff had fallen in the conflict. I did see the helmet at my feet.

Gripping the helmet's chin, I prepared to use it as a club to the skull of my unsuspecting victim. I advanced on his exposed back. Whether I made too much noise, he saw the look of joy in the little girl's face, or some sixth sense told him he was about to be brained, the Somu turned around, blaster in hand.

I swung out with the hard helmet, slamming the metal into his hand holding the blaster. The Somu screeched in pain as the blaster went skidding to the hard floor beneath us. A satisfying crack told me he wouldn't be using all his fingers, either.

A left fist cut me above my right eye, and I staggered for a moment, allowing him an extra shot as he screeched once more. He slugged me, splitting my lip and sending me reeling to the floor. The second shot came from his right hand that was already broken. On contact, he screamed again, hugging the limb to his chest.

I fell to my knees under a sheet of my own blood. My face felt both hot and wet at the same time.

Past red vision, I saw the mother and little girl again. If I didn't stop him, I knew what would happen to them. I felt anger. Sadness turned to rage in my chest. I used it all now as the Somu searched the ground for his blaster.

"Raw!" I roared, not sure where the strength came from but knowing it needed an outlet. I rose to my feet, sprinting at the Somu as fast as my legs would carry. Rima would have been proud. I hit my target with all the weight of a man possessed with rage.

The armor I wore made me so hard, I nearly snapped the Somu in half when I tackled him. We fell to the ground, me on top and him below. I took my training to heart now, using the pain I felt as a vehicle to fuel my action. I thought about how angry I was at losing her. I thought about how much I hated myself for letting her go that day. I let it consume me as I lifted my helmet and brought it down on the head of the Somu again, and again and again.

I didn't have a specific number of times I wanted to hit him, but by the time I was done, I couldn't lift my arms. I knelt on top of him, heaving for breath. My arms felt like lead weight. The gore-splattered helmet rolled from my hands.

Blood mixed with my sweat, mixed with my tears as I tried to find some shred of understanding in that moment. I looked down at my grisly work. The Somu's head was unrecognizable. Somehow he was still alive, sucking in breath through a ruined face.

"Who—are—you?" he wheezed.

I didn't answer.

"They'll—still—die," he managed to gasp.

"Maybe, one day," I said, rising from on top of the soldier. "But not today."

"Christina, no!" the mother shouted as the little girl ran to me and tackled me in a hug so hard, I thought she was going to take me off my feet.

"Thank you, thank you, thank you," the tiny girl cried.

"What did you call her?" I asked as the mother approached, tears in her eyes. "What did you say?"

"Her name, her name is Christina. Thank you. Who are you?" the mother asked, embracing me in a hug.

I knew it had to be a coincidence. The young girl did not have the same name as my dead wife. It was the all-water Tem made me drink that translated our languages. The young girl's name was probably something I couldn't even pronounce.

The little girl reached for me, trying to climb my armor to wrap her arms around my neck and sob. Who was I to deny her that?

I lifted the kid that weighed close to nothing.

"Who are you?" the mother repeated as the three of us

held on to each other like we had somehow known each other all our lives.

"Max," I answered. "Max Tyco."

I caught movement from the corner of my eye. A figure cloaked in shadow at the end of the alley stepped forward. Rima in her dark hood, sword poking over her right shoulder.

She didn't say anything. She just stood there.

I gave the kid, Christina, an extra squeeze and then slowly lowered her to the ground. The mother let go, still crying.

"Were you just watching the whole time?" I asked, wiping the blood from my eyes. My right eye was beginning to swell and I think a molar had been knocked loose. "You couldn't have, oh I don't know, lent a hand? I could have been killed."

"You could have been," Rima answered. She looked at the mother and child. "Follow the main road to the side gate. There are Ursonians there who hold it now. I've radioed ahead. They'll provide you safe escape."

"Thank you, thank you both, bless the Rowki. May the Father bless you, Max Tyco," the mother said, lifting her daughter and running the way Rima instructed.

"You didn't need to go save the chancellor or king or whatever from the warlord, huh?" I asked Rima, pretty pissed. "You could have killed these guys in seconds."

"I could have ended them in three to four moves, without breaking a sweat, yes," Rima answered. "But this was your journey. We still must continue on, but I wasn't going to stand by and let a mother and child be harmed. Not while I draw breath. Now get your gear. We have a mission to complete. And do something about your face. You're bleeding all over my armor."

I ground my teeth, but that hurt so much from the shot I took to my jaw, I stopped. What else was there to do but what she said? As I lifted my helmet from the ground, I realized it was spattered with Somu gore now inside and out. I clipped it to my belt and searched for my extending staff. I found it in a puddle of rainwater.

Although the rain had lessened now to only intermittent sprinkles, puddles of rainwater lined the alley.

I heard heavy footfalls arriving up the street. Preparing myself for another altercation, I looked for Rima to make sure she wasn't going to make me do this on my own again.

The female Rowki stood at the entrance to the alley and waved to someone. With a sense of relief, I joined her to find Ero and Bull with Tem behind them.

Ero gave a brief report, staring at me in shock the whole time. "Gate is secured. Captain Akel has taken a small unit and confirmed the slaves and militia are free and arming themselves now."

"Well done," Rima answered. "We move to the main building now and free the Chancellor. Once he is safe, we give the word to take back the city. Follow me."

We fell in line behind Rima as we continued up the street.

"What happened to you?" Tem asked, his mouth a big circle as he took in my battered face and scorched armor.

"I got my ass kicked," I told him truthfully. I looked over at Bull, who slowed to look at me as well. I expected some kind of jab at my manhood or to be called a pig species or something.

"I saw it all," Rima answered over her shoulder. "Tyco here took out three Somus by himself. Not bad for his first time in real combat."

I was surprised Rima would interject into the conversation. Although she still hadn't said good job.

"Were they dwarfed or already wounded?" Bull asked, looking at me skeptically. "Perhaps the ones he came in contact with were drunk."

"They were true warriors, all three," Rima answered.

"Is that right?" Bull answered through his red visor. "Well, there might be hope for you yet, little brother. Come now; there are more lives to take before the night ends."

EIGHTEEN

WE TRAVELED up the side road of the city. There were still echoing screams of the dead and dying around us, coupled with manic laughter and glee from those doing the plundering.

I wanted to help them all. I wanted to track down each sound and make them pay. Rima seemed content to head to her destination and help those along the way that we ran into.

Halfway up the sloping street, a pair of unwary Somus exited a house from our left. Rima drew her weapon so fast, all I saw was white light as the sword decapitated the first, then stuck fast in the gut of the second.

As the head and body of her first target fell to the ground, the second Somu looked down at his gut where a sword handle sprouted. He looked at us, trying to figure out what was happening. He didn't know he was already dead.

With one smooth move, Rima ripped the weapon upward, ending the alien's life. He too fell to the ground next to his companion. As if it were nothing at all, Rima cleaned her blade on their bodies, sheathed the weapon, and we were off again.

"Oh my," Tem said, shuddering. "No matter how many times I see her in action, her skill still impresses me to no end. Rima is unparalleled. She belongs on the High Council herself."

"How come she's not?" I asked.

"Rima is too much a warrior. Her own past still haunts her," Tem said, looking at me as if he shouldn't have said that last part. "The Rowki High Council aren't in the field much. They have their hands full with meetings, discerning where the next catastrophe is bound to take place and such."

We moved through the night until Rima lifted a closed fist and ushered us to take shelter in a doorway to our right. We hid in the shadows, crouching low. It was a miracle how the Ursonians could remain undetected. They were practically the size of Volkswagen Bugs themselves.

Bull crouched on all fours with Ero behind him. I followed Rima's gaze as we looked up through the dark street to a sizable building at the top of the hill. A small moon gave some light through the angry storm clouds. There were orange lights placed in streetlamps sporadically stationed every few houses.

I could see three, no four guards outside the house carrying blasters. The house was made of the same clay-colored coral, at least two stories tall.

"Four at the entrance," Ero whispered.

"And a fifth on the second story," Rima answered. "Third window on the right."

I followed her direction, looking up and seeing for myself. There was in fact a shadow of a Somu in place.

"If you three can breach the front door, I'll take out the

one on the second floor," Rima said, looking to the three of us, excluding Tem.

"Affirmative," Ero answered.

"Give me a two-minute lead," Rima said, melting into the shadows before I even got a word in.

"Just don't get in our way," Bull said, looking over his shoulder. "I might mistake you for one of them and crush your skull by mistake."

"We're still frenemies?" I asked, not giving him the satisfaction of getting under my skin. "I thought we had a moment back there. You called me little brother and everything."

Bull huffed and was about to say more when a harsh squeaking noise made us all turn and look over to Tem. The historian had removed his glass-looking helmet and was cleaning the inside with a rag.

I stared at him deadpan.

"Oh, sorry," Tem said with one last rag-on-glass squeak. "It gets foggy inside so—you know what, you don't need to know that. I'm done now. I'll stop."

"Prepare your recording equipment for this one, historian," Bull said. "You will not want to miss it."

"We'll cover you," Ero said to the massive Ursonian. "Rowki, are you ready?"

It took me a second to realize she was talking to me. "Oh, yes, right, me. Yeah. I don't have a blaster, so I'm not sure how much good I'm going to be at long range."

"We'll manage," Ero answered.

"And we're up and ready," Tem said, resecuring his glass helmet. He moved his puffy armored arms around as he pressed a few buttons on his datapad. The black hovering camera zipped through the air to get an arial view of what was about to take place.

"For the ancestors," Bull said, beginning his lumbering run. He transitioned to two feet, wielding his Mauler T-19 with both hands.

I wasn't sure if it was my imagination or not, but I swore I felt the ground shudder when he took off. Red laser fire came from his weapon as Ero and I followed. The Ursonian medic and second in command walked forward, aiming carefully down the barrel of her weapon.

"Well, there goes the element of surprise," I said under my breath. I thought about putting the gore- and blood-filled helmet back on my swollen head. I wasn't exactly a fan of getting Somu blood in my eyes and mouth, so I passed.

The Somu guards at the front, seeing our approach, opened fire on us, but mostly Bull, who moved incredibly fast for his size.

Rounds hit and clipped off his armor. Bull's own fire was too sporadic to be effective. Ero, on the other hand, took one of the Somu in the head with a burst of fire.

I didn't see Rima kill the one on the second story, but I noticed no fire came from that level. Neither was there any sign of the shadow figure that had been there minutes before.

A blue bolt whizzed by my head. It reminded me to focus on the here and now, not that there was anything I could do without a firearm.

Bull reached the three remaining Somu a moment later. I almost felt sorry for them. They were closer to my own size and weight than the Ursonian's. Bull swung his massive Mauler T-19 in a wide arc, biting deep into the side of a Somu with his ax end. Ripping it free, he swung again, caving in the skull of a second attacker with the sledge-hammer side of his weapon.

The last Somu shot Bull point blank, but it was too late. The behemoth brought the weapon straight down on him, crushing him to the ground.

Ero and I skidded to a halt beside the heaving Bull as he dislodged his weapon. He looked over to me and lifted three armored fingers. "That's three of my own and my face looks better than yours."

"That's debatable," I answered.

"Bull, the doors," Ero said.

"On it," Bull answered, rearing back with his weapon. He hammered the weapon into the doors one, two, three times. The rock-like coral the doors were made of cracked inward and then fell off the hinges altogether.

We entered a courtyard decorated with exotic plants and even a stream. Past that, the house door stood open. A Somu stood there as if he were going to greet us. Minus the sword sticking through him, he looked like he could have been a nice guy. He fell to the ground a second later when Rima pulled her weapon free from behind him.

"Hurry, they know we're here," Rima said.

We continued on with Tem bringing up the rear, still recording all of the night raid for later study.

The inside of the building was actually pretty nice; there was marble here with pillars and tall ceilings. Mirrors hung on the walls and a table and vases with brilliant-colored flowers of every hue stood nearby.

The one thing that was missing was the lack of opposition. I was no war expert, but I knew Bull had made enough noise at the front of the house to wake the dead. If there were enemies here, they should be rushing us.

Apparently, I wasn't the only one to notice this.

"I have a bad feeling about this," Tem said in a sing-song voice. "Maybe I should just wait outside. I'm a non-combatant. I can just maneuver my drone in here with you and see what's going on that way."

"Tem, quiet," Rima whispered. "Do you hear that?"

We followed a corridor on our left until it opened up into a wide room. No one was there that I could see, but the place was lit with orange lights strung across the walls, bathing the room in an eerie glow.

The sound Rima was referring to was a kind of singing. Not just one voice but many voices, male and female, singing a sad slow tune with no words, just tones. Prickles of goosebumps rose across my arms and the back of my neck.

"Ero, hey, Ero," I whispered to the female Ursonian beside me. "Let me borrow that blaster on your hip."

"No, be quiet," Ero snapped back.

"So rude," I mumbled.

A far door opened, making Bull and Ero bring their weapons to bear. A lone figure walked through the door. This person was neither a Somu nor human. He walked closer to us, smiling with a crooked grin.

Rima inhaled sharply, as did Tem. It was obvious they knew who this was.

He was tall with a black robe; no nose or hair, but eyes like a serpent made him look like a demon. He opened his arms wide.

"How appropriate, the student has come back to her master," the man said, taking us all in and zeroing in on me. "Oh, and she's taken her own pup under her wing. How sweet, Rima. I never pictured you as a teacher, at least not a good one."

"What are you doing here, Nok?" Rima asked. "You're wanted by the Galactic Government throughout the galaxy for war crimes against our own."

"Am I now?" Nok asked, rolling his eyes. "If you knew

what else I've been up to, war crimes would be the very least of your concerns. Look."

Immediately, feet slapping against the cold marble ground echoed in every direction from both the door we entered and the door Nok came from. A dozen, no, two dozen Somu at least, surrounded us with smug smiles. They were all armed.

I rethought putting my helmet on despite the gore that lay inside.

The thickest Somu I had yet to see joined Nok on his left. This Somu had face tattoos and was better armed than the others. I guessed he must be the warlord.

"Easy," Rima cautioned as Bull and Ero formed a circle.

"I knew I should have stayed back," Tem chided himself. "But no, Tem had to go see what he could see. Now I'm never going to finish that book I've always wanted to write."

Slowly, I moved the helmet to my head. I caught a whiff of the brain fluid and blood inside before squishing it on. It sucked, and that was putting it lightly.

I held my staff ready, not sure if I'd even be able to get within reach of anyone for it to do any good. I'd learned how much getting hit by one blaster hurt. I couldn't imagine being hit by a dozen.

"I should have guessed it was you," Rima said, picking up the conversation. "Where is the ruling family? What have you done with them and what are you doing here?"

"They'll be used for ransom," Nok said with another smile. "Oh, the Rowki, always a step behind, always a day late."

"You were one of us once," Rima said. "Have you lost yourself so much that you can't remember what it's like, standing for something?"

"Oh, I still stand for something—for myself," Nok said, opening his black robe to reveal the hilt of a blade at his right hip. "It pays so much better and I don't have to put up with all the Rowki propaganda. What are they telling you? Yes, you, are you on one of their designated meal plans?"

"Who, me?" I asked.

"No, the other husky Rowki wearing armor." Nok laughed. "Why are you wearing a helmet? Oh, is this your first time?"

"No," I lied. "I've done this plenty of times."

"I'm sure." Nok laughed. "Well, Rima, you have two choices, but I know you're not going down without a fight, so should I even ask? If you surrender, I promise we'll keep you alive. I'm sure the Rowki would pay a fistful of credits for you. Oh, and is that Tem?"

"Oh, hello, good to see you," Tem squeaked. "Nice weather here."

"You didn't answer my question," Rima said. "What are you doing here?"

"I told you, ransom pays well," Nok answered. "When I heard there was a warlord in position to overthrow one of the Rowki allies, I knew—"

"Nok, the real reason," Rima interjected. "Give me the truth for once, you piece of dunghill crip."

Bull coughed a laugh.

Tem inhaled sharply.

I wasn't sure what a dunghill crip was, but I got that it was pretty bad. I looked over at Nok and that plastic smile he had worn since he entered the room. It cracked for a bit and I saw the hate that molded him.

"There are rumors of war, Rima Noble, or should I call you Lady Death?" Nok answered. "You must have discerned the whispers for yourself. I'm sure that's why you're here. The Rowki council has sent you to find out what's happening. They know, and that's why they have commanded their best to investigate."

Nok moved his snake-like eyes from Rima and took me in. "They have sent their Lady Death, and then whoever this pig species is. Are the Rowki so short-handed they're sending their new recruits on missions like this? Tsk, tsk, tsk, times do seem dire for the Rowki."

"Put your weapons down and surrender yourself, all of you," Rima answered, her voice not betraying a hint of doubt if she felt any at all. "If you refuse, the only thing that lies down your path is death."

No one moved.

"Well then, shall we?" Nok asked. His sword moved from its sheath on its own. A rune on the blade glowed with a blackness so deep, it wafted off the weapon like smoke. "Who wants to die first?"

NINETEEN

SO MUCH HAPPENED NEXT, my senses had a hard time keeping up with it all. Nok and Rima lunged forward, clashing. Ero opened up with her Mauler T-19, sending a shower of red laser rounds into the Somu who'd entered the door behind us.

Tem yelped and dove for cover.

Bull followed Ero's example, sending his spray of weapons fire with a roar that echoed in my chest. There was so much incoming fire, I was hit in my left leg, chest, and head at once. I went down to a knee, trying to make sense of it all and find a way I could help.

Seeing that I had no long-range weapon, Bull took it upon himself to aid in my problem.

"Little brother!" Bull raged, lifting me in one giant arm. He flung me through the air like a ball into a group of waiting Somu. "There's enough for us all!"

The weapons around me cracked as I crashed against not just any Somu, but the warlord himself. The one with biceps the size of Arnold Schwarzenegger's and the face tattoos.

He stumbled back under the weight of my armor, recovering quickly. He unsheathed a long, thin sword from a sheath on his hip and struck out so fast, I barely had time to block the blow with my staff.

I fought to my feet under a flurry of blows I could hardly keep up with. I remembered my training at the hands of Captain Akel. I moved not to meet force with force but to redirect the force of my enemy.

I'm not sure if you've ever been in a real fight, but you get tired quickly, especially if you're the aggressor spending energy at every blow. I moved in a circle, blocking incoming strikes and letting them slide off my staff.

Unlike my previous run-in with the Somu, these soldiers were not willing to fire on me for fear of hitting their own warlord. Out of the corner of my eye, I could see sparks erupt from the blades of Nok and Rima.

Ero mowed down the Somu while Bull preferred an up-close and personal touch. He cleaved enemies in half with single blows as he waded into them, roaring unlike I'd ever heard any beast before.

I saw all of this from my peripheral vision. I knew war was hell, but I wasn't prepared for the sheer insanity physical conflict brought. On top of the sounds of weapons cracking and the ring of steel on steel were the grunts and screams of the dying, and those still in the fight.

I did my best to block all of this out as the warlord came at me, again and again, and again. I missed a sideways cut that my armor turned and then another to the side of my helmet.

Each blow landed was painful, but failed to penetrate the hard metal. It also served as a reminder of how much I had yet to learn.

I weathered the blows, allowing the war chief to tire

himself out. Sooner or later, he would make a mistake. I could weather the storm. I'd been through enough in my life to understand that much about who I was.

Exhausted rage soon twisted the warlord as sweat poured from his brow. Was it my imagination or were his strikes coming in with less force and slower now? Just a half-second or so more between attacks, but yes, he was slowing.

I knew exactly what he felt—muscles burning, joints and ligaments screaming for a rest, even if it was a few seconds. The warlord screeched something as he came down with his latest failed attack.

I knew this was my chance. That brief moment of hesitation was all I needed to go in for my own offensive feint. I held my staff parallel with my chest in a two-handed grip. I struck out with the left end of my weapon, and when he transitioned to block the blow, I changed the direction of the attack, now swinging with the right end of my weapon.

Everything I had went into the blow, connecting with the left side of his head. A resounding crack of steel against skull met my ears. The shock of the blow sent tremors from my staff into my hands and up my arms.

The warlord staggered back. I followed, offering blows to his legs and the side of his rib cage, if this species even had ribs at all. Whatever they had under their skin broke with my strikes as the warlord tried to defend himself and failed.

He finally tripped, falling backward and losing the hold on his weapon. He snarled at me, reaching for a blaster at his hip. I saw it too late.

I prepared to take the round in the head or chest, hoping I would remain conscious. Instead of the blaster bolt to my gut, a black orb swooped in and cracked the warlord across the left temple.

The warlord's eyes rolled into the back of his head and he fell unconscious. I followed the black orb to the right corner of the room where Tem controlled it from his data-pad. He gave me a nod and went back to work, zooming his camera this way and that across the battle.

I'd never admit this to Bull, but he was a beast. With Ero, the two were mopping up the last of the Somu soldiers who didn't decide to turn and run.

Rima and Nok were still going at it in a fight that I could only describe as the promise of death in motion. I watched in awe as the combatants clashed under the shower of sparks their swords made each time they met.

The black and white blades moved so fast in their hands, it was like watching rays of light instead of actual weapons. Then more insanity took place when I witnessed Nok release the hold on his weapon on purpose. His blade slashed out at Rima on its own from her left as Nok moved in and dealt a kick to her chest.

Rima blocked the sword that struck out at her as if an invisible hand were wielding it, but failed to stop the incoming kick.

I moved forward to help. I mean, not that I thought I was going to do any serious damage to Nok, but maybe I could at least offer a distraction to buy Rima some time.

It turned out the woman didn't require any help. She turned her backward fall from the kick into a roll and came up throwing her own sword at Nok. Nok dodged the weapon but failed to see it stop in space right behind him and fly back to Rima's hand. The hilt of her weapon hit Nok in the back of his head as it returned to her palm.

Nok called his sword back as he reached his free hand to the rear of his head. It came back covered in blood.

"Well done, well done, my pupil," Nok said with a smile

across his lipless mouth. "You have grown into the warrior I always knew you were capable of being. I knew I saw fire in you when you were in the fighting pits."

"You saw a young girl you could manipulate," Rima answered. "Don't pretend to be the hero you never were."

"That hurts," Nok said, feigning a frown. "If it weren't for me, you'd still be a slave in the fighting pits of Termonium. Show some gratitude."

Bull and Ero had joined the conflict now as any Somu still able to stand had decided going up against blaster- and ax-wielding war bears was a bad idea. Bull limped, but Ero looked unscathed.

"Well, it seems I'm outnumbered here, now that the warlord and his soldiers have been routed," Nok said with a sigh. "We'll finish this at another time, Rima Noble."

"We'll finish this now," Rima growled.

"I think you have a more pressing engagement," Nok said, pointing over to where the warlord lay on the floor.

I looked over in time to see the Somu who had been unconscious a moment before reach around his neck for a whistle. He blew on it, but no noise I could hear came forth.

"No!" Ero screamed, lifting her weapon and unloading at least a dozen rounds into the warlord's body. He spasmed, then lay motionless on the ground.

Apparently, Ero knew what the whistle meant. I had no idea, but what I did know was that Nok had used the moment of distraction to sprint for the back door he came out of.

Rima sent her sword flying through the air after him a second too late as Nok slammed the coral door closed behind him. Rima's sword stuck fast in the barrier.

"We should go after him," I said as Rima ripped the

weapon free with her mind and it flew back to her waiting hand. "We can catch him."

"No, we need to secure the ruling family before the Tulrog comes awake," Rima said as if she hated the very word. More than anything, she had to want to go after Nok, I could see that.

"Who's Tulrog?" I asked at the same time a clicking sound came fast and low.

"He had to ask," Bull said with a sigh as if it were my fault this sound was coming from the walls themselves.

"Not who, what." Ero shuddered as she looked from each entrance to the chamber with unease. "It's a creature used by the Somu as a weapon."

"You're a noncombatant, you're a noncombatant, why do you have to come on these things?" Tem was muttering to himself as he joined us. "It always sounds so fun and exciting when you're gearing up for it and you always regret it."

"We need to get the ruling family out of the building," Rima said, sending coordinates via the screen on her left forearm to Ero. "Take Bull and Tem with you. I sent you directions to where they are most likely being held. The Rowki will deal with this."

"Right, good idea," I said before I realized the Rowki also included myself. "Wait, what? We will?"

That eerie clicking came louder now, fast and ominous, like an insect. It was everywhere at once, all around us as if it lived in the very walls.

"No, we can't leave you," Ero answered through gritted teeth.

"The mission is more important," Rima answered, removing her black cloak.

"Oh, she's taking off her cloak," I muttered. "It's never a good sign when the hero takes off their cloak for a fight."

"I will stay," Bull answered, removing his blood-stained helmet to reveal a sweat-soaked face. "Ero and Tem are more than enough to rescue the family. Let me stay and even the odds. The stories of the Tulrog are legend. If we die, then I would die fighting a creature like this."

TWENTY

"OR WE COULD JUST HAVE a glorious life instead of a glorious death," I said, quickly removing my helmet. The piece of armor was stiflingly hot. It smelled like a rest stop toilet, thanks to the Somu gore that lived in there now. "We could live through it and kill this Tellamock thing."

Everyone looked at me like I was an idiot.

"Go now," Rima ordered Ero and Tem. Reluctantly, the two left.

Tem hesitated another second and gave me a nod before he left. "You can do this."

Ero and Tem ran out the entrance where we came through as a shadow covered the rear door Nok had escaped from. The ticking stopped now as something large moved on the other side of the closed door.

"What exactly is this thing?" I asked, trying to prepare myself for whatever kind of night terror creature I was about to see. "Are we talking a dragon, or a snake creature, or some kind of bigfoot?"

"I don't know why you'd be afraid of big feet," Rima said, taking up a stance in front of me on my right. "It would look like a spider to your kind. They are rare, but legend has it the Somu once used them in battle, with blood whistles only they can hear."

"Hail, my ancestors waiting for me at the gates of the otherworld," Bull growled out as he moved to stand on Rima's right. He reached down to where a wound on his leg soaked his fur with blood. He drenched one paw then smeared it across his face. "Hail, do I swear to uphold the bloodline of rage and courage. Hail, do I swear to give my last with tooth and claw."

I swallowed hard.

"None of that's helping me, like at all," I said, looking from my allies back to the door that slowly began to creak open. "Maybe it's giving you some kind of mental hype, but I feel like I'm going to throw up."

"Steady, little brother," Bull answered. "You're not as big of a sissy as I deemed when I first met you. Don't ruin that now."

The last thing I was worried about was ruining whatever Bull thought about me. I didn't have the focus to tell him as much now, as the door opened and skinny legs poked through.

The Tulrog was so long and slender, it had to crouch low to get its legs through the door. That same ticking came from it again as if it were playing with us, as if it knew we hated that sound.

The creature maneuvered through the door one leg at a time. It did look like a spider, except one with no body, and just a head and legs. A round head that was mostly a mouth of sharp teeth made up its body. From that head-like appendage, a series of seven long legs rose up in an arch before descending to the ground. Each leg ended in a spear-like point.

The ticking sound came from the creature's feet hitting the floor. It was taller than even Bull—nine, maybe ten feet.

"Spiders," I muttered. "Why did it have to be spiders?"

The creature tapped on the floor, moving to the left. Its head tilted forward with a wide-open maw showing us its rows of blackened teeth. It screeched at us as it came.

Not to be outdone, Bull roared a challenge before he flung himself forward. Rima was a bit more methodical in her approach, choosing to juke to the left and attack the creature from the side.

To say I was afraid would have been the understatement of this entire journey thus far. I was terrified. What drove me forward now wasn't what I wanted, or courage, or being heroic or noble. It was the idea that Rima and Bull were putting themselves in harm's way and I wasn't going to let them down.

I even gave a war cry of my own that sounded like a whimper compared to Bull's.

Bull unloaded with a burst of red laser rounds that struck the Tulrog without affecting it in the least. Two legs stabbed out at Rima as she ducked under one and batted away the other with her sword.

The Tulrog reared back on two legs, sending five out at us to skewer us where we stood. I dodged to the left of the leg meant for me as three more shot at Bull. Bull used his Mauler T-19 as a bat, slamming two of them to the side and being stuck in the gut by the third. Unlike me, Bull was a large target.

The Tulrog's leg went through the Ursonian armor like a box opener through plastic wrapping. Bull gasped, looking down at his ruined stomach.

"Bull!" I shouted, unsure what to do.

Blood dropped from Bull's maw as he grabbed onto the

leg in his gut and tore it, not out of his stomach, but ripped it from the Tulrog's joint.

Dark viscera poured from the Tulrog's ruined limb as it screeched in agony. The sound was so high-pitched, it made me want to slam my hands over my ears from the sheer torture.

Rima pressed her own attack, slicing through another of the creature's legs and sending a shower of blood in our direction. The blood coming from the creature was like a wild hose loosed from its owner's grasp. I was painted in the black blood as I broke off my own attack and went to Bull to see if there was anything I could do.

Bull fell to his side, the Tulrog's leg still in his massive gut.

"Hey, you're going to be okay, you're going to be okay," I said, having zero medical training and not having the slightest clue what to do. I pressed my hands on the wound, trying to stop the bleeding. "We're going to get Ero here. She's going to help."

"This won't kill me," Bull said through a mouthful of blood. "Get me up."

"Yeah, that's not going to happen; you're like a thousand pounds in your armor," I said, looking back as another screech filled the room. Rima had succeeded in severing a third leg of the Tulrog. Right now, she was going in for the kill and might have even succeeded in ending the creature there and then, if it wasn't for all the black liquid covering the floor.

Rima placed a right foot, trusting it to hold her maneuver. Her boot slipped on the soaked floor. The Tulrog realized what was happening and sent two of its remaining four arms slamming into Rima's body. Rima flew through the air, landing against the far wall with a crack. She slumped to the ground, unmoving.

The Tulrog screeched in victory as it slipped itself, trying to walk on four legs now, instead of seven.

Whatever happened next, it was on me. I understood that. With Rima unconscious and Bull unable to stand, if we all died or lived rested on my shoulders.

Bull was still trying to get to his feet. I left him there and stood in front of him, facing down the overgrown daddy longlegs. I closed the extending staff in my hand, forming it into a baton once more.

Maybe dying wasn't so bad an idea. Maybe Bull had it right when he was saying his little death chant. No more pain, no more suffering with my memories. I could die here and maybe, just maybe I could do something stupid enough to take the Tulrog with me. That would be something, wouldn't it?

The Tulrog continued to whine in pain as it headed for Rima's limp form. Its mouth snapped open and shut as if it were eager to take revenge on the creature that had done it so much harm.

"Hey! Cuteness, over here!" I shouted. "That's right, sweetheart. Here. Right here."

The Tulrog jerked its head in my direction, still leaking its own blood all over the wet floor.

I had a plan. Not much of a plan, but it was all I had. It would probably end us both if it worked, but Rima and Bull would be saved.

"Tyco, what are you doing?" Bull wheezed behind me.

"Come on!" I roared at the Tulrog. "I'm right here!"

The creature came for me, sliding in its own blood. I saw one leg that acted as a spear descend on me. Suddenly, I knew what fish must feel like when spear fishers paid a visit to their neighborhood.

I spun to the side just enough to avoid the leg entering my chest. Instead, it went through my synth suit between my chest and shoulder plate.

White-hot agony took my breath away. I screamed out, turning in my resolve from a cry to a roar of rage.

The Tulrog, having me in its grasp, stood up on two of its good feet, showing off its height as it brought me in toward its mouth. Another leg stuck me through the left shoulder.

It was hard to breathe. I had to remain conscious. Just a little longer, I had to hold it together. Tingling fiery pain ripped through both shoulders as I was lifted off the floor and brought to the Tulrog's mouth.

Its head-slash-body with teeth was deceptively large. It was nearly the size of my torso; it had just looked smaller from so far away.

The teeth on the top and bottom of its mouth were stained and cracked. I got a good look at them now as I fought to stay conscious. I told myself I was about to see her again. I wanted to believe there was an afterlife, and if that was the case, maybe she was there waiting for me.

The Tulrog opened wide.

"Eat this, you ugly son of a gun," I said, finding the strength somewhere deep down to lift my right arm forward and into the creature's mouth. I made sure the extending staff was vertical when it entered its mouth. It was hot in there, and muggy like some swamp's ecosystem. Just as the teeth came down to take off my arm at the elbow, I opened the extending staff.

Blood leaking from my shoulders and in more pain than I could ever remember, I sent the staff rocketing through both the skull and the bottom of the Tulrog's chin. More blood oozed as brain and skull fragments exploded in the air around me.

Unlucky for me, the act did not keep the creature from biting down on my arm. Razor-like teeth clamped down over my armor, crushing it into my skin and muscle.

The last thing I remembered was falling to the ground with the Tulrog on top of me.

TWENTY-ONE

UNLIKE THE WELL OF ENLIGHTENMENT, this time I was myself in the dream, not watching myself as events took place in the past. I was overlooking a vineyard of sorts from a balcony. The sky was beautiful, with warm rays touching my skin and a fresh breeze that felt so good.

I looked around, trying to remember where I was and how I got here. It came back to me in a flash—being teleported aboard the *Oni*, the Rowki, the fight with the Tulrog, and now this.

"Am I dead?" I asked myself in a soft voice. "Did I die?"

"You're not dead," a voice said from behind me on the balcony.

I turned to see a man who had not been there before. He was tall, with a white beard and eyes that were good without being kind, if that made any sense.

"Where am I?" I asked. "Who are you?"

"You are unconscious, being operated on by the Ursonians as they try to save your life," the man said as if that were a simple statement to grasp. "We're speaking in your mind. My name is Edmod. I am a member of the Rowki High Council."

At any other point in my life, that explanation would not have been acceptable. How insane had things become where that even made a shred of sense?

"So I'm not dead," I said, thinking back to the pain of getting stuck like a shish kabob by the Tulrog and then having my arm bitten off.

"No, despite your best efforts, you are still very much alive, my friend," Edmod said, joining me near the railing of the balcony. He didn't look at me; he just stared out into the vineyard. "Tell me, Max, do you want to die?"

Of all the things Edmod was going to say next, I didn't expect that to be one of them. No one had ever asked me that question before. To be honest, I wasn't sure how to answer.

"I don't know," I finally responded. "I don't know if she's waiting for me on the other side. I don't know how much longer I can deal with the pain I carry."

"There is another side," Edmod answered without hesitation. "She is there waiting for you, but your work is far from over."

I blinked a few times, wanting to believe what Edmod was telling me. But was I willing to put that much stock in a figment in my head?

"There are people here that need you now," Edmod continued. "Your wife is happy. She's safe now, free of pain and taken care of. But there's suffering here, and there are things you can do to alleviate the suffering for others."

"I don't want it," I said, shaking my head. "I didn't ask for this. I didn't ask to be a Rowki."

"And yet here you are," Edmod said, turning to look at me now. "Here you are faced with a decision. There is so much good you can do. What you've endured in your life has equipped you with a spirit of resolve and determination. We—the universe needs you, Max Tyco. Take heart that your wife is alive and well. If she were here, what would she say?"

"But she's not here," I answered, gritting my teeth. I couldn't hold my pain and anger at bay at the mention of what she would want. "I let her go that night."

"It's not your fault," Edmod replied. "The events of that night happened just as they were always supposed to. It's not your fault."

"I could have stopped—"

"It's not your fault," Edmod repeated, sterner now, as if he were challenging me to deny him this point. "It's not your fault."

Tears stung my eyes. Unlike most people, I didn't really care who saw me cry or not. I didn't try to hide the tears that were a testament to the years in silent torment. The truth was I did blame myself for that night. I always had.

"Know she's safe and happy. You don't need to cover your guilt with alcohol anymore." Edmod continued. "You know she would want you to be happy as well. With the time you have left in this universe, use it to mean something, Max. Use what you have become and allow yourself, not to move on from her—she'll always be with you—but allow yourself to live in the here and now. The past is a memory and the future is a dream. Live here; live now."

I took a deep breath, thinking about what Edmod had said. He didn't look like Yoda at all, but he sure fit the role of some kind of wise master.

"I want to believe that she's okay," I answered, letting the tears drip down my cheek before I wiped them away. "But how do you know?"

"I have faith that beyond this life there is another," Edmod answered. "But you didn't answer my question. Will you use what strength you have accumulated over the years to become the Rowki I know you can be? Or will you choose another path?"

"Now you're saying I can choose?" I asked with a raised eyebrow. "What was all the talk about fate and things only working out one way?"

"Think of life as a stream. It's only ever flowing in one direction," Edmod explained. "You're going with the stream one way or another, but you can maneuver within that stream. You can avoid or crash into obstacles, you can speed up or slow down, choose to go in a straight line or a zigzag pattern, yet still you flow with the stream. Does that make sense?"

"It does," I answered. I felt a strange sense of relief. I knew he was right. If Christina could see me now, she wouldn't want me to suffer.

"Are you ready, then?" Edmod asked.

"Ready for what?" I asked.

"Ready for the pain?"

He wasn't kidding. One second, I was standing on the balcony, finally sensing a bit of peace and understanding. The next, I couldn't help but scream out in agony. I opened my mouth so wide to scream, the muscles in the bottom of my jaw locked up and began to spasm.

I blinked, trying to get an idea of where I was. There were so many people around me. Ero, Tem, and others, but right in front of me, demanding my attention was the fiery, breathtaking agony coming from my shoulders and left arm.

"He's awake, he's awake," I heard Tem shout.

I tried to get an idea of where I was. Outside somewhere, it was cold. Voices and shouts all around me.

"Hold on," Ero said, appearing over my prone form. "We got you out and the nanites will kick in soon. I have to administer some skin spray to stop the bleeding."

"Rima, Bull?" I gasped, thinking about the other two I'd seen go down.

"I'm here, I'm here; is he asking for me?" Tem said, appearing on my right. "I'm fine, a little chafing in this suit, but I'll live, Max. You shouldn't be worried about me, my friend. I'll be okay."

"Rima suffered a concussion, but she'll be fine," Ero answered, ignoring Tem. She moved her paws around a heavy needle and a white bottle. "Bull's path to recovery is more serious, but he'll live. You saved them, Max."

"You hear that?" Tem asked, trying to hold back his own tears. That stupid glass helmet he wore was fogging up. "You're a hero. I knew you had it in you."

"I don't—I don't feel like a hero," I said, sucking in a sharp inhale of air as Ero stabbed me with an ice cold needle that felt like an icicle in my arm. My vision exploded with stars, so much excruciating aching, I couldn't help but pass out again.

This time when I was out, there were no dreams or visions or visits from Rowki masters, just blissful quiet blackness.

Tem's voice woke me from my sleep.

"Oh no, no, please no, oh father of the stars no," I heard Tem say from somewhere in the darkness.

I opened my eyes expecting danger, not really sure if we were under attack from another Tulrog or the Somu, or maybe Nok was back.

I opened my eyes to the inside of an infirmary. White walls and floor, with pods lined up against each wall and a wide walkway between. I looked over to my right where

Tem sat on a stool studying his datapad. I squinted, trying to see what he was going on about.

I could barely make out a game he was playing that looked like Pong.

"No, not again, please not again, you infernal AI. You won't beat me—"

"Tem?" I meant to say it in a normal voice, but my throat was so dry, it came out as a raspy whisper.

"Max Tyco?!" Tem said, jumping from his seat and coming up to my bedside, or I guess more like podside, in my case. "Max Tyco, you're awake. How do you feel?"

"I feel—I feel," I said, trying to search for the appropriate words. "I feel numb and tired."

"Good, that's good," Tem said, touching his datapad. "I am to call for Ero as soon as you awake. The nanites are in your body repairing you from the inside out. You're in the infirmary ward aboard the *Oni*."

"How long have I been out?" I asked.

"You were unconscious the return trip and all night," Tem answered. "This is the morning after the encounter with the Somu. You'll be happy to know Rima is already up and around and Bull is in the bed next to you. His healing process will be slow, but he owes his life to you."

I looked over to my left. Sure enough, the big brown bear lay in his own oversized pod. The pods, like the rest of the room, were white and shaped like half an egg cracked lengthwise. They hovered about a foot off the ground.

I heard Bull snoring from his pod. It was like we were in the newborn wing at a hospital.

"Oh, Max Tyco, or should I call you Blood Wolf? You are a legend already on your first mission," Tem was going on excitedly. "Not only did you slay the Tulrog, but the mission was a success. The ruling family was placed back in power and the Galactic Government Alliance has remained whole. Very impressive. Very impressive, indeed."

I didn't tell Tem that I was pretty much committing suicide when I went up to the Tulrog, and I knew it. Instead, I let him think I had wanted to live past that encounter. I didn't know what I wanted anymore after my talk with Edmod, if that had even really happened at all.

"Blood Wolf?" I asked instead.

"Oh yes, that's what the Ursonians are calling you now," Tem said, bobbing his head energetically. "Not just the Ursonians, the Somu as well. The blood moon and the wolf moon were perfectly aligned over the planet Somula last night. An event that happens only once every ten thousand years."

"Blood Wolf." I repeated the nickname. "I guess it could be worse. At least the chicken moon and the shi—"

Ero came into view from my left, walking down the aisle between the pods that lined the walls. She carried a datapad of her own.

"Max," she said, looking up at me with a smile. "Everything points to you healing well. The nanites have reacted to your anatomy better than expected. How are you feeling?"

"Good, I mean, considering I was used as a pincushion for Charlotte's web and lost an arm," I said, raising my right arm. I wasn't sure if I was going to see a nub or a hand. My arm was there all right, hand and all. I flexed my fingers, staring at a scar that ran the circumference of my forearm. The scar was jagged and ugly as far as scars went.

"The scar can be removed," Ero said, noticing me staring at mine. "It's a simple procedure now, with the technology we possess aboard the Oni."

"No," I told her, almost surprised at my own words. "No, that's okay. I think I want to remember this one."

"Of course," Ero answered. "I'd like to keep you another day just to monitor you, but you should be well. Are you hungry?"

"I'm hungry for some real food," I answered. "Do Tulrog killers or Blood Wolves get any sort of perks in the food department?"

Ero looked over to Tem.

The little historian chewed on his bottom lip. "If Rima finds out, I will deny it all. Everything, you hear me? This conversation never even happened. I'll deny it all."

"Deal," I said with a wide grin. "I want pizza. Can you make pizza with the works?"

Ero and Tem looked at each other, confused. Apparently, the word didn't translate well in either of their respective languages.

"It's okay. I'll tell the food printers what ingredients to put together in what order," I answered. "You two are in for a treat."

TWENTY-TWO

"MAX TYCO, I LOVE PIZZA," Tem said, shoving another piece in his mouth. "I mean that. I'm in love with what you call pizza."

"When Max first said the word 'pizza,' it translated in my language as 'dairy pan,' and I wasn't sure what to think of that," Ero said with both her cheeks bulging like a chipmunk's. "I have to agree with Tem. This is so good. Where has this dairy pan been all my life?"

The three of us sat at a table in the mess hall. The *Oni* was in between meals, so most of the mess hall was empty. I bit into my fourth piece of cheesy goodness with all the toppings.

The food printer hadn't done half bad when I told it how to prepare the food. I kind of wanted some hot sauce on it, but that was a battle left for another day. In fact, there might even have been a crate of hot sauce back in my trailer.

"I'm going to eat this every day from now on," the bear across the table from me said, licking her lips. She noticed my look. "What? You're on the restricted meal plan, not me. I still need to get my Red Bulls from you, too."

"Hey, you said it right that time," I answered.

"What else can you make?" Tem asked in between bites. "What else like this glorious pizza can you create? Your world must be full of legendary chefs and their creations."

"Oh, for sure," I answered, racking my brain for any chefs I could think of. "There's Captain Crunch, Chucky Cheese, and the most desirable of all, McDonald."

"Tell me of their creations and we will add them to the food printer," Tem said like an addict after his first hit. "We will taste all of them. In fact, I—"

Tem stopped himself mid-sentence.

Ero's eyes went wide as they looked over my shoulder.

"It's Rima, isn't it?" I asked, not really caring if she heard me or not.

Ero nodded, swallowing quickly.

I don't know what Tem was thinking, if he could deny eating the pizza, or if just not swallowing the food in his mouth would absolve him from the fact. He spit out the chewed food in his mouth back onto his plate.

"What is going on here?" Rima asked, coming to the head of our table to look at all of us at once. "What is this food?"

Tem was in too much shock to answer.

"It's called dairy pan, I mean, pizza?" Ero offered as if it were more of a question.

"You should try some," I said, willing to brave the storm that was Rima's wrath. "We just lived through a Tulrog attack and we completed the High Council's mission. I think they would be okay with a cheat meal."

"I am not cheating on anything," Rima said, joining us as she sat next to me at the table. "However, I don't see how one celebration meal would set us off course. I'll try two pieces."

The look on Tem's face was priceless. Everything he knew of the Rowki was shattered as Ero served Rima a pair of the deep dish, works pizza slices.

Rima lifted a piece, smelled it, and then took a measured bite. I saw her eyes widen despite how cool she played off the taste.

"Not bad," Rima said as we waited for her to chew.

I remember reading an article a long time ago on how the same part of the brain that was fired up from taking drugs was activated when eating cheese. I wasn't sure if it was actual fact, but I believed it.

Tem looked as if this whole meal was a trap and the Rowki High Council was about to storm in and discipline us for not sticking to my designated meal plan. Still, I saw him give Rima a sideways look and take another nibble from his slice of pizza.

"It's been a long time since I shared a meal with, well anyone," Rima said, taking another bite out of her pizza. "It's not as unpleasant as I thought."

"I don't think I've ever seen you eat outside your own quarters," Ero said around another slice. "It's usually Tem and Max in here on their own."

Rima nodded but didn't say anything at first. She chose her words carefully as if they pained her to say. "I guess we all still carry old scars."

I wasn't going to push the subject. It was a small miracle that Rima didn't slit our throats for breaking my meal plan. The fact that she was actually sitting with us was enough for me.

I thought about our meeting with Nok and what he'd said about Rima's past. What was it? Some kind of slave fighting pit he saved her from? I decided to save those questions for another time.

For now, we sat at the table talking about food. Ero shared how her culture celebrated a holiday called Bloodstein, where loved ones gathered around a smoked fish she swore was to die for, but sounded so gross in my ears.

Tem told stories of his mother baking bread for his graduation year that I guessed was like a birthday. Rima didn't contribute much, but she smiled with the others as they recounted their favorite dishes, family, and home.

"How about you, Max Tyco?" Tem asked. "Besides pizza, do you make any food yourself? What does your home look like?"

"Well, I mean you all can pretty much see my home," I answered. "It's parked in the circuit room. My home's on wheels. I have a small apartment to go to on my time off, but I try to spend as much time as I can on the road. It's not bad; it's cozy. It's a kind of adventure, and freedom on the road as well, if that makes any kind of sense."

"I think it does." Ero nodded. "Home doesn't have to be a stationary object. It can be any place with any people."

"I like your rig, as you call it," Tem said with a sigh. "It must be like an adventure every day to travel the lands of your world."

"Oh, it's an adventure all right," I answered. "But this, this is more of an adventure than I ever dreamed. Rowki, Tulrogs, and historians using their hover cameras as weapons."

"As what?" Rima asked.

"Oh yeah." Ero laughed out loud. "Our non-combatant friend here was using his hover camera like a wrecking ball."

Ero laughed again and Tem looked so embarrassed, it

made me chuckle. We even got a huff out of Rima, what I guessed passed for a laugh.

It hit me then how much I missed people. How much I missed friends. I couldn't recall the last time I shared a meal with anyone. Yet, here I was, traveling the universe with a lizard mouse, a polar bear, and a teacher who I was pretty sure wanted to kill me half the time.

Was this what I had been missing out on? So lost in my own pain, I couldn't see it?

"As entertaining as this meal has been, we have training to get back to if Tyco is going to be ready in three days' time," Rima said, reeling us back in. She looked over at Ero. "Is he cleared to continue his training?"

"He really should take it easy at least for a day, to make sure the nanites are finished and he urinates them out of his system," Ero said, patting a content belly with a sigh. "If you have any light work he's able to do, as in in-class studying, he should be fine."

"I feel great," I answered. "I can continue."

"All right," Rima said, standing from her seat, all business once again. "Tyco, I'd like to show you something. Follow me."

I looked over at Tem, who shrugged.

I grabbed one more slice to go despite the fact I was already pretty stuffed. I wasn't sure when I'd get the cheesy goodness again and I was a glutton. Let's just call it what it is.

I followed Rima to the lifts and we went below to the level designated for Rowki use. Rima didn't try to make small talk as we walked; that really wasn't her way. She led me to the room Tem used for instruction, the one with the orb in the center of the chamber that projected holographic displays.

"You handled yourself well," Rima said as we stood in front of the orb and she began pressing buttons on the command screen. "I've never second-guessed who the Rowki High Council chooses to undergo the training, but I had my doubts about your willingness to see this through."

"Fair enough," I answered, thinking about the talk I'd had with Edmod. I decided to tell Rima about it now. No sense of keeping secrets. "Rima, I have something to tell you."

I spilled it all to her, vaguely touching on the parts about my wife. I mainly told her about speaking with the Rowki and what he said about fate and choices.

Rima didn't say a word as I relayed the news to her. When I was finished, she stared at me as if I had grown an extra head. An awkward moment passed, and then a second and a third.

"Okay, and now that I decided to trust you with this, I'm wishing I hadn't," I said, clearing my throat. "What's wrong?"

"Was he tall?" Rima asked. "Edmod. Blue eyes, older male with a white beard?"

"Yes, that's him," I answered. "Why?"

"Tyco, Instructor Edmod is, in fact, one of the Rowki High Council; at least, he was. He died hundreds of years ago, facing a force like this universe has never seen," Rima explained slowly. "If he's coming to you now, then…"

The way her voice trailed off was beyond ominous. I was having serious second thoughts about telling her anything at all.

"No matter; that doesn't change what we have to do now, or the course set before us," Rima finally said. "After we talk, I'll speak with the High Council and see what orders they may have for us given this news. However, right now, I've brought you here to tell you about our main mission."

I watched in silence as Rima activated the projecting orb. All around us, the lights in the room dimmed and a picture of a solar system appeared around us. Of course, I didn't recognize any of the planets or moons, but my eyes were drawn to a particularly lush planet at the center of things.

"This is the planet of Ivandor," Rima explained. "Our mission from the Rowki council has been to travel to this planet and assess the situation."

I thought she was going to give me more, but she stopped there and just looked at me.

"And?" I asked, frowning.

"And what?" Rima asked.

"Assess the situation to find some kind of zombie virus, or is there like a sentient AI here, or killer robots?" I asked, listing off the premises for *I Am Legend, Terminator,* and *I, Robot* in that order. "What do we know about the planet?"

"Ivandor has yet to be explored," Rima explained. "We have opted to let it be. However, the High Council has sensed the need now to go there and investigate. Ivandor is the center of our universe, and as such the events taking place there are of utmost importance."

There it was again. The idea that I was being sent with Rima on a mission of paramount importance. Me, a brand-new recruit.

"I'm with you," I told her. "I've made up my mind. I'm in this. I'm here to help, but let's not pretend I'm stupid. If this mission is so important, why send me? Why not send a dozen trained Rowki? Hell, why not send the Rowki High Council?"

That struck a nerve I might not live to regret. I could see

a vein in Rima's forehead pulse right below her tight braids and tattooed scalp.

"Because there aren't nearly enough of us left," Rima explained honestly. "We uphold the balance in this galaxy. The truth, Tyco, is that we are a dying breed and will remain so unless something changes very soon."

TWENTY-THREE

I HAD EXPECTED AS MUCH, but it was different hearing it said out loud. Not just that the level of worry etched in Rima's face really drove home the point. The woman was a bastion of courage and ferocity. What I saw now was apprehension wrapped in fatigue.

It was like a mask had been taken off and Rima was letting me see a little more of who she was. As soon as that mask slipped, Rima recovered and continued.

"We go to Ivandor," Rima said, clearing her throat. "We have a few days left to get you ready. After what you did, I can see that your—you are..."

As Rima searched for the word, I thought I might help her out. "Heroic? Courageous, brave?" I asked.

"Suicidal," Rima answered.

"Oh well, I wouldn't say that," I said, surprised Rima had been the only one to pick up on the true motive for my actions. "I mean, I saved you and Bull."

"And you knew you would die doing it," Rima said with a raised eyebrow. "When we go to Ivandor, there is no telling what we'll meet there. I need to know you want to be

with us. As a last resort, yes, we would all sacrifice ourselves
to save each other, but only as a last resort. I need to make
sure you're not suicidal, and that you're sober."

I got it. Anger flashed for a moment as I tightened my
hands into fists. But she was right. I knew that much. After
what I had been through and my strange encounter with
Edmod, I felt a sense of peace. I had to hold on to the idea
that she was okay and, yes, she would want me to help as
many people as I could. The face of the small Somu girl
named Christina I had saved played in my mind as well.

"I'm with you," I answered.

"No more drinking, or taking unnecessary risks?" Rima
asked.

"No more drinking, but you're going to have to give me
some kind of long-range weapon if you want me not to take
risks," I said, seeing an opening for me to finally get my
hands on a rifle or blaster. "Come on, I don't have all my
Rowki powers yet. I can't move my weapon like you can."

"You seem to do well enough with your extending staff,"
Rima answered. "You killed a Tulrog, after all. Those are
creatures of legend."

"Let's just call a stick a stick," I answered. "Come on, I need,
like, blasters and swords and maybe a cool heat-seeking weapon
that will hone in on multiple targets and take them all down."

Rima had a way of looking at someone and making
them feel as tall as Tom Thumb. She did that to me now.
My butt tightened on instinct for what was coming next.

"All right," Rima said, crossing her arms. "Tomorrow
morning, I'll have Captain Akel instruct you in the proper
use of a ranged weapon. I can see the value in that, at least
until you find your own sardonium and are able to imbue a
weapon with the metal."

"Yes!" I shouted so loud, it echoed in the room. "Thank you, thank you, Rima."

Maybe it was my brush with death, finally getting some peace about my wife, or the pizza overload, but I moved forward as if I was going to give Rima a hug.

"Tyco, control yourself," Rima said with a growl and violence in her eyes.

"Oh, right, right," I said, clearing my throat.

"I will hug you, Max Tyco," Tem said, appearing in the doorway and coming over to me with open arms. "If for nothing else, than introducing me to dairy pan. I think I want to try it with all kinds of—what did you call them? Toppings?"

"Yep, wait until you try pineapple and ham on it," I said with a grin, giving the small historian a fierce yet brief embrace. "Some people hate it, but I don't think it's that bad. I mean, I wouldn't order it myself, but if it was at a party I'm not saying no."

"Yes, your previous weight suggested you didn't know how to use the word 'no' when it came to food," Rima said, heading for the door. "Enough hugging, now; we have work to do."

"Of course, of course," Tem said with a sigh as Rima left the room. "Max Tyco, we should continue your lessons today even if you are supposed to rest your body. You can still use your mind."

"You know what, Tem," I said with a sly smile. "I think you're right. I would like to learn a lot today and I think you can teach me."

"Max Tyco, I do not like the way you're looking at me," Tem said, taking a step back. "Eating dairy pan is the most illegal thing I've done in my time aboard the *Oni*. I'm a reformed man. I would like to stay on the right side of the law and not go back to my dark ways."

"You had dark ways?" I asked incredulously. "You?"

"Oh yes, I was quite the, how would you say, 'bad boy'," Tem said, nodding with all seriousness. "I was known to sleep in on my days off and once, once, Max Tyco, I even designated myself as ill one day when I was not ill at all."

Tem looked over both shoulders as if he were expecting someone to jump out of the shadows and catch him in his confession.

"You mean you called in sick?" I asked

"I said I was ill, but I was in reality not ill at all," Tem said in a whisper. "To get off work."

I just stared at him.

Tem took my silence as shock. "Oh, there are stories, stories I could tell you, Max Tyco. But I'm changed now. Have no fear. I am on the side of the light."

"Okay, well, that was weird," I said, trying to get us back on track. "What can you tell me of Rima's past and this Nok character we ran into?"

Tem cleared his throat uncomfortably. "I'm not sure Rima would—"

"Ahh, come on," I said, interrupting him. "You know she's not going to offer up that info. I'll be better equipped to help if I have some background information. Who is this Nok guy? He used to be a Rowki, I gathered that much, and Rima's instructor?"

"Perhaps it would be better to show you," Tem said with a resigned sigh when he realized I wasn't going to let this one go. He moved to the large sphere in the room and brought up an image of the man I knew as Nok.

He was easy to recognize with his smooth features, almost nonexistent nose, and snake-like eyes.

"Nok Marrow was one of the most powerful Rowki, a true believer and in line to take his seat at the High Council one day," Tem said with a sad twinge of pain in his voice. "He fell in love with credits and power, more than the Rowki code. From there, it was a short step to joining the Sait."

"The Sait are those who found a way to use sardonium outside of the Rowki?" I asked, trying to get a better idea of exactly who they were. "How many are there?"

"Yes, they've mastered the use of sardonium like the Rowki but serve a different purpose, one of greed, power, and ultimate control," Tem explained. "There are a few ex-Rowki like Nok, but most of them have been trained from the very beginning to be Sait. As to how many there are, I am not sure. I do know there are two Rowki who have left to join the Sait, Nok being one of them."

"He said he rescued Rima from fighting pits? Was she a slave?" I asked, making Tem uncomfortable yet again. "Just blink if that's a yes, Tem. You don't have to say anything; just blink if I'm right."

"Max Tyco, how can I not blink?" Tem said, blinking furiously.

"All right," I answered as more pieces of the puzzle began to fit together. "I get it now. We only have a few days left until we touch down on Ivandor. I need to be ready. It's time to get to work."

TWENTY-FOUR

THE NEXT FEW days aboard the *Oni,* I really laid into it. I was at the training circuit early to work with Rima, I memorized as much as I could from Tem about Rowki lore, and what it meant to be one of the members of this elite force of warriors.

I trained intently with Captain Akel like I had never before. I even managed to land a few punches on Rima when we sparred. She made me pay for them, of course, but it was worth it. I was getting better. I had months and years of training to achieve the skill level of those teaching me, but still, I could see the improvement.

It was the night before we were supposed to touch down on the planet of Ivandor when I invited Tem, Rima, Ero, and Captain Akel to my rig for a bit of celebration.

I'd had a full load, fifty-two pallets in my rig I had been hauling for Amamart when I was teleported to the *Oni.* No use in letting it all go to waste if we weren't going to make it back. That wasn't any kind of suicidal thought in there, just facts.

Ero was the first to arrive. When she did, I took her to

the back of my rig and opened the rear doors. I jumped in and handed her a case of Red Bull.

Ero accepted the gift, sniffing the cans with a wiggling black nose.

"No, you have to open them," I answered. I took one of the cans and popped the top. "Here, you drink it. It's a stimulant full of caffeine and bull testicles or something, but it works. It's going to keep you awake, just giving you a heads up."

"Please," Ero said, accepting the Red Bull with another sniff. "I'm not sensitive to stimulants. I'm very aware of how they affect the anatomy. I'm a medic, remember?"

Ero sniffed the contents of the Red Bull one more time before downing a huge draught. She may have taken down half the can before she came up for air.

I'm not sure about the science behind what I saw, but I swear I saw her pupils dilate as the Red Bull hit her system. A huge pink tongue came out of her mouth and licked her lips.

"I feel, I feel excited," Ero said, maneuvering her tongue around her salivating lips even more. "My heart is going fast. I like this Red Bull."

"Okay, okay, before you start scratching yourself asking for another fix, just slow it down," I warned. "If you've never had it before, it's going to be a kick to your system."

Ero nodded, trying to read the ingredients on the can, which I wasn't sure was feasible since she couldn't read English, as far as I knew.

The rest of our merry party arrived together. I use the word "merry" flexibly since Captain Akel wasn't saying anything and Rima looked somewhere between pissed about being summoned and annoyed at not knowing why.

"Thank you for coming," I said, waving them forward. "I have something to share with you."

"If you can make this quick, Tyco," Rima answered with hands on her hips. "We have preparations that still need to be made for our trip to Ivandor tomorrow."

"Right, right," I said, jumping back in my trailer. "I wanted to thank you all for what you've done for me. Taking your time to teach me and not letting me give up at the beginning."

I grabbed the case I was looking for on one of the pallets on the left. I came out carrying the packs of chocolatey goodness. "Back on Earth, this stuff is highly coveted and reserved for only the best."

I jumped down from the trailer and began opening the cardboard casing of Snack Packs and handing them out.

"Ohhhh, more Earth food," Tem said, licking his lips.

"Only for the best, you say?" Rima asked, looking at the plastic cup of Jell-O Pudding sideways. "What is it?"

"It's a treat," I answered, showing them how to peel back the lid. I pulled out plastic spoons I'd carried with me from the cabin of my truck. "Here, cheers?"

I lifted my open Snack Pack out in front of me to clink with the others.

Captain Akel sniffed his.

"Oh man, I can't wait to try this," Ero spat out in a rush of words. She shifted her weight from one foot to the other. "If this is anything like dairy pan or Red Bull, I think I'm going to like it."

Ero was speaking so fast now, it was difficult to tell where one word stopped and the other began.

Rima looked at her with a raised eyebrow.

Ero swallowed hard, then did her best to try and stop fidgeting under the stare.

"What is this 'cheers' you speak of?" Tem asked, looking at the snack in my outstretched arm. "Why are you giving me another one? I already have a Snack Pack."

"No, I'm not giving it to you," I explained. "Here, we clink them together, like. tap yours against everyone else's in celebration."

"Us touching our Snack Packs signifies celebration?" Rima asked

It was Captain Akel who lifted his eyebrow this time.

"Just go along with it. Come on, come on, tap my Snack Pack," I said as the others relented. We dug into the chocolate mana and everyone's eyes widened.

"This planet of yours is truly a magical place of gluttony," Ero said, abandoning the spoon and licking her snack pack with a large pink tongue. "I want to go to Earth one day."

Even Rima and Captain Akel seemed to agree with her. Both of them were quiet as they ate. Captain Akel kept on smacking his lips.

"I will miss treats like this in the field," Tem sighed. He looked over at me with a grateful grin. "Thank you for sharing your wondrous knowledge of food with us, Max Tyco."

"Yes, thank you," Ero echoed.

Rima didn't say anything and neither did I expect her to.

Captain Akel caught my eye and rubbed his stomach.

"It was a kind gesture," Rima finally said as she sucked on her spoon. "But now we should be focused on tomorrow, and what the day will bring as we touch down on Ivandor."

"Where exactly are we landing?" I asked. "I mean, did the High Council give us a certain place to search?"

"We do not have exact coordinates, but the area we have

chosen to land in is the one with the most likely chance of being inhabited," Tem explained as he traded his empty pudding for his datapad. "We'll know much more as soon as we touch down. Scouting parties will be sent out to get the lay of the land."

I nodded along with his words. We really were going in blind. If I'd known what the next day would hold for us, I would have had another Snack Pack.

THE NEXT MORNING was not one of routine. I was woken by my own internal alarm. After so many days of five AM wake-up times, it seemed my body was getting a nasty habit of waking itself up early.

After a quick meal with Tem, we headed to the armory. The energy around the *Oni* was practically palpable. Everyone was aware of what we were doing, even though not one of us had any idea what to expect.

Ursonians walked faster, chattered more excitedly, and even Bull was out and around.

I saw the massive soldier on the way to the lift to gather my armor. He walked with a slight limp, but otherwise seemed no worse for wear. Whatever nanobots Ero injected him with worked just as well as my own.

He was with two other Ursonians when they saw me.

"Little brother!" Bull boomed in a voice that I wasn't sure was friendly or not just yet.

"Bull," I answered, looking his dark gray uniform up and down. "You healed up."

"As did you," Bull said, extending a massive paw. "I owe you an apology for how I treated you before."

"You don't owe me anything," I answered, accepting the

show of friendship. His paw grabbed my forearm right below my wrist. "You would have done the same."

"But I was skewered like a dying Mongrowth and could not. You killed the Tulrog," Bull said, squeezing my arm so hard, I thought at least one of my bones would break. "You have my blade and blaster whenever you call."

"That's nice to hear; just let go of my arm," I said, wincing.

"Of course, of course," Bull said with a grin as if he was doing it on purpose. "Word of the Blood Wolf, the slayer of the Tulrog has been traveling over the *Oni*. Our females, it seems, are not as repulsed by you as I am."

I looked at the pair of giant Ursonians behind Bull that were, in fact, female. They pouted their lips in what I guessed was supposed to be a seductive way, but just seemed wrong.

"Well, I have to get to the armory," I said, waving at Bull and his companions as I walked to the lift where Tem waited, chuckling.

"I'll see you on the ground, Blood Wolf," Bull said, using the name again.

I stepped into the lift with Tem. As the glass doors closed, I caught the historian holding his side, barely able to contain his merriment.

"What's the joke?" I asked.

"No, no, nothing," Tem lied with a high-pitched laugh. "I'm sorry, I'm sorry, it's just the idea of you with an Ursonian. I mean, they would crush you. Could you imagine?"

Some pretty messed-up images came to mind and I shook my head. "No, Tem, I don't want to imagine."

We made it to the bottom floor and stepped outside the lift together. Tem wiped away the last of his tears from the laughter as we joined Rima in the armor bay.

"Good, you're here," Rima said, handing me an extending staff. "Captain Akel said your training with ranged weapons has begun, but with limited time, there is still much to learn. Here's the blaster you requested."

I accepted the object, looking over at Tem, confused. "Um, Rima? I'm not sure if I've had one too many concussions from all of our training, but this is just a staff."

"I had it augmented for you," Rima said over her shoulder as she began to change into her armor. "You'll see a button on the other side of the weapon now, opposite the button that allows the staff to extend. Don't touch it. That is your trigger. A bolt will come out of the end of the staff now."

I didn't want to seem ungrateful, but what I really wanted was some giant mini-gun to wield and unload on my enemies, not a blaster that came out the end of my staff.

"Is there any room here to negotiate?" I asked, scratching the underside of my jaw. "I mean, I appreciate the gesture, but I was hoping for something with a little more boom in it, if you know what I mean."

"That is what you'll be using. Trust me, it has plenty of boom," Rima said without even looking around. "You've trained with the staff thus far, and as much as I wish we had more time to train you with other weapons, we do not. It served you well enough against the Tulrog. It will serve you well now."

"I'm going to get my gear," Tem said, bowing out of the room like a kid when mom and dad had an argument. "I'll see you on the bridge."

"The bridge?" I asked Rima as I joined her, putting on my armor. "We get to see the bridge?"

"We'll be there when we land," Rima answered, pulling on her synth suit. She handed me a small circular device.

"This will attach to the space behind your right ear and provide communication with the rest of our team when we land, should you not desire to wear your helmet."

"About that helmet," I said, looking over at mine. "Why don't you wear one?"

"Helmets are optional. There are no standard rules for how a Rowki must dress. Most of our missions will be investigations, not full-out war. I would wear a helmet if I thought we were going into heavy danger. Otherwise, I prefer my hood."

"I guess that makes sense," I said, securing my suit. "This is just a discovery mission, right? I mean, there are no Tulrogs on Ivandor?"

Rima didn't say anything, which made me sweat. "Rima, tell me there are no Tulrogs on Ivandor."

"The truth is, we do not know," Rima explained. "Ivandor has not yet been explored, as I've said before. There could be Tulrogs there, there could not. There could be creatures much worse."

"Wonderful, well Merry Christmas to us," I said with a sigh as I finished gearing up. I really didn't know what to expect, so I clipped the helmet to my magnetic belt opposite my extending staff, just in case.

I had to admit, with both Rima and me walking down the hall to the lift, I felt like a badass. Her cloak fell down her back and her sword poked over her right shoulder.

I'd been meaning to ask what the tattoos on her head meant and never had the chance. As we rode the lift up to the bridge level, I took the opportunity.

"Rima, what are those tattoos on your head in between your braids?" I inquired. "What do they mean?"

"It's the Rowki code in my own language," Rima explained.

"The code you recited that day we were looking at the stars?" I asked. "The one that repeats 'send me'?"

"The same," Rima answered. "It reminds me of what I am. Of who I am when things get hard and when much is asked."

I didn't want to push the subject further. Rima seemed pretty jacked up and ready to go at the moment.

The lift stopped and let us out on one of the upper levels I'd never been to before. That in and of itself wasn't a big deal. I hadn't had the opportunity to explore a whole lot of the ship between my training sessions and almost getting used as a toothpick for the Tulrog and all.

This level, like many of the others, was well lit, with wide white walls. We passed through the corridor to a closed door with a pair of Ursonian guards.

They saluted us with heavy thumps of their right fists against their chests before allowing us entry.

The doors separated from the middle as we walked into what I could only describe as Star Trek. The bridge was a large half circle with stations set up in front of me and on the right and left. A few steps down, a command chair was placed in the center of the room with more stations to the right and left of that.

A crew of Ursonians worked blinking boards and read flashing lights on their monitors.

A massive front window showed me a grand display that stole my breath.

TWENTY-FIVE

WE WERE APPROACHING the planet of Ivandor. A lush green landscape covered most of the planet, with blue clear oceans. It was perfect and beautiful. The baseball-sized orb continued to grow in size as the *Oni* approached the sphere.

"Let's take her nice and easy," a female Ursonian said from the captain's chair. "We don't have any reason to expect a hostile welcome, but let's make sure our shields are up just in case, Mr. Vulkni."

"Aye," a black-furred Ursonian said from one of the control stations to my left. "Shields on full."

I knew the feeling of dread encompassing me was unfounded. We had no idea what to expect from the planet. There could be a cuddly puppy species here for all I knew. Still, as we approached, the sense of wonder I held in my heart was overshadowed with worry.

"We'll be setting down as discussed," the ship's captain said, looking over to Rima and then to me. "Is this the Rowki I've heard so much about? The one they're calling the Blood Wolf, that overtook the Tulrog single-handed?"

"I wasn't alone," I said, blushing under her measured eye.

"He is," Rima answered for me. "Tyco, this is Admiral Marm."

"Blood Wolf, your reputation precedes you," the admiral said, turning from me back to the massive window in front of her. "We'll need you and all the Rowki the Galactic Government can offer if we are to prevail."

"What did I miss?" Tem asked, joining us in his over-stuffed marshmallow costume. He held his clear glass helmet in the crook of his right elbow.

"We're about to set down now," I answered.

"Entering the planet's atmosphere, Marm," a female behind yet another control panel stated.

"There should be minimal turbulence," Admiral Marm warned us. "Take us in."

A slight shudder under my feet served to confirm the admiral's words. Heat warped and slid across the front screen as we descended to the planet of Ivandor. The vibrant greens of the jungle canopy welcomed us. The roof of the jungle was so thick, it was impossible to see what was actually on the ground itself.

A mountain range to the north and sea to the west hedged in our landing spot, with nothing but jungle to the east and south.

Our landing area wasn't really a landing area at all, but rather a location in the jungle where we were going to set down and crush the trees beneath us.

"Landing gears down," Admiral Marm barked.

"Landing gears down, aye, Marm," an Ursonian answered.

The *Oni* came down gently with barely a shudder through the craft as our gears reached the jungle floor.

Our craft was so large, the main window still overlooked the jungle. I could see both dark and light neon greens, nothing like the plants on Earth.

"Contact, contact, at one o'clock," Rima said way too calmly.

Every eye in the room swung to look out the window in front of us and just to the right.

Rima wasn't wrong. As far as I could tell, there was no breeze moving the jungle canopy from side to side. Yet something large, no, something massive moved through the trees. It was impossible to tell what it was. The only reason I knew there was something there at all was because the tree tops shifted to the right and left as whatever it was lumbered through.

"Do we have exterior audio?" Admiral Marm asked.

"Exterior audio, aye," was the answer.

Everyone on the bridge held their breath as we listened in.

Nothing.

I looked around as we all started to exchange glances now. The distant cracking of wood and the echoing footfalls of something in the distance. A wail came, not high-pitched, or even scary; maybe sad or in a song.

The only thing I could compare the sound to was recordings of the noises whales make when they sing to one another. Goosebumps rose on my arms as the sounds faded in the distance.

"Suddenly, I'm having very strong thoughts about sitting this one out," Tem whispered. "I can send my drone with you and remotely control it from here. I mean, you really don't need me at all. I—"

One look from Rima and Tem shut his mouth.

I didn't want to voice my thoughts at the moment. I

didn't need to. I knew we were all thinking the same thing. No one was eager to volunteer to be the first out the airlocks and into the jungle depths.

"Air quality, gravity?" Rima asked.

"All reading out as we expected," Admiral Marm said, looking down at one of the two screens set inside the arms of her command chair. "Air is breathable and gravity is slightly less than expected, but nothing that you should feel."

"Then we go forward as planned with the scouting parties," Rima said, nodding to Admiral Marm in thanks.

"May the ancestors protect you," Admiral Marm said to all three of us.

I followed Rima from the bridge and back to the lifts. Tem walked beside me, tapping away at his datapad.

"We'll rendezvous with Captain Akel at the bay and then join one of the scouting parties," Rima explained as we stepped inside the lift. "The sooner we can discern exactly why we're here, the sooner we can fix it and move on."

I couldn't disagree with her there. As the lift descended, I couldn't stop thinking about that noise we heard, and whatever large beast made it as it lumbered away. I still thought I needed a bigger blaster.

The lift reached the cargo bay floor and we stepped out to a show of force. Captain Akel had marshaled the Ursonian Corps in full gear. Unlike our brief layover in Somula where only a unit of soldiers came with us, the entire hangar bay was filled with bear people preparing for the expedition.

Hundreds of soldiers stood ready or carried crates and supplies to and from one location. There were also smaller ships in the hangar and land vehicles I had yet to see before now.

The smaller air ships, unlike the dropships, were made

for no more than six or seven soldiers. The land vehicles couldn't be for more than four Ursonians. I did notice some pretty heavy fire power on the vehicles, as well.

Rima headed straight for the center of the hangar bay, where Captain Akel and Ero stared down at a holo-projected map floating just above a table.

The map was like a miniature layout of the land, complete with the mountain range to the north and the sea to the west. Captain Akel was in the process of pointing to our center location, then moving a large finger out from our location in four directions, one to the north, one to the east, one to the south, and one to the west.

"Four scouting parties on foot, with the Hogs ready to go in case we need backup," Ero said out loud as the captain motioned to the heavy-duty land cruisers. "At the same time, we'll deploy the Razors overhead to let them scan in each direction. Whatever they can't see through the jungle canopy, our scouts will get a good look at on foot."

Captain Akel looked up to Rima.

"I like it," Rima explained. "We should take all precautions on this first trip out. What are your unit sizes looking like?"

Captain Akel lifted both hands, showing five fingers, then closed his left hand and showed two more fingers on his right.

"Twelve unit teams." Rima nodded in agreement. "Assume for the sake of argument everything out here wants to kill us. Let's get our teams back safe."

Captain Akel nodded again.

"So which way do we go?" I asked, staring down at the map. With no real idea on what was out here, each direction seemed as good as the next. "Do we flip a coin or something?"

"At least to the north and west, we know what we are headed toward," Tem explained, looking at the map. He pointed to the mountain range to the north and then the ocean to the west in turn. "To the east and south, we have no real idea."

He was right. In those two locations, only dense jungle brush opened up to us.

"East or south?" Rima asked herself with a click of her tongue. "East or south? The creature we saw took off to the south of us. That is where we'll go."

"You know, I thought you were going to say that." I said. "Most people, when faced with an opportunity to follow a giant mysterious beast into the unknown, would go in the opposite direction, not try and follow it."

"Well, we are not 'most people'," Rima explained.

Captain Akel and Ero, who had allowed us to talk it out, nodded their agreement. Both Ursonians moved now to dole out orders to the four units that would be heading out into the jungle interior.

Unlike the first time I visited the hangar bay and the red force field shields were up, the walls on each side of the hangar bay were closed.

A deep click was heard through the hangar bay as the walls to the ship were now lowered, granting us access to the planet of Ivandor. I looked out into the bright morning, noticing for the first time there wasn't just one sun but two.

I wasn't sure how I had missed the second much smaller star giving warmth to the planet. There had been so much to see before and the second sun was so small, I had missed it in all the action.

The first sun was yellow and reminded me of the Earth's one star. The second much smaller sun was more orange and bright.

All around me, as the doors to the hangar bay opened, Ursonians gathered in ranks, ready to move out as directed.

The Razor crafts also fired up, four in all, each going out in a different direction to get a better look at the overall landscape of the area.

Captain Akel took a position at the head of the four units of Ursonians ready to be deployed. Ero spoke for him as he motioned with his paws.

"We are here for a reason, to do our job," Ero shouted over the roar of the engines. "No one gets left behind. Remember your training. You are the best. The Ursonian next to you is the best. What we do here on this planet echoes into the rest of the universe. Do your job!"

Captain Akel finished that last remark with a heavy thud as his right fist came across his chest to pound his armor.

A roar from the Ursonian Corps that rattled my chest vibrated through the hangar as they also returned the gesture, thumping their own armored chests.

I could feel my adrenaline begin to flow as the Ursonians filed out of the hangar bay into the jungle. The Razors took off overhead into the bright morning sky.

"Be safe out there," Ero said as I moved to follow Rima and Tem.

"You're not headed down to the south?" I asked, realizing I had just taken for granted that Ero would be coming with us.

"No, headed north," Ero answered. She moved her right hand to a side pouch where she opened the top and revealed a can of Red Bull sitting in her satchel. "Took one for the road. We'll be back in no time."

"Be safe," I answered.

"You as well, Blood Wolf. May the ancestors watch over you," Ero returned, turning and jogging off to join her unit.

I had to run to catch up with Rima and Tem, who followed Captain Akel and another unit out the opposite hangar bay door.

I took a deep breath before stepping off the ship onto the planet of Ivandor. I knew technically we were already there, but there was something about actually taking that first step onto the planet that meant something special.

TWENTY-SIX

THE PLAN WAS to move out slowly and methodically as we searched the area. Each unit would set out to go four miles into the jungle, and then return to the ship before dark. Our aerial support would double that number, reaching eight miles in every direction and mapping the terrain before they, too, returned.

I found myself in the middle of the column of Ursonians between Rima and Tem. The interior of the jungle was so dense and the Ursonians so massive, a pair of the large soldiers took turns in the lead forging a path for us through the underbrush.

This pair of trailblazers was swapped out every mile for a fresh pair of arms as they used their Mauler T-19's as brush-clearing tools.

Not only was I much smaller than the typical Ursonian, but since they were clearing the path for us, my job was pretty easy. I walked along in the column, eyes open and alert.

The sounds of the jungle were like nothing I had ever

experienced. Clicks and ticks from insects mixed with throaty caws from the colorful birds overhead. I even thought I saw some kind of monkey-like creature swinging from tree to tree.

It was wonderful and worrisome at the same time. Who knew what could be in the brush? It wasn't long before we caught the trail of whatever had been moving through the jungle in front of us.

The column stopped short as a clearing twice the width the one the Ursonians made for us opened out to the south. Trees had been pushed to the side and bushes trampled underfoot. The dark rich soil under that was nearly black, stomped with heavy footfalls.

I heard a series of clicks over the radio unit Rima gave me. The small circular piece of alien tech was a sticker thing, and I forgot I was wearing it behind my right ear altogether.

"The captain has found something, come," Rima said to Tem and me.

We moved up the column to the front where Captain Akel pointed to a particularly clear track stamped deep into the soft soil. It was huge. I could stand in the single print with both my boots comfortably and have room to spare.

"Whatever it is came through here recently," Rima said, crouching down to inspect the print. Her hand was dwarfed by the track. "We should follow."

"That is not what I was thinking at all," I answered. "We should let this creature go ahead and go home or wherever it's headed. It didn't bother us."

"She's right," Bull said, coming up from my right. "It's an easy path for us to follow and not have to cut through the brush for the next few miles."

Captain Akel motioned to two of his scouts. In a

moment, they were gone down the path, fearlessly headed after whatever creature made the prints.

"Well, on the upside, at least these aren't Tulrog prints," Tem offered. "It would be worse if they were Tulrog prints."

We continued on with the jungle so dense around us, at times it was difficult to see the suns through the canopy. The heat was getting to me as well, a wet, humid kind of warmth sending droplets of perspiration down my back.

If the heat bothered the Ursonians, they didn't show it. Despite the level of humidity and exertion the Ursonian Corp continued on, helmets and all. The red visor across the eyes of their helmets was lowered along with the center of their helmets to allow in air as they pushed ahead. Once opened, the helmet appeared in a T shape, allowing their muzzles to poke through. The helmets reminded me of something ancient Vikings would wear in this altered state.

"They train in harsh conditions to prepare for any planet," Tem said, handing me a water canister from his belt. "Ursonians are well known for their ability to fight in heat or cold."

"I can see that," I said, taking a long swig of water and handing it back to Tem. "Thank you."

"Oh, not to worry. I must say you are handling everything extremely well for this being your first actual mission." Tem gave me a smile with the word of encouragement. "Many new Rowki have been known to—"

The familiar sound of a whoopee cushion ripped through the air, interrupting Tem's next words. "Oh my, excuse me. I seem to pass gas when I'm nervous. It didn't affect me much on Somu because I had an idea what to expect. But here, there is no knowing what we will encounter."

A few of the Ursonians chuckled.

Rima didn't say anything.

"It's my nerves," Tem said, swiping the air behind his rear end as if that was going to help.

"Hey, don't push it back to us," the Ursonian behind us who happened to be Bull complained. "Bless the ancestors, that's the foulest scent I've had to rest my nose on since the food printers started to smoke."

"Sorry, sorry," Tem said, trying to keep it together. "My bowels seem to not agree with me this morning."

"You might want to check your underwear after that one." I coughed. Bull was right, it did smell like burned food. I was about to crack another joke when a scream ripped through the air to our left.

The column halted.

The bellows and shrieks weren't human or any kind of alien being I had yet to encounter. It sounded like the calls of predators fighting over a kill.

Captain Akel gave a command with a closed fist he opened and then motioned all of us to move forward in the direction of the sound. We had to be two or three miles from the *Oni*. Not that I could see it through the dense jungle interior anyway.

I felt my heart pick up in speed as I withdrew my extending staff equipped with a blaster from its place on my hip.

We moved into the jungle depths to our left as Rima spoke in our comms.

"Remember, we're here to figure out what's going on, on this planet first," she said to our unit. "Engage only if given the command. We need to make contact and speak with the locals, not kill them."

I understood why she was reminding us, but the crashes

coming from the interior of the jungle sounded more like creature or beast, not intelligent life. There were yelps now along with the snarling and cries.

We moved into the jungle depths, the Ursonians having to move sideways and trample bushes to get through. Fifty or so yards in, we arrived at the scene of all the commotion.

A pack of gorilla velociraptors—at least that's what I'm going with, because that's as close a frame of reference as I had—surrounded a heavy creature on all fours that was skin and scales. If the biggest pit bull in the world hit the gym every day, didn't have hair but scales instead, it would look something like this.

The pit bull creature was wounded and ripped open in a dozen places. It stood guard in front of a small opening in the ground.

The creatures attacking it had velociraptor-like bodies, from powerful hind legs to their sweeping tails. Long arms extended from their torso to the ground, resting on knuckles.

These creatures were all hard leather hide, except for their front arms, which were covered in a thin layer of black fur. Their faces were reptilian, with razor-sharp teeth extending from the top and bottom of their gums.

"Stand down, stand down." Rima gave the order when she saw it was not the native population making the noise but instead the local wildlife.

Too late. With this many Ursonians moving through the forest, they were bound to make enough noise to tip off these giants to our presence.

The hybrid velociraptor gorillas turned around to take us in. They roared and growled to one another. One particularly scarred member of their order leaned forward and gave off a challenge, showing an incredible mouth of teeth that reminded me of a shark.

The other creatures charged our position, kicking up dirt and foliage on their way.

Captain Akel took a step forward from his position near the head of the column and opened fire.

TWENTY-SEVEN

THAT MAY AS WELL HAVE BEEN an order to open the gates of chaos themselves. Every Ursonian on the line fired their Mauler T-19 with deadly accuracy. Red laser beams ripped into the oncoming creatures, tearing them apart.

I even got to use my new weapon. I pointed my new blaster forward and pressed the button on the handle.

Vroom!

I wasn't prepared for the level of kickback from the weapon. My right arm jerked to the side as my round went off. It was impossible to see if my round was the one that took down the charging creature I aimed at. Nevertheless, under the extreme amount of firepower being pumped into the creatures, they all fell within seconds.

Only a few of the beasts survived the attack, including the scarred one. The survivors yelped and ran into the woods.

As soon as the firing began, it stopped. Smoke wafted from the ends of the Mauler T-19's as the Ursonians again moved into the clearing, examining the bodies.

I thought Tem's gas smelled bad. The stench coming off

the downed bodies of these creatures was like burned hair mixed with rotten eggs. I spat to the side, trying to breathe through my mouth instead of my nose. It didn't help much.

"Historian, it smells of your defecation," Bull said, sidling up to Tem and me as we looked down on one of the dead creatures.

The thing shivered and twitched a little as if its brain was still realizing its body was deceased. There had to be at least ten of the creatures down. They were slightly taller than I was but slender, all muscle and built for speed.

A groan reached my ears as I was reminded of the scaled pit bull these creatures were attacking. Cautiously, I made my way to the thing's side. It was dead before I got there. Deep lacerations covered its body, and half of its lower jaw was missing.

From behind the beast in the hole, a much smaller version of the creature, with fat rolls and big green eyes looked up at me, yelping. Its cry made more sense to me than it might have had it not been trying to nudge the dead protector I now assumed to be its mother or father.

The little thing yelped, showing off tiny stubby teeth. It nudged the larger version of itself as if it were attempting to wake it from a deep slumber.

"Oh my, what truly horrific beasts there are on Ivandor," Tem said, joining me and getting a look at the little creature. "Well, survival of the fittest, right?"

"We should keep moving," Rima said, joining us. "With all the noise we just made, I doubt we will find much today, but perhaps one of the other scouting parties had better luck. Come."

Everyone turned to go like this little creature wasn't crying his heart out.

"Wait, we can't just leave this thing," I said, looking at

the scaly chubby thing that was pretty much a puppy. "We need to take it."

"No," Rima answered. "We move on and finish our mission, and then return to the *Oni*."

"I agree," Tem said, waving me forward. "Come, Max Tyco. That creature is repulsive to look at and will only be a nuisance."

"It's not that bad," I said, reaching a hand down for the creature to smell. It gave me a few sniffs then nudged against my hand and licked the tips of my gloved fingers with a tiny pink tongue. "Look, it's friendly. It's just a baby."

"We're not an orphanage," Rima called back as the rest of the Ursonian column began to move along. "Let's go, Tyco."

I stared into the green orbs this little thing called eyes and I knew there and then, there was no way I could leave the little guy there.

I scooped up the fat alien creature and cradled it in my arms as I joined the others.

"No, don't—don't do that," Tem said, shaking his head. "It's going to imprint on you."

"What's that even mean?" I asked, ignoring the laughs and eye rolls from the Ursonian Corps.

"When a newborn looks to its mother or caretaker, it imprints on them, forming a bond and marking them as provider," Tem explained with another disgusted look on his face. "Throw it away, Max Tyco, throw it away."

I held the little thing at arm's length as we stared at one another. Two tiny fangs protruded from its bottom jaw and stuck out over its top lip. Its ears looked like tiny bat wings that spread out wide from its head. It was horrific, but it needed someone, and it didn't have anyone. I knew how it felt to be alone.

"Nope, I'm taking it," I said, cradling it in my arm. "It'll be my responsibility. I'll look after it."

Rima lifted an eyebrow and was about to say something, then thought better of it as we moved on. We took up the creature's trail again that moved through the jungle, but stopped after we reached our designated four-mile mark.

The trail continued on as far as we could see into the jungle depths. We took a noonday meal of protein packs that were flavored like fish, I guess because the Ursonians loved that taste. I washed mine down with water and shared both the pack and water with my new little friend.

The fat creature lapped up the water greedily and went to town on the food. I had to get it its own ration. It didn't really have a tail as much as a nub it wiggled in glee.

"Little brother, it seems like you have an offspring," Bull said, slurping his protein pack next to me. "The Blood Wolf has a pup of his own."

"Yeah, I'm probably going to need help carrying it back," I said, wiping the silly grin right off Bull's face. "It's heavier than it looks."

"I will not carry an alien pup," Bull said as if I were crazy. "I have no emotional weakness for orphans. It is yours."

"What about all that talk about you owing me one for saving you from the Tulrog?" I asked. "What did he call it, Tem? What did he say he owes me?"

Bull looked to Tem with an imploring plea on his face. He shook his head so fiercely, his jowls swayed.

"I think he said he owed you a life debt," Tem answered, playing along.

"Yes, that's it," I said, looking over to Bull. "Does your life debt include you just laying down your life for me, or carrying small things as well?"

"Not a word of this to anyone," Bull said with a growl as he scooped up the small creature in the crook of his arm. "Not a word."

When the other Ursonians smiled and laughed at him, Bull shot them with an angry expression that shut them up straight away.

Our column headed back to the *Oni* after our rest. Tem asked if we could pick up one of the dead creatures who'd charged us for scientific purposes on the ship. He was sure some Ursonian scientists would love to get their hands on it and he wanted to catalogue the discovery.

Rima agreed, and one of the larger Ursonians slung a dead carcass over its shoulder on the way back to the *Oni*. The twin suns overhead were just beginning to set when we arrived at the *Oni*. It appeared the unit going to the east had already returned and the unit from the west was due in any minute.

There was no word from the column headed for the north. They had failed to check in the last four hours, and the Razor sent in that direction wasn't able to pick up any sign of them due to the dense foliage.

When I heard the news, I thought of Ero and her goofy smile when she showed me the Red Bull she planned to take with her.

"Location and last transmission," Rima said to an Ursonian tech as we reentered the *Oni* hangar bay and heard the news.

The tech had a table set up against the back side of the hangar bay. All around us, each team leader was making their report to Captain Akel. The Ursonian captain, it seemed, trusted Rima enough to allow her to gather the intel on the missing unit.

"Last check-in was at noon, when they stopped for their

meal," the tech said, pushing a pair of thick goggles up over his eyes. He was skinnier than many of the other Ursonians and younger too, if I had to guess. "When they missed their second check-in, we sent the Razor to look after them, but they couldn't see much from the sky. A drop team rappelled and went in but reported no sign of them."

It all felt wrong. I felt warmth spread from my gut outward. I looked down to see the little creature asleep in my arms. It had peed down my stomach and legs. It wasn't a feeling at all; it was just urine.

The sky was transitioning to dark now as not one or two moons, but three began to appear in the sky along with a myriad of stars.

Captain Akel returned after confirming with the other two unit leaders. He shook his head toward Rima, then began with a series of hand gestures I didn't understand.

Rima, however, did.

"It'll be dangerous at night. We don't know what's out there," Rima answered. "Let me go. I might be able to find clues where a unit of Ursonians may not. You heard the report. A Razor did drop a squad in and they didn't find anything."

I could tell Captain Akel wasn't a fan of not going himself, but Rima's reasoning did hold up.

"Trust me, old friend," Rima said, placing a hand on the scarred arm of the captain. "I'll bring them back with no loss of life to your brave soldiers. Let me try."

I could see the war raging in the eyes of the older Ursonian. I could imagine the level of responsibility he felt for his soldiers. When he didn't respond, Rima pulled him to the side and spoke in a low tone I couldn't hear.

"So you're him, huh?" the Ursonian at the desk said, adjusting his goggles over his eyes.

"Him who?" I asked.

"The Blood Wolf. I thought you'd be, you know, more..."

"Bigger?" I asked

"No, more intimidating, maybe? More teeth or arms or something," the Ursonian said with a shrug. "I'm Ted, by the way."

The fact that Ted looked like a big teddy bear was not lost on me.

"I handle the tech and communications around here," Ted said, as if he felt like he needed to explain more in light of my silence. He nodded to the creature in my arms and then scrunched his nose. "I think it peed on you."

"It definitely peed on me," I said, looking down at the hunk of chubby mass in my arms. The little guy was fast asleep.

"What is it?" Ted asked.

"No idea," I answered.

"What's its name?" Ted asked.

"Doesn't have one," I answered.

"Let me see what I can find out," Ted cracked his knuckles and then went to work typing on his holo-projected screen. The symbols were in his own language, as well as the readout, but I could see from the pictures he was looking for a species similar to the one I held in my arms.

After a few seconds that stretched on and felt like minutes, he shook his head. "Nothing here like what you have in your arms. You may have discovered a new species only known to this planet."

Rima and Captain Akel joined us again, with the latter pointing to one of Ted's screens. The last transmission from Ero's unit before they disappeared.

Ted nodded and played the transmission.

"This is Lieutenant Ero Tambers of the Ursonian Corps reporting in. We haven't seen much on our scouting journey besides wildlife indigenous to the planet," Ero said, taking a moment to cough. She hacked something ferocious like she was trying to get something out of the back of her throat. "Allergies are acting up, probably from some of the plants in this area. We're going to stop for our noonday meal and then head back to the *Oni*."

Captain Akel pointed to his throat and shook his head.

"That cough was pretty telling," Rima agreed. "If you play it back, Ted, I thought I heard others coughing in the background."

Ted leaned into the screen, rewinding the transmission and playing it back again, this time minimizing Ero's voice and enhancing the background noises. Rima was right. There were sounds of other Ursonians coughing.

"What is it?" I asked, straining to hear anything else I could pick up.

"No idea," Rima answered. "But we're going to find out."

"By 'we' that's a singular we, right?" I asked with a hard swallow. I didn't consider myself a coward, but neither was I eager for a trek into the jungle at night.

"That's a Rowki 'we'," Rima explained. "We leave Tem here. It's too dangerous for him. Gear up; we head out now."

Apparently, the Rowki, or at least Rima didn't believe in a democracy, but rather a dictatorship.

I looked around for Bull or Tem. The former was removing his gear at the far side of the hangar bay. The latter was doing the same but only a few yards away.

"Tem, Tem," I said, jogging over to the historian with the little mound of meat in my arms. "Can you watch this little guy? Rima says we need to go after a predator in the jungle."

Tem looked at me and the dried piss on my armor and then the little animal.

"Well, actually, I had this thing, you know, this really important thing to do," Tem said, shaking his head.

"Come on, it's like a pet. I'm sure it'll sleep the whole time it's with you," I said, forcing the chubby creature into Tem's arms. "Just don't let it kill itself and you'll be fine."

"Max Tyco, Max Tyco!" Tem's voice rose in pitch as I turned away. "I do not like this one bit."

I joined Rima at a supply station near the center of the hangar bay where supplies in crates and shelves had been set up. The gear ranged from weapons and ammunition to water and protein packs.

Rima threw me a few water cartons and rations.

"How long are we going to be out there?" I asked.

"I am unsure, but we should be prepared," Rima answered.

Captain Akel approached us with Ted at his side.

"I have a camera for each of you to wear on your shoulder armor," Ted said, showing us what looked like a small black dot with a glass dome. "We should have had every soldier wear them on their outing the first time. The captain will have a Razor in the air with him and a strike team to call down on your position as soon as you require aid."

Captain Akel nodded.

Rima and I took turns being fitted with the small black camera. The black glass dome couldn't be larger than the end of my pointer finger. It stuck on my right shoulder much like the comm piece connected to the area behind my right ear.

Amazing what kind of technology one got to see when you were a part of an intergalactic federation.

"We move quickly and quietly," Rima said over her shoulder as we headed out the hangar bay door. "Whatever took the unit did so without leaving a trace. Our best effort will be to sneak up on whatever this is and take it by surprise."

TWENTY-EIGHT

I FOLLOWED Rima into the night. Three moons shone high overhead among the myriad of stars. The suns were long gone. The night was total.

Eerie jungle sounds echoed into my ears, from the screeches of creatures to the ticks and clicks of insects. The path the Ursonians cleaved through the jungle was clear to see.

Rima followed the trail, ducking in and out of the moons' light as we ran. I kicked myself mentally for not including a stimulant in my load out before we went. Coffee or an energy drink would do the job right now.

I was grateful for my cardio training and I didn't say that every day. Don't get me wrong, the light jog Rima set still sucked and I could feel my lungs on fire, but two weeks ago, if you asked me to jog a mile, I would have laughed at you around a mouthful of powdered donut.

We headed into the night like a pair of wraiths. At every mile marker, Ted was in our ear giving us updates.

"Cameras are operational, Captain Akel is in the air with a strike team ready to descend on your position as soon as you give the order," Ted reported. "Am I supposed to call you Max Tyco or Blood Wolf?"

"Max—is fine," I huffed.

"Max, it seems you're beginning to slow a bit. Are you okay?" Ted asked.

"Oh, just peachy, running through an alien jungle at night toward an unknown entity that makes you cough and then disappears you," I said, huffing. "I'm fine."

"Okay, good," Ted answered, missing the sarcasm gold I was mining.

Just when I thought I couldn't keep the pace any longer, Rima called a halt. Not so much called out anything as stopped in her tracks and lifted a closed right hand.

I nearly collided with her. I was just concerned about putting one foot in front of the next.

"What—what is it?" I gasped.

Rima darted off the path to our left. She grabbed my arm, taking me with her, and slapped a hand over my mouth as we crouched in the darkness.

Releasing me, she lifted a finger to her lips and then used a knife hand to motion further down the path.

I nodded, trying to control my breathing.

Six seconds in through your nose and six seconds out through your mouth, I reminded myself. *Control your heart rate.*

I leaned forward from behind our cover along with Rima to peer down the path.

A beam of moonlight cut through the foliage overhead and shone on a humanoid figure crouching in the middle of the path. It was difficult to tell how large the creature was. It looked like it had two arms and two legs, with copper skin that nearly shone.

It wore clothes way more suitable for the weather here.

Bare feet, a short skirt, and a top that wrapped around its full-figured body. Long black hair fell over the female's face. She carried no weapon I could see.

She looked down at the ground in front of her, searching for something. Of all things, she didn't look hostile.

"I don't think this is who we're looking for," I said, turning back to Rima. "I don't think she took out an entire unit of..."

My whisper broke off to silence as I realized Rima was gone.

"Rima? Rima?" I whispered as loud as I dared into the dark jungle around me.

Nothing.

A loud grunt and bodies hitting the ground with a thud drew my attention back to the figure in the path.

In the space of a few seconds, Rima had circled the woman on the path and ambushed her from her blindside. The woman was taken off guard as the two went down, but then quickly recovered as the Rowki and the stranger struggled to their feet.

"Oh snap, it's going down," Ted said over the comm line. "Captain Akel and his unit are inbound."

I ignored the chatter over the channel, rushing forward to help Rima. I saw Rima slam a boot followed by a fist into the woman's gut and face. On her part, the stranger accepted the punishment in stride, leaning in to Rima's attacks instead of backing off. She landed a punch of her own across Rima's jaw.

Even at a full sprint, it took me longer than I would have liked to join the fight. Rima and the stranger had each landed a series of blows, with Rima gaining the upper hand and putting the stranger in a rear headlock.

I came to try and grab her hands.

Bad idea.

The wild female in front of me clawed at Rima's hold across her neck with frightened abandon. Now that I was up close, I could see how truly terrified she was.

Instead of trying to help Rima choke out the woman, I slowed and tried a different approach.

"Rima, she's scared. Maybe—"

That was when the wild woman kicked me in the groin. The flat top part of her foot struck my huevos rancheros with all the force of an expert punter. She hit me so hard, my non-existent grandkids would feel that one.

Even with the cup the armor provided, it didn't feel great getting kicked in the balls. It felt like a hippie playing a super aggressive version of hacky sack.

I grunted and stumbled.

The wild woman used her legs to run up my kneeling form and flip herself over Rima. Rima lost her hold and the wild stranger might have escaped there and then if it weren't for the series of armor-clad gummy bears dropping from the night sky like it was raining giant pandas.

The ground practically shook as each armor-clad Ursonian made their jump from the Razor overhead. Bright lights shone from the sides of their helmets and shoulders as they circled the stranger.

"Stand down!" they ordered. "Stand down or you will be killed."

"No, don't kill her," I said, regaining my feet and squinting into the bright lights. The treetops around me were getting kicked in every direction as the Razor overhead lowered as close as possible to help with supporting fire should the need arise. "She could know where they are. She could tell us where the missing unit's gone. Look at her. Does it look like she killed twelve Ursonians?"

The moment was silenced with only the Razor above making sounds from its thrusters as it remained airborne just above our location.

The wild woman hunched low, looking from side to side for any hint at a chance of escape. Her eyes were alive with fear and wonder. I knew how she felt. I remembered my experience witnessing it all for the first time only weeks before.

"Rima?" I asked.

"We need her alive!" Rima shouted over the engines overhead. "We need to know what she knows."

The largest Ursonian stepped forward, wearing the insignia of the Ursonian Corps with the three slash marks across his shoulder.

She looked at him and darted to the side too late. Captain Akel brought his Mauler T-19 to bear, sending a red electric round into her that stunned her on the spot.

My heart seized then relaxed in my chest as I realized the round wasn't lethal. I didn't even know the Mauler T-19's could do that. Red vines of energy crackled around the woman's prone form then dissipated altogether.

I knelt by her side as her chest rose and fell in perfect rhythm. She was beautiful. Other than the copper skin and white eyes, she appeared nearly human, as well.

"Magnetic cuffs and let's take her back to the *Oni*," Rima said, staring down at the woman with resolve. "Tyco was right. We need to know everything she knows."

While the Ursonians secured the prisoner and cleared a landing zone for the Razor, I had a chance to get a good look at the area. This was where Ero and her unit had last checked in.

Far from any kind of tracker, I surveyed the landscape, looking for anything out of the ordinary. As far as I could tell, it was a pretty normal area in the jungle. The brush was trampled, but there were no clear tracks of beasts or other people.

I noticed a very faint sour smell in the air I couldn't place, but it was definitely present. Then a glint of metal caught my eye. To the right, a metallic container lay mostly buried under a thick bush. I pulled out the full can of Red Bull.

Not that there was any question before, but it was even more evidence to tell me something had gone very wrong here. Ero loved Red Bull like an extrovert loved socializing. No way she'd drop it and wander off into the jungle.

The Ursonians felled enough trees for the Razor to land and we hopped on board with our prisoner in tow. The hairs on the back of my neck rose as I stepped aboard the craft. I looked back into the jungle interiors to see nothing but darkness and warped shadow.

Still, I swore we were being watched.

"You feel it too," Rima stated more than asked. "They're in there watching us, studying us. Sooner or later, they'll know where the *Oni* rests. We must prepare our defenses."

"Who?" I asked, finding a seat inside the Razor, which had to break all kinds of safety restrictions, by the way. Not only were there no seatbelts, but only a single bench provided anywhere to sit and there were no doors on either side of the craft, only heavy gunner stations.

"Her people, I'm guessing," Rima said, nodding toward the unconscious woman. "The *Oni* is no longer safe here on the planet's surface. We can't risk anything happening to it and sacrifice our way off-planet. It must return to orbit."

I held on to my seat as the Razor lifted off into the sky

and headed back toward the *Oni*. Warm wind whipped into the aircraft. The Ursonians swayed and rocked with the movement of the craft, mocking my white-knuckled hold on my seat.

The truth was it just wasn't the ride that was giving me second thoughts. The idea of losing the safety the *Oni* provided gave me pause. The ship was so large, it seemed impenetrable in my mind. Without it, we'd be out here, open and exposed.

The return trip to the *Oni* was uneventful. Tem was already asleep with the new creature when we returned, and as much as I wanted to see the little animal, I wanted answers more.

The strange woman was taken to an interrogation room aboard the *Oni* as Captain Akel went to make preparations for the *Oni* to return to orbit. I made a quick trip to my truck onboard to make myself a hot cup of coffee.

The food printers in the mess hall made a pretty close replication of the life-giving substance, but right now, I needed the real stuff. With a mug of Black Rifle Coffee, I rejoined Rima in the interrogation room.

The interrogation room just happened to be on a mid-level along with the prison block. As of yet, I'd had no reason to visit this floor. Like the others, it was well-lit with wide halls, enough for four Ursonians to walk shoulder to shoulder.

I sipped on my coffee, wondering, and at the same time, not wanting to know what time it was. It had to be the early hours of the morning. How I was still functioning was beyond me.

Following Rima's directions, I rendezvoused with her at a closed door off the main corridor.

Rima had removed her armor and had a medic look at

her superficial wounds. Skin spray had stopped the bleeding on her left cheek. Her right eye was swollen.

She looked at me with a raised eyebrow as I showed up in my full suit of armor. As soon as we had arrived back at the *Oni,* Rima had given me fifteen minutes before meeting her at the interrogation room. Apparently, she had meant that fifteen minutes for removing my armor and tending to any wounds, not coffee and a quick Snack Pack.

Rima jerked her head for me to follow as we entered the exterior door. Her handprint on the reader to the left granted us access as the door slid open into the wall.

A pair of Ursonian soldiers stood guard at an interior door. They nodded to us, and once again, Rima placed her hand on a digital scanner set into the wall before the door opened into a smaller room.

A single chair with our prisoner slumped forward in it, still unconscious, was the only piece of furniture in the chamber. The stranger's wrists were still bound by the magnetic cuffs. The cuffs had been separated from one another, now connecting her wrists to the chair itself and not each other.

An identical pair of cuffs were around each of her ankles, also attached to the legs of the chair. The Ursonians didn't mess around.

The door clicked closed behind us.

TWENTY-NINE

I BLEW ON MY COFFEE, savoring the heavenly aroma that made me salivate.

"She's awake," Rima said, staring at the woman, hands crossed over her chest.

"How can you tell?" I asked, looking at the prisoner. She was hunched forward, raven-black hair covering any of her facial features. She didn't move besides a steady rise and fall of her breaths.

"She's only pretending to still be unconscious," Rima said. "I'm listening to her breathing pattern. Her heartbeat spiked when we entered the room."

My admiration for Rima and her years of training grew. I had no idea she could tell something like that. It also reminded me I had years of my own training to undergo before not getting my balls kicked in, in a fight.

"She needs to drink the all-water to be able to speak with us," Rima said, removing a vial from her belt. "I'm going to guess she's not going to take it down willingly."

Before I could stop her, Rima crossed the distance to the chair, grabbing the woman's head, forcing it back.

Rima was right, our stranger was not unconscious at all. She moved to lash out at Rima with the only thing she still had, her teeth. Rima had anticipated all of this, shoving the vial down the woman's throat instead.

The woman coughed and choked on the liquid, trying to spit it out even as the all-water began to take effect. I could see her clench her eyes in pain. She rocked from side to side, straining in vain against her bonds. A scream ripped from her throat, one half pain the other half frustration.

I couldn't watch her like this. I had undergone a lot of what she was being subjected to, but at least I'd known what was going on. I was talked through it, not bound and forced to take the all-water.

I placed my coffee cup at my feet and approached, making sure to stay out of biting range.

"Hey, hey, it's okay," I told her. "It's okay. I know that may be hard to believe, but we don't want to hurt you. We're not the bad guys here."

The woman coughed again, staring daggers at me through her wild black hair. She spit in my face, spraying me with a well-aimed shot. She screamed something in her own language that sounded like "you son of a monkey's mother's milk," but I knew the all-water was just beginning to work.

"Okay, okay, I'll take that for the sake of our future friendship," I said, wiping the spit from my face. "Do you understand me yet? We are not your enemies. We are here to help you, as hard to believe as that may sound."

Apparently, a few of my words were beginning to make sense to her as a look of bewilderment crossed her eyes. The all-water was kicking in, allowing her to start comprehending a few of my words in her language.

"What is this?" she asked, looking at me as if I had sprouted an extra head. "What witchcraft is this?"

"There we go. Give it some time and that pain in your head will go away," I told her, taking a step back out of what I hoped was spitting distance. The girl did have a set of lungs on her. "We're not going to hurt you."

The woman heaved a few more times, staring at me through that curtain of black hair. At least, I thought she was staring at me. It was hard to tell with her all-white eyeballs.

"Who are you?" she asked.

"There we go now. We're making some headway," I said, placing a hand on my chest. "My name is Max. What's your name?"

The woman didn't respond but looked to Rima instead.

"Oh, that's Rima," I said, looking over my shoulder at Rima's severe face. "Don't worry, she's not going to hurt you either. She just always looks like that. You know, RBF and all."

The native looked at me, confused. "What is RBF?"

"Never mind, poor choice of words on my part," I answered. "I need to know what you were doing out there on the path tonight. We're missing our friends. The Ursonians. You know, big walking bears in armor. Have you seen them?"

"Where are we?" the woman asked. "Where have you come from?"

"We don't have time for this," Rima said, stalking forward with ill intent. "Every minute that passes is another minute the missing unit could be dying. Tell us where they are."

That last part was more a growl at the woman chained in front of us than actual words.

If she was intimidated by Rima, our prisoner didn't show it. She stared at Rima defiantly, as if she weren't going to talk at all, then smirked. "We didn't take your people. And if you didn't have help from Max and the giants, you wouldn't have had a chance against me, either."

I knew Rima well enough now to know she was not above torture. Already I could see her balling her hands into fists.

"Whoa, whoa, okay, ladies, ladies," I said, stepping between the pair. "Aren't we all just getting along nicely. Rima, a word?"

Rima didn't move her gaze from our stranger.

"Rima, please," I said, whispering in her ear. "Please let me talk to her for just a few minutes. You said it yourself. All the inhabitants of this planet aren't our enemy. We're here to find out who is. Give me ten minutes with her. Ten minutes. Please."

The muscle under Rima's jawline quivered like it was doing reps in the gym. Rima turned to me with a nod. "You have five minutes, Tyco. Then it's my turn."

"Thank you, thank you," I told her with an audible sigh. Part of me thought for sure she was about to lay into our prisoner with the full nine yards of torture. "Good job with the good cop, bad cop by the way."

Rima had already turned to walk out the door. My last comment made her stop and look over her shoulder. "Who is this good cop and bad cop? Are they at war with one another?"

"No—no, nothing like that, it's an expression," I said, kicking myself for even bringing that up at the moment. "You did good. Just saying we're doing good here."

"Later, when time permits, I would know more of these cops," Rima said, leaving the room. "You have five minutes."

The door slid open and closed and she was gone.

I was left in the room with the woman bound in front of me. Right now, she was staring at me with those pure white eyes of hers. I got the idea she was trying to figure me out. Good luck with that one. I was still trying to get an answer there as well.

"Sorry for all of this. I wish it could have been done another way," I told the woman. "I'll get those magnetic cuffs off you and we'll get you out of here. I don't think you took the unit of Ursonians, but if you know who did, that would go a long way toward my being able to help you."

"You ambush me, take me as prisoner, pour magic water down my throat that lets me speak your language, and now you want my help?" the woman asked in disbelief. "Why would I help you?"

"Because right now, I'm the only one that can get you out of here," I said, taking a knee in front of her. "Because I know exactly what it's like to see fantastic things your eyes tell your brain is real, and still you have a hard time fathoming what it could all mean. I know you're in shock and a bit scared, if you'll admit it or not."

"That's where you are wrong." The woman gave me a legitimate grin. "I am not afraid to meet my creator. I welcome the day. And I will embrace the moment with a roar on my lips and violence in my hands."

"Man, if you're even half serious about the words coming out of your mouth, you and Rima have more in common than either of you would like to think," I said, scratching my forehead. "We are not your enemies. Can you believe that?"

"Then why are you here?" she asked. "Why did you ambush me?"

"I told you, we're looking for our friends," I said. "We

came to this planet because we believe there is something going on here. Something dark that we can help stop."

That brought a physical reaction from the woman. She sat up in her chair a little straighter. Instead of malice on her face, a glimmer of hope could be seen.

"You know something," I told her. "Please, tell me what you know. We can help. We're here to help."

She opened her mouth as if she were going to say something, then stopped herself. I could see she was on the brink. I needed to come up with something to push her over the edge.

"I'll be honest with you, I'm not the wise veteran you think I am, although I know I give off that vibe," I told her, rising to my feet. "Under the swagger and rugged good looks, I'm just a guy trying to figure this all out, too. It's hard to believe I know. I know."

She held my stare and when I broke into a smirk, she realized I was joking.

I caught her smile then a flash of her teeth, so brief but so beautiful.

"Honestly, I am trying to figure this out as well," I told her. "Give me something, and I can get those magnetic cuffs off you. We'll get you out of this room and cleaned up, with some food, and you'll be free to go. Just give me something."

"Swear to me, Max," the woman said. "Swear to me you are who you say you are on what you hold most precious in this world."

"What I held most precious was taken from me a long time ago," I said, clearing my throat. "But I give you my word on my truck, on my reputation, for whatever that's worth."

A moment of silence passed. I was wondering how much time I had left on the timer Rima set. There was no doubt in my mind that Major Payne had an actual timer she was using before she barged in.

"That will be enough," the woman said after holding my eyes for a moment longer. "I can see in you that you are telling the truth. I will help you, Max. You, not her or the giants. But I trust you."

"Thank you," I answered with a sigh of relief. "Who are you? Who took our friends?"

"My name is Aiya Stormbringer from the Plains Walker tribe," Aiya answered. "And it is not *who* took your people but *what*."

THIRTY

MY MOUTH WENT dry when she said that. We'd already witnessed a colossal mystery beast moving through the jungle, and the smaller reptile-looking gorilla things. What else was out there?

"Okay, I'm pretty sure I'm going to regret asking this, but, Aiya Stormbringer from the Plains Walker tribe, *what* took our friends?" I asked, swallowing hard.

"Did you not notice the smell in the air at the location where they were taken?" Aiya asked. "It was practically palpable. I could taste it on my tongue. When the plant-eaters come, they always leave that scent behind."

"Plant eaters?" I asked with wide eyes. My mind went back to *Jumanji* and that crazy plant that tried to suck in the kid that turned into monkey boy later in the movie. "Regret number two, what's a plant-eater?"

"They are large meat-eating vegetation in the jungles," Aiya explained. "They secrete a sleeping toxin. That is what you smelled. It lulls their victims to sleep. They are then taken by vines of the creatures and carried through the jungle to be slowly digested. Your friends are not far from the location where you kidnapped me. The plant-eaters' vines will only reach a few dozen yards. If you move now, you can still save them."

The door to the room burst open. Rima ran in, her eyes alive with relief. It was obvious she had been watching and listening somehow from the other room. Small hidden cameras in the corners of the room was my guess.

"Where?" Rima asked Aiya without so much as a thank you. "In which direction do these plant-eaters live?"

"If you free me, I will show you," Aiya said, motioning to me with her chin. "No, free me, and I will show Max. I trust him."

I saw the flash of anger in Rima's eyes once more. Negotiating this deal was more work than I anticipated.

"She's helping us, just like we asked," I said, jumping into the conversation before the two could go at it again. "Let her show us and build some trust."

"And if she's leading us into a trap?" Rima asked.

"If I were leading you into a trap, you would never even suspect it, witch," Aiya answered with a genuine smile that really disturbed me. "When I come for you, you'll never see it coming."

"Okay, that's not helping, Aiya," I said from the corner of my mouth. I turned back to Rima with open hands and a shrug. "Come on. Come on, we'll be on her like Tem on that pizza I printed the other day. He was all over that stuff."

Rima hesitated for a moment then nodded to Aiya. "Magnetic cuffs stay on. If this is a trap, know the last sound you hear will be my blade removing the head from your body."

Rima moved forward, disconnecting Aiya's feet from the cuffs on the chair. She did the same to the cuffs on her wrists, but instead of freeing her, she locked the cuffs together in front of the woman.

Aiya, for her part, didn't do anything. I sighed a pent-up breath of air I didn't know I was holding. Half of me thought Aiya was going to lay into Rima as soon as her legs were free.

"Come, we have little time before your friends are digested," Aiya said hurriedly. "The plant-eaters will be sleeping now as they work on their food. We must go, now."

Rima, Aiya, and I left the interrogation room, heading for the lifts on this level. Rima was barking out orders to the two Ursonian guards, who looked surprised to see all three of us walking out of the room together.

"Contact Captain Akel and tell him we have a lead on the missing unit," Rima rattled off. "We need a strike team ready to meet us at the hangar bay in five minutes. Fuel two Razors as well."

As the lift took us down to the hangar bay level, I caught sight of Aiya and the wonder in her eyes. Despite the lack of pupils or irises in her white eyes, I could see their size and the way her mouth hung open.

"You'll get used to it after a while," I explained. "I know it's a lot to take in."

"You are a star traveler?" Aiya asked. "You come from another world?"

"Another galaxy," I told her, trying to figure out the simplest way to phrase things. "Space, what you see in the night sky, is called the universe; inside this universe are many galaxies made of many planets."

I couldn't tell if her eyes were glazing over or that was just how she looked.

"There will be more time," I said, thinking I wasn't doing that great of a job explaining to her. "There's a guy here named Tem. He'll be able to explain everything to you in better detail."

"No, no, I understand," Aiya answered. "I've dreamed of this day for years, ever since I was a girl. Of knowing what is beyond the stars, of meeting others who travel the night sky."

The lift came to a stop, and we filed out into the hangar bay. I kicked myself mentally for forgetting my cup of coffee back in the interrogation room. There was still a good swallow or two left. I was running on fumes.

Rima explained the situation to Captain Akel and his strike team, who arrived moments after we did. It was no surprise to me that Bull was among those chosen for the mission.

He looked at me sideways as everyone geared up to go out once more.

"Little brother?" Bull asked, looking from me to Aiya, whose head turned this way and that, taking it all in. "Can this thing be trusted? Is she also a pig species like you?"

"Who are you calling a pig species, you oversized furball?" Aiya asked, staring at Bull who towered over her without so much as a hint of doubt. "Take these cuffs off and say it again."

Bull and the other Ursonians within earshot looked at each in shock at first. They hadn't seen Rima shove the all-water down her throat. Once they recovered, they broke into a cacophony of laughter.

Even Bull threw back his massive head and chuckled so deeply, I saw his belly shake through his armor.

"I like this one, little brother," Bull said, slapping me so hard on the back, I almost fell. "Let's keep her as a pet."

"A pet!" Aiya said, taking a step forward as if she were going to take on Bull right there and then.

Two deep thuds as Captain Akel pounded his armor quieted the group. The veteran looked tired and worn, just like I felt. Still, he didn't let his hand gestures relay any of that; they were as determined and quick as ever.

He divided his unit in half and pointed to two Razors refueling on the opposite side of the hangar bay. He motioned to Rima after making another series of hand gestures toward Aiya.

"We have a lead on our missing unit," Rima announced. "Move quietly, be ready for anything, and let's bring them home safely."

The Ursonians present roared as one and pounded their chests as we moved toward the Razors. This was Aiya's first time in an aircraft. At least the first time she was in one, conscious.

She hesitated when we reached the ship. I could only imagine the things going through her mind.

"It's okay, it's just a machine that's going to move us through the sky back to where we found you," I reassured her. I jumped into the Razor first. "Come on."

She accepted my offered hand with hers still mag-cuffed together. She sat between Rima and me on the bench seat while the Ursonians piled in.

There were six of the large warriors that fit in the Razor along with the three of us. They checked and double-checked their Mauler T-19's along with their armor and gear.

When the Razor lifted off the floor of the hangar bay and moved out into the night, Aiya tensed.

I had to admit I felt a little uncertain myself. I mean, the Razor had no doors. I wasn't afraid of heights; at least I didn't think I was. But when I looked out the open side doors to the jungle canopy whizzing by below us, I felt a touch of vertigo. Maybe that coffee and pudding on the go wasn't such a good idea.

"In what direction from where we found you do these plant-eaters lie?" Rima shouted over the hum of the thrusters.

"Set down as quietly as you can where I nearly killed you, and we will go into the jungle from there," Aiya yelled back. "The plant-eaters are heavy slumberers, but will awaken if you make too much noise."

"You didn't almost kill me," Rima corrected her. "You did kick Tyco in the balls hard enough to fell an Ursonian, though."

"Right, sorry about that," Aiya shouted in my ear. "Once we rescue your friends, I will make you a salve and apply it to your bruises."

"What? No," I said, shaking my head, suddenly nervous.

"Are you a eunuch?" Aiya asked, confused. "Are you not sore where I kicked you?"

"No, I mean, yes. Yes, I am sore and, no, I am not a eunuch," I shouted back. With that last part, for whatever reason, the pilot slowed the thrusters, causing the sounds around us to nearly disappear altogether.

Everyone in the Razor looked at me in stunned silence.

"Little brother, that is nothing to be ashamed of," Bull said, leaning over from across from me and placing a heavy paw on my shoulder. "Once when I was stationed at the outer rim of the galaxy, I went through a swamp that had a parasite that swam right up my—"

"Okay, okay, that's enough," I said, stopping Bull in the middle of his story. "I'm not a eunuch. Can we please just drop this?"

"Does that mean you don't want to hear the rest of my

parasite story?" Bull asked in disbelief. "It's popular at parties."

"No, Bull," I sighed. "I don't—"

Bull cracked a grin, unable to keep in the laughter. The entire Razor erupted in mirth. Even Aiya was chuckling.

"Wonderful," I shouted. "I'm glad I can bring you all so much joy."

"And did you see his face?" Bull was already immortalizing the moment in his memory as he traded laughs with his fellow Ursonians. "He was all like, what? And I was like, yep. And he was like, oh gross, don't tell me more."

The mirth quieted down just in time as the Razor slowed then lowered quietly to the jungle floor in the clearing the Ursonians had made before.

We jumped out, Rima on one side of Aiya and me on the other. I didn't think our new ally would run, but I had been wrong once or twice before.

Our unit moved to the side to allow room for the other Razor to lower and drop off its soldiers as well.

"Where?" Rima asked Aiya as soon as we were clear of the next descending Razor. "No games. Where are they?"

"Let me smell," Aiya said, placing a finger in the air for silence. "You should be able to smell it as well. It's a bitter taste on the wind. The aftermath of the toxins the plant-eaters secrete."

Extending staff in my right hand, which was more like a blasting staff now, and helmet clipped to my belt, I smelled the air. Aiya was right. It was fainter, barely recognizable, but the air smelled wrong.

"This way," Aiya said, motioning to the path. "Keep close. Keep quiet."

THIRTY-ONE

ALL THOUGHTS of sleep were wiped from my mind as my adrenaline kicked in. I gripped my blasting staff so tight in my hands, they shook. We maneuvered through the jungle with me, Rima, and Aiya in the lead. The Ursonians followed close behind, moving as quietly as they could, but let's face it, a thousand-pound bear creature trying to maneuver through a dense jungle wasn't quiet at all.

Aiya stopped in her tracks. The moons found a spot through the canopy overhead and played silver light across her fair features.

"Can you tell the furballs that if they keep stomping on the ground like this, we will lose the element of surprise?" Aiya asked, annoyed. "One of our little ones could hear them a mile away."

"That's the first thing you've said that I agree with," Rima whispered. "Wait here."

Unlike the Ursonians, Rima moved like a shadow in the night. She retreated to confer with Captain Akel, leaving Aiya and me alone for a moment.

"So these plant-eaters," I said, trying to bring up the

question I so badly didn't want the answer to. What exactly are they?"

"Huge stationary foliage with massive petals that close and open, covering a mouth and a sack where they digest their prey. They grow in clumps across our lands," Aiya whispered. "You do not have anything like this on your planet?"

"No, nothing as large as you're describing," I answered. "There are Venus fly traps, but those things are tiny. I vaguely remember some other plants in that same family that eat insects, but again, they're small. Our foliage on Earth doesn't really try to kill us."

"Must be a nice place," Aiya mused. "Everything here is dangerous. My people have learned to adapt over the years to survive."

"Back on the ship when we were first talking about why we were here, to combat an evil, you tensed. You knew what I was talking about," I said, trying to get more out of her despite this not really being the time or place. "What is it?"

"There is another tribe," Aiya said, licking her lips. "Another tribe that has come across something and— changed. I don't know exactly what they found, but they are different now. They feel...wrong."

"The Ursonians will drop to all fours and follow single-file to mask their presence," Rima said, rejoining us. "Aiya, lead the way."

I wanted to continue our conversation. I felt that what-ever Aiya was going to tell me next might be the reason we were here on Ivandor in the first place. However, Ero and the rest of her unit, if they were still alive, needed us right now.

Aiya nodded and crouched low. Her bare feet made no noise at all in the rich soil. Like a wraith, she maneuvered her way through the trees. It was still hot and humid, even at night. I was sweating again, from my brow to my armpits and nether regions. I'll spare you the details there.

The jungle was alive with the sounds of insects and night mammals. They maneuvered through the jungle on their own agendas, no doubt picking up our presence and steering clear, although they had to be intrigued by our alien scent.

The smell here was stronger. That bitter aroma gnawed at the back of my throat. It made me want to spit. Aiya stopped at the edge of a clearing and hunkered down low. Rima and I joined her on either side.

Without a word, Aiya pointed to the clearing in front of us.

I was reminded of the movie *Alien* with those egg sack things that let out the face huggers. It was like that, but plant-like and much, much larger. A closed green bulb rose from the ground into the sky with pink and purple petals opening up around it.

A cool mist rolled around the grouping of plant-eaters. Massive vines that were nearly the thickness of my arms coiled around each plant. I got the feeling that although the closed bulbs of the plants were what we could see on the surface, the rest of the things were buried underground.

There had to be ten, no, fifteen of the bulbs scattered around the clearing sporadically. From the sky, it wouldn't look any stranger than the rest of this alien planet.

"Your friends," Aiya whispered so close her lips tickled my ear. "They are in the ground sacks of the plant-eaters. Be careful when you free them so you do not cause them harm."

I nodded, not sure if my heart picked up tempo because

Aiya was so close or because I was about to get into a fight with a group of overgrown Pokémon.

Aiya was right. I heard the soft impression of a massive paw behind me as Captain Akel joined me on my left. His visor was open. I could see his dark eyes in the light of the moon.

"They're in sacks just below the surface of the ground," I told him. "Be careful when we kill these things."

Captain Akel nodded. Slowly, he rose to his feet, looking behind him to his unit. He lifted his hands, going through a series of motions to his force. That started with a finger over his lips and ended with a thumb across his throat.

Whatever prearranged communication plan he'd worked out with his team, they seemed to understand. Quietly, we moved into the clearing. I knew it was my imagination, making every noise the Ursonians made seem ten times amplified. Still, I couldn't help but think these plant-eaters were going to wake up at any moment and realize they were standing in the middle of a traveling buffet.

I followed Rima and the Ursonians' lead, then thought twice about it as I witnessed one of the vines from the plant-eaters wriggle. Not sure if it was experiencing a weird dream from digesting Ursonians or what. I know sometimes if I had dairy before bed it gave me some strange dreams. I couldn't imagine what a whole Ursonian would do.

They've got this, I reasoned to myself, rethinking my move to join the others in the field of man-eating plants. *There're more than enough Ursonians to handle all the plant-eater things. You should stay behind to act as backup in case they need it.*

I was struggling with these thoughts when I saw Aiya step forward to help. Magnetic cuffs still on her wrists, she walked into the field of sleeping man-eaters to lend what aid she could.

I saw her take up a place opposite the man-eater Rima was standing over. The Rowki gave Aiya a nod of respect.

Okay, well now, you can't be the only one to stay behind, I told myself. *Don't be that guy. Nobody likes that guy.*

I bottled my fear and followed the others. Every Ursonian stood in front of one of the sleeping plants ready to strike with his or her Mauler T-19. I took up my own position along with Rima and Aiya.

I held my blasting staff out with one hand ready to unload on the creature as soon as I was given the order. I also made sure that my rounds would hit the top of the thing. On second thought, I took a two-handed grip on the closed staff that also shot death. I remembered the kick back from last time.

Not sure if we were supposed to wait for a signal or not, I looked from Rima to Captain Akel; surely one of them would be giving the call. I wasn't disappointed.

Captain Akel made eye contact with everyone in the field and then nodded.

I held my breath in anticipation.

BOOM! BOOM!

Captain Akel slammed his armored fist against his chest armor, making a loud banging sound.

RAAA! Every Ursonian soldier bellowed. Rima even added her own battle roar. I added my voice to the mix as the plant-eaters came alive in front of us. All around, I could see Ursonians slashing at their plants, but that was secondary to what was happening in front of me.

THIRTY-TWO

THE BULB of the plant that pointed to the heavens above twisted and opened in four equal sections. A pit of teeth was revealed in the center of the plant as it woke from its slumber.

Vines that had been wrapped around it and on the ground whipped to life.

Rima was so quick with her sword, it was difficult to track the movement. Like some gunslinger, she unsheathed her weapon and turned the move into a slash, taking off the head of the plant-eater, right where the four petals met and turned into a throat of teeth.

The move was beautiful and deadly at once. The top of the plant-eater fell to the ground quivering. Thick vine-like arms swung wildly in its death throes.

One of the vine arms came for Aiya, who rolled out of the way. The other made for me. I pointed my blasting staff and sent a round into the vine arm that totally annihilated the limb, splattering me with green gooey gore.

The vine fell to the ground, quivering there like a fish

out of water. The arm intended for Aiya was doing the same as the plant died at our feet.

It was almost sad to see the thing squirm in pain. It was just doing what it needed to survive, but weren't we all?

"In there, they're in the stomach of the creature," Aiya said, pointing down the severed throat of the plant-eater.

Rima didn't hesitate reaching in, way into the dead plant's throat. She was armpit-deep in the thing before she stopped groping and began to pull.

"Help me," she said as she heaved.

"I would, but apparently, I'm not to be trusted," Aiya said, extending her cuffed hands to Rima.

Rima shot her a dirty look but placed the thumb of her free hand onto a scanner on the mag cuffs. They fell away without a sound.

Both Aiya and I reached our arms into the mouth of the plant-eater, grabbing on to the Ursonian inside.

"This is probably the most disgusting thing I've done since being a Rowki," I said, coughing on the stench of the dead plant-eater. "Scratch that; I also put my hand into the mouth of the Tulrog. Why does this job entail putting my hands in so many alien mouths?"

My armored forearm scratched against the teeth of the dead plant-eater's throat. I felt through saliva and a soft gullet until I finally made contact with something hard under my fingers.

As one, Rima, Aiya, and I heaved. We probably still wouldn't have been strong enough if the Ursonian within wasn't semi-conscious and at least able to stand up and help us.

The Ursonian stumbled out covered in digestive juices, but at least alive.

All around us, the fight was going our way. Half the

plants were already dead as soon as Captain Akel gave the kill order. The other half fought wildly with vines, lashing out left and right, but an aware Ursonian wasn't as willing to go down as one drugged and surprised.

Rima, Aiya, and I moved to give aid. I aimed my blasting staff at a vine, evaporating the limb as I saw another vine head for me out of the corner of my eye.

I extended the staff, batting away the limb before twirling my weapon so the blaster pointed at the vine again, and fired.

Once again, the vine exploded on contact, unable to withstand the force of the round.

In seconds, it was over. The Ursonian Corps stood victorious over the plant-eaters, helping their unconscious and semiconscious comrades from the pits of death.

There were two casualties: one lifted from the pit with a broken neck and another of our number strangled by one of the vines before it could be freed.

I searched for the survivors, finding Ero among them. The big white Ursonian was still coming to, peeling off her armor and trying to dry her fur from the digestive fluids of the plant-eater.

"You didn't even get a chance to drink your Red Bull," I said, handing her the can. "I knew things had to be bad if you left that behind."

Ero looked at me with a sigh and took the offered can. "Your legend is growing, Blood Wolf. Killer of the Tulrog, slayer of the plant-eaters, and now deliverer of the holy mead known as Red Bull."

We shared a chuckle but only for a moment. I could tell how shaken up she still was. I didn't blame her. Although I'd never been taken as a lunch for a man-eating plant, I had been almost eaten by a Tulrog, and that definitely sucked.

"You good?" I asked not because I thought she was really all right, but I didn't know what else to say. "I can help you with your armor."

"Thanks," Ero answered, rising to unsteady feet.

The order was given to head to the Razors, and all around us, Ursonians supported their brethren back to the crafts. Captain Akel coordinated two additional Razors to meet us at the clearing.

The two Ursonians who would not be walking home were carried reverently by their brethren.

"I see now you are who you say you are," Aiya said as we traveled through the jungle back to the waiting Razors. "I will help you if I can. Even the one you call Rima. She has a warrior's spirit, even if she is a witch."

"I've called her worse in my head, trust me," I said. "I'm not making excuses for her; she's rough around the edges. She's been through a lot. But when it comes down to blood being drawn, she's loyal."

Aiya nodded along with my words.

We traveled back to the *Oni* in relative silence. I was beyond exhausted as my body now told me it was out of adrenaline, and with no caffeine, I was about to shut down.

When the Razors landed back at the *Oni* I had no idea what Rima was going to say about Aiya. I hoped against hope she wasn't going to order her bound and chained again. We'd come a long way to build trust in a short time, and even I knew trust was something we all needed if we were going to see this through.

"Can I rely on you to make contact with your people?" Rima asked Aiya as the Ursonians unloaded from the Razors. "We need to find out what's happening on your planet. If they can help, we would appreciate the gesture."

I noticed nowhere in there did Rima say 'thank you for

helping us save our missing unit', but for Rima, it was a step in the right direction. I mean, she did use the word "appreciate" and hadn't ordered Aiya back in mag cuffs.

"I will speak to my people and tell them why you are here," Aiya answered. "They will wish to help, I'm sure of it."

"She can't travel at night," I said, stifling a yawn. I was barely able to stand. I looked over to Rima. "It would be polite to offer her a place to stay for the night and some food."

I saw the muscles in Rima's body tense like it physically pained her to be polite. Despite this, she turned to Aiya with a forced smile that showed way too many teeth. "Would you like to stay for the night? We can serve you a meal as well."

Aiya looked out at the dark night and stifled her own yawn. "Yes, thank you. I can leave at first light. My village is not far. If you give me two days, I can be there and back with news."

"Agreed," Rima answered, looking over at me. "Tyco can show you where the food is and where you can sleep for the night."

Without an official goodbye or goodnight, Rima turned on a heel and walked away to confer with Captain Akel.

"Don't worry, you'll get used to Rima," I said, motioning Aiya to follow. "Believe it or not, that was pretty polite for her."

Aiya followed me to the mess hall, where I showed her the food printer. She stared open-mouthed as I ordered us a pepperoni and olive pizza. We sat down at the table to share it.

"This is amazing," Aiya said, closing her eyes as she

savored her first bite of the pizza. "Not just the food, but all of this. How—how can all of this exist?"

"Years of learning and technology, I guess," I answered, thinking back to how humans had evolved through time. I had to assume the Ursonians did the same, but were just a few thousand years ahead of us. "Trial and error, learning and growing."

Aiya nodded, looking around the room in awe.

It was nice to have someone to talk to that felt like I did. Tem, Rima, and the rest of the Ursonians were so used to the tech, nothing seemed to faze them.

I was still growing accustomed to it, so geeking out with Aiya was like a breath of fresh air for me. We talked about Earth, her people, and the vastness of the universe. If I hadn't been so punch-drunk exhausted, I would have progressed the conversation to what was going on with the neighboring tribe she'd alluded to before. Right now, I was barely keeping my eyes open.

"You can have my bed for the night," I told her as we headed to the circuit room that carried my rig. "You'll get a great night's sleep, the best. I didn't skimp when it came to the quality of my mattress."

"Mattress?" Aiya said the word as if it were the first time she had ever heard it. "Is that like a grass bed?"

"Oh, you're in for a treat," I answered as we walked into my training room. My Peterbilt 379 sat in the center of the room where it hadn't moved since I had teleported aboard the *Oni*.

Aiya's eyes lit up when she saw the steel horse I rode.

"It is amazing," Aiya said in awe. "Does it fly as well?"

"It can do anything except fly," I told her, opening the door for her and offering her a hand up. "It's my home."

Aiya stepped inside with a playful smile on her lips. "It's like a steel tent."

She sat on the bed and lay down with that smile I was starting to enjoy more and more.

"Max, this is true luxury," Aiya said with a yawn. She scooted over on the bed as far as she could, lying on her right side. "Come, we can share it."

Heat rushed to my face. I hadn't been on so much as a date since I'd lost my wife. Well, there was that one time I used the dating app, Lonelyroad, for truckers, but that just got weird really fast.

"Um, no, no, I'm good," I said with a cough. "I'll sleep in one of the front seats. I mean, not that I want to offend you. I would like to."

Why was it so hard for me to talk to women? I sat in the passenger side seat and took a breath. "It's just, you see, where I come from, a man and a woman sharing a bed it—it's not really just sleeping. I mean—"

Light snores wafted from Aiya before I could stick my foot any further into my mouth. I looked over to see the woman sleeping peacefully.

"Right," I sighed, grateful her fatigue had saved her from hearing most of my rambling. I went over and covered her with a blanket before returning to my front seat and descending into blissful sleep.

I swear to the Nutcracker king himself I had my eyes closed for a handful of minutes before Tem opened the driver side door and shoved the little chubby creature we'd found in the jungle into my arms.

"I have had it, I have had it, Max Tyco, up to here," Tem said, using a hand to motion somewhere around his chin. "I even gave you a few more hours to sleep than I got last night. I heard about your night raid, but even a historian can only take so much."

I blinked the sleep away from my eyes, sitting up as I cupped the little scaly animal in my hands. The chunky thing panted happily and licked my fingers.

"What—what happened?" I asked, having lost track of all time.

"I need my sleep, I need my sleep, Max Tyco, and that devil spawn was up howling all night."

I took a better look at Tem. His eyes were bloodshot and heavy bags hung under them like hammocks.

"I said to myself, 'Self, be a good friend to Max Tyco. He's a new Rowki, he's just trying to do something nice for this alien wildlife'." Tem took a deep inhale. "But the little demon was playing mind games with me. Sleep deprivation is a form of torture, you know."

"Max, is all well?" Aiya asked with a yawn from her bed behind me.

"Oh, oh my," Tem said, craning his neck into my rig to get a better look. "Max Tyco, you bad boy."

"No, it's not what you think," I said, shaking my head. "Aiya, this is Tem Fan. He's an historian. Tem, this is Aiya Stormbringer. She lives on this planet and helped us find the lost Ursonian unit."

"Pleasure to meet you, Aiya," Tem said, looking back to me with a wink.

"No, no winks," I told him. "Stop winking."

"If you say so," Tem answered with another wink.

"It's a pleasure to meet you too, and oh, I didn't know you had a wolfhound with you," Aiya said, moving over to pat the little chubby monster in my hands. "What's his name?"

"Wolfhound?" I asked, surprised at the term. The thing

in my arms resembled a lot of creatures, but a wolf or a hound was not one of them.

"Yes, of course," Aiya crooned with a smile at the little guy. "They are bred to be hunters by my tribe. There are wild ones, of course, but they are great and loyal companions. What is his name?"

"I don't know," I answered. "We just found this chunky meatball yesterday."

"Ahh, Meatball," Aiya said, mistaking my words. "That is a good name, although I am unsure of what it implies. May I hold him?"

"Sure," I said, handing Meatball to Aiya, who cuddled the little guy like a stuffed animal. There was no argument from him. He yipped and licked her cheek.

"Meatball is the devil," Tem said under his breath.

A beeping from Tem's datapad brought us back to our current responsibilities. The historian took one look and I knew it wasn't going to be good.

"Do I even want to know?" I asked.

"Probably not," Tem answered. "Do you want the bad news or the worse news?"

"I'll take the worse news first," I answered.

"The *Oni* has been ordered to return to orbit. The jungle floor is too dangerous and we cannot risk it being damaged," Tem told me the news I already knew. "An expedition for Aiya's tribe is leaving within the hour."

THIRTY-THREE

"THAT WASN'T part of our agreement." Aiya exchanged heated words with Rima in front of the *Oni*. "I was to go to my people first and then come back to you. You will not force your military into my village."

All around us Ursonians, under the direction of Captain Akel, were unloading supplies and equipment from the large ship. I understood why the *Oni* was to return to orbit, but it still left an uneasy feeling in my gut. Out here exposed without the protection of the massive ship, was not what I would have chosen as my first option.

"We will travel with you," Rima told her, holding up both hands to calm her. "You have proven yourself an ally, but time is short. You said it would take you a full day to travel to your village and another to return. On our vehicles, it will take a fraction of the time. Only three of us will travel with you, leaving the rest of our force here."

That seemed to calm Aiya a bit.

"Max, Tem and I will travel with you to your village in one of our Hogs," Rima said, pointing to the sturdy all-terrain Ursonian vehicles that looked like a tank and off-roader had a hovercraft love child. "We'll make it to your village in hours."

Aiya chewed on her lower lip, looking over to me as if I had any kind of say in this.

I wasn't sure how much my opinion was worth, but I nodded in agreement.

"Okay," Aiya relented. "When we get to my village, you must remain out of sight until I can speak with them. "Our elders may not be so trusting. Our young will be fearful."

"Agreed," Rima said, motioning to Tem and me. She looked at Meatball in my arms and gave me an eye roll so hard, I thought her eyes were going to fall out of her head. "We're leaving in five minutes. Get your gear. We'll eat on the road."

Tem and I rushed to obey. The historian packed our food for us while I grabbed my armor and staff. I saw Bull carrying out a crate of weapons from the *Oni*, working with the other Ursonians to unload the large craft before its departure off planet.

"Bull," I said, running up to the large Ursonian. "Bull, I need a favor."

"Little brother, I know I said I owed you a life debt, but that was more a figure of speech," Bull said with a grunt as he lowered the crate to the ground. "What is it?"

"Well, I know the *Oni* is taking off to orbit, but I'd like to keep my truck with me. If you can make that happen, I'll make it worth your while."

"How so?" Bull asked with a raised eyebrow.

"You know those cans of Red Bull Ero's been drinking?" I asked.

"You refer to the god's blood she found that increases heart rate and reaction time?" Bull asked with large eyes. I knew I had him. "Yes, she hoards the items and respects them above all else."

"You get Ted or whoever's in charge of teleportation to leave my truck here, and I'll make sure there's some god's blood flowing in your veins, too."

"It will be done," Bull said, licking his lips. "Little brother, I take back everything hurtful, mean, degrading, rude, derogatory, and downright uncalled for that I have ever said about you. And trust me, there has been a lot."

"Wait a minute," I said with a sideways look at the big bear. "What have you been saying about me?"

"Well, before you saved me from the Tulrog and earned your name of the Blood Wolf, I thought you were kind of a sissy-lala," Bull said as if that were a normal term. "I also continued to call you a pig species, dense, a slow learner, a Rowki mistake, and—"

"Okay, okay, that's enough." I waved Bull off. "I get it."

I jogged to the racks of weapons where my armor and weapons were waiting for me. I barely had enough time to get my gear on and make a run for the Hog before Rima started the engine.

A deep, throaty bark came from the thrusters on the vehicle as it lifted from the floor and hovered a foot or so above it.

Rima sat behind the wheel with Aiya in the passenger side seat to give her directions. Tem and I sat in the rear with Meatball between us. The Hog was made for Ursonian use; as such there was way more space than we all needed.

The front of the Hog was equipped with an open top like a jeep. The rear was exposed like a truck bed, with a large blaster mounted on a swivel should the occasion arise.

It did cross my mind that I should be the one behind the

wheel. It was hard to imagine Rima had more experience than I did driving, but this was a Hog, not a Peterbilt 379. Still, I believed I could drive anything.

With the cool morning air already giving way to heat and the suns rising in the distance, we advanced into the jungle.

The drive would take us only a handful of hours. We could have made better time, but the Ivandor jungle was so dense, there was no direct path or route to Aiya's village.

Meatball stood on unsteady feet as the Hog maneuvered over rough terrain. The little guy sure could eat. Tem had brought eggs, coffee, and a mystery breakfast meat back with him from an outside food printer.

I shared my portion with Meatball and the little chunk went to town on it, licking his lips and wagging his nub of a tail like a maniac.

"How can you not like this guy?" I asked Tem, pointing to Meatball. "Look at him; he's just so chubby and happy. How can you not smile just looking at him?"

"Easy, like this," Tem said, staring at Meatball flatly. "I do not understand your infatuation with him or with your overall desire to take in those in need."

"I don't have an overall urge to take in those in need," I said around a mouthful of eggs. "What are you talking about?"

Tem looked at Meatball then pointed to Aiya in the passenger side seat. "I do not fault you, it is a trait of a Rowki, just not one I share for little creatures that torture one all night."

Meatball yipped, his little bat ears opening wide as he sat down hard and smiled at me.

The trip was rocky but not long. Aiya directed us to the fastest route the Hog would be able to travel, and within two hours, we were stopped on a large hill overlooking a flat grassland area.

The jungle had begun to spread out a bit, giving room to more and more plains and wide-open areas of grass and shrubs. Down below our hill we could see a series of small structures, as well as cooking fires and tiny moving dots that had to be people.

"Give me a few hours to get down there and explain who you are," Aiya said, hopping out of the Hog. "It will take time to start the meeting and longer for them to be open to meeting you."

"Two hours," Rima said, regaining control of the situation. "Two hours. We're here to help. The faster we know exactly how to help, the safer everyone will be."

Aiya nodded to me and left. I watched as she jogged down the steep hill toward her village. I thought now would be a good time to tell Rima and Tem what Aiya had told me about her sister village and their strange behavior.

When I was done, their response was not what I expected.

"Could be nothing, could be everything," Rima said with a shrug. "Perhaps this sister tribe has been touched by something. or maybe not. Either way, we should look into it."

"It's something," Tem confirmed.

"We should use these hours to prepare," Rima said, backing the Hog down on the other side of the hill. "Your training has only just begun."

I didn't complain. Between the Tulrog and the plant-eaters, I actually wanted to know more and be in better physical shape to deal with these new threats. More practice could be the difference between life and death out here on Ivandor.

Rima took me through an hour workout and another hour of instruction with my staff. I looked on in awe as she blocked my staff strikes with her sword, barely breaking a sweat. Her sardonium rune glowed vibrant white in the light of the suns.

By the time we were done, I was soaked in sweat. That was something that was becoming a common occurrence on Ivandor.

Tem kept watch for Aiya, and Meatball slept in the sun with his belly pressed against the ground and his limbs splayed outward. A pink tongue hung from his lips as he snored little Meatball dreams.

"She's coming back," Tem shouted from his lookout spot on the top of the hill. "She has someone with her. An old man, I think."

"Did you bring some all-water?" I asked Rima as we headed back up the hill. "You're not going to shove it down an old man's throat, are you?"

"I was thinking about it," Rima answered.

We reached the hill at the same time Aiya and the elder did. The old man's shimmering copper skin and all-white eyes mirrored Aiya's own. Unlike her raven hair, his was snow white, with a thick white beard.

He looked at us in awe as Aiya reassured him all was well.

"Elder Niko, this is Tem, Rima, and Max, the ones I was telling you about," Aiya said in a slow, soft tone. "They are allies who have come to help us. I have seen them in action; they are honest and true warriors."

"By the gods, the stories are true!" Niko exclaimed. "There are travelers among the stars."

The all-water translated his words in my ear, making it easy for me to understand him. He would be able to understand us via the translators built into the collars of our armor. However, Tem must have thought asking Aiya to translate for us would be the best at the moment.

"Please tell him hello for us," Tem said with a slight bow.

Aiya did so in their own tongue.

"If he would be willing to drink the all-water, we could speak with him directly and without the aid of you translating or our technology doing the work," Rima said, reaching for a flask on her hip. "Would your elder be open to this?"

Aiya explained to the man, who nodded hurriedly. It seemed he had a much different reaction to us than Aiya. But then again, Aiya was ambushed in the middle of the night, stunned and bound.

Elder Niko drank the all-water greedily. After his intense but brief headache, he was conversing with us in no time. Man, could this guy talk.

You ever hear of an extrovert? This guy was like an extrovert on crack cocaine. He rattled off question after question, all smiles and grins. He asked to see our armor and weapons up close and even requested to drive the Hog.

Rima told him no to that one.

"I knew it, I knew I was right for keeping the customs of our old ways and never forgetting the teachings of those generations before us," Niko said with a wild laugh. "The other elders are going to be so jealous! I can't wait until they see this."

"What's he talking about?" I asked Aiya. "You have teachings about this?"

"There are caves where my people used to live," Aiya answered. "Ancient caves that tell stories through pictures of what our ancestors say were star travelers that visited our planet many, many years ago."

"We would very much like to see this cave if at all possible," Tem chimed in.

"Of course," Aiya agreed. "But now the rest of the village would love to meet you, and it is time for our noonday meal. After that, I will show you the caves of our ancestors."

Rima nodded, relaying our plans through her communication link back to Captain Akel and the Ursonian encampment. Rima had made sure to keep them up to date on our movements and location should anything go awry.

We followed Aiya and Niko back down the hill toward their village. Tem and Niko chatted away about everything from alien species to space travel. The older man was getting a thrill out of hearing it all.

Aiya set Meatball down on the ground and the little guy played with her, zigzagging between her legs.

Rima touched my arm and fell back a step. I followed suit.

"Be on guard in the village, Tyco," Rima warned. "They will outnumber us a hundred to one. Tem, as you well know, is not much of a fighter."

"Do you think this is a trap?" I asked, stunned. "After Aiya helped us?"

"I think everything's a trap," Rima answered. "That's why I'm still alive."

THIRTY-FOUR

I KEPT my right hand near the blasting staff at my side as we entered the village. Men, women of all ages, and even children and animals I took to be pets came out to greet us. There had to be a hundred, maybe two hundred villagers all together.

I said a prayer of thanks they were humanoid and not a grotesque squid species I would have to learn to make eye contact with.

They greeted us with looks of awe and wonder. It was strange. The last time someone had looked at me with such shock was the guy who cleaned dishes off the table at the all-you-can-eat buffet in Vegas.

Murmurs rippled through the crowd as I did my best to smile and seem as friendly as possible. Rima, I was surprised to find, did the same, although I could tell how tense she was. The smile she put on almost seemed to cause her actual physical pain.

The village was a series of tents that led into a circular central area that served as their town hall. Outside, I could smell a spiced soup cooking. As far as I could see, there were no traps ready to be sprung or weapons in the hands of the villagers, just genuine curiosity and wonder.

When the all-water was mentioned, they were practically falling over one another to take it. It was decided that the village elders would be the ones to consume the all-water Rima had brought. There simply wasn't enough to go around.

We were shown to the village center, where we sat with the elders, the rest of the village crowding around to hear what was going to be said. Those in attendance wore clothing much more suitable for the humid weather. The men were mostly shirtless and shoeless, with either pants or shorts. The women wore skirts and what I knew as tube tops and crop tops, but I'm sure there was a better name for them.

Bread was brought for us along with the soup that made me salivate. Rima stayed my hand before I dug in, making sure others were eating the soup before we began.

"If I wanted you dead, I would have done so already," Aiya said to Rima around a plastic smile. "Still don't trust me?"

"I don't trust anyone," Rima said with a smile of her own.

"Our village is run by our elders," Aiya explained, changing the subject. "They will have questions for you, I'm sure."

And questions they did have, from how our armor was made and what we called our home worlds, to how many other planets were out there. I let Tem and Rima do most of the talking; they were better suited for it anyway. All of this was still pretty new to me. I just put down a few bowls of their delicious soup and looked friendly.

"I am sure you have more questions," Rima said after a good thirty minutes of conversation and food. "However, you should know why we are here. Our High Council has foreseen a conflict here on your planet. We are here to investigate and help. Do any of you know of what that darkness or evil may be?"

At this, there was a rush of whispers. I saw some of the elders shake their heads; others seemed on the verge of saying something. I kept hearing the words "Stone Dwellers."

"Forgive us," Niko said from his seat to our left around the meeting area. "It's only that our elders are hesitant to say too much lest we turn your attention on nothing at all. You see, we have no proof, just—a feeling."

"Intuition can be a powerful thing," Rima answered. "Speak freely. We are friends, here to help. There are no enemies present."

"Well, you see, there is a tribe to the north, called the Stone Dwellers," Niko began.

"Niko, stop; we barely know these star travelers," a woman not that much older than me said. She was tall and thin, with a perpetual frown. She hadn't said much yet. "We cannot throw our sister tribe under suspicion."

"Peace, Cator," Niko sighed, leaning his head forward and closing his eyes. "There will only be fact here. The fact is we have no proof other than their strange behavior. That is fact."

The woman named Cator swallowed hard but didn't say anything. She eyed me with disdain but remained silent.

"What has been strange about this sister tribe of yours?" Rima asked. "Are they near?"

"No, maybe three to four hours by your transportation," Aiya explained. "The last time we met to exchange goods, they were—how do you say it?—worried or anxious, like they wanted to tell us something but couldn't. They missed our last monthly meeting to trade goods. When we sent a party to them, a group of their warriors turned us away. Even then, it was like their warrior wanted to tell us something."

"It is strange behavior for them indeed," a relic of a woman said. Even in this heat, she wore a shawl over her wrinkled arms. "We would be remiss not to check on them. Perhaps there is something going on that these star travelers can help with. If not, then there is no harm done."

Cantor didn't look like she was buying it, but she kept her mouth shut. Apparently this older woman carried some serious weight with the tribe.

Tem changed the subject then, telling them of the wonders of space and curious planets. I stopped eating long enough to chime in when they asked me questions about Earth.

"And on your planet, are you a warrior there as well?" the old woman asked.

"Not a warrior, but I am a traveler," I told her. "I guide supplies from one side of my country to the other. It's honest work and keeps me busy. You could call me a product relocation specialist."

"An admirable calling!" Niko nearly shouted. "No reason to be so humble. Why, without supplies moving your tribe would not be able to survive."

I didn't really think of my country as a tribe, but I was picking up what he was putting down. Maybe we'd all be better off if we thought of each other as one tribe.

"These roads you travel, are they dangerous?" Aiya asked. "Filled with horrors?"

"I mean, some of those driver showers are pretty

horrific, lot lizards can be downright terrifying," I told her. "But we travel through all means of weather and dangerous roads."

"There are more like you?" Niko asked, intrigued. "More of these travelers braving the roads and carrying supplies?"

"There's an army of us," I told him, not remembering the last time I had to really describe to someone what I did. I didn't talk to a whole lot of people interested in my profession back home. To be honest, I didn't really talk to a whole lot of people, period.

Here, everyone waited to hear what I was going to say with bated breath. Some were even leaning in from where they sat, as if that was going to help them pick up on any lost words.

"It sounds like an honorable profession and one much needed by your tribe," the ancient woman said with a smile. "You must be a hero to your people."

I didn't tell them about the lonely nights. The other drivers on the road cutting and flipping me off, the others I knew who had died in their trucks. I just gave them a smile and a nod.

"Well, this has been very kind of you all," Rima said, getting to her feet. "If it's appropriate now, we'd like to see this cave you've spoken of and to go meet these Stone Dwellers."

The tribe elders rose along with us, chattering away about who would lead us to these caves. The whole village was going to come until Niko and a few of the other elders shooed them off.

I didn't blame them. Anyone would be intrigued by a visiting alien species, and there were three of us here.

In the end, it was decided that Aiya, Niko, Cantor, and

the older woman whose name I didn't know yet would come with us to the caves. They assured us it was a short walk from their village into the tree line and a cave opening just beyond.

As we began our trip, the older woman chose to walk beside me. She stared at me with a smile I tried to ignore by smiling back and looking away, but she never turned her head.

Her white frizzy hair was wild in the kindest way, her wrinkles earned and worn with pride.

"You are watched over by the spirit of another," the woman said, finally breaking the silence. "Did you know that?"

"I'm not really familiar with ghosts or spirits," I told her, trying to be polite. "But thank you for telling me. Is that a good thing?"

"Of course, the bwolf watches you from the tree line," the old woman said, motioning to the trees in front of us and to our left. "She watches not us, but you. The spirit of another compels her."

I followed the woman's gaze to the tree line. I didn't see anything at first. There were just trees, a lot of them. Not really jungle trees or foliage, but taller trees and more spread out like ones you'd find in a forest.

Then I caught movement, something large shifting through the trees like a shadow. This one, unlike Meatball, had fur and looked like something between a bear and a wolf. Just as soon as I saw the creature, it was gone.

"When the bwolf comes it's to check on the living. The bwolf is sent by someone from the dead lands," the woman explained. "You are watched, Max Tyco, and you are loved."

I didn't trust myself to say anything. This wasn't the place or the time. It was just a story, a story by this old woman.

I did more thinking rather than talking as we found the cave entrance. The mouth of the cave was wide enough for two of us to enter shoulder to shoulder. The roof of the entrance was at least seven feet tall.

The rock outcropping vanished into the side of a short hill.

"We can start a fire for light," Niko said, looking around for fuel for his fire. The cave is dark but not deep."

Rima activated the lights in her armor, then revealed what she called a torch but what I knew as a high-powered flashlight.

Aiya, Cantor, Niko, and the old woman each gave off a sigh of admiration at the light. There was so much I took for granted, light being one of them.

I activated the lights on my armor as well. Two beams shot forward from my shoulders, cutting into the dim cave entrance. Tem withdrew a torch from a bag he carried around his shoulders.

"What witchcraft is this? You can make light?" Cantor asked with disbelief. "How?"

"Uh, you want to field this one?" I asked, looking to Tem. It struck me then how little I knew about how things actually worked.

"Max Tyco, I thought you'd never ask," Tem said, adjusting his shoulder strap on what I called a purse, but what he insisted was a satchel.

Tem began to educate our alien friends about the inner workings of a flashlight as I joined Rima at the cave entrance.

She drew her sword that carried a light from the sardonium metal rune in the center of her blade. Without a word, she entered the dark cave.

THIRTY-FIVE

THE CAVE WAS cool and damp. But it wasn't just the temperature that gave me pause. There was a feeling in this cave. Not bad or creepy; just old, if that made sense. As if the very stone walls we walked beside had been there for millennia. I got the feeling we were in the presence of something that had remained for a very, very long time.

Meatball, who was growing more independent by the day, had taken the walk with us thus far on his four feet. Now as we entered the cave, he whined and trotted over to Aiya, who picked him up and held the chunky animal in her arms.

The cave floor sloped down and opened to a circular cavern free of either stalagmites or stalactites. The walls were smooth, not full of crevices and bumps like I would have imagined, as was the ceiling.

It was obvious to me that something had made this room, or at the very least worked on smoothing the rock. It had to be a machine that did this, not any human or alien I had seen.

I ran my hand over the smooth rock that felt like marble.

"Fascinating," Tem breathed.

"Who did you say made this cave?" Rima asked.

"Our ancestors," Cantor answered with pride.

"Rima?" Tem asked what I was thinking. "How did they manage to smooth out the walls and ceiling like this?"

"That has always been a mystery to us," Niko explained, directing us to a portion of the cave wall near the far end of the room. "However, our ancestors have left us clues in the form of images."

I moved over as the light bathed the far side of the room. Pictographs lined the walls, not etched into the smooth walls, but painted with ink. They were mostly black, but here and there, colors were used as well.

It started off with images of the universe, or at least what I took to be planets and stars. As the images ran to the right side of the room, there were creatures—aliens, beasts and plants.

It seemed what I saw here was trying to explain the passing of time as the images went to what looked like a doorway or a portal. The doorway was silver, with a gold interior. A black shape was set in the middle of this yellow gateway. All the other figures around this door were kneeling.

"I've seen Stargate enough times to know what that is," I said, leaning in closer to the image of a figure exiting the triangle-shaped door. "Rima, what's going on here?"

"I don't know," Rima breathed.

I felt a rush of goosebumps race down my spine.

We separated, looking for more clues or anything that might be useful. As large as the cave was, it seemed whoever wrote this message however many years before, was not interested in using all of their canvas.

There was little else left on the walls. A few more

images of creatures and the natives here, and that was it. There were no words or runes to decipher, just these pictures.

"You must have other writings to go along with this," I said, looking over to Aiya. "There are no books or texts your people have passed down?"

"None that have survived," Aiya said sadly as she stroked Meatball's scaly head. "It has been a mystery to us as well for so many years. Niko is the leading mind on what it may represent."

"It all has to be speculation of course," Niko answered with a shrug. "It seems our ancestors discovered an advanced technology many years ago, but what happened to this technology and why it disappeared is a mystery that has plagued us for so many generations."

"There is the story of Amin," the old woman said.

"Mother, that is a fable," Cantor scoffed. "The lost city of Amin is something we tell our children, a myth."

"Even in myth, there can be some truth," the old woman reminded Cantor. "It is said the city of Amin is where our people came from. They discovered a magic that allowed them to travel from one dimension to another. Their greed to know more was their undoing. They let something in from another dimension that was their end. Neither the city of Amin nor this evil has ever been seen or heard of."

"That's because it's a story," Cantor answered. "Stop trying to scare them."

"Too late," Tem breathed, then let out a tiny little fart. He followed this up quickly with a question. "May I take pictures, ummm record this event for future study?"

"You may," Niko answered. "We would love to learn anything you are able to uncover."

While Tem and Niko got to work, the rest of us moved to the side of the room.

"It's clear to me that we are in the right place," Rima said with a furrowed brow. "There are no coincidences. I've seen enough of the universe to know that is true. We must visit this sister village of yours to see what ails them."

Cantor opened her mouth to protest.

"We're going to go as friends, just like we came to you," I told her. "We just want to talk. Maybe they know what's going on here, or have information that can help."

Cantor didn't say any more on the subject but it was clear she was far from pacified.

Our short trek back to the village and then our Hog was uneventful. I could tell Aiya's people were disappointed we had to eat and run, but Rima insisted our time was short.

With promises to return as soon as we could, we loaded up in the Hog once more. Aiya had to practically wrestle Niko for the right to show us where the next village was, but in the end, I was surprised to hear Rima request our original guide to go with us again.

A three-hour trip, this time to the north, would see us to the next village. The suns would be setting then.

Rima let Tem take the wheel. Both the pedals and steering wheel adjusted for the little historian as he chatted away with Aiya. It still bothered me a bit that I wasn't asked to drive. I don't know why.

With Meatball fast asleep at my feet, Rima radioed Captain Akel and the Ursonians back at base camp.

"The *Oni* has returned to orbit?" Rima asked. "Good, our communication relay should be fine. We are headed north to the next village where there has been strange activity. You have us on GPS? Good, we'll keep you updated. If we do need backup, the Razors should be able to reach our new position in no more than thirty minutes. Have them standing by. Over."

"I would ask if you're expecting trouble, but I know now you're always expecting trouble," I told my teacher. "Paranoid much?"

"Just because I'm paranoid doesn't mean everyone's not out to kill us," Rima reminded me as the Hog rocked back and forth. "I wanted to sit back here with you to tell you I have an idea what that symbol was in the cave."

"I can't help but notice your voice dropping to just above a whisper," I said in the same low tone. "Still don't trust Aiya? Then why ask her to come with us?"

"Because of all the natives here, I trust her the most," Rima explained. "The drawings in the cave, the triangle with the man in the middle and light all around... The Rowki have stories of such portals as well. Like the story the old woman told us, the Rowki also believe there were portals with the ability of not just taking us to different parts of the universe but different dimensions altogether."

I felt the walls of my mouth dry as I tried to wrap my mind around an interdimensional portal. Of all the sci-fi stories I'd seen and read, from *Ghostbusters* to the *Avengers*, *Poltergeist*, and *Big Hero 6*, other dimensions never, ever ended well.

"We won't know for sure until we find one, of course, but I want you to be as prepared as possible," Rima continued. "If we do find one of these portals, we handle it with extreme caution, Tyco. Do you understand me? Nothing good can come from it. If there is one on this planet, we handle it with care."

"I get it, I get it," I answered, witnessing the determination in Rima's eyes. She wore her hood, but those eyes of hers shone with an intensity I understood well. She was committed.

We made small talk off and on the rest of the journey. By "we," I mean Tem, me, and Aiya. Meatball snored most of the way and Rima was silent, popping in here and there for clarification or to answer a question.

As the suns descended and the trio of moons shone brighter and brighter in the sky, the landscape began to change as well. Gone were the lush, thick jungles where we'd landed the *Oni*. The ground around us was dotted with trees as we headed to the north. A mountain range that became larger and larger with each passing minute loomed in front of us.

"We will enter the territory of the Stone Dwellers soon," Aiya said as a mountain pass came into view. "What is your plan?"

"Would these Stone Dwellers fire on us with any kind of weaponry if we were to slowly enter their territory and show ourselves?" Rima asked. "Would it be better to go in quietly? At night or during the day?"

"Their weapons would seem like sticks and stones compared to your own," Aiya answered, turning in her seat to look back at us. "However, it may be best if we did so like the last time. Let me go in first and tell them and then we will come back for you."

I didn't really like the idea of Aiya going alone in the dark to the Stone Dwellers. It was nearly full dark now, with the last oranges and reds touching the sky before the night took reign over the heavens.

"Agreed," Rima answered as Tem pulled off to a forest of trees to the left before we reached the mountain pass.

"It'll take me one, maybe two hours at the most," Aiya

said, looking at the large cream-colored mountain range. There were two main peaks and the road between.

Tem maneuvered the Hog between a pair of rather bushy trees that gave us cover in the night. He cut the thrusters and we disembarked. Meatball yawned then scratched at an ear with his hind foot. He looked around, smelling the air and wagging his nub.

I really didn't have a sixth sense about things. I wasn't a natural worrier either, but something just felt off. It didn't seem right to send Aiya alone to a settlement, even if she was familiar with it. Not if we suspected something was wrong.

Aiya hopped out of the Hog and gave me a smile before she left.

"Wait," I said, joining her. "Maybe I should go with you. In case there's something going on with the Stone Dwellers."

"They would go into a panic if they saw you without an explanation first," Aiya said with a grateful smile. "They are a good people. Even if something is happening to them, they are not evil. I am in no danger, and even if I was, I can take care of myself."

I opened and closed my mouth, trying to find words for how I felt, but there were none. I sensed something was wrong, but I had no evidence for this.

"Here," Aiya said, taking off one of her bracelets and pressing it into my hand. "Our old woman said you are favored by the bwolf. Her spirit watches over you. Keep this for me until I come back. Maybe your spirit bwolf will watch over me as well."

Aiya gave me one of her easy smiles and glided into the night. I looked down to see what she had given me. It was a simple bracelet of mostly black stones and one green. In the middle was a metal head of what looked like a wolf, worn and scratched with time.

We waited for Aiya the full two hours, then three and four.

She didn't come back.

THIRTY-SIX

THERE WAS no need to set up a watch. Rima was on high alert all the time. Dinner was a simple meal of protein packs and water. Meatball finished off an entire pack by himself. His little belly looked like it grew a full size.

When Aiya didn't come back at the designated time, I was already worried. I wanted to go after her, but Rima insisted we wait. After the first then second hour passed since Aiya was supposed to return, Rima was finally ready to take action.

"We should have given her a comm device," Tem said with a sigh. "It goes against the rules to hand over Galactic Government technology to less developed species, but still, we should have given her something."

"We lost contact with the native," Rima said in her own comm, relaying the news to the Ursonian base camp. "Stand by with Razors. We're going in."

"Let's go," I said, jumping into the Hog's front seat. "I'll drive."

Rima and Tem exchanged a worried look.

"I know you don't think I can handle Ursonian tech, but

trust me, I can drive anything," I said, familiarizing myself with the pedals at my feet and the wheel in front of me. I'd kept a close eye on Rima and Tem driving. "This is what I do."

Rima shrugged and Tem nodded.

"All right," I said, pressing the ignition button that lit the thrusters. "Hold on to your butts."

Tem sat next to me with Rima on the weapon in the rear truck-like bed, that swiveled this way and that. Meatball jumped in beside her.

"Take it slow," Rima corrected me. "There is no doubt we are approaching a much larger force. Surprise will be a better ally than—"

I heard it when she did, a snapping of twigs to our left. I peered into the darkness, trying to discern if it was an animal or a person. The previous rustling of feathers, chirping of insects, and natural wildlife sounds had ceased.

I held my breath as Tem turned on the Hog's high beams. Not one or two, but five, ten, more men and women descended on our location. Like Aiya, they had copper skin, long dark hair, and those white eyes. Except with these people, there was something wrong with them. Deep bags hung under their eyes, and they were malnourished, sickly even.

Weapons ranging from clubs to spears and slings were held in their hands. For a split second, we just stared at one another. Us shocked they were so close. Them surprised, I'm sure, at the "magic" light and our vehicle.

"Kill them!" the shout went up loud and clear.

I slammed the Hog into gear just like I had seen Tem and Rima do. I pressed on the pedal that was a circle, not a square under my right foot.

The Hog leapt to life, hovering backward as it sped

away from the attack. Weapons were flung in our direction, bouncing off the armored exterior of the Hog. While stone and wood were no match for the dura steel the Hog was made from, I knew it only took one lucky projectile to hit Rima in the back or sail into Tem and me via the open roof.

VROOM! VROOM! VROOM! VROOM! VROOM!

Rima lit the darkness around us with her red rounds fired from the turret just behind me. There were so many of the Stone Dwellers. So many more than I'd expected. They must have been sneaking up on us the whole time. We were surrounded.

Instead of getting out of the Hog's way when I reversed, they charged us, throwing themselves at the vehicle and trying to climb aboard.

The Hog made a sick crunching noise as I rammed a handful of natives behind us.

One managed to climb into the truck bed. As much as I wanted to look back, I knew Rima could handle herself. I pulled a hard left, then gunned the thrusters, shooting us forward as weapons bounced off the exterior of the Hog. A rock sailed through the top of our open roof, crashing into my right shoulder with numbing pain.

A spear whistled through and buried itself deep in the seat Tem sat in right between his legs.

"Get that gun back up!" I shouted over my shoulder. At first, I had almost felt sorry for the natives attacking us with sticks and stones; now I was just pissed. I couldn't feel my right arm and Tem had almost been castrated. "Rima?!"

A man' head fell through the roof into my lap, leaking blood from a severed neck.

"What the...?!" I yelled, doing a seated panic dance to get the head off my lap like it was a hot potato. I threw it over to Tem, who farted.

"No, Max Tyco, no, I do not want it!" Tem screamed as the Hog waved this way and that.

Rima was up on the gun again and I heard it barking, or more like zipping into the night.

Tem batted the head over to me again.

I grabbed the thing and threw it out the top of the roof.

With no clear order of where to go, I headed for the pass in the mountains. The Hog drove like a dream. It was so responsive to every press of the thruster or turn of the wheel. It handled like a Tesla while being the size of a tank.

Soon Rima's weapon silenced as we put distance between us and the chasing Stone Dwellers.

"I think I need to change my undergarments," Tem groaned.

"Are you two all right?" Rima asked as I decelerated and continued to move us forward at a steady pace. "Are you injured?"

"No, no, I'm fine," Tem said, grasping the spear shaft in between his legs and pulling it out. "Although I was about an inch away from an early retirement."

I moved my right shoulder around in my armor. The rock failed to penetrate the steel of course, but it still hurt like a mother.

"I'll live," I answered. "We're heading in after Aiya, right?"

"It seems we have the answer to the question whether there is something going on or not with the Stone Dwellers," Rima said with a nod. "Move slowly. I've already radioed in the Ursonian Corps. They are en route."

I thought how deadly the Ursonians were, and how much larger and better armored they were as well. It would be a massacre if the Stone Dwellers insisted on a fight.

But I had seen the madness in their eyes as they

advanced on us through the dark like a zombie horde. There was no doubt in my mind there was something very wrong with them. Instead of awe or wonder at our vehicle and weapons, they'd charged our position.

I thought on this, even though I knew there were no answers to be found, only more questions at the moment.

I concentrated on the road. Strangely, it felt good to be behind a wheel again. No, it felt great. For more than two weeks, I'd just been training and sleeping. I didn't know how much I'd missed the open road in front of me. Even if that open road was leading to a maniac-infested village.

The only thing I was missing now was some chrome and my chicken lights. A little *Welcome to the Jungle* or *Juke Box Hero* would be nice as well.

Darkness greeted me to the right and left, with high sloping hills morphing into the twin mountains. To say I followed a road would be pushing it, but there was a path for sure in the canyon. The light from the stars overhead and Ivandor's three moons was more than enough. Add in the headlights from the Hog and I had no problem seeing the path.

What did bother me was how much I couldn't see. My mind played tricks with me as shadows morphed and twisted in the light. Was that a rock or a hunching zombie Stone Dweller, ready to impale my manhood with a spear?

The terrain was different here as well. Fewer trees and shrubs, with more rocks. Before this, I couldn't have thought of myself as necessarily courageous, or a coward. I was just a guy. Right now, I could feel what courage I did have being put to the test.

That same indescribable ominous feeling was in the air. We were headed toward something bad. I didn't know how

I knew, but I knew. I looked down on the bwolf bracelet on my right wrist.

If you really do exist, bwolf creature spirit animal thing, I thought to myself, *now would be a good time to pull something magical off.*

"Do you remember the code of the Rowki?" Rima asked from behind me. "The mantra we profess?"

"No," I told her honestly. "I remember you repeated it for us when we were on the *Oni*, but I don't remember the words besides the part that repeats 'send me'."

"That is all you're required to remember at this time," Rima answered. "Tem, if you would?"

Tem cleared his throat and began. "When the world of men stands defenseless against the dark."

"Send me," Rima and I answered.

"When the ancient ones come to reclaim their throne," Tem continued.

"Send me," we replied.

"When all hope is lost and no one can see the way."

"Send me."

"And when the light trembles to regain its feet, who will go?"

"Send me."

Our voices trailed off into silence as we finished the mantra and rode on into the night. The canyon's road was ever inclining until we crested a ridge on a plateau somewhere inside the mountain range. We'd been traveling for ten, maybe fifteen minutes at this point.

I killed the lights as the Stone Dwellers' village opened up in front of us. It was quiet. Not tents but wood-made structures lined the main street. There were torches for light and fires, but that was not what caught my eye.

What grabbed my attention now was chanting of some

type and a brilliant glow that came from no fire I had ever seen. It was on the other side of the village. The huts blocked our line of sight.

"We can't take the Hog and not be detected," Rima thought out loud. "We park in the woods, scout the perimeter."

"I'm not going crazy, am I?" Tem asked. "Everyone hears that chanting?"

"I hear it," I answered, obeying Rima and parking the Hog just inside the tree line surrounding the village.

We hopped out of the Hog and moved in a circle to our right, flanking the houses and moving toward the glowing light and sounds of the unknown.

THIRTY-SEVEN

AS WE MOVED through the woods, the warmth of the day just dying off, my heart rate spiked. Meatball huffed and growled, but I kept the little guy close to my chest. If I told him to stay with the Hog, it didn't seem like he would get the idea.

Rima in the lead with me and Tem close behind, the chanting and glow came into view.

I had to blink a few times to make sure I wasn't hallucinating. I actually wanted to hallucinate if this was reality.

Behind the village, an excavation site had begun. An indention in the ground going ten, maybe fifteen feet deep showed. One of the strangest things in this strange scene were the tools scattered around the site.

There were no tools I would have assumed to see, like crudely made shovels or picks. There were steel, highly-advanced digging instruments I could only guess at. Something that looked like a jackhammer, hovering wheelbarrows, and even a small machine with a digging claw attached to its arm.

A crowd of Stone Dwellers were on their knees in front

of a triangle-shaped structure chanting, not words the all-water could translate, but sounds and hums.

"That portal, it's the same one from the images in the cave," Rima confirmed as she crouched low in the cover of the trees. "It's an interdimensional gateway."

"Oh, they don't pay me enough for this," Tem said as another toot squeezed out.

"Wait, you're getting paid?" I asked incredulously.

"Focus," Rima breathed, the word barely above a whisper.

I searched the scene for any sign of Aiya, but there was none. I prayed she had only been captured and not the other thing.

The triangle-shaped portal was what was shining. A sheet of light stretched across the surface of the portal. And it was moving. No, something was moving on the other side. Something large.

The light rippled and bent as a behemoth of unknown origin moved and shifted.

Suddenly, the chanting stopped. Everyone present looked to the left. From within the city, three aliens moved out, holding Aiya prisoner between them.

The aliens were grotesque, and that was putting it lightly. Although they walked on two legs, they looked to be an alien bug species, with large eyes and an exoskeleton that acted as armor.

Mandibles protruded from their lower jaws, and they had bony foreheads. They were stockier than humans, but lacked the height and weight the Ursonians carried.

Whoever these intruders were, they looked to be the ones in charge. They marched Aiya to the portal that stood on a raised dais of a few steps, and forced her to kneel.

Rima was on her comms again, but I didn't listen to her as one of the aliens began talking.

"Children of the Eternals, your faith and effort to see your gods again will be rewarded," one of the three alien creatures said. Unlike the other two that seemed to be wearing blue armor, this one was robed in black. "This is just the beginning. Soon, as more portals across your planet are opened, our eternal gods will come forth. For now, we must be content with going to them."

I knew what was about to happen. Aiya yelled and threw herself at the two aliens who held her by each arm. She tried to bite them, shaking her body and kicking out.

I had to help. "Tem, can you hold Meatball?"

"Stay," I told the little guy. "Stay."

I rose from my spot in the tree line.

Rima grabbed my arm.

"We wait for backup," Rima hissed. "The Ursonians are ten minutes out. Going in now would be suicide. Remember the mission."

I'd already made up my mind. I jerked my arm free from Rima. "I'll buy us ten minutes. Get behind them and be ready to move in. What good is being a Rowki if we just stand by and watch?"

Rima opened her mouth but didn't have an answer. I didn't wait to hear her out.

"You!" I shouted as loud as I could, coming from the tree line.

Everyone swung their heads to look over in my direction. The two aliens holding Aiya reached for long blasters on their backs I hadn't seen before. One of them cracked Aiya across the skull and sent her down to the ground, unconscious.

"No one's going to be doing any summoning of Eternal

ones, ancient deities, or fairy godmothers today," I said, realizing now I had no plan or epic speech prepared. I just needed to buy some time. "So you all need to go home. Cult meeting's been canceled. You can grab some coffee and cookies on the way out."

The lead alien in the robe looked half annoyed and half amused. He waved a hand to his two soldiers, who aimed their blasters in my direction. They didn't lower their weapons, but they weren't firing at the moment, either. I'd call that a win.

"We've been tracking your ship as it came into orbit and then left," the alien said without sounding the least bit worried. "I was wondering when the mighty Rowki would make their appearance. Although I was expecting them to send more than one. Where are your Ursonians? On the way? Are you here to buy time?"

"No," I lied, suddenly realizing this might be a trap. Rima was never going to let me live this one down.

"Oh, you must be new," the alien said with a smile that turned his mandibles. "Do you even know what's going on here? What lies have the Rowki fed you? Have they told you they're a dying order? Have they told you their time is at an end?"

"I don't need the Rowki to tell me that manipulating a less advanced species is wrong," I said, looking out over the Stone Dwellers. They were all malnourished, with sunken eyes, just skin and bone.

"They do this willingly," the alien crooned. "They realize all life in our universe comes from Ivandor. They see they are descendants of the Eternals. They are happy to bring about a new era of rule."

"Yeah, they seem overjoyed," I answered. "Especially

that guy over there who keeps scratching himself and looks like he hasn't seen a bath this month."

All eyes swung over to the corner of the gathered Stone Dwellers. A man there slowly stopped scratching his dirty neck. He awkwardly put down his arm and coughed.

"Keep him talking," Rima said in my ear. "He knew about us. He knows about the Ursonians and he's not worried. This *is* a trap. I'll wait to tell you I told you so later. Right now, keep him talking. I'm going to scout the village."

"They are eager to assist in unveiling the mysteries of their origin," the alien in front of me said with a sideways stare. "That's what's always wrong with you Rowki. You travel across the galaxy, forcing your own ideologies on everyone around you. It has to be *your* way. Who's to say what is right and what is wrong? You?"

"Not me," I answered, shaking my head. "I'm just a trucker. I'm not someone crossing the galaxy to dole out knowledge. But there are universal truths. He who smelt it dealt it, never get into a fight with an Ursonian, and using and manipulating people to meet your own ends is wrong. What did you tell them? Did you tell them you were one of these gods? What did you promise them?"

The alien in front of me swallowed hard. I could see his hands tighten into fists.

"You'll die here today, Rowki," the alien said, regaining his composure. "But the Enzite Federation is as benevolent as it is wise. I'll give you this one opportunity to stand down. Join us in welcoming the Eternals once more. Join us in welcoming our creators. All you have to do is kneel."

"I found something in the huts," Rima said over the comms. "Ion surface to air turrets. That's why he's not afraid to have the Ursonian crafts come down on him. He's going to shoot them out of the sky. Tyco, the Ursonian

Corps will be here soon. I can disable the turrets with Tem's help in the next few minutes, unless you need assistance. I can always call the Ursonians back."

I paused, weighing my options. The truth was there was no real choice here. If the Ursonians didn't come now, my chances of getting Aiya out alive were slim to none. As brutal as we were, Rima and me against these numbers was asking a lot. We needed the Ursonians. For that to happen, Rima had to disable the turrets and I needed to buy more time.

"What's your name?" I asked the alien in front of me.

"Excuse me?" the alien asked, irritated.

"Your name, your faction, who are you?" I pressed.

"I am called Zion. I am an Enzite and I serve the Enzite Federation," Zion said, clearly annoyed. "Now answer the question. Will you kneel?"

"Well, Zion of the Enzite species serving the Enzite Federation," I said, taking a long breath and lowering my right hand to grab my blasting staff from my hip. "My history is full of stories of people like you. Those who manipulate the weak and try to intimidate everyone else. I can't kneel for you. I won't. You kneel."

"Then you will die this night, Rowki," Zion said, taking a step back and motioning for his pair of armed soldiers.

"Maybe," I told him, my fingers tingling in anticipation of grabbing the blasting staff. "But you first."

At the same time I reached for my weapon, the guards who had walked up on either side of Zion opened fire. I was able to get a single round off before the suck started. My blasting staff jerked my hand back with violent force as one of my rounds slammed into the head of the soldier on the left. The bolt tore through his helmet and into his face beneath.

He went down like a rock. It would have been an amazing shot had I not been aiming for the retreating Zion the whole time.

Zion ran back to the portal, screaming for the Stone Dwellers to kill me as he did.

I felt pain slap me across the chest and left thigh as I went down under the remaining soldier's fire. I might have died right there from the next barrage of his weapon, except the Stone Dwellers surged forward to attack me, blocking his line of fire.

I gasped, trying to regain my feet as the first Stone Dwellers reached me with crude knives, rocks, and makeshift clubs. My training kicked in as I extended my staff. Rising to my feet, I cracked my first attacker across the head. The next second I spun to my right and swiped his feet out from under him, sending him tumbling to the hard dirt ground.

More and more came. I took out two more with red laser fire from my extended staff, but there were too many. I swung the staff around my body, trying to create space and keep them at bay.

There was no strategy in my actions as they lunged for me with clubs and knives, only the will to live and keep living as long as possible. One brave Stone Dweller lunged at me. My staff came up and he got a mouthful of broken teeth in the process, but that was the move everyone else needed to lunge in as well.

Hands grabbed for my weapon. A club struck me in the back of the head so violently, I saw stars and stumbled, losing the hold on my weapon.

Not yet, not yet. You have more to give, I yelled at myself in my head. *Come on, Max, come on, you're better than this. Get back up!*

I don't know where the roar came from. Somewhere deep inside where it had been buried for so many years. I gave my pain and anger an outlet. I used it now, swinging for the fences. If I was going down, then I was taking as many of them with me as I could.

"Rawww!" I screamed, taking strikes to my torso and head.

I recovered from my stumble, trying to retreat. I grabbed the Stone Dweller nearest me with a hand on either side of his head and drove his skull down into my right knee, which came up to meet him.

I used the armor I wore to my advantage, striking out with my fists and connecting with jaws and bodies as I tried to find a way out of the circle of attackers. My staff was gone. I took another blow to the head. Hot wetness poured into my eyes. The metallic taste of blood filled my mouth.

I'd never been attacked by a mob before. It was horrifying. Just when I thought I didn't have anything left in the tank, I found a tree. Against all odds, I had retreated far enough to get to the tree line. I put my back to the tree and heaved. Breathing was painful; my body was numb with pain and fatigue.

I looked out to a mass of Stone Dwellers preparing their next attack.

THIRTY-EIGHT

THEY'D TAKE ME NOW. They knew it. I knew it. That didn't mean I was going to go lying down.

"Come on!" I roared. "Come on! You think I'm scared? You think this is pain? You don't know what pain is. Come now! Come now!"

They hesitated just for a moment. I could only imagine what I looked like to them. A bloody raving alien screaming at them in his own tongue.

"Turrets down," Rima said over the comms.

"Little brother?" Bull's voice came out of the comms next. "What are you yelling about down there?"

Red laser beams slammed into the ground around me, obliterating the Stone Dwellers two, three, four at a time. A pair of Ursonian Razors hovered above me as the side gunners ripped apart the horde of crazed natives.

I staggered forward as the walking battle tanks that were the Ursonian Corps touched down on the ground and made short work of any Stone Dweller crazy enough to still want to fight.

"You look horrible," Ero said, joining me on the ground.

"I feel horrible," I answered, moving around the landed Razors, stumbling toward the triangle-shaped portal and the last place I had seen Aiya.

"Contact, east," Bull shouted through the comms.

I really needed to get to know how to work these things and tune in and out of frequencies.

I looked to my right.

Out of the trees, more of the bug-like Enzites were emerging, firing their black blaster rifles at the new threat. It seemed Zion was well prepared for various contingencies.

As the Ursonian Corps met the Enzites head on, I ran for the portal.

The one remaining soldier with Zion had been reinforced with an entire unit from the woods. Aiya was still on the ground in front of the portal, unconscious.

"Kill him!" Zion shouted as I ran forward.

A dozen rifles pointed in my direction.

Before they could fire, two things happened.

Aiya wasn't really unconscious at all. At some point since she had been knocked out, she had played possum. She made her move now, jumping to her feet. She freed a blade from one of the soldiers' belts, slamming it up through the underside of his jaw and into his brain.

At the same time, Rima came from my left with her white sardonium sword lighting the path. A few rounds were still fired my way, but it was hard to concentrate on me when two Valkyries were on top of them cutting them to pieces.

A little fat ball of paws intercepted me right before I joined the fight. Meatball dropped my blasting staff at my feet. It was closed, back to its compact size. He looked at me and smiled with his tongue out of his mouth.

"Good boy," I said, picking up my staff. "Good boy, Meatball."

I wish I could say I joined in the fight in front of me and saved Rima and Aiya, but the truth was the two were making mincemeat out of the Enzite guards.

Zion stood next to the portal with pure rage in his eyes. Despite his contingency plans, things were still not going his way. Now that I was standing next to the portal, I could see how truly massive the thing was. It had to tower as much as three stories tall. Along the steel-like pillars that made up its outer sides, there were runes and carvings laid into the metal.

The golden energy waved along the front of the portal, with bubbles and splashes as if something on the other side was disturbing its peace. The portal itself stood on a stone altar with a short set of stairs leading up to it.

"You have no idea what you're dealing with here," Zion said, leaning down and removing a long, curved bladed weapon from one of his dead soldiers. "But you will. When the three portals around Ivandor are opened at once and the Eternals are allowed to reenter our dimension, then you will know!"

Something on the other side of the portal roared. There weren't any words I could decipher, but it sounded big and pissed.

Laser rounds and shouting flew all round the battlefield. I could smell burned flesh from blasters. Still, I needed to be focused. Sore and tired, I clashed with the insane cult member of the Enzite Federation.

He slammed his blade down. I extended my staff on Zion as he came slashing and hacking at me with a ferocity I was hard pressed to match in my fatigued state.

I tried pointing the blasting end of my weapon at him,

but he was too good. He'd seen what my weapon could do now. He remained close and refused to allow me to aim my weapon at him.

In the light of the portal so close to us that I could reach out and touch it, we traded blows.

I slammed him across the side of his face with one end of my staff, then used the other end to batter his ribs. He slashed me with his sword, sparking off my armor, then again finding a spot where my armor gapped . His blade passed between the armor plating and found its way through my synth suit.

I gritted against pain that took my breath away.

I stumbled and fell, the portal on my left, the war raging to my right.

"This is why you'll die," Zion said, stepping on my staff as I tried to lift it to blast or block him. "Because you are too empathetic to the weak. I saw how you exposed yourself. To save the Plains Walker we captured. Now you will die alongside her."

Zion lifted the wickedly curved blade in the air. I kept my eyes wide open. When death came for me, it wouldn't find me trembling in the corner.

The steel weapon arced down then stopped. Zion screamed in pain. I looked down to see that little hunk of meat attached to Zion's left ankle like my life depended on it.

Zion screamed again in pain. Blood oozed down his ankle around Meatball's mouth. Zion tried to kick the little guy off, but Meatball might as well have been a bear trap.

Move, Max, move, I yelled at myself in my head.

I stood up, closing my staff as I did so.

Zion finally managed to free himself of Meatball, kicking him to the side.

I opened the staff, pointing it at Zion. The force of the staff opening was so violent, it was enough to punch through Zion's right shoulder.

The alien dropped his weapon, screaming in pain.

"You're wrong," I told Zion, gasping for breath as I used my left hand to stem the flow of blood from my open wound. I looked over at the little animal I had saved a few days before. It had been his turn to save me now. "Empathy doesn't make us weak. It makes us stronger, together."

Zion's right arm useless, he quivered on his feet. He used his left hand to grab clumsily at my staff. The portal was right behind him now. Whatever was on the other side groaned and rippled the surface in manic glee as if it could sense Zion so close.

"You think this is over?" Zion growled out. "You think I was the only one opening the portals? The Enzite Federation will not be stopped. They will kill you. You will see the afterlife."

"Maybe," I said, rearing back with my right boot. "But you first."

I slammed my boot into Zion's chest, sending him reeling into the portal. I couldn't be sure it, happened so fast, but I swore a clawed hand grabbed him right before he disappeared.

With their leader gone and the Ursonian Corps obliterating their numbers, the Enzites announced a full retreat. That was fine with me. I didn't have anything left in my tank to give.

I stumbled down the steps, deciding to take a seat as Meatball trotted over to me wagging his nub. Despite the kick, the little guy didn't seem to have any lasting injuries.

"You did so good," I told my four-legged friend as I scratched behind his floppy ears. "You did so good. You saved me. Did you save me? You did, that's a good boy. Who's a good boy? You are, yes, that's right, you are."

That was how Rima and Aiya found me, deliriously talking to Meatball, full of cuts and bruises and bleeding all over the portal steps.

"We need to get you looked at," Aiya said, joining us. "Are you seriously injured?"

"Not Tulrog serious," I said, looking down at the wound on my side. "But yeah, it's definitely going to leave a scar."

"Should I say it?" Rima asked, spitting blood to the side from a split lip.

"Say what?" I asked.

"That this was a trap?" Rima smirked.

"You can tell me, " I said as the Ursonians routed the prisoners and secured the area. "You called it, but even a broken clock is right twice a day."

"Oh my lort!" Tem said, joining us and taking us all in, especially me. "Max Tyco, you require medical attention right away. I'll get Ero."

Tem hurried off, leaving us there at the front of the portal. Rima stood staring at the object like she had seen one before.

"I have a bad feeling about this," I said with a sigh. "Something tells me this isn't the end and is just the beginning."

THIRTY-NINE

THE URSONIANS' base camp was moved to the portal. The Stone Dwellers put down their weapons as the long process of educating them to the trickery of Zion began.

Between the skin spray that stopped the bleeding and cleaned my wounds, and the nanites Ero injected me with to repair my body from the inside out, I was up and running the next day.

My wounds were closed and I was sore, but nothing was broken. I was getting a better idea of what life as Rowki meant. A sick little part of me kind of liked it, although I would never mention that to Rima.

I stood with her now. It was midday, the day following the battle. We stared at the portal together. Her mysterious and brooding, me crouching down to tickle the back of Meatball's neck.

"Should I ask how much you're not telling me?" I said, breaking the silence. "Would that even help or is it confidential?"

"What would you know?" Rima asked, not removing her eyes from the portal. Tem and the tech

Ursonian, Ted with the goggles, worked with a team, mapping everything from the width of the portal, to the steel it was made from and the runes etched into the frame.

"Is this the first time you've seen a portal?" I asked. "What do you know about them?"

"It's the first time I've seen one in real life," Rima explained. "There are stories and theories, of course, that something like this could exist, but one has never been built, much less unearthed."

"Unearthed," I said, playing with the word. "What does that even mean?"

"Oh, this is a great day for science and revealing the mysteries of the universe, Max Tyco," Tem said, leaving his place in front of the portal with Ted and the Ursonian team. "This was already here. Do you understand what that means? This advanced alien tech already existed. It was dug up."

It was strange for me to hear Tem, who I considered alien, to talk about other alien technology, but I understood what he was saying. I stared at the triangle-shaped portal, still reflecting that golden glow of light.

After I'd kicked Zion inside, the sounds of whatever was in there had died away. The rolling and swirling motion of the golden light stopped as well. Now it was just a smooth surface of undisturbed yellow light.

Tem mistook my silence for not understanding.

"Oh, Max Tyco, how can I explain this to a human who has only just begun to explore outside of his planet?" Tem said, not in an unkind way. "You see, some advanced species had to have been here before to set up the portals many, many years ago."

"I get it, I get it," I said with a deep sigh. "Didn't you say the Ragmar galaxy is the center of the universe and Ivandor is the center of Ragmar?"

"It is," Rima answered. She didn't move her eyes from the portal. Her stance was tense, back rigid as if she expected something to jump out at any moment.

"What if ancient aliens created these portals here to move back and forth between their dimension and this one?" Tem asked excitedly. "What if they hold answers to questions we don't even know to ask yet? What if? What if? What if? This is so exciting. So very exciting!"

"I'm overjoyed," I said in my best monotone voice. I wasn't sure I wanted to open the portal. Whatever had been in there, whatever grabbed Zion when he fell through...well I wasn't sure I wanted to meet it. "Zion said he was part of the Enzite Federation. What is that?"

"A faction of fanatics that have broken away from the Enzite Empire," Rima answered, still not moving her eyes from the portal. "They believe they are the superior race and wish to exterminate all other species. They see the portals no doubt as a weapon."

"We need to send out the call for scholars," Tem said, rubbing his hands together like a kid at Christmas. "I know my limitations. I'm a historian, not a scientist. We need to send a call to the High Council and the Galactic Government requesting help."

"You're going to need more muscle, too," I said, thinking to myself.

Rima actually broke her gaze from the portal and looked over to me.

"Zion said there were three portals on this planet. The other two will need to be found and secured," I said, chewing on my lower lip. "And when word of this gets out to the rest of the galaxy, you bet you're going to have your share of treasure hunters on Ivandor looking to make a quick buck."

"Sometimes you surprise me," Rima said with a nod. "Now you're thinking like a Rowki."

No sooner had those words left her lips than the portal in front of us snapped with an electrical sound. The glowing golden light disappeared a moment later.

"What did you do?" Tem asked, rushing up the steps to Ted and his Ursonian team. "What did you touch?"

"Nothing," Ted shot back, adjusting his goggles. "Nothing, we were taking pictures of the portal and it just—just closed. We can open it again. We just have to figure out how."

Aiya joined us as Tem worked on the portal with the others. I for one was not disappointed it was closed.

"I spoke to a few of the Stone Dwellers who weren't happy with Zion," Aiya told us. "Most of them bought into his propaganda, but a few refused to help him dig and were held as prisoners. You should talk to them. They aren't a bad people as a whole. Many of them were tricked and brainwashed."

"It would have been easy to manipulate them," Rima agreed. "Coming to them in ships with advanced technology, Zion no doubt set himself up as a sort of demigod."

"I'll show you," Aiya answered, taking the lead up the incline of earth from the excavation site.

We made our way through the Stone Dwellers' village, which was now teeming with Ursonians as they worked to relocate their camp here and create a perimeter around the portal.

I caught sight of Captain Akel speaking with his hands as he doled out orders. He looked ever the leader, not weary or unsure, but certain and decisive.

There was one main dirt road in town with wooden buildings on either side that weren't much better than log cabins. Aiya led us to one of these structures on the right about halfway down the road.

Inside, a small, bent man rocked next to a fire. His gnarled hands hovered over the flames for warmth. When we walked in, he neither turned nor acknowledged our presence.

"This is Geo," Aiya explained. "He was one of the ones who refused to work with Zion and the Enzites. We freed him along with a handful of others. He drank the all-water."

I looked over to Rima.

"I gave her the all-water and permission," Rima said to my questioning glance.

"Geo," Aiya said softly, going over to the old man and placing a gentle hand on his shoulder. "Geo, this is Max and Rima. They are Rowki. Can you tell them what you told me?"

Geo broke his gaze from the fire and looked over at Rima and me. I could see his eyes sunken from malnourishment, bruises across his face, missing fingernails on his hands. Zion hadn't just placed him in captivity. He'd tortured him.

Despite all of this, Geo smiled through broken teeth.

"Are these our saviors I've heard so much about?" Geo asked. "I hear stories of legendary beasts being killed by the Rowki, the freeing of my people and rumors of a Blood Wolf."

"We are the Rowki," Rima said, looking over at me with a sly smile. "Although I can't claim the title of Blood Wolf, this one can."

"Just doing my job," I answered.

"Well, we are all better off because you just did your

job," Geo said, motioning for us to sit. "No doubt you've come not to listen to an old man ramble on about the meaning of life. You'd like to know about Zion and the Enzites."

"Whatever you can tell us may be of use in the coming days," Rima answered. "Aiya says you have information that can help?"

"What you see here," Geo said, pointing to the bruises across his face and then extending his torn fingernails for us to examine. "Was not simply torture."

I forced myself to look. I forced myself to remember what was done to this man. Something told me the conflict with the Enzite Federation was only beginning. When it came time for action, I needed to remember this to spur me on to doing what would need to be done.

"They were experimenting on us," Geo said with a hard swallow. "And not just me—men, women and children."

"Why?" Rima was the first to find her voice. "The portal wasn't enough?"

"They told me nothing, but I overheard a few of their scientists talking of weapons, genetic mutation, and even cloning," Geo said, looking into the fire now as if he were back there remembering the conversations he'd overheard word for word. "They are looking for weapons to wage their war."

Geo started to cough. I reached for a cup of water and handed it to the man, who accepted it gratefully.

"Rest now," Rima told him, standing up. "I'm sure we'll have more questions for you later, but rest and get some food."

Geo nodded as Aiya stoked the fire for the man and gave me a stern nod.

I walked out of the hut with a mixture of anger and

confusion as to how someone could do this to another living being. But mostly anger. I didn't know what to think. It was difficult for me to imagine putting people through experiments.

"Walk with me," Rima said, already traveling down the main road of the small town.

I did so, looking up at the twin suns, which beat down as hot as ever. I shrugged in my armor, wishing I could kick Zion into the portal all over again for what he did to Geo and the others.

Rima took me off the main road and to the left where a slight incline in the ground rose just inside the tree line. We stopped there, looking back on the small town. Some of the natives were already in their homes, trying to piece together their lives after the events that had transpired.

From where we stood, we could see through a window of one of the homes to a family. At least I guessed they were a family: a mother, a father and three small children sharing a noonday meal around a table.

Despite what happened to them, they looked happy. The kids were all giggles and laughs, the parents no doubt grateful the Enzite occupation was over, and now not sure what to think about our presence.

"This is why I fight," Rima said, breaking the silence. "I haven't told you much about my past, but I can tell you about my present. Every planet I go to, every evil I over-throw is for this. So others can live free without the fear of wolves at their door."

I didn't say anything. I let Rima speak her piece. She was right, she hadn't opened up much directly to me at all. I didn't want to interrupt her and make her think twice about what she was doing.

"But make no mistake, Tyco, we too, are wolves," Rima

continued. "And we will protect these families and little ones. This is why I fight. Why do you fight?"

I'd sensed the question was coming. To be honest, I didn't have an answer to recite. Everything I said now came straight from the heart.

"I fight because if I can do some good before my time is up, I will," I answered. "I'm not afraid of dying. I've been through a lot, but maybe somehow that's prepared me for all of this. I don't fear physical pain. I've been through enough emotional torment to know what true suffering feels like."

"The Rowki are chosen not for their current levels of skill or strength, but for their capacity of potential," Rima said as if she were quoting a line out of a book. "You, Tyco, have an unlimited potential for growth if you just apply yourself. I know you have the heart to do just that."

I let the moment linger for a moment longer.

"All right, well, where I come from, you're called a creeper for staring at a family eating their lunch through a window," I said, looking over to Rima. "Come on, I need to train. I still have to find some sardonium and, apparently, there are portals to unearth."

FORTY

I WOULD LIVE to regret those words as Rima put me through a gauntlet of training over the next few days. But, to be honest, I was learning to enjoy the pain. I don't know what that says about me. Maybe I'm a masochist, but as the days turned into weeks and we trained on, I could see my body changing. A pudgy belly gave way to flat and then toned abs, my stick-like arms began to show definition, and I went from a size B cup to full-on muscular chest.

I still had a long way to go, that was for sure. I'm not saying I could give Rambo a run for his money; still, progress was progress and I loved it.

Weapons training progressed in a similar fashion, with my skill level reaching new heights as I drilled day in and day out with my staff.

A larger Ursonian presence was stationed around the triangular construction now, as attention was drawn from other corners of the galaxy. Along with the Ursonian Corps, a trade element grew. Where soldiers were, there was a profit to be made on extracurricular activities. Merchants peddling alcohol, tattooists, restaurants, and more popped up on the outskirts of town.

I could only imagine what the Stone Dwellers thought about this. Then, one day, I didn't have to. Aiya told me.

I had just finished a training session with Captain Akel. I was in my designated quarters preparing for a shower and a hot meal when a knock on the door came.

"Come in," I said, removing the box of water that tasted like heaven's cool touch from my mouth. "It's open."

Aiya opened the door. She was wearing a flowing orange dress that contrasted her copper skin like a dream. She stepped through the door and then closed it gently behind her. She didn't have to say much for me to realize there was something wrong. Her body language, the expression on her face—it was all worth a thousand unsaid words.

"Uh oh, what's that look for?" I asked with a raised eyebrow, trying to lighten the mood. "Did Tem get into another case of Red Bull? Talk your ear off for hours about the interweavings of stone structures in the galaxy?"

"No, no, nothing like that," Aiya answered with her best attempt at a smile. "It's the Ursonians and what's happening here."

"What's going on?" I asked, looking for a place to sit in my meager hut. The structure had been given to me by the town officials. It seemed there were many houses unoccupied now after the events of the Enzite occupation.

"These people," Aiya began, choosing her words carefully. "They're not fighters or warriors like you and me. They are mothers, fathers, farmers, and masons. They don't understand wars and politics."

I nodded along with her words, taking in the meaning of everything she was and wasn't saying.

"They're scared and not sure what's going to happen to

them," Aiya said, shaking her head. "It's so much for them to wrap their minds around. Not only is there an army of life out there in the universe, but day after day, new wonders come to meet them whether they are ready or not. First you and the Rowki, and then the Ursonian Corps, and the dozens of others flocking to the planet. When does this stop? When do they get to have their lives back?"

Aiya would never admit it, but she was talking about herself, whether she knew it or not. She was in the same boat. She had been introduced to a wondrous and terrifying new universe where anything was possible.

"Do you want the truth, or do you want me to try and make you feel better?" I asked in the kindest tone I could muster. "Because I'm sorry, Aiya, they're not the same."

Aiya, straightened slightly at my words. Caught off guard by my bluntness for a moment, she recovered quickly. "Please, be honest with me."

"I don't think life as you knew it is ever getting back to normal." I shrugged, trying to dull the blow as much as possible. "Not that I really know what normal is. You know the truth now and there's no going back. Instead of fighting the knowledge, embrace it. That's what I've done. Find comfort that there's a lot more out there to be explored, and enjoy the adventure."

"Are you enjoying the adventure?"

"Change isn't easy," I answered honestly, looking down at the many bruises across my knuckles and forearms. "But it can be good."

We stood there for a moment in silence, each shifting the invisible weight on our shoulders that this new scenario brought.

"What about you?" I asked, trying to change the subject. "Are you going back to be with your people? The

Stone Dwellers aren't part of your tribe. What about the Plains Walkers?"

Aiya shook her head slowly, staring at me with those pure white eyes of hers. "I feel called to aid in this situation in whatever way I can. I'm not sure any of this makes sense, but there is something far greater than any of us at play here, and I believe I am to play a part before this is all over."

"I think I understand."

"Do you?" Aiya asked with a hint of hope that someone might actually get what she was feeling.

"Fate, destiny, whatever you want to call it," I said, thinking back to my wife. "I don't know if I'm at the point yet to think that everything happens for a reason, but it's hard to believe in the alternative."

"What alternative?" Aiya pressed.

"That there is nothing but chance," I said, shaking my head. "I'm not sure which is better, that there is no order in how things happen and everything is pointless, or that there is a grand plan set in place and that things happen for a reason."

Images of my wife came to mind and a bad taste was left in my mouth. If things happened for a reason, then what reason was it that she had to be taken from me?

Before I could spiral down that rabbit hole, there was scratching at the door accompanied by a few heavy huffs and whimpers.

Aiya opened the door for Meatball. The little guy was growing like a super soldier. His chunky leathery body was already filling out, front and back legs beginning to elongate.

The nightmare of a creature plodded into the room, wagging his nub of a tail. He went to Aiya first, sniffing her, pink tongue lolling to the side, and did a little jump of greeting and then made his way to me.

I took a knee and rubbed the top of his head. His thick skin felt like aged leather; his batwing-like ears bent under my hand as I gave him a good scratch. Meatball leaned into me, closing his eyes and enjoying the moment.

"So, what happens next?" Aiya asked, taking a seat on the edge of my bed. "The Ursonians and the Galactic Government run tests on the portal to see if they can restart it again?"

"I guess so." I shrugged. "I'm not really involved in the strategy here. It's not exactly like Rima or Captain Akel are asking for my advice. I—"

Boom!

Before I could finish the thought, an explosion rocked the ground under my feet. Meatball jumped to attention as Aiya and I looked to one another for answers neither one of us possessed.

We ran for the door of my hut as shouts and screams ripped through the afternoon air. As soon as I ran outside, I saw a cloud of dark smoke coming from somewhere deep in the Ursonian encampment around the gateway.

The Ursonians had set up defensive fortifications around the portal and excavation site just outside the Stone Dwellers' meager town.

Huts built from stone and wood gave way to thick metal blocks that reminded me of shipping containers. Bull told me the metal pieces were made of dura steel and were easy to fabricate, while being as reliable as any piece of armor.

Aiya and I ran to the danger now as a siren pierced the air. Stone Dwellers exited their huts as well, looking first at the smoke rising to the air in gray tendrils, and then to us. I didn't have any answers to give them, so Aiya and I, with Meatball at our heels, rushed forward.

The Ursonian walls were two stories tall, with a catwalk built on the inside. I could see a pair of guards on the battlements now looking back into the encampment.

Aiya and I skidded to a halt in front of the massive metal door that led into the Ursonian camp. It was square and had to be at least ten feet tall and just as wide.

"What's going on?" Aiya yelled up to the pair of Ursonian guards. "Let us in!"

I didn't recognize either of the soldiers. There were so many Ursonians coming and going these days, it was difficult to keep track of all the new furry faces.

"Can't do that," one of the soldiers shouted back. "We're on full lockdown. All civilians are ordered to return to their homes and remain there until given further instruction."

This was it. This was my time to shine. I didn't really care about my new title as a Rowki inasmuch I never used it to gain an advantage in any situation, but maybe this was it. Maybe this was the right time to pull rank.

"Maybe you'll make an exception for the Blood Wolf," I shouted back, making use of my new nickname.

"Who?" the other Ursonian soldier called back.

"The Blood Wolf. I'm a Rowki," I shouted back, trying to keep my voice firm and in command like Rima did when talking to—well when talking to pretty much anyone.

"This pig species guy says he's a Rowki?" one of the Ursonians said more as a question than anything else to his counterpart. "You ever heard of a Bloody Wolf?"

"Blood Wolf," I corrected.

"Never heard of him," the other Ursonian answered, looking over his shoulder to the inside of the compound where shouts and orders rang out. He turned back to me.

"Listen, we've got some serious matters going on here, so if you're done, return home. We'll get this figured out."

I knew Meatball couldn't really laugh—he was an animal after all—but I swore a deep chuckle came from the beast now. I looked down at him with a scowl. Immediately, he stopped and coughed, which led me to believe that he actually was laughing at me.

I straightened my posture, puffed out my chest, and fixed the pair of Ursonian guards with my best Rima Noble impression.

"I'm not trying to get anyone in trouble here, but we can help," I said in a commanding tone, or at least what sounded like a commanding tone in my ears. "But if you don't open this door right now, I'll have to inform Captain Akel."

The Ursonians on the gate smirked and were about to say something when their appearances changed drastically. From a bit annoyed to exasperated, they turned to surprised and even scared.

"Doors are opening now," one of them said, fumbling for the controls in front of him.

"Please come right in," the other Ursonian soldier sputtered.

I let out a big sigh I didn't know I was holding in. The square metal door in front of me began to slide open with a hiss of hidden hydraulics. I looked over to Aiya. "See, sometimes you just need to—"

Rima brushed past me on my right, not breaking stride and heading straight for the Ursonian encampment. Both Ursonians on the gate were already on the ground level to greet her.

"Rowki Noble," one of them said with a smart salute.

"I think maybe they opened the door for Rima and not

for you," Aiya said as if I were slow and not getting what was taking place here.

Meatball chuckled again.

"I know—I know," I muttered, following Rima inside. "Come on."

We entered the Ursonian compound set around the excavation site. It was really amazing what the Ursonians had done with the space in such a short time. Barracks had been constructed along the right side of the enclosed area along with mess halls, a docking bay for ships and of course, the portal site itself to the rear.

Whatever had caused the explosion was coming from the portal. The dark smoke lifting to the clear warm sky was mostly gone now. A heavy Ursonian element surrounded the portal.

It was difficult to see much around the massive bear soldiers armored and ready for a fight. A large group of them were near the portal, looking for something or someone to hold responsible now that the immediate danger of a fire was off the table.

"What's going on?" Aiya asked Rima as we reached those gathered.

"I'm not sure, but we're going to find out," Rima answered.

The portal's outer border, which looked like a triangle, was charred but undamaged at its right base. Whatever had happened, it had happened to the portal itself.

"Understood," a familiar voice said from behind me. "No casualties; they were going after the gateway, not us. At least this time it wasn't us."

I turned around to see Lieutenant Ero talking into her comm. She carried an unused medical bag in her right hand.

"What happened?" Rima asked before I could get the same words out.

"We were attacked," Ero answered, shaking her head as if she too were still trying to figure out how it happened. "Early reports are no casualties on our side, but someone saw an Enzite sneak over the wall."

"An Enzite?" I asked. "I thought they were all captured or killed."

"Apparently not," Ero said, going over to the charred spot at the base of the gateway. She leaned down to pick up what looked like an overcooked finger. "We routed them and they fled into the forest. Maybe a few are still hanging around, biding their time to suicide bomb the structure."

"Why would they want to destroy it?" Aiya asked. "Didn't they say this was a weapon they wanted to use?"

"Why indeed," Rima mused.

A cold chill touched my spine as I stared at the portal and then over the wall to the forest beyond. I felt eyes watching me, a sixth sense telling me I wasn't alone.

The portal projected a coldness, if that feeling was even possible coming from an inanimate object. Being watched wasn't a sensation I had felt often, but I swore out there over the wall and in the dense forest, we were being measured.

"There could be more Enzites in the forest just biding their time," Rima said, following my gaze. She must have felt it too. "If they are cut off from their faction, perhaps desperation is leading them toward this course of action. The age-old thinking that if they can't have the gateway, no one can."

Before any more speculation could take place, the Ursonian soldiers parted ranks to allow Captain Akel in. The colossal bear man nodded in our direction before looking over the damage. Ero handed him the bit of charred finger.

Akel looked pissed. I was glad at that moment that I was on the side of the thousand-pound bear people and not one of the Enzites in the forest.

Captain Akel glanced at Rima and Ero before forming hand gestures that started with what looked like him giving them the finger and ended with a knife hand toward a structure to the right of the Ursonian compound.

They nodded and together followed the captain toward the designated building.

"Would anyone like to share with the rest of the class what's going on here?" I asked. "I didn't get—"

"I'm here, I'm here," a small figure yelled across the encampment. Tem was running out of breath, the little historian's floating black camera trailing behind him. "What —what did I miss?"

I thought it was sweat at first but then realized Tem was wet. Not just was he wet, but a towel was wrapped around the lower half of his waist and he was nude from that point up.

And just when I didn't think I could be more confused, Tem's towel fell.

FORTY-ONE

TO SAY I was puzzled would be a drastic misrepresentation of the word. I didn't want to see what I saw, trust me, but before I could look away, my eyes went through a crash course of the anatomy of a male Ublec.

"What in the name of the Maker," Ero said under her breath.

"Why?" Aiya sighed.

"Oh my," Tem said, skidding to a halt and then doubling back to bend from the waist, exposing his rear to pick up his towel.

I felt sick.

Tem finally joined our party, heading for the communication building, still securing his towel around his waist. "I heard the explosion while I was doing some—personal washing and grooming. I came as fast as I could."

"You really didn't have to," Rima told him. "You could have taken an extra minute to put on some clothes.

"Why, Rima Noble," Tem said, aghast. "You of all people should know I am a professional. As soon as I heard the explosion, it was my sworn duty to come and support the Rowki and document the incident."

"Why didn't I look away," I said under my breath. "I should have just looked away."

Thankfully, before we had to continue down the thought process of what we had all just seen, we reached the communication building. The building, like the rest of the compound, was made from the thick, slate gray dura steel crates. Captain Akel pressed his paw to the door. It opened on command.

Inside, the room, like much of the Ursonian structures, was immense. Another pair of soldiers saluted as we walked in. The room was open, with an army of soldiers seated and working at various control stations. Each control station had its own holographic screen the Ursonian soldiers navigated, pressing commands and scrolling through information.

I saw our buddy Ted near the front of the room. He sat with his back toward us, leaning over his control station. He maneuvered around his holographic screen so fast, it was a wonder he knew what commands he was pressing.

He had to have heard us coming, but he was so entranced in his work, he didn't budge until Captain Akel stood next to him. Ted stopped and stood, ready to salute. Captain Akel placed a hand on his shoulder as if he were allowing him to ignore the formality in light of the current situation.

Instead of words, the silent captain pointed to the screens in front of Ted and shrugged as if he were asking *What happened?*

"Right," Ted said, adjusting the goggles over his face that made his eyes look twice as large. "As soon as the reports came in of the explosion, I had my team go to work," Ted explained as he returned to his near magical movements of the screens in front of him. He brought up a recording of the view of the triangle-shaped gateway and then zoomed in to the right bottom of the gateway's frame where the explosion had taken place.

We all watched on with bated breath as we witnessed a figure crawling on its belly toward the portal.

Ted zoomed in. Most cameras I had seen when zoomed in lost their quality. This camera, when enhanced, was just as clear and crisp as ever. An Enzite soldier painted with who knew what over its body to match the terrain was barely visible. It carried something shaped like a football in its right hand.

The insect-like Enzite moved inch by inch until it was near the base of the gateway and then, without a second's hesitation, detonated the bomb, sending itself to kingdom come.

I'd heard of suicide bombers, but they always seemed so far away. To see one at your doorstep was something else entirely. There was no hesitation or second thought. As soon as the Enzite reached its destination, it detonated the bomb as easily as if it were pressing the snooze button on its alarm clock.

But these Enzites probably didn't have alarm clocks. They were awakened each morning by their need to kill and maim.

Captain Akel reached for one of the windows in front of Ted, dragging it through the air to stand in front of him. He then brought up the holographic keyboard and started typing in commands.

The captain searched the video files for angles on either side of the gateway and behind it. I knew he wanted to uncover how the Enzite had managed to get into the compound in the first place.

A myriad of cameras and angles popped up in front of us, tracking from that morning to the afternoon.

"There, right there!" Aiya said, pointing a finger to a screen in the upper left hand corner. "Can you rewind it?"

Ted jumped into action, enlarging the window and then rewinding it like Aiya asked. We all saw it. The ever so slight movement of the Enzite cresting and then lowering itself over the wall as the sun rose. He was nearly impossible to see with his camouflage. Paired with the rising of the suns, he would be invisible to anyone unless they were standing at the very spot where he climbed over the wall.

"They'll send more," Rima said as much to herself as anyone else. "Once they know they can't destroy the gate, then they'll try to start killing us."

"We have to go after them," Aiya said firmly. "There can't be many left that escaped into the jungle, maybe a dozen? Two dozen at the most?"

All eyes swung to Captain Akel, who nodded and then went through a series of hand gestures that ended with a pointer finger across his throat. I wasn't privy to the language he used, but it seemed there was a universal sign for killing someone.

"I'll have Sergeant Bull put together a hunting team," Lieutenant Ero answered, already turning to go. "I can have them ready to depart within the hour."

Captain Akel nodded.

"Oh my, I still have to finish my cleaning program," Tem said, hugging the towel around his waist. "Within the hour?"

"The Rowki will go as well," Rima stated with no room in her words for question.

"And me," Aiya joined in.

"This is a matter for the Galactic Government," Rima

said with a shake of her head. "The Ursonians act as the hammer, the Rowki the tip of the spear. Leave this to us."

"This is my home," Aiya said without backing down. "They came to my home, enslaved the tribe right next to mine. It could have very easily been my tribe. I'm not going to sit by and watch. I'm going with you."

For a moment, I thought the women were going to come to blows, again.

"Well, let's remember who we're fighting here," I said, placing myself between the pair of warriors. "Rima, maybe it would be good to have someone who knows the general terrain? You're always telling me to be prepared, or was that the Boy Scouts?"

"I know nothing of your scouts of boys, pervert," Rima said with a lifted eyebrow. "But if Aiya agrees to let us take the lead, I see value in having someone familiar with the terrain."

"There's not a better tracker in my village," Aiya said, looking at me, disgusted. "You should not speak of scouts of boys in such a way."

"What? No, it's a group, like a club of boys that learn valuable life skills. It's nothing weird," I told them.

"It sounds wrong to me," Tem said, shaking his head. "Perhaps an appointment with a psychologist would help."

"I'm fine," I told them, shaking my head at how sideways this conversation had gone. "Let's be ready to go in an hour. We have an Enzite faction to track."

The next hour was full of prep work. Armor and weapons checks, to food and water. The suns were already setting. That meant another trek into the alien landscape at night.

Now that the *Oni* was in orbit, I used my truck as a staging area for my gear. My truck was parked inside the

Ursonian defensive encampment, and to my relief, on the opposite side of the excavation site from where the attack had taken place.

The inside of my truck, normally filled with to-go wrappers and dirty clothes, was beginning to take on a different appearance altogether. Like me, my truck was beginning to change. There was no need for things like food or clothing in my rig since they were provided for me now. Instead, I used the space to store my armor and weapons.

Plus it kind of made me feel like a bad-ass to have the armor and weapons in my truck. It was like my very own Batcave or secret headquarters; you know, like the ones where the hero presses a button and the bookcase moves and slides around to reveal an assortment of weaponry.

As far as weaponry went, all I had was my blasting staff at the moment, but hey, I needed to start somewhere. I mean, even Superman's Fortress of Solitude began as a hunk of ice.

I grabbed my armor and my blasting staff and stepped outside to dress. Meatball followed me, going around to the rear of the truck and whining while he scratched at the closed doors.

I wasn't positive what kind of nose he had, but it had to be something next level if he could smell through the closed doors and packaging to whatever food had caught his attention.

"Wolfhounds are known for their noses," Aiya said, approaching me in hard leather armor so different from our own. She wore it tight-fitted and it breathed a lot easier than our synth suits and dura steel armor plating. "She's an insistent one, isn't she?"

"She?" I asked, glancing over to Meatball as I shrugged on my chest armor. "Meatball is a boy."

"I'm not sure how much of an anatomy class you need, but Meatball is very much a girl and not one of your scouts of boys," Aiya answered, picking Meatball up and showing me what she was talking about.

"Oh, right," I said, shaking my head. "Okay, okay, I believe you."

"We're moving in ten," Rima said, ignoring Aiya and looking at me. "You wearing a helmet this time?"

"Is that like a trick question?" I asked, remembering Rima always wore her hood. "Why don't you use a helmet?"

"It would be beneficial for you since you're still so new," Rima said, ignoring my question. "Get something in your stomach now. We'll take rations with us, but we didn't do our job well if this takes until morning."

Rima finally looked over to Aiya and her armor with an approving nod and then left.

"Is she always like that?" Aiya asked.

"Actually, I think she's in a good mood," I said, going over to my truck and placing the helmet on my magnetic belt opposite my blasting staff.

Aiya, Meatball, and I made our way to the mess hall for a quick bite. Unlike the *Oni* mess hall, this one was staffed by a crew of Ursonians working behind a buffet counter filling trays of food as soldiers ran through the line.

"What will it be?" the Ursonian behind the counter of food asked before looking up. When she did look up and our eyes locked, her jaw dropped. "Oh, oh my, I heard there was a new Rowki, but I didn't—I didn't expect to see you myself."

The Ursonian sneezed, spraying mucus all over the food in front of her. She didn't seem fazed in the least, grabbing for a dirty towel on her apron and wiping her nose and hands before replacing the towel and gripping a serving utensil with her hand.

"Please, what can I get you?" she asked eagerly.

Half of me was grossed out at the display of mucus, but the other half realized I had a golden opportunity here. Neither Tem nor Rima were present to remind me of my designated meal plan. I could go buck wild.

"Whatever's the most unhealthy thing you have to eat," I told her, eyeing the dishes in front of me of who knew what. I searched in vain for something that looked like cheese, bread, or sugar. "What's that over there?"

"Oh, goulash surprise," the helpful Ursonian offered with a wag of her eyebrows. "Here, have a double serving."

She ladled on the stuff and then added scoops from two other steaming plates. I wasn't really sure what I was eating, but it smelled great and looked full of carbs and fat, so I was in.

Aiya followed behind me, more selective in her food choices.

We found the first unoccupied bench and went to town. Whatever goulash surprise was, it tasted like cheesy stuffing and I was on board with that. Meatball sat her chunky little self down beside me, wagging her nub and licking her stubby teeth, which protruded from her lips.

I ran over to the bin of trays and scooped some of my food portion onto the tray for Meatball, who attacked the food with zeal.

Aiya, Meatball, and I spent the next few minutes eating in peace. If I'd known what waited for us that night, I wouldn't have rushed through our meal.

FORTY-TWO

WE LEFT as the suns disappeared over the horizon. Lieutenant Ero had put together a squad of ten Ursonians that included Bull and Captain Akel. The other seven soldiers were ones I recognized in the day to day movement around the facility. I remembered seeing them because of the scars they all carried, across their knuckles, snouts, and faces.

These weren't new Ursonian recruits, these were trained killers, and I was glad they were going to be on our side of the fight. We set off together, the unit of Ursonian elite, two Rowki, a historian, Aiya, and Meatball.

Aiya wasn't kidding when she said she could track. She took the lead along with an Ursonian named Artio.

Rima, Tem, Meatball, and I traveled in the middle of the pack. This part of the planet of Ivandor was more forest and rock than jungle. I thought it might be a welcome change from the dense jungle that we had moved through when we first arrived, however, it presented its own problems.

Night calls from nocturnal predators echoed through

the trees. Yes, there was more room to move, but visibility was minimal, thanks to the way the trees rose to the heavens and blotted out the sky.

I had no idea what trail we were following; the ground all looked the same to me. Blasting staff on my right hip and helmet on my left, we traveled deeper into the nightmarish woods.

"When the world of men stands defenseless against the dark, send me. When the Ancient Ones come to reclaim their throne, send me. When all hope is lost and no one can see the way, send me. And when the Light trembles to regain its feet, who will go? Send me," Rima said slowly to herself.

She caught my eye before I could look away.

"It helps center me at times," Rima answered my unspoken question. "The creed is one I have sworn my life to."

"I get it," I whispered back. "It's starting to make more sense to me now."

"How so?"

"I've seen a lot of bad, but not what I'd call pure evil," I said, thinking out loud as I recalled images of the suicide bomber. "He didn't hesitate to blow himself to kingdom come. There's no doubt in my mind the other members of the Enzite Federation feel the same way."

"What you say is true, Max Tyco," Tem answered, walking on my right. "But we must not confuse the Enzite race as a whole with the faction known as the Enzite Federation. There are many Enzites of the Enzite Empire who have given their own lives fighting their Enzite Federation counterparts."

"Still, what you say about the Enzites we hunt this night is true," Rima added. "They are committed and beyond reason. If you have the chance, you kill first, or they will without a doubt kill you. Do you understand?"

"I do," I answered, still wrapping my mind around the idea of killing another being. In the moment, it was instinct and self-preservation; it was me or them. But when the cries of battle faded and I was left to my thoughts, that was when the real question of whether I was doing the right thing plagued my mind.

But you are doing the right thing, I reminded myself. *You've seen what the Enzite Federation is doing. You've seen them enslave, torture, and knowingly suicide bomb their own. How could stopping them be bad?*

We traveled with minimal talking for what felt like an hour, heading ever deeper into the forest and toward a slight incline up one of the many mountains that jutted every so often over the tops of the trees.

With each step, I felt my resolve growing. We were on the right side of this. I was on the right side of this. I understood how important the Rowki were if they were the ones to put an end to the evil that existed in the galaxy, like the Enzite Federation.

While I was wrapped up in thought, the column came to a halt. Rima and I crouched low along with the others, waiting to see why we had stopped. Meatball sniffed the air greedily, her stubby tail going rigid.

Something whipped through the air. A small craft hovered over us. All weapons raised to meet this new threat. My hand reached for my blasting staff, and in one smooth move, had the business end pointed at the craft.

It was silver, smaller than my truck, with short wings and a cockpit that couldn't fit more than one, two at the most. I had seen enough Ursonian spacecraft to know this wasn't one of theirs. My only guess was that it was a lone

Enzite fighter that had somehow managed to remain hidden.

I braced for the moment to shatter in dozens of rounds from the Ursonian Mauler T-19's as they opened fire on the craft, but they never got the chance.

"Stop, hold your fire," Rima said in a voice that wasn't a shout, but carried all the weight of one. "He's one of ours."

My muscles relaxed and shoulders dropped as the ship lowered to the ground. The wings folded on either side of the ship as thrusters supported its descent between a pair of trees.

"Negative; it's a friendly," Ero said into her comm channel, coming up beside us more than a bit peeved. "Rima, who is this? We could have shot him down. Razors were already scrambling to intercept."

"He's Rowki," Rima answered, sounding just as frustrated herself. "The High Council said they might send reinforcements, but there was never any confirmation or I would have told you."

A hiss spewed from the cockpit of the ship as a figure stepped out. He wore a long jacket, and handles to a pair of blades rested on his hips like a cowboy would wear his pistols. If he was worried that he might have scared us he didn't show it. He walked like a man who had traveled a million miles, his gait sure yet tired.

When he came into the light, what stood before me was another human. Or at least what looked like another human, if humans had deep blue skin. I could guess he was in his fifties, with dark salt-and-pepper hair. His eyes twinkled: one part mischievous, one part—okay maybe two parts mischievous.

"Rima," the man said, coming over to us and looking over our party. "So, who are we supposed to kill today?"

"Geister," Rima said, barely audible. "You know the rules. You should have radioed ahead."

"Oh, did I forget to?" Geister asked with a shrug. "I thought the council was going to do that. I swore they'd let you know. So, what are we doing today? Putting down another insurrection, protecting a political asset? It must be important for the council to have sent me when you were already here. You know how thin the Rowki are spread."

Captain Akel joined us before Rima could answer. He looked pissed. I didn't need any sign language to tell me that. The mammoth bear wore it all over his face.

"Akel, it's great to see you again." Geister waved and offered a hand. "When did we serve together last? Oh, right, pinned down by the Grogian militia on Amperstand, wasn't it? Fun times."

Akel shook his head with a sigh of forgiveness only brought on by spilling blood with one another. He offered Geister a paw in greeting.

Geister took it before Akel signed a few more motions I didn't catch.

"Don't worry, don't worry, I did a high-altitude scan coming in," Geister said, both hands up and pointed to Akel. "The group you're hunting didn't see me coming in. They're still a good three miles east. My scanners picked up at least two dozen of them."

A few of the Ursonians huffed, but this seemed enough to put the captain at ease. He nodded and then regrouped with Ero to plan their next move.

"And you must be the new recruit," Geister said, offering a hand. "I've heard some pretty horrible things about you in the reports."

"What? What did you hear?" I asked, looking between

Rima and Tem for answers. Tem looked away and whistled a low tune, rocking back on his heels and toes.

"We logged your progress from day one," Rima answered honestly. "I was truthful. You weren't much to see."

"Well, why don't you just tell me the truth," I said sarcastically. "Don't hold back, Rima. Tell me how you really feel."

Rima ignored me, turning back to Geister. "Where is your historian? Is she still in the ship?"

"Oh, yes. Weren't you assigned Trek Alan?" Tem asked, hopeful to see another of his order. "She was so excited to be paired with you. It was to be her first assignment. I have not heard from her in some time."

"She's dead," Geister said, reaching inside his coat for a silver flask. He took a long pull. "Died trying to protect a family on some god forsaken rock. I can't even remember the name."

"Oh," Tem said, lowering his eyes to the ground. "I—I didn't know."

"We should move. If what this Rowki says is true, then we'll be there soon," Ero ordered, waving us forward. "We'll take them in the night."

Our column moved on with more questions than answers. I didn't know what meeting a new Rowki would feel like, but this wasn't what I'd expected. Geister was, well he seemed normal. Not heroic or all powerful, or even tough as nails like Rima. He was just a guy, a guy trying to do the right thing like me.

Rima hadn't seemed overjoyed to see him either. Neither did she try to make small talk with him now. It wasn't her way.

Geister, on the other hand, had no problem with talking

as we moved through the night. He and Tem were carrying on a conversation I joined.

"Enzite Federation again, huh?" Geister asked the historian. "What are they doing this time? Cloning, creating super soldiers, portals to another world?"

"At least two out of the three," Tem said, trying his best to get over the news of the death of his friend. "They tortured the local species and found a gateway they tried to open here."

"A gateway," Geister said, playing with the words as if he had never heard them before. "A gateway in the oldest galaxy on the oldest planet."

"They went on about releasing the Eternals or some gods they worship," I added, trying to be helpful. "It almost worked; there was something on the other side of the portal, but it closed before they could get out."

A look of realization passed over Geister's face. He was about to say something when the party halted again and word was sent down from the front. We had arrived.

FORTY-THREE

THE DARKNESS WAS TOTAL NOW, save for the giant moons and many stars that twinkled from above. The forest area was still dense, but more bushes and shrubs dotted the landscape now with the occasional rock outcropping.

Rima and I, along with Geister, moved to the front of the party to see what we could. Aiya, Captain Akel, and Ero lay on their bellies or crouched as they looked out over a slight drop-off. Beyond that and through the trees, I caught movement and the orange glow of a fire.

The wind carried faint voices from those gathered. I could see the occasional movement past the trees; any more than that was lost to sight.

"Sentries on either side of the camp," Aiya breathed, looking to the right and left.

I didn't see anything, but apparently I was the only one, as both Rowki and Ursonians nodded.

Captain Akel performed hand motions, relaying the plan to his second in command.

"Rowki will remove the sentries," Ero translated for the rest of us. "The Ursonian Corps will move in from the west and take as many of them alive as we can. It's time to get some answers."

"Or we can just kill them all," Geister said, taking another pull from his canteen. We all stared at him. "What? I don't have enough to share or else I'd offer you all some."

"That plan is acceptable," Rima said, looking at me and then Geister. "Geister, take the sentry on the left. Tyco, you and I will take the one on the right."

Geister nodded before walking backward and disappearing into the shadows. Rima motioned to me to follow and we moved around the right side of the encampment.

Before I left, I looked Meatball in the eyes with the best stern whisper I could muster. "Stay, stay with Tem. I'll be right back."

I don't know how much Meatball got, or maybe she just wanted to stay with Tem anyway, but she waddled over to the historian and sat at his feet.

Rima moved quietly through the night in a large half circle around the right side of the Enzite encampment. I tried stepping where she stepped and moving just as quietly as she did, but she was a pro with years, maybe decades of experience. I was a truck driver. I knew how to navigate around lot lizards and the I-10.

I made a wrong move and cracked a tree branch. I knew the noise was minimal at most, but it still sounded like a firework exploding in my ears. Rima looked over her shoulder, annoyed.

I mouthed the word *sorry*.

We moved forward, always keeping our unexpected enemy to the left of us. When we had circled enough to satisfy Rima, we moved in. I didn't see our intended target at first, but a few yards in, I saw the silhouette of a figure sitting on a low tree branch.

We were on his left now as he gazed out into the forest depths. Even in the darkness, the fact that it was an Enzite was easy to see. The large black eyes, the protruding mandibles, and the boney exoskeleton were enough for me.

Rima took the lead once more. Low to the ground, she silently unsheathed her weapon. The sardonium imbued in her blade flashed bright right before it flew through the air, impaling itself in the forehead of our enemy.

The last thing the poor SOB saw was literally a flash of white. As easily as she sent the weapon forward, Rima called it back with a thought. It flew to her hand. The dead Enzite slumped backward into the tree, sitting there as if he were still awake and on watch.

Rima motioned me forward. Blasting staff in hand, I followed. We crested the copse of trees in front of us to see an area leveled out and cleared of trees or brush about twenty yards wide. Crude lean-tos made of wood surrounded a fire in the middle. Geister was right: there had to be almost two dozen Enzite Federation soldiers, all in various stages of sleep. Most were already sleeping, but a few stood by the fire. Others played with cards against a crate.

While they were far from fully supplied, it seemed they had managed to take a few buckets of rations and ammunition with them on the run. No doubt they planned to play guerrilla tactics until their reinforcements arrived.

Across the fire and into the far side of the trees, I saw Geister appear in his long coat and then disappear so fast, I had to question if he really had been there at all.

"That's the signal," Rima said as a bird hooted in the night. "Get ready."

Rima made the same bird call that sounded like an Earth owl. The night noise didn't seem to interest the

Enzite soldiers, and why should it? Through the night, there had been various bird calls and the chitter of different nocturnal animals.

Something was off; I felt it as Ero called over the comm channel in our ear.

"Ready to engage," Ero said.

I didn't know what it was. I wasn't sure what I felt. Rima was going to need something more than a feeling from me if she was going to step in and call this off. But what was it? What was off? What felt so wrong?

I searched the Enzite soldiers in front of us, realizing too late what seemed wrong. While yes, there were soldiers milling about the camp, most of the soldiers were asleep. Their armor showed around blankets and just inside the lean-tos, but there was no movement. There was no snoring or heavy breathing. Besides the five Enzites moving around, it was quiet.

"Rima," I hissed in her ear. "Rima, it's a trap."

Rima looked over her shoulder, about to tell me to shut my trap. The panic on my face made her rethink her words. "What?" she asked instead of snapping at me. "What are you talking about?"

"The soldiers, the ones sleeping; there's no sound, no movement from them. It's a trap," I said, staring into the camp, now more sure than ever I was right. "Call the Ursonians off."

Rima's head snapped back so she could get another look at the camp.

"Stand by, contact in ten seconds," Ero said over the comm channel.

"Rima," I warned.

"Stand down," Rima said in her comm. "I repeat, stand down. Something's not right."

"Repeat? Rima?" Ero asked.

"She's right," Geister said over his radio. "Something's off. Let us go in first."

I mentally kicked myself right then. Of course the Rowki would be the ones to go first if there was indeed something off.

You just had to go on and open your big mouth, I chided myself. *Good one, Max. Way to go.*

"Understood," Ero replied. "Standing by."

"Well, shall we do this?" Geister asked. "I'm not getting any younger. Remember the Planes of Oblivion?"

"I do and, no, let's not do the Planes of Oblivion again," Rima growled. "That ended horribly."

"Sorry, you're cutting out; you said yes to the Planes of Oblivion?" Geister pushed. "I'll go in first."

"No—I—" Rima said, cutting off the rest of her reply, understanding that Geister was beyond reasoning with. "Curse you, Geister."

"What's the Planes of Oblivion?" I asked, eager to see how deep we were in it. "Is it bad? It's bad, isn't it?"

"It's not good," Rima said right before Geister blew his cover and walked right into the middle of the Enzite camp.

"Enzite brothers and sisters you heard of our lord and savior, the tentacled one?" Geister asked, stepping into the camp. He held both hands up beside his head in the air.

In seconds, five blasters were pointed at his chest. But only five. None of the supposed sleeping Enzites moved, just the ones that had been playing cards and patrolling the camp.

"Who are you?" one of the Enzites shouted. "Hands up."

"My hands are up," Geister replied. "They couldn't be

any more up. I'm going to go out on a limb and say you're not the one in charge here. Am I right?"

The Enzite soldier's mandibles clicked nervously. He looked to his right and left, unsure.

"It's okay, there's no shame in that," Geister said with a reassuring smile. "We can't all be the hammers. Some of us have to be the nails."

"It's a trap," Rima said to me and in her comm. "Scout the surrounding area. The rest of the Enzites have to be close. There are only five currently in the camp."

Geister whistled at the Enzite who was clearly not in charge. "Yoo hoo, hey, can I put my arms down now? I've had a long day and they're starting to get tired."

The Enzite nodded as if he were about to comply then thought twice about it and sneered two words to the other four soldiers. "Kill him."

Rima bolted from her position beside me so fast, I almost tripped trying to keep up with her. Two of the Enzite soldiers pivoted to train their weapons on us as the other three opened fire on Geister.

Geister was as quick on the draw as anyone I had ever seen. A pair of knives zipped through the air like arrows, impaling themselves on two of the guards.

Dark bolts of black laser beams peppered Rima and me. I returned fire with my blasting staff. The weapon kicked in my hand, but my aim was true, striking one of the soldiers in the chest.

Ero yelled something in my comm that sounded like, "You're surrounded," over the sound of the weapons fire being exchanged. My mind couldn't process the words fast enough, but my eyes tracked the shadows as they converged. Enzite soldiers smeared in mud and cloaked in the shadows fell on us.

I saw Rima go down under an onslaught of weapons fire. Geister was lost to view. Pain hit me like a heavyweight boxer smashing his fist into first my chest and then my left leg, sending me down to a knee.

Black tendrils sought to rip away my view of the world around me. We were exposed and out in the open. Why did I never wear my helmet? I was definitely going to start wearing my helmet wherever I went from now on.

A roar that shook the ground underneath me tremored outward as the Ursonian Corps joined the fight. Unlike the first time, this time, we were outnumbered and ambushed.

My vision cleared enough for me to see the Enzites clear the way for the Ursonians to rush in and then close their outer circle again.

"Max!" Aiya yelled, skidding to my side. "Max, are you okay?"

"I, I think so," I lied, reaching for my right leg. My hand came back bloody. "Rima?!"

I looked over to my right to see the Rowki Guardian on her hands and knees. She was bleeding from a wound on her side, but at least she was moving. Her sword shone in her hands like a beacon of hope in the night.

Screams of the dying and wounded Enzites, roars from the Ursonians doing the same ripped through the night. No, this was not like the first fight at all. We were the ones on the ropes this time.

Aiya helped me over to the right side of the camp. We took cover behind one of the many wooden lean-tos the Enzites had constructed in their fake camp. All around me, the fight raged on. Rima bled furiously from a gut shot. Both Ero and Geister were with her. Bull and Captain Akel were in charge of the unit now as the tank-like Ursonians regrouped, reloaded, and redeployed out into the field.

At the moment, we were surrounded by nearly invisible enemies camouflaged in the dark forest interior. We would have been swiss cheese already had it not been for our armor. The Ursonians were walking battle tanks, their armor accepting the punishment with not much more than a scratch or a dent in the metal to show anything had happened at all.

But even the strongest steel weakened over time. Captain Akel wasn't about to give the Enzites the time they needed to use them as target practice.

"Rawww!" Captain Akel bellowed, lifting his right hand into the night air that carried his Mauler T-19. With quick precision, he motioned with his left hand. Even as he did so, rounds from the Enzite pulse rifles found him and battered across his chest plate and helmet.

Captain Akel remained unfazed as he thundered again. This time, howls from the Ursonians in the hunting party returned the roar. As one, they advanced into the darkness. It was a test of sheer massive durability versus stealth and cover.

"Can you walk?" Aiya asked, looking down at my leg.

I followed her gaze down to my right thigh where the dura steel armor connected to my synth suit. One of the Enzite rounds had found its way to the left side of the armor and scorched my leg. It wasn't anything life-threatening, but it didn't feel great either.

"I'm fine," I lied, pushing pain out of my head and running over to Rima. I did my best not to limp to show Aiya I meant what I said.

"Stop gawking over me," Rima was saying to Geister and Ero as I approached. "I'm fine. Get me back into the fight."

I was no doctor, but it was clear to even me that Rima

was very far from fine. The right side of her stomach was a mess of blood and char. Ero worked on her, injecting her with a vial of nanobots and applying skin spray to the exterior of the wound.

"I can give you something for the pain," Ero said, reaching into her medical bag.

Rima grunted. She pushed the Ursonian off, fighting to her feet. "I told you I'm fine. Drugs will only cloud my head. I can't have that now."

I always had respect for Rima, but that feeling in my heart only grew as I witnessed the warrior shake off the serious wound and look toward the fight.

"Go, go, I'm fine," Rima said, reaching for her blade. She looked at me. "Go. If I have to tell you again, I'm going to kill you myself."

Rima's warning and Tem's voice in my ear were enough to shake me from my shocked trance.

"I thought I was in the rear of this fight, but they're in the forest," Tem squeaked. "Why does this always happen to me?"

"We're coming, buddy," I said. "Stay where you are. We're on our way."

"Use the waypoint in your helmet," Tem whispered. "I think they can hear me. I—Ahhhh!"

Tem's voice trailed off in a strangled scream.

"Tem! Tem, can you hear me?" I asked.

Nothing.

"Let's go!" I shouted to Aiya, slamming my helmet on my head. Over the training I'd had since we secured the excavation site, I had also had time to explore the many uses of the helmet. I cursed myself for not always wearing it now.

The heads-up display in the helmet showed a readout of

the terrain, provided night vision, and also marked friend-
lies on the map with green dots. I searched the display to
find the little green dot that read "Tem."

There it was, ahead and to my left. I took the lead with
Aiya beside me. We crashed into the fray of Enzite and
Ursonian conflict, helping where we could but always
heading deeper into the forest toward Tem.

Pain was a secondary thought as my injured leg
screamed at me to stop and threatened to buckle. I crashed
deeper into the nighttime foliage, my heads-up display
painting everything in a bright green. I nearly ran right into
an Enzite soldier so fully camouflaged, he looked like he
was part of the forest itself.

Okay, that might have been a lie. I did run headfirst into
an Enzite soldier. But seriously, can you blame me? These
guys were as good as any professional cosplayer you'd see.
You know, the ones who get the makeup perfectly and look
just like the character they are trying to portray?

I crashed into him and we went down together. Scrambling to my feet, I reached for my blasting staff, too late.
The Enzite Soldier was on his knees, aiming his weapon at
me point blank. I had yet to see how dura steel would hold
up at this close of a range. I guessed I was about to
find out.

Vroom, vroom, vroom!

A volley of dark laser rounds pummeled the Enzite,
chewing him up from his torso to his skull. The Enzite
soldier shuddered then slumped over dead.

Aiya skidded to a halt beside me, an Enzite pulse rifle in
her hand. "I feel like I was just asking you this, but are you
okay? You've got to stop putting yourself in harm's way like
this. One of these days, I'm not going to be here to save
you."

It was crazy to think that something as beautiful as Aiya could be so deadly.

"Why are you looking at me like that?" Aiya asked, leaning in closer to get a look at my eyes through my visor. "Max, Max, are you in shock? By the gods, are you hit, again?"

"No, no I'm good, I'm good," I said, rising to my feet with a wince. "Thanks for the help. Come on; we've got to find Tem."

We continued our night run through the dark forest. I crashed into a clearing where an Ursonian struggled to get an Enzite off its back. The much smaller species hooked a blaster lengthwise under the great bear's chin in an attempt to strangle it to death.

Not on my watch.

Without pausing to slow my run, I aimed and fired my blasting staff at the alien's head. A red light erupted, and where the Enzite's skull had been a moment before, only red vapor and bone fragments remained.

The Ursonian fell to all fours, coughing. "Blood Wolf," the Ursonian managed to hack out in thanks before I was gone again.

Aiya and I finally reached the waypoint in my helmet where Tem was supposed to be. It was near a cliff where a group of trees gave way to a short clearing and the edge of the cliff beyond.

Tem lay slumped on the ground, his little black floating camera broken beside him. There was no sign of Meatball.

I skidded to my knees, my heart seizing in my chest.

"Tem, Tem, talk to me, are you okay? Please be okay," I begged, gently rolling Tem's little body over and into my lap.

A gash over his left eyebrow showed where the damage

had been done. But he was breathing and even blinked his eyes open as I called his name.

"Max? Max Tyco, am I dead? Are we both dead?" Tem wondered in awe.

"Sorry, no such luck," I told him. "I guess our job's not done yet. What happened? Can you move?"

"An Enzite, a big one with armor and rank on his chest that led me to believe he was their leader, ambushed me," Tem said, sitting up with a wince. "Meatball attacked him, but then I don't know what happened. I didn't realize the conflict would spill so deep into the forest or I would have taken greater care to ensure more distance between myself and the battle."

"Just take a seat, take it easy," I told him, showing my lack of proper first aid training. "We'll get Ero or someone with medical training here to get you checked out. I'm just glad you're okay."

Thus far, as I talked to Tem, Aiya stood with her back toward us and the edge of the cliff, looking back into the forest. Her body tensed, which made me look at her and then the black forest beyond.

"What is it?" I asked.

Aiya lifted her rifle to the trees, craning her neck forward to see more. "Why did he leave Tem alive?"

"I don't know, maybe he thought Tem was dead or not worth his time," I suggested.

"Hey," Tem grunted indignantly.

"Sorry," I offered.

"Maybe, but what if he knew he was still alive and let him live for bait?" Aiya asked without taking her eyes off the tree line.

The hairs on the back of my neck lifted as I witnessed a shadow emerge from my peripheral vision. I was turned, looking to the tree line with Aiya at the moment, but that was not where the shadow emerged. Something big pulled itself up over the edge of the cliff.

"Aiya, behind us!" I shouted too late.

The Enzite pulled himself over the edge of the cliff where he had been hiding. He sprinted toward us at full stride.

I rose from tending to Tem as the Enzite smashed a fist into the back of Aiya's head. She slumped without a sound.

I pointed my blasting staff at my opponent and fired a round. The Enzite anticipated this, batting my staff away, sending the round to careen aimlessly through the forest interior.

Before I could line up another shot, the Enzite produced a serrated blade. The piece of steel was as long as my forearm. With menace, he slashed out toward me.

My staff was a ranged weapon and, as such, I played to my strength, taking a step back and pressing the button on my weapon to extend the staff.

Without hesitation, the Enzite came for me, using its tough exoskeleton skin to parry and absorb the strike I laid down with my staff. This Enzite was not like the others I had encountered. This was a trained soldier with years of experience. It used its exoskeleton forearms like weapons themselves, blocking my blows.

The moon glinted off the hardened steel as the impressive blade slashed down at me over and over again. I was outmatched, that was for sure. I fought to steady my footing as we maneuvered around the edge of the cliff. One false step and I was done. I didn't want to see how lucky I could be at my dura steel turning his blade, or if the synth suit underneath would be able to stop it at all.

Sparks flew off the impact as the Enzite knife met the

Ursonian metal of my blasting staff. Each strike sent tremors of pain down my hands and arms. But this was pain well-known and endured from my hours of practice with Captain Akel. Yes, this Enzite was tough, but not stronger than an Ursonian.

We parried and blocked, moving around the threshold of the cliff in a dance where one misstep meant death. I always gave ground, hoping to tire the Enzite out. My hopes would not be realized as our conflict turned into minutes. Minutes might not seem long to anyone else, but with adrenaline flowing, heart pumping at max, it can feel like an eternity.

Then it happened; my lack of training compared to that of the Enzite cost me. In a cheap move, the Enzite kicked up a spray of dirt into my face. While my helmet kept any grains of dirt from getting into my eyes, it did obscure my vision for the briefest of seconds.

I moved to the side, batting away the cloud of dirt but losing track of my opponent. He lunged at me, taking me off my feet and toward the edge of the cliff.

FORTY-FOUR

WHILE THE ENZITE wasn't that much larger than I was, every part of him was built with muscle and bone. His armor scraped against mine as we went down. He tore off my helmet, dealing a series of crushing blows to my head that had me seeing stars.

The metallic taste of iron in my mouth told me I would be missing a few teeth when this was done.

I brought up my staff, slamming it against his face. I brought it back to hit him again, but he caught it, forcing it against my throat. I gripped the weapon on either side of the shaft, trying to squeeze out from under the weight. I moved up, but there was no room. The hard-packed ground my head rested against was gone within a few feet. My head wavered over the edge of the cliff.

"Die, Rowki," the Enzite said, his considerable bug eyes shimmering with glee. His mandibles clicked a few times in excited anticipation. My Adam's apple felt like it was going to pop out the rear of my neck.

He was too heavy. The Enzite pressed down on me

with the full weight of his body. I was getting better with the bench press and pushups, but not that good.

Come on, Max, come on, you've got more to give, I yelled at myself inside my head as I fought to lift the weight from my neck.

The strangest war cry I had yet to hear emanated from somewhere behind my enemy. Tem came flying through the night air like a spider monkey. He jumped on the Enzite's back, grabbing onto his face and raking at his eyes.

"You leave Max Tyco alone!" Tem screamed, scraping at the Enzite's face. "He's still new. He's learning."

The Enzite howled in pain, rising from on top of me and grabbing at the back of his head.

I gasped, coming up for air, coughing as I removed myself from the edge of the cliff. Aiya was also struggling to her feet, looking a bit woozy. She placed a hand to the back of her head. It came back bloody.

Tem's valiant attempt was short lived as he was thrown to the side with such ferocity, his little body cracked against one of the trees. In that moment, the idea of family not related by blood was driven home to my core.

I wasn't related to Tem or Aiya; heck, I wasn't even the same species as either of them, but here they were, willing to put themselves in harm's way for me. Each of them was willing to do anything to help protect each other.

As if it were an exclamation to the thought, Aiya gritted her teeth and ran at the Enzite, slamming into him so hard, he stumbled backward toward me and the edge of the cliff.

I knew in that moment what I had to do and I was more than at peace with it. I missed her. If I could go out saving others, then maybe that would be a death worthy of reuniting me with her.

The Enzite finally found his footing with his back to me and mine to the cliff. He grabbed Aiya by the head, twisting a handful of her hair. She screamed in pain.

I moved into action, placing my forearm under the chin of the Enzite. Like a bulldog, I dragged him to the edge of the cliff.

He released Aiya, trying to find a grip in my chokehold around his neck. Like a crocodile in a death roll, there was no way in this life or the next that I was going to let go. It would take an act of God for me not to see this through to the end.

If the Enzites could be so devil-may-care with their own lives and their suicide runs, then I was going to be just as dedicated in protecting the lives of the people I had come to think of as family.

Without a second's hesitation, I dragged him off the cliff and we fell together. Except we didn't fall far. As much as I was ready to sacrifice myself if it meant Aiya and Tem could get away, instinct made me reach for the edge of the cliff at the last moment.

I failed to grab any hold, but Aiya's hand grabbed my wrist. She had thrown herself to the edge as I went over, making a wild attempt to catch me. She had. She wasn't the only one. Our Enzite friend also latched on to my boot.

Aiya screamed in effort, trying to hold both of us up.

I looked down at the Enzite who held on to my right boot with both hands fighting for a better grip. I also saw what waited for us below. A river of rushing water nine or ten stories below. I was bad at gauging this kind of thing, especially dangling from the cliff's edge.

"Max, Max, I can't—I can't hold you," Aiya managed as her fingers slipped from my wrist to my hand.

I held on to hers as well, the knee jerk fear of death coming into play even when I knew I was okay with falling.

"Let go," I told her. "I'm okay, let go."

Aiya stared at me with that look someone gives you when they want to ask if you're an idiot.

"Max—" Aiya said with a scream as I released her hand. Her grip alone wasn't enough to hold up two armored soldiers.

We fell, Rowki and Enzite, to the water below. I didn't know if there was a shallow bed of rocks waiting for us or if the water would be deep enough to absorb our fall, and my armor would weigh me to the bottom and drown me. To be honest, I kind of hoped that the fall would kill me. The idea of drowning to death wasn't one I wanted to realize.

They say when you're about to die, your life flashes in front of your eyes. It happened so fast that maybe it did. What I remembered in that moment, falling to the rushing water below, was her.

I remembered the way she rolled her eyes at me when I was intentionally or unintentionally being silly. How she would slap my butt playfully on the way in or out of our tiny kitchen. How she would hug me for no real reason but to be close. I remembered how her hair smelled, how her voice resonated in my ears. I remembered it all in painful slow motion as I fell, and then, nothing but blackness.

I saw my body slam into the water and the current take me deeper and deeper into the inky darkness of the river. But I saw it all happen. I didn't experience it. It was as if I was having an out-of-body experience.

I stood on the bank of the river watching my body being taken away.

"You know this all only works if you want it to work."

I knew that voice. I whipped around to see her. My Christina stood on the river bed not with a halo or wings, but with jeans and a shirt from the Salvation Army. She had never been into fashions or trends.

My knees felt weak. I had dreamt about her so often, and yet I had forgotten what she actually looked like. The cut of her strong jaw, the playful fire that danced in her eyes.

I took a step and then actually fell to my knees sobbing like a child.

"Max, shhhhh, Max," Christina said, coming down and kneeling in front of me. She placed her hands on my chin and lifted my eyes to hers. "Hey, hey, shhhh, I'm here. I've never left. I'll always be here."

"I'm so—so sorry. I should have never let you go that nigh—"

"Stop." Christina placed a finger to my lips then used her hands to wipe away my tears. She lifted me up from the ground and pressed herself into my arms.

I stood there, not caring at all that I had seen my body drifting down into the depths of the river. I only lived in the current moment. In her arms. I couldn't stop the tears. They came flooding down my cheeks, unwilling to be denied.

"None of it was your fault, and I'm so proud of the man you are choosing to become," Christina said, gently removing herself from my arms and looking up at me. "You are everything I hoped for. You are enough. You are more than enough, Max. And we will be together again one day."

"Will be?" I repeated her words, looking behind me to the river and my body that I could no longer see. "No, now, we can be together now. I saw myself die."

"Did you?"

"What do you mean?"

"Do you want to die?"

"I want to be with you, whatever that means," I answered honestly.

"Max, I am with you already," Christina said with a shake of her head. "I've always been with you. The parts of you that carry my thoughts, what you learned while we were together; those parts that have become you are me, too."

"What do you mean?" I said, trying to understand but falling short.

"I'm not really gone," Christina told me. "I'm with you. Anything that you took from me or that I taught you while we were together lives on through you. Do you still burn the chicken and stuffing casserole?"

"What?"

"Do you still burn the chicken and stuffing casserole?"

"No."

"Well, who taught you that, your appreciation for Johnny Cash, the way you put the toilet paper back on the roll?" Christina asked with a playful smile and hands on her hips. "Being a Rowki? Where do you pull that willpower from? What keeps you going?"

"I've learned it from you," I told her, realizing now what she had been getting at the whole time. "You, your memory."

"Right, and the universe still needs you, my Rowki Guardian," Christina said, turning me around by the shoulders. She stood on her tiptoes to speak in my ear. "Can you have faith we will be together again? Have faith, but know your work here isn't done. I'm waiting for you, Max, but not yet. No, go do what you do best."

Christina slapped me on the butt and gently pushed me forward.

"Go and be stubborn, be too stubborn to die," Christina said with a wink. "Oh, and before you get to the surface, reach down."

"What?" I asked, looking back to her as the river water rose to envelop me.

"Just do it," Christina said with a bright smile. "I love you, Max. Go be the hero I know you are."

I was going to return the words, *I love you*, but the water was rising too fast. It reached my chest and then covered my mouth. All of a sudden, I was under water. Oxygen was in short supply. Cold darkness I could barely navigate pressed in on me. I remembered Christina's words before I fought my way to the surface.

I looked down to see a shimmering rock at my feet. Scooping it up, I propelled myself upward, but my armor was too heavy. Like a madman, I released the latches for first my chest armor and then the pieces of dura steel on my forearms and legs.

I kicked to the surface not a moment too soon. Lungs burning and head about to explode, I came up from my watery grave.

Gasping, I made for the shore that wasn't more than twenty yards away. I didn't stop moving until I made it to dry ground. On my back, staring up into the night sky, I lay there still sucking in breath. The nights on Ivandor were hot like the days, and for once, I found myself grateful for the warmth.

My mind raced with my near-death experience. Tears ran down the corners of my eyes, along with a smile as I remembered her.

A moan from my right killed any other images of my wife. I looked over and couldn't believe my eyes. The Enzite had also survived. He was crawling out of the river on all fours, retching and coughing.

Oh, you got to be kidding me, I thought to myself.

FORTY-FIVE

I WAS BEAT UP, leg still charred, face used as a punching bag, and half drowned. The strange thing was I didn't feel that bad. Maybe it was the jolt of energy I got from seeing her again, maybe it was that I was just really pissed off at this Enzite for not dying. Whatever the case, I found the strength within to rise to my feet and make my way over to the gasping Enzite.

"You—you should be dead," the Enzite croaked, struggling to stand on unsteady feet. A long gash across the left side of his face showed that his skull had made contact with some river rock on his journey down toward me.

"I guess my work's not done here yet," I said, balling my right hand into a fist. It was then I realized I was still holding on to something. Something that felt like a rock, hard but not sharp.

Whatever I'd lifted from the bottom of the river would have to wait for closer inspection. I slammed my fist into the face of the Enzite so hard, I thought I might have broken my hand in the process.

The Enzite's head snapped back as he crumpled to the ground. I winced, shaking out my hand.

"Son of a Baptist preacher," I said, examining my hand first to make sure it wasn't indeed broken. Next I examined the item I carried in my fist.

It wasn't a rock at all; rather, a kind of metal. Or at least to my untrained eyes I thought it was metal. Shiny and silver, it seemed to glow with a warmth of its own. It was light and slender, no more than a few inches long.

Memories of what Rima had explained to me of what sardonium was teased my mind. But this couldn't be that, could it? She told me how rare the metal was. I just found it because I was willing to kill myself, and my dead wife came to me in a vision?

"Just when you thought things couldn't get any crazier," I muttered to myself. "You have to go and discover some rare Rowki metal."

I sat down hard, all the adrenaline wearing off and letting me know how beat-up I actually was. I'm not sure how long I sat there thinking about my wife, what was happening in my life, and what was to come.

"Max Tyco! Max Tyco!"

I heard Tem long before I saw him. Both he and Aiya were making their way down the sloping cliff that paralleled the river. The historian was at a dead run with the river to his left, Aiya behind him warning him not to shout should there be other Enzites in the area.

Tem didn't seem to care. Still fifty yards away, he slumped to all fours, picking up something from the water. It was my helmet, which had fallen down the cliff with us and now bobbed in the water like a boat.

"Oh, Max, you were so young, why do you take them so

young?" Tem wailed to the heavens. "We just met. You were the best of us, Max."

I rose to my feet and hobbled over to Tem. He didn't see me as he cried his laments, but Aiya did. She lifted her pulse rifle for a moment and then lowered it when she realized it was me. A smile of relief crossed her face.

"Oh, oh, the injustice of it all," Tem said, weeping. "Why, tell me why he had to go?"

"Tem," I said, getting closer.

"No, don't, do not offer me comfort," Tem said, still not looking in my direction. He hugged the helmet to him like a life preserver. "Let me be. Just let me mourn for my friend."

"Tem," I said louder as I approached. "It's me."

"Max Tyco, please, I'm in the middle of—" Tem's head whipped around to look at me. "Max Tyco?!"

Tem jumped to his feet, dropping the helmet, and rushed me. He wrapped me in a hug so strong, I couldn't breathe for a moment.

"Max Tyco, you're alive, you're alive, but how?" Tem asked, finally releasing his hold. "How are you alive? I saw you fall. And—"

Tem cut off the rest of whatever it was he was going to say as he stared at my open hand.

While he searched for the words he wanted, Aiya came over with a smile. "You look horrible."

"I feel horrible," I told her.

"Remind me to punch you once you've healed," Aiya snarled, the smile on her lips vanishing in a moment. "And don't ever do that again or I'll kill you myself."

"Yes, ma'am," I answered. "If I'm ever dangling on the edge of a cliff again with my enemy hanging on to my boot and you're holding us up, I'll hold on right back."

"Good," Aiya said, ignoring my sarcasm.

"How—when—where—" Tem asked the words, looking at the metal in my hand like it was a holy relic long lost and now found once again.

"Here, you can hold it," I said, tossing him the sardonium.

"Oh, oh my," Tem gasped, snatching it out of the air. "Max Tyco, have some respect. Do you realize how rare this is?"

"Yes, but I have a feeling you're about to tell me again anyway," I said, grunting as I took a seat by the river.

Aiya pressed her fingers to her ear, listening to something on her comm channel. I had lost my earpiece during the fall.

"It is unknown how much sardonium exists in the universe, or the origins of its creation," Tem said, examining the piece of metal in his hand with reverence. He stroked the item in a way that I was pretty sure was inappropriate. "Rima, in all her years, has only found a sliver to imbue into her blade, Geister has found two. That you would be able to find one in such a short time being a Rowki, well, it's unprecedented."

"Understood, I have Tem and Max with me," Aiya said into her comm channel. "We will remain here for pickup. Max is wounded—yes—yes again. He's hurt again. Understood."

Tem and I looked over to Aiya for answers. "The Enzites have been routed and a team is on their way down to us now. Meatball was found in the forest, tearing at an Enzite corpse."

"Good girl. Oh, that reminds me, we should probably restrain Mr. Personality," I suggested, throwing a thumb over my shoulder. "He survived the fall as well."

The three of us walked over to where the unconscious

Enzite lay on the riverbank. His breath was even enough. Can't say that I was overly concerned about his well-being, but I knew we wanted him alive. The more Enzites we could take in, the more answers we would be able to get from them.

Aiya secured his hands behind him with her belt while Tem sat on the riverbank examining the piece of sardonium like a kid with a new toy.

It wasn't long before Captain Akel and Ero made it down to our position with a handful of Ursonian soldiers.

They secured the area and I found myself in Ero's' care again.

"You know we need to stop meeting like this," Ero teased as she injected a healthy supply of nanites into my shoulder and then examined my leg. "You keep this up and we're not going to have much of you left for the return trip."

"Do Rowki get sick days or vacation leave?" I asked, only half-joking. "I didn't read the fine print when I agreed to all of this."

Ero barked a laugh and then proceeded to use the skin spray on my face and clean up the wounds I had our Enzite friend to thank for.

While Ero worked on me. Captain Akel secured the prisoner and called in Razor support. We'd had to come in quietly to track the Enzites, but now that the deed was done, we were able to signal air support to give us a lift back.

"Rima?" I asked as Ero packed up her medical kit.

"Rima is the last person we should be worried about," Ero said with a shake of her furry head. "I think death itself is afraid to come near that woman. She'll be fine."

For once, our trip to the Ursonian encampment around the excavation site was uneventful. I actually fell asleep in the Razor on the way back. It wasn't like the ship was comfortable either, so that was saying something.

I was a zombie by the time we landed and all I could think of was sleep. It had to be in the early hours of the morning. I stayed up long enough to get eyes on Rima to make sure she was indeed fine. Rima just scowled at me when she saw me staring.

Part of me wanted to tell her about the sardonium and see her eyes widen in shock. That could wait until tomorrow. Meatball, who had joined us when the Razors came to give us a ride back home, now followed me to my truck.

I needed rest; my aching body told me that as much as my drooping eyes. I shed what parts of my armor remained and fell into my bed. The feeling was euphoric. There was nothing like sleeping in the cabin in my truck; this was home. Meatball curled up at the foot of the bed, and I fell asleep like a dead man.

No dreams dared to come that night and disturb the slumber of a man who had died and come back. I woke after a nine-hour escape from reality to Meatball panting heavily and scratching at the inside of the driver door.

"Okay, okay, I'm up, I'm up," I said, rubbing sleep from my eyes. The motion of sitting up from my bed sent aching pain through my entire body, most notably my leg and head.

I winced through the light of the windshield and made my way to the door for Meatball to get out. The little chunk of energy hopped out and proceeded to do its business on the front tire of my truck. She peed like a guy, one leg up and everything.

I needed to pee myself, come to think of it. Still squinting, I gingerly stepped out of the truck in my black shorts and a Metallica t-shirt. Furry slippers that looked like animal claws padded my feet.

Inside the barracks, the Ursonian Corps was already busy at work. I could tell by the number of guards on the walls that we were on lockdown. Drills were being conducted in the middle of the grounds. Ursonians walked to and from their duties, looking at me with one part awe, one part curiosity.

I was getting used to it by now. Most hadn't ever seen a human, and some had never seen a Rowki. I nodded to them and waved. This got some to look away quickly and others to smile or send a wave back my way.

I reached into my truck for my *Infinity System* robe, from a TV show that I had enjoyed watching before I was abducted.

"Good, you're up," Geister said, joining me in front of my truck. "We need to talk."

Something in his voice told me this wasn't going to be an average "how did your night go last night" conversation.

FORTY-SIX

"OKAY, good morning, good to see you too," I answered, jerking my chin toward the mess hall. "I've just really got to pee. Can we talk and walk?"

"What are you wearing?" Geister asked, looking at my claw-footed slippers and then my *Infinity System* robe. "What is that? A dress?"

"No, it's not a dress," I told him, wrapping the robe around my waist and tying it there with the cord. "It's called a robe and it's comfortable, thank you very much. Now can I go take a piss and come back or—"

"I'll go with you," Geister said, taking the lead. "What I have to tell you can't wait."

"Rima? Is it about Rima? Is she okay?" I asked, hurrying to catch up with Geister's long strides. "Ero said she'd be fine."

"Rima?" Geister asked with a laugh. "No, that old bag was up this morning before the suns, running laps. Rima is going to outlive both of us. What I wanted to talk to you about was the Enzites and what's going on here. I have a feeling you're in way over your head and, well—I remember what it was like to be a new Rowki. I feel like you should know."

We entered the mess hall, with the familiar delicious smell of cooking meat. I listened to Geister as we walked into the rear restroom section of the mess hall. Ursonians were massive, so it made sense that their latrine would be as well. I'm not sure what kind of fragrance they used to mask the smell of their fecal matter, but whatever it was, I was going to take it back to Earth with me one day and make a killing.

Instead of smelling like doo-doo, the scent from the latrine I caught was a whiff of one part honey, one-part cinnamon. I wanted to hang out in the room all day. I went to a trough used for going number one and began undoing the tie in my robe cord.

Geister stood next to me, looking me in the eye as he continued. "The portals or gateways, whatever you want to call them, the ones the Enzite Federation is trying to open. Do you know what they are? I mean, exactly what they are?"

"Can you—do you mind?" I asked, feeling that urge to pee so strong now I was about to have an accident.

"No, go ahead," Geister said with a shrug. "Your species shy or something? Can't go when the moment calls?"

"I'm not shy," I told him, fighting and losing the battle against my bladder. "You're also standing two inches away from me looking at me in the eyes while I'm trying to pee."

An Ursonian walked into the latrine, took one look at us, then nodded and took a step back out.

"Humans are touchy," Geister huffed under his breath. He raised both blue hands in a sign of surrender and took a big step back. He even turned his back to me. "Better?"

"Yes, thank you," I said, pulling down my shorts and letting loose.

"Like I was saying before all your strangeness took over," Geister continued. "Do you know what the portals, what the Enzite Federation is doing? Do you know what's on the other side of said portals?"

"Another dimension?" I asked, trying to remember the exact details. "I'm not exactly the scholarly type if you haven't noticed. Basically, the Enzite Federation wants to open the portals to unleash the Eternals and that's bad for us."

"That's a very simple way to put it," Geister said with a shrug. "The more precise 'why' of it would be that these Eternals are an advanced alien race we suspect left this galaxy in exploration ten thousand years ago through these portals. If these portals are opened again and we invite them back—well, there's no telling how good or bad that might be for us."

"Why did the Eternals leave at all?" I asked, finishing the deed and retying my robe. I went over to a hand purifier that used light to wash any bacteria away. Again, something I was going to have to take back to Earth with me one day and make a killing off of.

"No one really knows," Geister explained. "Up until now, it's all been working theory mixed with myth. The portal is the best evidence we have that an advanced civilization once existed and created these portals in the first place. But if the portal exists, then maybe the rest of the story is real after all."

We walked out of the latrine to the mess hall. I was always hungry, and since we were already there, I looked over to Geister, who nodded, picking up my train of thought. We stood in line together. I gathered an assortment of strange new food the Ursonians dished out. It all smelled good to me.

"And if the story is true, then there are two other gateways on this world that, when activated with the first, are going to open said portal and we're going to be really surprised, in a good way, or in a bad way." Geister continued, shoveling hot food into his mouth. "You get me?"

"I get you," I answered, trying to decide where I stood on the matter. On one hand, we could open the portals and hope that the powerhouse on the other side was friendly. On the other hand, keep them closed and not roll the dice. Images of my only interaction with the activated portal crossed my mind. I remembered the beastly figure on the other side of the portal, how it had devoured the Enzite I'd battled.

"My thought is that we never open them, and if we do, we'd better have the full power of the Galactic Government behind us ready to rain down unholy hell on the portal if whatever does come through the other side isn't friendly," Geister said around a mouthful of food. "I for one am not a fan of opening Pandora's box."

"And what else could be in this other dimension, or wherever the portal leads?" I asked, thinking back to the monster I had seen. It sure didn't remind me of any alien advanced civilization I had ever seen in *Star Trek*. "What if we open the portal and these Eternals don't come out? What if something else does?"

"Then there's always that, too," Geister said, reaching into the folds of his jacket for his flask. He opened the lid and offered it to me. "Drink?"

Truth was I did want a drink. I didn't want to have to deal with all the emotions and pressures inside of me that came with seeing my dead wife, and bearing the weight of a

Rowki Guardian and everything that came with it. But I knew I couldn't. I had to say no to one drink, or one too quickly became twenty.

"I'm good," I answered, looking down at my plate and forcing myself to think of anything else but drinking.

"Your loss." Geister shrugged, pressing the flask to his mouth and throwing his head back. He smacked his lips when he was done. "Love me some Heston. Finest whiskey in the galaxy, maybe even the universe."

I was about to ask where the Rowki Council stood in the conversation of whether to open the portals or not when we were interrupted by Captain Akel and Rima.

The former looked like he hadn't slept all night. Bags dangling under his eyes did nothing to quell the respect he demanded when he walked into a room. Rima, on the other hand, looked great. She didn't seem fatigued or in any kind of pain. To the contrary, she was in her PT clothes of a black tank top and pants, looking like she was ready to go another ten rounds on the training floor.

Every Ursonian in the mess hall stood to show respect, and the ones already on their feet went rigid with a paw across their chest.

Captain Akel pounded his chest in salute. He along with Rima walked over to our table.

"I'm getting the feeling this isn't a social call," I said, wishing I had grabbed some coffee before all of this started. "Do I have time to get some caffeine before you say whatever it is you're going to say?"

Captain Akel performed a few sign language moves with his hands that Rima translated. "The prisoner will only talk to you."

"Me?" I asked uncertainly. "Why me? All of them will only talk to me?"

"The lower-ranking Enzites spilled their guts, but the officer, the one you battled on the cliff is—tougher to crack than we anticipated," Rima said, cleaning the knuckles on her hands of what I realized now were specks of blood. "We can use drugs, of course, but this would be faster, and we'll be able to use him again if you can get him to talk. The drugs sometimes leave lasting effects."

Rima relayed this information as if she weren't rattled in the least by what she was talking about. It seemed the interrogation of prisoners didn't faze her, nor was she bound by a law or rule of the Rowki Council.

I looked over to Geister, who shrugged and took another swig from his flask.

"All right, I'll talk to him," I said, rising from the table. "Why me? Why does he want to talk to me? We nearly killed each other."

"I think that's why he wants to talk to you," Rima answered. "The Enzite Federation breeds warriors. They respect strength and brutality above all else."

I moved along with the group out of the mess hall toward my truck. "Can I at least change and/or shower?"

"No time," Rima said as Akel shook his head. "The faster we can discern exactly what the Enzite Federation is up to, the better. You can change out of your dress when we're done."

"It's a robe. It's a robe! For the last time, how have you people never heard of a robe?" I asked incredulously. "You have spaceships and lasers but not robes?"

"Whoa, whoa, whoa, what do you mean by 'you people'?" Geister asked with a raised eyebrow.

"You know, you, all of you people as a whole, Ursonians, whatever blue species you are, and the near-human species Rema is," I said with a sigh.

We walked toward a building I hadn't been inside yet. It was tucked in the rear corner of the encampment behind where my truck sat. It was small and shaped like a square, with a pair of Ursonian guards in front and another pair on the catwalk above.

Captain Akel saluted the soldiers, who returned the gesture then moved to the side and allowed us entrance. Inside, another Ursonian sat at a counter in front of red laser beams that acted as bars. Beyond that, I could see individual cells and rooms with Enzite prisoners.

The guard on duty saluted. He maneuvered around his control panel, turning off the first set of red laser beams separating us from the rest of the cell block.

"There won't be much here other than holding cells," Geister informed me. "Ursonians aren't keen on being prison wardens. They get what they need, holding prisoners for a time before those in question are shipped off world to stand trial in front of the Galactic Government."

I nodded in understanding as we crossed a hall with doors to our right and left. Ahead of us were larger cells with the same red laser bars keeping the Enzite prisoners at bay. The Enzites I did see looked like they had been worked over pretty good. I felt conflicted about this. I could guess where they'd received their wounds and they weren't all from the fight the previous night.

I followed Captain Akel and Rima to the left where the hall ended in a T intersection. Another left brought us to a closed steel door.

"He's in there," Rima told me, narrowing her eyes at the door as if she could see through it. "Get as much out of him as you can. We need to know if there are more of them out there, what the Enzite Federation plans to do, and of course, the endgame with the gateways."

"Okay, are they portals or gateways?" I asked, trying to buy some time before I was stuck in a tiny room with a bug alien that wanted to kill me. "How is he going to understand me? I'm not wearing my armor with that translator in the collar."

"Call them whatever you want." Rima shrugged, opening the door of the cell. "The chamber is equipped with translation tech. Just get our answers."

There was no room for discussion in those words. With a sigh, I tightened my robe and stepped into the room.

FORTY-SEVEN

THE ROOM WAS NOT AT ALL what I expected. Unlike the interrogation room aboard the *Oni*, this one was devoid of any furniture. The Enzite stood against the far wall, bound with magnetic cuffs on its hands and feet. Each cuff wrapped around one of its limbs and was secured to the wall behind it.

In this way, the Enzite was forced to stand up, arms over his head. His armor had been stripped as well as his shirt. He wore loose-fitting pants. It was my first good, up-close look at the Enzite anatomy. I was trying to go in with an open mind here, but the bone structure of an Enzite seemed almost painful.

A thin layer of skin wrapped around hard bone and the exoskeleton that grew over their body. Chest, forearms, and thighs looked like hard coral.

I jolted when the door shut behind me. If the Enzite noticed my jump, he didn't say anything. He stared at me with those two giant black eyes of his.

"You—" I cleared my thought to remove the squeak and

tried again with my best baritone impression. "You asked to see me?"

A translation device hidden in the room changed my words into a series of clicks and chitter the Enzite understood.

The Enzite let a moment pass before clicking his mandibles. "Yes, nice robe."

"Thank you," I said, looking over my shoulder to the closed door behind me. I was sure everyone on the outside was listening in. There were probably micro-cameras in the room I couldn't see as well. "Finally, someone who understands what a robe is."

"You do not seem like any warrior I have ever encountered before," the Enzite said, looking me up and down. "Where do you come from? Why are you interfering with the Enzite Federation's glorious purpose?"

I was about to deny him answers when I realized I might be able to leverage the conversation for my gain. "Okay, let's play a game. I'll answer your questions and you answer mine, and around and around we'll go. Fair?"

The Enzite dipped his head in agreement.

"I come from a planet called Earth; I'm a human," I said, also going out on a limb to answer his next question before I got my answer. I had to build trust if I was going to get him to spill the beans. "I'm a Rowki Guardian. We were sent here to stop you."

That was pretty much the truth.

The Enzite tilted his head and clicked his mandibles again, an act that I took as him thinking.

"My turn," I began before he could ask anything else. "I answered two of your questions, so here are two of mine. "How many of you are left hiding in the forest? If they surrender, I can promise they'll be taken alive."

"None, there are no other Enzite forces on Ivandor for now," the prisoner answered. "But there will be, and not just us. As word of the portals spreads, more and more factions, treasure hunters, and mercenary groups will come to see for themselves and lay claim. This is just the beginning. The beginning of a new era."

"Now you're starting to sound a little culty," I warned him. "Your buddy Zion was raving about that too, before I sent him to go meet his Eternals through the portal."

"There are some amongst the Enzite Federation that are more religious than others. I am not one of them. I fight for my leaders, not a deity," the Enzite prisoner stated. "What's your next question?"

"What does the Enzite Federation plan to do next?"

"It's no secret. I just told you. They'll come, as will countless others, and Ivandor will turn into a battlefield where millions will die trying to secure the portals," the Enzite answered. "What do you plan to do with me and the rest of my soldiers?"

"Have you sent off-world to stand trial with the Galactic Government." I repeated word for word what Geister had told me that morning at breakfast. "What's your name?"

"What?"

"You heard me, that's my question to you," I repeated. "What's your name? I'm Max."

"Max," the Enzite said, clearly not used to being dealt with in such a civil manner during an interrogation. "First interrogation?"

"No, second, actually," I said, thinking back to my time with Aiya before we had become allies. "How am I doing so far?"

"Could use some work. I'm Ezra," he answered.

"Ezra the Enzite, huh?" I asked with a raised brow. "Bet school was hard for you."

"We do not have school in the Enzite Federation," Ezra responded with a bite to each word. "We have the militia, where hatchlings are trained from birth to fight for the glorious cause."

"Fight and die," I added, remembering the suicide bomber. "You send your own out to die without a second thought."

"It is considered a great honor to die in the name of the EF."

"EF?"

"Enzite Federation," Ezra answered with a look that told me to try and keep up. "It's something I know you understand. That's the reason I agreed to speak with you and only you. I can see why the Rowki chose you. I see the potential you carry. Most would not have been willing to sacrifice themselves back there on that cliff."

"I can't tell a lie." I shrugged in my robe. "People have called me special my whole life."

"Perhaps they were using that term not in the way you imagined," Ezra said, adjusting himself uncomfortably in his cuffs. "Regardless, you carry the heart of a warrior and that is something we respect. There was no point in me keeping anything from you. The planet is revolving, and plans are already in motion. There is nothing you, the Rowki, or the Galactic Government can do, no matter what I do or do not tell you."

"Great, so last question, and this one's for all the marbles," I said, staring the alien directly in his black eyes. "The portals—what does the Enzite Federation think is on the other side?"

"Eternals, our forerunners," Ezra answered simply.

"The more religious of our order think that opening the portals for the Eternals to return will broker a partnership between us and them, and they will aid us in raising the EF banner for all to behold."

"And if they don't?" I pressed. "If they come in and annihilate all of us or, just as bad, something else besides the Eternals comes through?"

"It's a risk those in power are willing to take," Ezra explained. "I'm a soldier. I do what I'm told."

"And you were just going to blow that plan to hell with your suicide run?" I asked, reaching for the last piece of the puzzle. "You were going to disobey the order and close down the portal forever?"

For the first time, Ezra was silent.

"Maybe there's a storyline here where you wanted the portals closed, this war not to happen," I said, playing Sherlock Holmes. "Maybe you ordered the suicide run because you told your unit that was the order given from on high when, in reality, you were hoping to blow the portal and save everyone from what comes next."

"You're not as ignorant as you seem," Ezra answered.

"I get that a lot," I answered with a grin. "Ezra, I'm not sure I can say thank you, but I'll do my best to make sure you're treated fairly and sent off-world for the trial you deserve."

I turned to go, content that the questions I had set out to ask were indeed answered.

"Max," Ezra called to my back as I opened the door.

I looked over my shoulder.

"One warrior to another, be cautious," Ezra told me. "The Rowki have been operating across the universe as long as time can remember. Along the way, they have acquired many enemies, and now those enemies are yours."

I didn't have a cool response. Even if I did, I got the sense that, in a twisted way, Ezra was trying to help me.

I nodded and left the room.

When the door closed behind me, I stood in the hall with Captain Akel, Geister, and Rima.

"We heard everything," Rima said, pursing her lips. "We'll be able to use the information you uncovered to plan accordingly."

Captain Akel placed a huge paw on my shoulder and gave me a jerk of his chin, signaling he approved.

"Well done," Geister added. "I think he likes you."

"Great, can I shower and change now?" I asked, looking down at my slippers. "I could use some coffee, too."

"Go, change out of your dress," Rima said, already exchanging a knowing look with the other two. "We have much to discuss with both the Rowki and the Galactic Government."

I skipped the part where I corrected Rima that I was not in fact wearing a dress. I think at this point she knew and was doing it on purpose. I saw myself out of the brig and went to my truck to gather supplies. Meatball was waiting for me in a spot she had found underneath the truck.

"Hey, you." I smiled at the little alien wolfhound.

Meatball jumped up and trotted over to me, her pink tongue lolling out the side of her maw.

I bent down and tickled her leather ears. Since the attack on the Ursonian compound, I decided I wanted to stay close to the action. The Stone Dwellers had been kind enough to offer me quarters in their town, but this was where I belonged. I could sleep in my truck and make use of the Ursonian showers.

Said showers were attached to the latrine and mess hall. I gathered the supplies from my truck and made my way there now. The showers were much like everything else the Ursonians constructed: large, no nonsense, and simple. I went to a stall where a hole in the ceiling would let down the water from a dial in the center of the wall I would press for heat and pressure.

Half the stalls were already in use by various Ursonians preparing for or getting off their shift. Meatball, it turned out, was not a fan of water and opted to wait outside.

I let the warm water wash over me, stretching as much as my aching body would allow. I felt like one massive walking bruise, but even that I was getting used to. The wound on my leg was healing well, thanks to the nanites Ero used, along with the skin spray.

I washed, changed, and headed back to my truck. Clothing was provided for me by the Rowki and Ursonians. They both went out of the way to make sure the threads would fit me. Or I should say, Tem went out of the way to make sure I had clothing my size.

But on days like this when there wasn't a synth suit to put on under my armor or PT clothes to sweat in, I preferred my own pair of jeans, Converse, and whatever shirt wasn't dirty. Speaking of dirty, I wore a *Dirty Harry* shirt at the moment that asked the age old question, "Are you feeling lucky?"

After washing and new clothes, it was coffee time. I was in my truck licking my lips with anticipation as the Keurig machine brewed a cup of Cerberus coffee when I heard a commotion outside.

At least it wasn't an explosion this time, just the shouts and orders from a dozen Ursonian throats. They weren't panicked, but stressed. I really didn't want to even go outside. I wasn't, in fact, but Tem Fan popped his head up outside the driver side window and waved, motioning to me to come quickly.

"I'll pass," I said, taking my *Star Wars* mug from the Keurig. "I'm good. Whatever's going on outside, I'll just sit this one out."

"Max, Max Tyco," Tem Fan knocked on my door frantically. "You must come, you must come to the gate and see what's happening."

"Must I?" I asked

"Max Tyco, you must," Tem answered, waving me out of my cabin.

FORTY-EIGHT

AGAINST MY BETTER JUDGMENT, I opened the driver side door, coffee in hand still untasted. Tem jumped down and motioned to the sky. There was so much happening at once, I didn't know where to look first. Dozens of ships lined the horizon, coming to dock outside the Ursonian camp. Again, I didn't know much about spacecraft, but I did know they weren't Ursonian.

These ships were heavy freighters, cargo ships, and maybe even a few fighters? I guessed that at seeing the weapons mounted on the ships. They were every shape and color, from bright yellow to pure silver.

Along with the ships landing outside the walls was the commotion inside the Ursonian camp. Soldiers were running for the walls, not like they were going to open fire, but more like defend the line.

"Nope, I'm good," I said, closing the cab door and settling in the driver seat. I sipped on the hot nectar of the gods we call coffee.

"Max, Max Tyco, you must come," Tem said, appearing on the other side of the door again. "What we thought is happening. Treasure seekers, merchants, soldiers of fortune; the news of the portals has reached the universe and species are coming from all corners."

I sat in my truck, savoring one last sip of silence and peace before I opened the door and all hell broke loose. I wasn't sure what the Rowki role was going to be in playing safety officer, but I was sure Rima would be prepared to be on the front lines.

"Max Ty—"

Before Tem could finish my name, I opened my cab door with him still on the other side. "I'm coming, I'm coming."

I stepped down to the ground, closing the door. Tem rode the exterior of the door until it closed and then stepped down with me.

"I understand you must be tired, but this is certainly exciting times," Tem said, blinking furiously. "This may be the single greatest discovery save for the uncovering of the celestial phallus."

"Nope, not going to take that bait," I said, walking to the front of the encampment with my friend. A thought made me stop in my tracks and look at Tem in the face. "I forgot to ask how you're doing. Geister came in with the news that his historian was dead. You said you knew her. Was she a friend?"

Tem's jaw dropped. Tears welled in his eyes.

"Or we don't have to talk about it," I said as Meatball joined us, sniffing the air and practically bouncing with excitement. "I just knew with everything going on, that was kind of brushed under the rug and wanted to make sure you were okay."

"Max Tyco, the fact that you would be willing to unbrush my rug and ask me how I'm doing means so much,"

JONATHAN YANEZ

Tem said, coming to me before I could stop him and wrapping his arms around my waist. His head pressed against my stomach. "I'm all right. I knew her, but not well. But to think she is gone is such a hard thing. She had such life to her. I wish I'd known her better. Hold me."

"All right, all right," I said, securing my coffee cup in my right hand as I patted Tem on the back with my left.

"Hey, you two weirdos, something's going on at the front," Aiya said, walking past us and motioning us to join her.

I didn't know if she really had called us weirdos or that was the closest term the all-water had used to translate her real words. Either way, I got her point.

"All right, all right, that's enough," I said as gently as I could. Tem released his hold, wiping his eyes. "We can talk about it more when we're done here. But I want you to know that I'm here for you."

"And I am here for you too, Max Tyco," Tem said, looking around him. "We should honor this moment by exchanging fingers."

"What?"

"An ancient ritual of my people when a blood brother is found. We each will cut off our pinky fingers and present it to one another as a gift," Tem explained, looking in the folds of his cloak. At that moment, Geister passed us on his way to the front wall. "Rowki Geister, do you have a blade we might be able to use for a moment?"

"No, no, we're all good here," I said to a confused Geister. The Rowki had not yet broken stride for the front wall. "We'll join you in a moment."

Geister gave me a confused frown as he continued on.

"We also have an ancient tradition on Earth, that brothers share who hold a bond closer than blood," I told

Tem, extending my right pinky. "This bond means I've got your back and you've got mine, no matter what happens."

"Yes, yes, teach me, teach me, Max Tyco," Tem said excitedly, nodding his chin like a bobblehead on my truck's dashboard. "I wish to learn of these mysterious Earth ways."

"It's called a pinky promise. It's just as strong as cutting off and exchanging fingers, but twice as deadly, and we get to keep our fingers." I explained. "Here, you wrap your pinky finger with mine and then we shake on it."

"Oh, the historian in me loves learning new alien traditions," Tem said, slipping his pinky finger in mine. We both pressed hard and shook.

"All right, there we go. Let's not pinky promise too long and lose the magic," I told my friend. "Come on. If we're not at the wall soon, Rima is going to make us do extra laps or something."

"Yes, of course," Tem said, breaking the pinky promise hold. "Let's go, pinky promise brother."

We hurried to the wall where a line of Ursonian soldiers led by Bull were manning the inside of the gate. Once again, I didn't get the sense of impending danger, but excitement and tension was thick in the air like a heavy blanket resting on everyone's shoulders.

Tem and I found the stairs on either side of the main gate that led up to the catwalk. Rima, Geister, Aiya, Captain Akel, and Ero were all there looking out toward the Stone Dwellers' city.

It was a sight to see. Craft were landing, ramps opening, and alien species with all kinds of different intentions and goals were filing out. I saw some wild stuff, like aliens with squid faces and tentacles for their beards, walking out carrying large floating boxes. There were reptile races, little gnome guys smaller than Tem, and even a bird species with hooked beaks and piercing eyes.

I let out a low whistle. "We're not in Kansas anymore."

"There will have to be strict rules in place," Rima said to Geister and Captain Akel. "The Galactic Government will need to send more troops to strengthen our foothold here."

"What about kicking them off the planet?" Geister suggested. "We tell them you don't have to go home, but you can't stay here."

"Privateering, commerce...entrepreneurs will always find a way in," Captain Akel signed as Ero translated for him. "We'll spend more troops and effort trying to lock down the planet than policing it."

I looked over to Aiya, who stood staring over the wall, jaw clenched and rigid. I understood from our previous conversation that this was what she had feared the most, her people, the Stone Dwellers, and other less advanced tribes being taken advantage of by various species.

"We'll look out for them," I told her, catching her eye. "It's our job. We won't let them be hoodwinked."

Aiya tried a smile of thanks, but I knew her mind was already running through the possibilities.

"We'll get through this," Tem offered as everyone quieted, lost to their own thoughts. "We always do."

"Whatever we face, we'll do it together," I said, convincing myself of that idea even as the words escaped my lips. I quoted my wife with my next words. "We're here for a reason. Our time's not up yet."

"Tyco, shut your mouth," Rima said without looking at me.

Everyone looked over, confused, as a small smile played across Rima's mouth.

"Instructor Noble, are you trying to bring some levity to

the moment?" I asked with a mock expression of shock. "I didn't know you had it in you. In light of this, I have something that's really going to cook your noodle. Look what I found."

I turned with those last words to Tem, who blinked. A look of recollection crossed his face a moment later as he dug the sardonium out of the folds of his cloak and presented it for all to see.

Eyes widened, and none more so than Geister and Rima.

"How?" Geister asked in awe.

"Where?" Rima followed up.

"Oh, you know, I do what I can," I said, accepting the light metal from Tem, then tapping the side of my head with my right pointer finger "I may just look like a pretty face, but there's a lot going on in here. All right, now how do I get this into my staff?"

EPILOGUE

"ZION WAS a fool who took a small unit to Ivandor to search for his so-called portal," Ul said with an exasperated sigh. "He wastes his time trying to tame the local indigenous species."

"Well, that fool, as you call him, succeeded," Keyra answered from her seat at the table. "Brother, you didn't even bother to look at his reports?"

"I have a federation to run," Ul sighed, rubbing at weary eyes. "Not every report from a mad scientist reaches my desk."

"You need rest," Keyra answered. "But do so after you see this."

Keyra tossed a holo disk on the table between them. A holographic display of Zion popped up in the air above the projector.

"Your Excellency." Zion began clicking his mandibles together in excitement. "I know not many resources were invested into my research, but I have great news for you. We have succeeded. We have discovered the portals spoken of by past generations."

Ul perked up at this, removing his boots from on top of the table, and leaned in closer. He knew his sister had to be loving this. In that moment, he didn't care. He needed something to turn the tide of battle with the rest of the Enzite Empire. If he could show them he had something, maybe they would side with his splinter faction.

On the holo screen, Zion stepped to the side, allowing whoever was filming to get a clear shot of the structure behind him. A large triangle on a raised platform jutted into the sky.

Ul's breath stuck in his throat.

"My research says there are three of these portals around the planet known as Ivandor," Zion chattered away excitedly. "The species here are primitive and easy to manipulate. They have made wonderful slaves and test subjects for my other work. If we can discover and open all three portals, there is no telling the amount of wealth and knowledge lying on the other side with the Eternals."

Zion paused here to let whoever was operating the camera zoom in on the portal. It was beautiful. The ancient metal and runes etched into the frame of the object took Ul's breath away.

As Enzite children were raised, stories of myth and legend were told about the portals able to take one, not just to another world, but another dimension. The creators of these portals were long lost, thought to have gone through for some unknown reason and never returned.

"As you can see, this is no speculation or hoax," Zion said, appearing in front of the camera again. "Along with this break-through, my studies in cloning have also advanced. I will send you coordinates so we may join together and usher in this new era for the EF."

The holo film shut down, leaving a multitude of questions yet unanswered in Ul's mind. For so long, the EF, or Enzite Federation, had been the weaker splinter group from the much larger Enzite Empire. But this, this could change everything.

"Oh, how I see the wheels turning in your eyes," Keyra hissed, with a tongue groping each mandible and then retreating back into her mouth. "This is it, Ul. This is what we've been waiting for."

"How long ago was this transmission sent?" Ul asked, drumming his fingers on the stone table. Already he was making calculations of how quickly he could get to Ivandor.

"A few weeks, but much has happened since then," Keyra sighed. "You should really read all the reports that come in. Even those from the lone unit you sent to Ivandor to appease Zion."

"Just tell me. Enough of your games, Keyra," Ul raged. "What is it? What aren't you saying?"

"That report was followed up by another, from some captain reporting in that Zion was dead. The site had been overrun, and our forces were in full retreat," Keyra answered, standing from her seat and walking over to her left where a massive window oversaw the hangar bay. "Who overran them was actually very interesting."

"You're going to make me ask, aren't you?" Ul asked with a sigh, also standing. He walked over to join his sister. "Who possesses access to the portal?"

"The Galactic Government," Keyra said, staring out down below to the hangar bay. "An entire Ursonian Brigade and at least two Rowki Guardians."

The mere mention of the Rowki sent a tremor of rage down Ul's muscular physique. He clenched the railing in front of him so hard, the metal dimpled under his grip.

"Easy, brother," Keyra said with a soothing tone. "Their

time will come. I haven't forgotten what they did to our family. This is a gift for more vengeance to be brought on the Rowki."

Ul saved his words. He looked behind them across the room and past the table where they had been sitting a moment before. A trophy case set against the wall showed medals, accolades, and awards, but his most prized trophy of all rested under a bright light in a glass case solely reserved for that one item. A spear, six feet long, marked with a rune that glowed white with sardonium.

After he'd killed the Rowki it belonged to, he opted to keep the spear as a reminder of how the Rowki had ruined and disgraced his family.

"Save your anger for the fight ahead," Keyra said, motioning to the thousands of ships below them in the hangar bay. "We've prepared for this moment. We're ready. And the Rowki will never see us coming."

STAY INFORMED

Get A Free Book by visiting Jonathan Yanez' website. You can email me at jonathan.alan.yanez@gmail.com or find me on Amazon, and Instagram (@author_jonathan_yanez). I also created a special Facebook group called "Jonathan Yanez' Reading Wolves" specifically for readers, where I show new cover art, do giveaways, and run contests. Please check it out and join whenever you get the chance!

For updates about new releases, as well as exclusive promotions, visit my website and sign up for the VIP mailing list. Head there now to receive a free stories.

www.jonathan-yanez.com

BOOKS IN THE GALACTIC GUARDIANS UNIVERSE

Made in the USA
Monee, IL
19 January 2024

52021315R00222